A Friendship of Thistles

E.L. Parfitt

To Joanne, who knew that 'purple' could take us so far!

Part 1

Let's drink to days gone by

Chapter 1

October 2020, Edinburgh

A brass bell chimes as an unexpected visitor pulls its cord. Its resonant clang reminds Heather of Maither's cowbell; a souvenir brought back from Austria from their only holiday abroad. Irvin had brought the bell back from Tibet in an October as grey as this one – dreary tarmac and sky, an airborne peppering of drizzle – he had joked that it would cleanse people's souls, releasing their suffering, before they could enter his house: *her* house now. She hoped, in death, that her friend had found his 'singing sun'.

'Hector!' Heather flings her sleeves wide open – the Scottish-wide ban on household visits be damned – a piece of her heart has returned to her. Small flecks of rain speckle Hector's glasses and raincoat, though not enough to dampen her woollen dress. 'Where's Fran?'

Hector's shoulders stiffen. 'Fran threw me out.'

She leads him into the kitchen, their staggered footsteps echoing on the sandstone tiles like a heartbeat; the late-blooming hydrangeas exploding outside the floor to ceiling windows to match the pigmentation in her cheeks. 'Want a cuppa?'

'If there's Earl Grey.' He moves, she notes, unsteadily, as he chooses a stool.

She pours her cold jasmine tea down the sink, eyes on his back as he inspects the garden, face pale – even for a Scotsman – against the contrast of his ginger tufts.

As they wait for the boiling kettle she fiddles with the end of her chestnut-grey ponytail and asks herself: what's wrong here? Hector is holding himself differently. Usually, he posed a risk to breakable objects or, and on more than one occasion, he'd poked someone in the eye. Yet his arms rest today by his expanding waistline. Well, they were all getting on a bit, touching middle age, feeling that once inner fire tarnish as their dreams hadn't panned out the way they'd thought.

Hamish speaks over banging his teaspoon against his wrist, 'The kids have missed you for Sunday lunches.'

The mugs in her hands knock the granite countertop as she jerks. What more to say: other than she agreed. She could've reached out. If she hadn't … if Fran hadn't … They'd both been hurt. An inadequate word for the rupture of a friendship.

'You didn't visit or pick up the phone.'

She waits for him to say Fran is ill, dying, dead. What could it be? She pictures tall, indelicate-boned Fran with her choppy bob.

The rain has given way to an autumn mist that insulates the house from the sun and emphasises the tick-tock of her feet from the kitchen island to the Victorian cabinet that holds the tea, and the tac-tac of the grandfather's pendulum in the dining room.

'There's a mathematical formula for rain,' he says. 'Well, not rain per se, but rainfall. Intensity, duration, frequency. It's about droplet concentration and—Sorry, I'm boring you.'

'Surprising me.'

He blinks, and stares outside as though it's the first time he's ever seen yellow-leaved birch. 'Still got their gold.'

Had Fran sent him? Her husband was the peace pipe that could always draw them together. 'Did Fran—?'

'Could've called,' he says.

'Is that what you want me to admit today?'

He laughs: a broken blast punctuated with missed notes. 'Except you … you couldn't … have called … because … because … our phone line … is dead,' he says, followed by more canned chokes.

How had he and Fran been these past months? More than

months. At least a year since the rupture.

He scratches the end of his nose. 'Me and you and Fran.'

Yes, she remembers. United over roast dinner, Fran often joked.

The primary school's canteen had been an organised war zone where adults unknowingly strode across enemy lines; the boundaries marked by plastic trays, jugs of water, and blocks of tables. The early level tables sat together: chubby hands and milk cartons on plastic chairs. Heather and Hector perched next to the older kids on wooden chairs, swinging their feet off the ground. Most eight to nine-year-olds in their own class were too immature for Heather and Hector's tastes.

Amongst the wooden tables Heather spotted lanky, cropped-haired Fran, with the body of fashion model Twiggy and the cheek bones of Mike Tyson, face-to-face with Alex – new boy and self-imposed know-it-all.

'Take that back, Alex Simons!'

'Or what?'

The kids at the nearest tables stopped shovelling beef, tatties and mushy peas into their mouths. Fran shuffled her shoes long enough for Alex's worm-like lips to wriggle into a smirk and retort, 'Just 'cause your mom is a dinner lady don't mean we eat this slop at home.'

Fran's knuckles whitened on her plastic tray. Heather imagined tatties, peas and an overcooked slice of beef sliding down Alex's sweater. Fran would get into trouble and her parents would have to pay for damage to his jeans and jumper.

Heather stepped between them. 'Alex, that was mean.'

'What if it is? You can't do anything.'

'We don't treat folk *that* way at *this* school.'

Confronted with his bored gaze, Heather had no notion what to do if he objected to the rules. But she kenned some of the teachers well enough to know what they would say.

'Do you ken the expression wee clipe?' she asked.

Alex regarded Heather's brown plaits as if tempted to tug on them for daring to call him a snitch.

Heather narrowed her eyes.

Alex stuck his hands in his pockets and said, 'Don't be a tell-tale.' He knew the meaning of 'wee clipe' all right.

'I can,' Heather said. 'Not to the adults. They've their own rules. I'm talking about our rules. I can tell every child at this school not to play with you …' She gave it time for her words to sink into Alex's thick skull. True. She was fairly well liked. Others regarded her as the default referee for arguments. She could see the cogs in his brain working that out. Liked by the quiet kids too because she made sure that no one sat out during a game. Fairness and the name Heather went hand in hand.

Alex's smirk wavered.

'You're new here,' Heather said, 'so I'm going to give you a break. Welcome to Our Lady's. Come on, Fran.'

'Awesome, Heather!' Hector stretched a palm above his fiery curls for their ritual high five.

Warmth spread across Heather's neck; relief, she guessed from escaping a tricky situation. She flinched as Fran slammed her tray on the scratched table.

'That twit annoys me,' Fran said.

Hector swallowed a mouthful of tatties and gravy. 'It's only his first week.'

Heather added, noting Alex squirting strawberry milk at his friend Fraser, 'I think that boy would annoy astronauts on the moon.'

A half-laugh ruptured Fran's frown. 'That's a strange thingy to say.'

Heather shrugged.

'Heather's mum's a dinner lady too,' Hector said, nudging back his glasses.

'Which one?' Fran asked.

'Ann.'

'My ma's Ruth.'

And, as it turned out, they saw more of each other outside school; their mums struck up a friendship, and the girls struck up a companionship of their own. That's why Fran often joked that Hector, Heather and Fran were united over roast dinner.

Heather nods to show Hector that she remembers, remembers so much that the distance between them yanks on a scar she'd thought healed.

Hamish sips his tea until she can't stomach not knowing.

'Why aren't you with your wife?' Heather asks.

April 2019

Edinburgh from above is a city hammered into an uneven finish: marked by the cobbles along its wynds and closes. Tall stone buildings and tall tales, trickster passageways, myths underfoot in its walls, lofts, cellars. Lies told by writers, painters, singers, and, of course, storytellers. There's not enough room in the walls, attics and vaults of Edinburgh, so stories must spill down the streets. Some sonnets sharpened a place in the paving near the Scottish Writing Museum, although most flowed between the people, carried on their heels to peaks elsewhere.

The old man in the thick woollen coat and trilby, who had designated himself in charge of Irvin's ashes, beckoned everyone round him on the hilltop. Heather and Fran didn't follow, as they'd been dubbed 'hangers on at best' – a remark made by the crabbit of the man in the heavy coat Fran had nicknamed Baneshanks.

Hands raised, the huddled group – sufficient numbers for a ten-a-side football match – halted.

'Bloody Nora,' said Fran, fist unclenching. Once that first billow of cremated ash broke free, the rest of the group cast their remains as the canny wind shifted direction.

'Huh, huh,' Heather half-coughed half-laughed. 'Irvin would have loved that one.'

Fran watched Heather brush her nostrils, with the back of her sleeve, as they drifted away from the others and their expensive wool coats. Heather's hair sported grey streaks beside her ears all the way to the tips of her tresses, but her face had barely lined in the last ten years. No kids. That was the secret. And genetics. Probably. Over forty now, Heather's waist was filling out, crafting two lines on her back where she held the excess weight, while Fran remained broomstick thin, aside from her belly, yet the mirror each morning showed deep lines bracketing her mouth and underscoring her lower eyelashes.

Heather said, 'It's as if a fine sheet of muslin has been drawn across the sun.'

Bollocks, and Heather called her the superstitious one because she daily checked her horoscope. 'If we're talking about veils between worlds ... he has the presence of Baneshanks, don't he?' Fran nodded towards the silhouettes of the mourners clustered around the cairn on the top of Allermuir – a foot-breaking trudge up a grassy and rocky slope beyond Edinburgh's ski centre.

'That's Irvin's brother,' Heather said. 'Blair ... or Blain. No, it's Blair like the siege of Blair Castle.'

'No way! That guy's seventy or more.'

Heather counted off the years on her fingers. 'Aye, that's right. Blair was born twenty years before his father married Irvin's mother.'

'What about the lady in her fifties with the pink lippy?'

'Fenella, Blair's daughter. Which makes her Irvin's ... niece? Um, she has a brother: see that silver-haired guy, blue and green tartan scarf?'

'A rhino, like his father.' Fran elbowed Heather in the ribs.

Two blond adults with glasses, and therefore academic-looking, squinted at the view.

'Fenella's children,' Heather told Fran. 'One at Glasgow studying dentistry, the other at St Andrews for international relations.'

Fran closed her eyes as the wind attempted a full facial exfoliation. 'Given May's bollocks, we'll need more students studying that. Fucking, politicians.'

Fran watched Heather's eyes fix downwards, as they always did whenever the topic of voting for the "wrong side" in the

EU referendum came up. Especially, when Hector ranted that folk would "vote wrong" again in the next general election. She suspected Heather had voted for Brexit; best not to say any more as friendships were rupturing all over the place over the Scottish National Party's press for independence.

'God, I could use a smoke.' Fran excavated her pockets for a ciggie.

'I've no idea about the others,' Heather said. 'They didn't visit the house those two years I knew him.' Her nose twitched, and her jaw tensed as she clamped her teeth together. Today was apparently a war between Heather and the others who weren't there to support Irvin as he died of cancer.

'You sure you're—' Fran lit her ciggie, swearing at each attempt against the gusts, and raised her eyebrows over the smouldering end. 'You sure you're fine, Heather? I know we're ancient according to my kids but don't mean we can't lose our cool. Gosh, I sound like Ma when she put her posh on. Like the queen. She thought.'

Against the wind's assault on her eyelashes, Fran glimpsed the grey currents of the estuary below merging into a golden sky as the guests added to the pile of stones.

'A prehistoric ritual, that,' Heather said, motioning at the pile of stones, a cairn, against the backdrop of the Pentland Hills on one side and the city on the other. 'Stones as burial markers. Later they became markers for trails all over the rolling heather hills of Scotland. Why do hills roll? Why do rivers sweep?'

Fran shrugged and drew a deep smoky breath, easing the tension within. She'd wondered, and still did, if there had been more between Heather and Irvin than a professional relationship. Admittedly, she'd been jealous of sharing Heather's time with this mysterious eccentric.

Heather said, 'Irvin would have cited poetry, like: "the sky that was grey is blue", and I'd have called him a numpty.'

Fran rapped her ciggie hand against Heather's head. 'You okay, Thistle? Fine, fine, I know, wrong question for a day like today.' She wiped a smudge of ash off Heather's hairline: either from her ciggie or Irvin's remains.

'Thanks for coming, Fran,' Heather said, a bit of an edge to the words, though the grounds for this escaped Fran. Unless it was because Heather felt too mothered. Not a feeling she must be used to after losing her ma so young.

'You're welcome, pal.' Fran punched her arm, to lighten the mood in a way only two people who had been inseparable since primary school could – even over forty and ancient in the eyes of Fran's kids. 'Hen,' Fran said.

'Queen.'

'Wifie.'

Heather sniffed. 'Don't. You'll make me cry.'

Fran's arms crept around her pal.

'Don't burn a hole in me jacket.'

'Aye, sure. I'll be careful.'

'That's what you said the last time.'

'Right, do you want a hug or no?'

'Aye.'

Fran stamped out her ciggie and threw both arms about Heather. The force swayed them, so Fran had to dig in her heels.

'Do you ever think about how you'll die?' Heather asked, her muffled face pressed against Fran's shoulder.

'From bowel or lung cancer leaving Hector and the kids alone.'

'Alone, eaten by my pet.'

Fran snorted, and pulled back to give Heather a frank stare. 'The pet you never buy?'

One or two individuals in the rest of the group were saying a few words. The wind blew away before Fran could seize them. Their faces appeared composed. Where was the sobbing, the anger or the regret? They should be shamefaced, this majority who, as Heather had said on their traipse up the hill, had feared death too much to haunt his deathbed.

Heather shrugged. 'Pets cost money. Easier to quit smoking

to salvage some pennies, isn't it?' Heather eyed the remains of Fran's ciggie on the rocky soil.

'I gave up for a week, you know. But they say stress is atrocious for our health.'

'Please, try again.'

Heather's request repeated a conversation Fran had multiple times with her ma. Donna hadn't listened and now she was dead the wrong side of sixty. *It isn't possible to control death,* Fran told herself. *Look at poor Irvin, their age and dead of cancer.* But at least she and Heather had each other. And because relationships demanded a certain give and take it might be time to revisit giving up smoking. Fifth time the charm?

'For you, Heather, that was my last one. Better, Thistle?'

'Ain't achievable today, but thanks.'

Heather's eyes flickered to one side as the wind rolled the ciggie across the bare earth, grass and rock. 'Go on, you ken you want to.' Fran nudged her.

Heather trudged towards the stub and picked it up.

Fran tutted. 'Anti-litterer. You won't see me mop the Royal Mile on me weekend off.'

Folk had begun to disperse. There would be a picnic at the Botanic Gardens later, in one of the glasshouses. Yet it was too early in the season and too soon after a death to be picnicking. A handful of ashes in the wind and life resumed.

Heather said, 'Feels too short, you know. I feel like I just answered his advert.'

'You didn't expect to like the guy.' Fran tried to sound casual, even as her remark hid a question. Did they? Didn't they? And why won't she flat out say it?

'That makes it sound like we were an item. We were ... kindred souls.'

That phrasing sounded like code for a relationship to Fran, but she pretended to misunderstand. 'Pals? You still got pals. Come on, no point to footer about, we're the last uns.' Fran clasped an arm around Heather's shoulders. 'You'll be all right. Could be worse.'

'Ach, you reek of smoke!'

Fran placed a hand across her heart. 'Long may your chimney reek, long may your feet nae stink.'

Heather stifled a laugh with the point of her thumb pressed to her lips. 'Don't. They're looking back. Judging.'

'Don't care for them, Thistle. Don't care for those folks. When Irvin got sick, they weren't nowhere. You were.'

'Aye,' Heather said, 'till the sky that was grey is blue …'

'What's that mean anyway?'

'That troubled times will pass. That this grief will fade.'

Hands concealed by her pockets, Fran dug her thumbs into the curve of her index fingers. Her ma had died a year and a half ago but it could have been today.

∞∞∞

Pluto's trajectory through Capricorn is shaking your foundations – prompting dramatic career changes, upheaval and even resettlement.

Fran's keys clattered into the battered wicker basket beside the phone. She brushed against the radiator in the lounge, and shivered towards the cramped kitchen, kneading her achy hands. Everyone has things they'd like to change in their life. She'd like to change her career and have more romantic time with Hector; proper dates instead of frantic couplings before one of the kids interrupted. However, she didn't object to returning home to find her husband in the kitchen.

Hector stirred Heinz baked beans in a pan, banging the wooden spoon off the pot. She slipped her arms around him, taking in the lavender-camomile smell of his jumper, and crawled her fingers underneath to warm them. The toast leapt with a metallic rattle as she touched the holes in the armpits of his thermal.

'Ouch! Icy digits, you crook. I thought I'd make you something hot. Just as well.'

She fetched the cutlery as he scraped butter across the toast and tipped the beans on top. Baked beans on toast was his go-to meal. She cooked, he washed the dishes, she bought food, he ferried the kids to school, she brought the kids home and cleaned, he emptied the bins and the never-ending laundry basket. She hoped Allan and Jack would grow up to negotiate the household chores with their wives. And that Patricia would also seek out a balanced role in the home – unlike Fran's ma who had sorted out the home while Da had worked, and ate and sat and read the Monday through to Sunday newspapers.

'How's Jack feeling?' she asked.

'Poor kid fell asleep on the toilet bowl. I tucked him into bed with a bucket on the floor.'

She shuffled across the soiled-beige carpet of the lounge to their faux-leather settee. One of these days she'd get around to bothering the landlord to replace the threadbare carpeting throughout the house.

'How was the funeral, my little penguin?' Hector asked.

She smiled at the term of affection. He handed her a plate and she handed him a knife and fork. 'Ta,' he said. The settee shifted as he sat, cushions wonky, his upper leg touching hers as he rested his plate on his lap.

The warmth of her plate seeped into her frozen-chicken thighs. He'd made the effort, the least she could do was respond to his question. 'Bloody freezing,' she said, tucking in, scalding her tongue.

'How's Heather?'

They'd gone back and forth about leaving Patricia to watch over her younger brothers, but Hector rightly argued that if Jack's stomach bug worsened and he grew dehydrated he'd need some fluid replacement solution which Patricia couldn't give him, and Fran didn't trust their usual babysitter, Fiona.

Fran could read from the pleating of his brow he was

annoyed. Of course, he'd wanted to be there for Heather. They'd both also wanted to stay with Jack.

'She understood,' Fran said. 'Sometimes, though, Heather and I are stuck in our teenage selves. We can't talk. I mean, not like we can.' She gripped her knife and sawed through the stale toasted bread. 'Bloody hard trek up that hill after work.'

'Are you happy enough?'

Every couple of months he asked the same question. Happy: what a loaded word. 'Why wouldn't I be? We're all in good health and getting by.'

'If you didn't want to go back to work tomorrow, I could understand. You could retrain. We could get by on my salary.'

'I'll think about it.'

They ate, listening to the scrape of their cutlery, and the tick of the gold clock that had been her ma's. It sat pride of place on a shelf above the dusty electric fire with its dusty on-off switch, beside pictures of the children. Patricia had been born at lunchtime, interrupting a ham salad sandwich, and shared her ma's pragmatic nature. Two years later, Allan had been born impatient and inquisitive, shooting out into his da's arms to explore the world. Two years after that Jack came prematurely and spent his first month on a ventilator, surrounded by so many wires they'd been scared to touch him.

Hector switched on the telly.

Simultaneously, the news smothered their silence and the phone cut across the presenter's report. As she answered her mobile Fran heard a clipped, high-class accent protesting over the People's Vote; the camera panned across a group of remainist supporters who wielded signs to mock those who wanted to leave the EU.

'Fran, can you pick Max up this Tuesday?' A female voice asked. It must be Beth, Max's ma. She was the breed of parent who had time to complain about not having time, yet found spare hours to self-publish a novel.

'Aye.'

'Thanks.' The line cut off.

'Campbell was provocative on social media today,' Hector said. 'He tweeted against Farage: "Sod off. Dulwich College. City trader. Member of European Parliament. Billionaire friends with private jets".' Hector chortled. Baked beans spilt from his mouth.

'Farage is Brexit Party and Campbell is …?' Fran tried to get her head around the names and political affiliations.

'Used to be Tony Blair's campaign director. Journalist now.'

'Do you think they'll be a second referendum?'

'In Scotland, aye.'

'That'll do for politics.' She pressed the mute button on the remote. 'How's work?'

'We've another new manager.'

'That's … good?'

'They're all incompetent.'

Phusss, phusss, clink, BANG! A rubbish truck grumbled by, shook the sun catchers on the window.

She winced as Hector's knife scraped his plate. 'What's wrong with this one?'

'Micromanager. Been shadowing each of us to "understand what we do".'

Hector had slaved for sixteen years to support her and the children. Hadn't been another option for either of them; God knows her job was hard enough for meagre wages. Fran fished for a positive word to support him. 'This new manager is more interested than the last one then?'

'Checking on us, more like. Arsehole.'

A wise woman knows it's unwise to poke a bear in the forest when he's got his head in a wasp's nest; an unwise woman can't help herself.

'Maybe you should apply for the management program?'

He licked his fork. 'Nah. Drop it.'

'Found anything you'd like to apply for?'

'Nah. Dumb office jobs.'

It wasn't hard for Fran to imagine an open-plan office, where someone else watered the plants and emptied the bins, polished the tables, dusted the computers, scrubbed the toilets and hoovered the carpets. All before 9 a.m. After which the office would fill the ears in its walls with telephone calls and keyboard chatter. The smell of cheap paper-cup coffee would soak into the carpet, spoons and bowls would wait in the breakroom sink, and toilet paper would be footed around the cubicles for her to tidy up the next morning.

Fran chewed her food for longer than usual to stopper a comment bubbling forth about 'lucky bastards' and 'bog-standard office job'.

She cocked her head. The usual thumps from the kids wrestling upstairs or playing karaoke were absent. 'Where're Allan and Patricia?'

'Sent them to the movies.' He moved the empty plate off her lap.

'Not, with Fiona?'

'Aye.' He pushed his heavy presence on her. He kissed her neck with baked bean breath.

'I don't like them out and about with Fiona. In the home is okay, but she's a teenager.'

'Humm, mmmm,' he muttered into her neck, squeezed her breasts too hard. This was as romantic as it got these days.

'Ma? Da?' Jack wavered in the doorway. 'I don't feel ...' He vomited onto the carpet.

'One more stain for the collection.' Hector grimaced, scooped up Jack and carried him upstairs.

The next day, during morning break, Fran's horoscope announced that if there were changes to be made in her life she should stop loafing about.

You might temporarily lose your ambition and be left wondering if it's all worth it. There is never a perfect time to start projects or engage in important discussions. So what's holding you back?

'Messy toilet,' Heather said. Entering late, heading towards the kettle.

They brought their own mugs. You couldn't be too careful in the Scottish workplace. Careless mug use was asking for your finest Where-there's-tea-there's-hope mug to vanish; or worse, stained with coffee and left unwashed in the sink – presumably by the same bastard who burnt food to the inside of the microwave.

Fran watched Heather over the top of her magazine: she poured the water, watched the teabag bleed out, and released a lengthy sigh. From the lack of make-up and her rough hair bun, it didn't look like she'd slept.

The clock read 9.10 a.m. Fran had tried to brainstorm new careers for ten minutes and only uncovered the obvious: starting her own cleaning business. Fran pretended to read as Heather sat opposite.

The tea room smelled of instant soup, floor cleaner and talc. The lack of windows hid them from the vertical rain that windshield wipers wouldn't shift when Fran left the house to catch the 4.20 a.m. bus. At a corner table, under a discoing artificial light, Mark, Bob, Joan and Henry played Ludo. Four cleaners and not one amongst them thought to call maintenance to fix the light. Well, it wasn't Fran's job either.

Heather pointed her chin in their direction as dice clattered across the table. 'They play with the concentration of gods determining the fate of mortals.'

Fran watched the players propelling their pieces round the board, and around again. What a stupid game. If the board was the Earth and the pieces people at least it would be interesting. Once she'd turned down an invitation to join in with a polite 'games aren't my thing'. She hadn't been invited to participate again. When Henry, still called the newbie after six years, started work their dedicated Ludo team was complete.

Fran waved a hand towards a discarded newspaper – the Metro? She couldn't remember. They were all the same with their apocalyptic attitudes – she'd keeked at the horoscopes page and the article opposite. 'Hector said I should consider retraining and my horoscope agrees – kind of.'

'I guess modelling's off the cards,' Heather said.

Surprising that Heather remembered that old dream. Yet the stretching of her breast tissue and a belly covered with scar lines had led Fran to put that dream aside after Allan's birth.

'I thought about starting my own cleaning business,' Fran said. 'Eco-friendly house cleaning seems popular.' Fran's mobile rang. 'Aye?'

'Could Max stay over on Friday?'

'Sure.'

'Thanks.' As Beth hung up Fran made a mental note to ask her for the latest news about her husband, away from the playground gossips.

'So?' she asked Heather. 'What do you think?'

'You're a bit of a control freak.'

'What's that got to do with it?'

'Because you can't control everything in business. I think that'll frustrate you, and you're not always willing to compromise or listen when our supervisor tells you to do something, which you might have to do with clients.'

'I'd be respectful to clients' needs.'

Heather winced as she kicked off her shoes and wriggled her toes. 'Best to consider the difficulties ahead of time.'

Fran flicked through glossy pages. 'Difficulties … difficulties … can't find any.' She threw the magazine in Heather's face.

Heather chucked it back.

It fell open on a page with BREXIT across the top, where the put-together businesswoman on the cover gave her middle-class opinion – with a smile and perfectly plucked eyebrows. Fran ran a thumb and finger over the ridge of one brow. 'The country's going to shit, the world's going to shit. All Hector wants to discuss is strikes in Chili and student protests in Hong Kong. I'm waiting for the folk around here to suggest donning yellow vests once Brexit isn't reversed. I ain't about to join them.'

'Forgot to ask, how was your anniversary?' Heather asked.

'Our neighbour, Nike, took the kids. Me and Hector got a takeaway and watched a rerun of *Takin' Over the Asylum*.'

Heather drew some typed-up sheets from her pocket. She'd bought a second-hand word processor, circa 1999, at a rummage-sale and refurbished it months ago to type up her stories.

'That last night's work?' Fran asked.

Paper shoes

In the story when the girl is offered a gleaming pair of red shoes, how is she supposed to know their danger? Youth is for dancing. To learn the steps to discover one's dance partners and position. The girl wants to skip to a reel, and the shoes are so delightful. She's warned as she knots the woven inky lacing: 'Paper shoes aren't for dancing.' A list of don'ts sail into her ears, and she intends to keep them: 'Don't dirty them on the pavement', 'Don't make any sudden movements', and 'Don't get them wet'. She dances out of the shop.

Her paper shoes are fraying. She wants to dance before they tear further. She pirouettes. And the thing about dancing is once you taste that freedom it's hard to stop. Spinning, once, twice, thrice. On the fourth unable to stop. On the fifth realising one's error as the shoes continue the spin, they are now spinning you.

Now you're a fish struggling on the line.

A paper fish curling on a hot palm.

You can't tug them off, your feet keep jigging, leaping, stamping, twirling. 'My feet hurt!' you cry.

Then a motherly figure appears, holds you still. Her face, though, is strange. A piece of broken pottery, glued back together with drips and spills of tree sap lacquer on her skin, painted over with silver dust. The face is someone you know, but it's chipped and grotesque. You wriggle away. The shoes clack together and continue the dance.

Trapped again, your feet feeling like swollen sausages, you dance out of the house into the street, the paper tips browning themselves on the pavements.

You remember the warnings: 'Don't dirty them on the pavement', 'Don't make any sudden movements', and 'Don't get them wet'.

A fountain comes into view. Don't get them wet. The shoes leap over the low surrounding hedge bordered with flowers and pirouette around the stone edge. An old man mutters under his breath that 'Dancing on the fountain isn't allowed. Young people are so entitled these days.'

Above, cast in disapproving iron, four female figures of art, science, poetry and industry, look down.

Art says, 'What a lovely dance.'
Science says, 'Paper shoes are impractical'
Poetry says, 'Watch those feet, how they can dance.'
Industry says, 'How can I manufacture paper shoes in bulk without deforestation?'

Only the grotesque motherly figure paused the dance before. Now you are on your own. Unlike the waters of a fountain, you can't split apart a person, nor mould and recast the broken parts, then fashion a person back together. You dance yourself into the water. The paper shoes come to pieces.

Fran examined the story. 'Dark. Imaginative.'

'First person to complete the game has to fill the kettle. That's the rules.' Mark argued with Henry from the Ludo table.

'Fran?' Heather asked. 'Do you ever think of doing something completely different?'

'I've got plenty on my plate.'

'Right. But,' Heather added, 'If you could … would you try modelling?'

Fran slapped the pages on the table, covering the well-dressed woman with her mocking smile. 'I don't have time for daydreams. Is this to do with your writing again?'

Bob grumbled as Joan landed on one of his pieces. 'I've to go back to the start. Again? Again?'

'Break's almost over,' Joan said, 'If you guys aren't willing to play fair …'

Heather fiddled with her fingers. 'It's nothing.'

'You should give up on this nonsense. It don't make you happy, Thistle.'

'Mm.' Heather sipped her tea.

After work, glad that the rain had eased into a gentle pat-a-cake, Fran splashed beside Heather up Candlemaker Row to a café where the tea was cheap and, as a bonus, tasteless, after which they caught the bus together. Fran rented a house and Heather a flat in adjacent streets.

Fran grunted in response to Heather's cheerful 'see ya!' and turned into her street. Being situated across the road from Allan and Jack's primary school, countless comings and goings were visible from her windows, and the dramas of everyone living in this row of eleven houses.

She pulled her scarf around her face to block the smell of burnt plastic that emanated from the house divided into council flats at the end of the street. In the distance she heard the chimes of the ice cream van. It even played in blustery February to March despite the snow and rain. What did people buy throughout winter …? Crisps? Chocolate? Handwarmers? Mable, at number 42, had joked about drugs, yet she might be closer to the mark than she realised.

Sandwiched next to the druggie house and where Mable lived was a scunner fixing a house up. He made metallic-grinding noises early on a Saturday and Sunday. Hector said he'd got the place as a fixer-upper and would move on when it was ready to sell. Today metal ground into wood from inside, and curls of waterlogged wood slumped around his doorstep. Fran shivered. Her breath steamed the air. Surely nippy enough for snow? Her fingertips ebbed purple.

Mabel's son, the DJ, lived with her, even though he was thirty-five. The whole neighbourhood had got used to tuning out his music. The dogs at number 43 barked and attacked the gate: three Labradors, one Border Collie and a Jack Russell. Five dogs were a bit obsessive but their owner Mirren always gave a broad smile when she saw you. The garden at number 44 was a haven for old broken toys because the young married couple fostered children. Now and then, before a home visit, they'd have a jumbo clean up. Yet, more often than not, the place was a regular mess.

Next to Fran and Hector, pigeon enthusiast Andrew kept his birds in a shed round back, along with an assortment of junk, broken sinks, bits of pipe, engine parts, and he'd parked a rusting van on the street that hadn't moved for fifteen months. On Hector and Fran's other side, Nike was to be avoided – to prevent being drawn into a discussion about her illness of the month. Then, at number 48, lived Nancy a prune-faced woman who confiscated balls that sailed over her hedge. Patricia called her 'the witch', though technically according to the urban legend of the playground, number 49 was the witch's house.

No one ever saw a soul go in or out, except for a slender black cat which was said to be the witch in feline form. In reality, Polish parents, Adrianna and Leon, were cleaners in Leith and insisted on sending their kids to the Gaelic nursery at New Kirkgate, so that they could get the best primary and secondary education.

At the end, in number 50, lived a retired couple, Jan and Rob, with their impeccable garden. They paid a cleaner in cash who was a suspected illegal immigrant. Fran saw Rob out on cold sunny mornings raking leaves, pulling up plants and moaning about plastic bottles and fish heads that escaped the recycling lorry and ended up in his vegetable patch.

There were worse streets to live on. Though, if the neighbours had been more considerate she would be able to feel more charitable. Their actions shouldn't matter. It was part of her faith to be charitable to others regardless. Time to go to church and confess to the priest, to unburden herself of these uncharitable thoughts. Though, whoever made up that rule didn't work a full-time cleaning job.

Fran used the time before she was due to collect Allan and Jack at the primary school to rebandage her blistered feet.

That night, kids in bed, following prayer and a story from the Bible, Fran dug out the scum under each nail and clipped her toenails. 'I have a business plan,' she would tell Hector. Fran smeared a fine layer of peppermint mask onto her feet. 'It's related to what I currently do.' She sat on the toilet seat to let it dry. Flicked through the same magazine from lunchtime, lingering on the businesswoman's interview, who had built up her confidence and assertiveness to jump in and go big! With savings from her previous financial services job, or the Bank of Mummy and Daddy – no doubt.

Fran skimmed the celebrity pages, then threw their glossy lives to the floor beside Hector's book of jokes. She dangled her legs over the edge of the bath, wet her hands, and scrubbed the mud into her feet, exfoliating them. Did she even want to remain a cleaner? What had this trade gotten her, except for lined and cracked hands, swollen joints, creaking hips? She rinsed her feet, brusquely towelled and massaged them with kitchen oil, as beneficial as overpriced massage oils. A pair of greyish bed socks, once polar bear white, finished off her ensemble. She tidied her 'beauty tricks' away in the medicine cabinet. The cupboard was divided into two: Hector's side filled with shaving items, plasters, dissolvable aspirin, and Vicks vapour rub; hers with foot cream, hair oil, nail varnish, monthly rags, and makeup. With kids in the house, medications and creams in tubes were best hidden out of reach.

She avoided seeing her face in the mirror: forehead lines, sagging cheeks. This was not the face of a business owner. Then again, no one would doubt her qualifications in the cleaning world with a face like this. She could raise that point with Hector when justifying the initial investment a cleaning business would require: a van, some equipment, possibly a logo of a dancing broom with a wink.

'Hello, I'm Fran of Eco-cleaning Services.'

So what's holding you back? the phrasing of her horoscope mocked her.

Heather could have been more supportive, considering how she'd been there for Heather when her ma died. And too many other times to count. Take the time that Heather, on a health kick, had bought a second-hand bicycle and promptly got a puncture on the first day she used it to go to work. She'd called Fran to let their boss know she'd have to walk the rest of the way, half-an-hour by foot as she'd forgotten her purse. Fran had hopped off the bus and run home to borrow Hector's car so they both arrived a little late, with bicycle wheels sticking out of the boot of the Hyundai. And there was all that onion soup she'd made whenever Heather got the flu. Even if it was such terrible soup her family wouldn't touch it. That wasn't the point. The point was taking soup in the first place.

Hector had always supported her no matter what. Yet it was best to think of the difficulties ahead of time in case he held reservations. Heather's reaction had made her see that. Besides, he was the one who had gone to business school, so running the concept through him would be invaluable after thinking through a few more details.

The phone rang. *Come on, Hector. Pick it up.* When it woke the kids it was her who would have to read them more stories until they nodded off.

Fran limped down the stairs on tender feet, avoided the Lego figures, and a used tissue, and a wooden toggle that didn't belong to anyone in the house. 'Aye?'

'Fran.' It was Heather. 'I've a house.'

The carpet felt wintery through her socks. Fran shivered, pulled her robe tight, wishing it could encase her like a cocoon from what lay ahead.

'Did you hear? Irvin's left me his house.'

'He never!'

'He did.'

'He never. Hector! Dear God, thank you for the blessing you bestow on us today.'

Hector entered the lounge with a dishcloth.

'Heather has a house!'

Hector hugged Fran's back. 'Brilliant news.' His hands caressed Fran's buttocks, his glasses dug into her neck.

'Must be a mistake.' Heather said. 'Irvin didn't mention— The sneaky devil.'

'You must have meant a great deal to him.' Fran waited for an acknowledgement that didn't come. Kneading fingers reached inside her soul and pounded firmly, reshaping the warmth that should be there, celebrating a pal's gain, instead of the burnt and hollow carcass between her ribs. Hector's fingers opened the front of her dressing gown.

Heather sniffed.

'You crying?' Fran asked.

'No.' Heather's voice cracked. 'Not much.'

'Why's Ma yelling?' asked Allan. His head poked around the top of the stairs.

Fran saw a mismatch of her and Hector's features in his face: lips, nose, eyes. Patricia had her mother's build and colouring, her da's chortle; Allan had the most blended features yet Hector's ginger curls and personality; while dark-haired Jack had Fran's frown and Hector's way of cocking his head to the side when he tried to puzzle something out.

'I'll sort it,' Hector said, with a pinch to her thigh.

Fran yanked her gown closed. 'It's a blessing, Thistle. Accept it with an open heart.'

'Aye, I will, I am. It's. A lot. Good night.'

'Night.'

Fran listened as Hector firmly told their kids to go back to bed.

'Is Mummy upset?' Jack asked.

'No, she's excited. Tell you in the morning.'

'We're awake now. You might as well tell us,' Patricia said.

Fran padded upstairs. 'Aunty Heather has been given a house. Go, back to bed.'

When the kids had settled, and she and Hector nestled, in the scuddy, under their blankets, Hector said, 'Would it do any good to pray for a house?'

'We're fine as is,' Fran said, reflecting on the words of her new horoscope: *it is important to be more sensitive towards other people's feelings today. You are likely to feel more vulnerable than usual, and you should do what you can to prevent yourself from becoming a victim.*

'We're fortunate,' Hector said.

She whispered a prayer for compassion.

'Pray for a parking space,' Hector said, misreading her plea. For Fran was thinking about the newspaper clipping she'd given to Heather, and the house that should have been hers.

Chapter 2

Heather's flat was one of eight: squat, pebble dashed blocks once home to people toiling at the gasworks. The best that could be said of the flat was that it had four walls and a roof. Cheap to heat too: sandwiched between flats above and below. All that grew in the shared space – a communal concrete square out back – were dandelions. The fencing, similar to chicken wire, didn't enhance the aesthetic. It was a place to dry washing that was never used because one tenant took it over for their bear of a dog and never cleaned up, attracting flies. Heather's street was largely quiet except for that fire in the boarded-up flat downstairs last October where everyone had stood on the pavement and watched the poor woman's belongings burn, or that time the police closed the street and questioned everyone about drugs, or that time at 2 a.m. one of the neighbours had a screaming fit with her fella for sleeping around (again). 'Just dump the arsehole and let us sleep love,' Fran's maither would have yelled towards their starlit fight.

Now, thanks to a newspaper article Fran gave her two years ago, she was about to inherit a house from Irvin.

Fran suspected an affair. Knowing Fran, she would take Heather's final confession as a betrayal. Demand a reason why Heather hadn't told her. The answer was simple: fear. But how to tell a pal that you feared their reaction when that pal had been nothing but supportive in the past. Not the fear of surprise, she would have to explicate, or that you wouldn't understand, rather *my own fears pinning me down, telling me I'm going to fail.*

She'd never had a job interview in her life. Fran had sorted out their cleaning jobs and following a brief meeting they were both hired. The week in May 2017 after Fran had given her the newspaper clipping, Heather had arranged to be interviewed by Irvin one afternoon at his home since that's where he needed help; though with what she wasn't quite sure as 'home help' could refer to various responsibilities. Fran had assisted Heather to prepare some competency-based answers to interview questions. Still, her knees stuck together as she'd stood at the top of his gravelled driveway, rocking, balanced on a precipice of self-doubt. *She could do this. Couldn't she?* She cast off the imaginary weights on her shoes and marched forward, gravel shifting underfoot.

A series of crisp mornings had softened into mild afternoons scented with hyacinths. Heather breathed in their scent, and paused on Irvin's doorstep to jot the thought down. She did the same with people; glancing at them then away, trying to recall a few details at a time to form an impression of a person.

The door opened inwards. A man her age, though deeper lines rumpled his forehead, filled the doorway. The mordant smell of citrus mixing with the asperity of his voice.

'You are a writer,' he said, clapping his hands, blue eyes brightened by the sun behind her.

'No.' She slipped her pad and pencil into her bag.

'Ah, well come in.' His sagging disappointment was overly externalised. The emotions too readily expanding and deflating in the movement of his arms and torso, and beneath his mossy eyebrows and patchy beard, to be anything but an act. Heather saw right through it. This was a man wanting to distract others from feeling sorry for him.

She followed his bouncy-castle step. Heather saw towers of books and notepads in every room and understood why he'd drawn the conclusion she was a writer: his house stamped him as a lover of books. It smelled like a library – almonds and ink. What a magical place to work. It brought to mind Carlos

Ruiz Zafón's *Cemetery of Forgotten Books*. Her jubilation rising, Heather stilled her quivering hands by clasping one over the other.

'Books are my obsession,' he explained. 'My muses.' He eased into a seat in a brown leather armchair with a wince that appeared genuine. The only sign so far that he required, as the advert suggested, bits and bobs done around the house. 'Sit.'

She carefully moved the books from the seat offered to her so she could obey.

'Excellent,' he said, as if taking care with the books had been a test.

'Who is your favourite author? Quick, now. No overthinking.'

'John Burnside.'

'Hum, atypical. Contemporary Scottish author and poet.' Irvin laced his hands behind his head and inspected the ceiling.

Eccentric, she would depict him later to Fran. A word often used to describe wealthy people who did what they liked when they liked. The type of man you would expect to drink rusty nails or Scotch sours: those lovable oddballs of British society almost extinct.

'I like how poetic Burnside's prose is,' Heather said. 'Each word carefully selected.'

'I am not going to ask you any competency-based questions because it is more pertinent that we get along.'

Oh shit, all that preparation for nothing. 'So, what else can I tell you about myself?'

He tapped one fluffy cheek. 'Nothing, because you are hired.'

'You're kidding.'

Irvin's eyebrows danced a skitter of perplexity. 'Not in this instance. I have been given a year or so to live, so I am going by gut instinct here. You have a problem with that?'

'With intuition?'

'With death.'

Heather recalled her maither's face, peaceful in the coffin.

She had been ready to get inside and curl up next to her. 'No.' It wasn't lying exactly.

Fran was the strong one, Heather reflected the next day walking home from work. A street magician entertained a crowd of tourists as Heather wove her way home through Edinburgh's streets. Smoke and mirrors. More and more these days the Fran that Heather grew up with seemed an illusion; if not exactly like the fake Victorian spiritualists who promised to reconnect people with their loved ones, for a price, at least a little like a man with white doves up his sleeves and a secret compartment in his top hat. Sure, Fran's empathy level registered at 'lost a parent' but had constantly stumbled over minor cuts or scraped knees. Fran had not been the kind of child, for instance, to run to others with a hug if they tripped on the tarmac, yet she acted decisively when emergencies arose. During one of their science experiments in his da's garage, Hector went awry with a penknife and sliced into his middle finger. Fran, unruffled, told a frenzied Heather to fetch Hector's da, and in the meantime sat Hector in the back seat of his da's rusty Ford, with a towel plucked from the heap of laundry beside the machine.

'He's cut his finger, Mr Rodd. Not too much blood. I suspect he'll need one or two stitches, that's all.'

That day Heather had considered Fran to be the bravest person she'd ever met. As an adult, replaying the scene in her head, Fran's competence replaced her bravery. Fran had known instantly what action to take as if she'd witnessed the scene before, and hadn't Fran's brother Scott a scar on one finger? At the connection, Heather's internal organs relocated themselves in her oesophagus. That said, give Fran her due, she'd courageously returned to that house night after night for Scott. Surviving years of physical abuse. No wonder her edges were sharp. So if Fran's empathy didn't quite rise to sliced fingers that was Dougie, her step-da's, doing. A practical manner was hardly a flaw when balanced by the times Fran had been there for Heather over the years.

To anyone watching, well they might draw their own conclusions about what type of person Fran was there and then. What they couldn't see were all the times Fran had looked after her husband and kids when they were genuinely poorly. Placing cool towels on feverish brows, dotting camomile lotion on itching blisters. It wasn't that being sick was unacceptable in Fran's code of conduct, it was rather being sick and moaning about it was unacceptable. Hector had once tried to get away, in boy-like fashion, with a cold, making too much of a deal of it. Fran had told him to stop sniffling. No sympathy there. Yet, numerous times when Heather had caught flu Fran had turned up on her doorstep with a food parcel – usually containing homemade onion soup – and she'd run a bath for her, and done her laundry while warming up soup, observing Heather slurp up every last drop. Then with a satisfied nod Fran would announce she'd be back tomorrow and the day after that, and after that, until Heather could return to work. You never felt alone with Fran around. Despite her brusque treatment.

Irvin treated Heather like a new friend as they settled into an easy routine. What had she been so afraid of? The pay was generous for an afternoon of playing cards, helping him shave and washing windows. Fenella dropped by, never without her pink lippy, pink coat, to check on him three times a week.

Irvin explained, 'My brother thinks I need a nurse. I disagree.' A compromise had been reached with some home care. Irvin chortled. 'They think I hired a nurse.' His naughtiness and eccentricity went hand in hand. In some ways Irvin reminded her of Fran; he easily put her in her place when she asked if he needed help clipping his toenails: 'I am not an invalid yet,' he remarked in an off-hand way as if closing the subject.

It reminded her of Fran's terse reaction to wedding planning.

Eighteen years ago, Fran had introduced Hector's proposal in their fifteen-minute work break by saying, 'The only thing I care about is the dress.' Then, with a cat-who-got-the-cream smile, she showed Heather her engagement ring: a simple gold band that would double as her wedding ring.

They'd never been the type of lassies to walk in their mothers' high heels and play weddings.

Heather's ribcage imploded. 'You're engaged?' she asked, forcing the question out.

'Aye, we discussed starting a family, so first comes marriage. Gosh, your reaction is supposed to be, congrats!, not—' Fran widened her eyes and dropped her mouth open, imitating catching flies.

Heather laughed. 'I do not look like that.' She'd rather stab her eyes out with a compass than say congrats. Though, to be fair to Fran, Heather had held herself back from pursuing what she wanted, and this was the consequence. 'Want me to help?' Heather asked, instead.

'If you and Hector want to sort things out, sure. I can't be bothered.'

Dice rattled at a nearby table where the game of the year was Monopoly, soon to be forever replaced by Ludo.

Fran rolled her clicking wrists. 'You and Hector are artier than me, so the wedding will look better if you two plan it.'

If she could do this, despite her reservations about Fran and Hector, then she'd be the best chum that she could be. To both of them. Agreeing to plan the wedding of a friend whose fiancé you coveted was bad, right? She wouldn't benefit out of this. The remuneration of her time and emotional endurance would be redirected to them and their relationship. This either made her a walkover or an imposter. In her best case, dream scenario: Hector and her bonded and he married her instead. Worst case scenario: she lost both friendships. Then she'd have nothing. Fran and Hector's wedding, sure, but deeper than that: a three-way friendship forged in anti-bullying campaigns, shared packed lunches and a lot of Scottish drizzle.

Heather said, 'Of course I'll help. I'll give Hector a shout later. Any venue preference?'

'My church,' Fran said. 'That's all. I'll ask the priest this Sunday what paperwork we need. We might also get the church hall for free since I volunteer at crèche. Keep it simple and save our pennies.'

Planning anything with Hector's easy. They slipped into an effortless two-way banter while selecting invitations and personalising them. Hector sneakily used the printer at work to print the invites. They sourced as many contributions as possible from family and friends: flowers, cake, music, buffet food for the church hall reception. On the day, people would take their own photographs and share them. It was surprising what skills existed within their community. One lady from Fran and Hector's church even did makeup.

Eleven months blinked by, and, in May 1999, Heather stepped down the aisle announcing the arrival of the bride. *Hector and Fran are getting married. Hector is getting married.* As the words of the ceremony wove their liquescent magic on Fran's maither, Hector's parents, six friends of Hector's from college and those of the church community, they crisped on her skin. A few concrete-grey flecks settled here and there, patches hardened and spread across her chest and arms and merged into one. Statuesque. She fought to outwardly curve her lips in a slight smile, to pass off traitorous tears as happiness.

It wasn't as if she'd been cut out of their circle of friendship, she told herself, during the ceremony. The honeymoon would be a weekend in North Berwick, then they'd form their usual triangle, similar to the chemical composition of water.

The wedding party progressed to the church hall: a shabby interior which she'd helped Hector and Fran decorate the night before with forget-me-not balloons and sunflower place settings. She sat, marblesque, during the buffet while the wedding from hell unfolded.

Her outline was pencilled in with a mellow numbness until the dull thwack of a plastic knife against a plastic champagne glass signalled Hector's attempt to get the room's attention. It made no logical sense, but she could have sworn the sound vibrated between her toes. Hector announced, 'Hey! Speech time!' If there had been a discrete way to stuff cheese in her ears the moment had passed.

During their first dance her heart swelled, until the ribs that were supposed to protect it tried, instead, to scoop their way out. A scraping of splintered bone on the fleshy wall of her torso, a desperate scratching from the inside out. It's going to tear its way out and, in its hunger, consume the nearest guests within arm's reach. Cleaving their bodies into spots of bloody confetti. Fran would watch that in a movie. Not so much at her wedding.

Hector is married. He struts on the dance floor to 1980's beats. People jerk their arms like zombies. Fran flounces from table to table, greeting everyone, lips parted, eyes bright, guffawing like a donkey. If only she'd chosen the monstrosity in the window so that people would only have to pretend that she looked lovely in her dress.

She does look lovely. Heather fought her festering emotions and focused on the positive. Fran shouldn't suffer because Heather had been too cowardly to admit she loved Hector too, so she should push this ill will aside. She'd missed her chance. Her alone. So quite rightly, Fran had taken him. *He's a fantastic guy. He's happy.*

Watch him. In time to the music, Hector pulls faces, and twists his arms into his body like their old Jurassic Park game. He's happy and she wants him to be happy. Ah, the contradictions of human feelings: desire combined with compassion and self-loathing.

Fran swirled into the space beside Heather.

'I'm so happy.' Fran gave a gaping grin. If crocodiles

could smile their happiness would contain teeth as bitter as grapefruit and as sweet as Turkish delight.

'I'm glad.' What else could she say?, aside from 'this is the most miserable day of my life'. To put Fran's needs above her own, like a good mate, wasn't easy. Fran, Heather reflected, didn't know this and feeding resentment couldn't be appropriate for a friendship. She wanted to be happy for them, so she would try.

'Come and dance, I've requested a tune for old time's sake.'

The DJ changed tracks; drumbeats replaced with the cheesy pop of Chesney Hawkes. Habitually, in clubs Heather watched the crowd, feeling distant from the fandom that carried people away. Even so, this song always had a transportive effect ... she joined Fran and Hector on the dance floor, feeling about eleven.

'I'll still be doing it the way I do it!' they sang. Two hydrogens covalently tied to an oxygen in their liquid state, none of them caring who were the hydrogen and who was the oxygen.

Their three-person hug ended abruptly at the end of the song; Hector lifted Fran by her waist, the flouncy dress almost engulfing him. A soft twirl and a kiss and Heather is forgotten. A lone gas molecule, watching the hydrogens split.

As she turned to leave, Fran grasped her hand. 'You okay, Thistle?'

She wanted to escape to curl into a ball where she stood, and at the same time to wipe the note of concern from Fran's face. Especially on this day. That's what friends do even when they're dying inside.

'Sure. Wonderful day. Parched, want anything?'

'Nah, thanks.' The couple danced a slow number as she gulped down a gin and tonic. She told the young man behind the bar, who didn't seem old enough to serve alcohol, that the drink was for the bride so she didn't have to pay. Remaining silent and amenable today deserved a reward.

Chapter 3

May 2019

It took a month for the paperwork to be completed on the house.

'As it says in the Bible: in my Father's house are many mansions,' Fran told the kids as they raced after Hector into Heather's new home, clearly a mansion, look at the size of the garden encircled by a privacy hedge under the rare blue sky.

Where their hallway was functional, Irvin's hallway held a cabinet, a coat stand and shoe storage – the draws hiding Oxford leathers barely worn, in both senses of the word – without being cluttered. Except for the piles of books sliding off and under the shoe and book cabinets.

While Patricia, Allan and Jack explored the house and Fran asked Heather what the strange objects in the dining room cabinet were, Hector stacked boxes like a person who appreciates law and order in the building-block sense of the word. Heather had asked him to stack her belongings in Irvin's dining room.

'Cheers, for helping me shift this lot,' Heather said.

Hector pushed his glasses up his nose. 'Always a pleasure, never a chore.'

Fran said, 'Two carloads. I don't know whether to be flabbergasted or jealous. Our house is a war zone of crap.'

'Except for books and clothes what else do we need?' Heather asked.

Hector gave a wry smile. 'Toys, games, ornaments, figurine collections, ugly inherited pieces of furniture. You name it and it's in our house. Looks like you've inherited stuff here.' He perused Irvin's cabinet of curiosities: a Tibetan singing bowl, a stone Ganesh from India, a Japanese puzzle box.

'He collected those from his travels,' Heather said. 'We still on for Sat, charity shops?'

'Two o'clock, as usual.' Fran examined each object. She loved a nosy through other people's stuff. It would be hard to explain to a person who was not standing in Irvin's house how many books he owned because paperbacks were jammed into bookshelves and cupboards until they burst. Spines were piled high in every nook. They weighed down the tops of cabinets, tables. And tumbled off windowsills. An armchair that would have taken up too much space at Fran's barely made a dent in the lounge; it was constructed with slots for books, like a mini library, with religious covers: *Muhammad in History, Thought, and Culture* and *The Heart of the Buddha's Teaching*. Heather showed them the crammed shelves in the toilet, the novels that carpeted the stairs and one of the upstairs bedrooms had bookshelves wedged behind the bed in an upwards arc.

Heather explained that Irvin liked to read several hardbacks at a time, and although she was responsible for keeping the rooms amply clean so that his family would accept he could stay and die at home, he would keep piles of hardbacks that she was not allowed to touch. Some piles waited to be read, others had been read but were waiting for notes to be taken. Heaps of notebooks toppled in the corners of every room; full of extracts he had written down, as well as piles to reread or find a place to store.

'All that dust would bring out Hector's allergies,' Fran said.

'It's—,' Heather said. 'This place doesn't feel like mine. It can't be. I'm not even family.'

She's so ungrateful. This should have been mine – ours. These rooms, these cabinets, the art on the walls, the bread machine in the kitchen. If she'd only answered that advertisement instead of Heather.

Fran turned her nose up at Irvin's taste in art; namely, the detailed wood etching with the name Katrine Lyck beneath it, and a photograph of a girl in yellow wellies who waved at a flock of swans.

'There's no family photos,' Fran said. She ran her finger over a silver tea set which left a line in the fine coating of dust. 'Plenty to clean.'

Hector sneezed. 'Aye, you might have to pack to unpack.'

'There's no rush to erase his presence.'

Fran understood, for Heather to say 'my house' would be too soon. They'd dreamt of owning a house. A place beyond the ring road like Penicuik. Not handy for a commute to work by bus unless you wanted two hours added to your day. Irvin's house was nestled in a leafy area of Ravelston, 20 minutes by bus, 30 minutes' walk, to the city centre. Shame all these books cluttered the place. It would take Heather weeks to sort through them and Fran had no time, or wish, to help.

Hector wiped his hands on his baggy trousers. 'I'm happy for you.'

'We're happy for you.' Fran wound her arms around his waist. 'Where're the kiddies?' Fran asked. 'It's too quiet.'

Patricia, Allan and Jack were rattling a handle.

'Why's this locked?' Patricia asked. 'We heard noises.'

'I'll show you the bodies of overcurious children I keep inside,' Heather said as she unlocked the door.

'She's joking,' Fran said to Jack, who had retreated behind her legs.

The creaking door revealed a room that contained two large cages and plenty of stands and ropes and a miniature rope bridge. A parrot, about 30 cm long from beak to tail, paused from wiping his beak on the vertical perch in his cage. He gave a greeting whistle.

'This is Schelle. He's a Green-cheeked conure,' Heather said. 'Let him get used to you. I'll open his cage.'

Despite the name of the species he had a grey head and cheeks, a pale belly graduating to yellow at the legs, green and blue wings, and red tail feathers.

Allan pushed forward to be the first to enter. Fran smelled

bird droppings as Hector sneezed.

Schelle wiggled his tail. Fran hoped this was a friendly gesture like a dog might make towards its owner.

'Why's the cage padlocked?' Patricia asked.

'Because this parrot is a master lock picker,' Heather said.

'Why does he wag his tail like a dog?'

'Because he's happy to see us.'

'Where's he from?' Allan asked.

'Edinburgh. His parents came from somewhere like Argentina or Brazil, I think.'

Fran's phone rang. It was Beth again.

'Max would like to go to church. I think it's young curiosity as Ronny and myself are both Atheists. Can he go with you on Sunday?'

'Aye.'

Fran overheard a male voice ask, 'You dropping him off?' Beth said, 'Oh, shut up. Shit.' and the line went dead.

Patricia said, 'Keeping parrots as pets is cruel.'

Fran hadn't been aware Heather was smiling until Heather's smile widened as she met Fran's eyes. 'I agree with you, Trish. That's why Irvin taught me how to keep him happy.'

Schelle flapped to the ceiling and hung off the light. The kids laughed. Schelle copied; his laugh an imitation of honking geese blended with a sorcerer's cackle.

Jack asked, 'Does he like to play?'

'Let me show you.' Heather ran through some hand signals with Jack. She fetched a strawberry. 'Stand by this perch. Take this.' She bit off the main part of the strawberry leaving the leaves and the juicy red flesh.

Fran resisted pulling Jack away. The parrot was friendly enough to be around the kids if Heather thought so.

Schelle skimmed the top of Fran's head to land on a perch close to Heather and Jack.

'He wants that strawberry,' Heather said. 'To get it he will have to go through the sequence of hand gestures I taught you.'

Jack stared at the parrot; the parrot stared at the strawberry.

Jack stretched one hand into a star-shape. Schelle copied, displaying his green and blue wings. Jack tapped one hand on the other and the parrot tapped his perch with his beak. Jack waved and the parrot raised one leg.

Patricia and Allan clapped, followed by Fran and Hector.

'Great. Now his treat,' Heather said.

Fran admired Jack's bravery as he began to hold out the strawberry leaves. She wouldn't approach the parrot's sharp beak and claws.

Then his hand changed direction as the parrot bobbed his head towards it. Heather took the treat from Jack.

'You'd make a great animal trainer, Jack.' Heather handed the strawberry to Schelle who balanced on one leg, shredding his treat.

'Why does he have two cages?' Patricia asked.

'One's for sleeping, the other's for playing during the day. Parrots need a lot of stimulation. They're smart. And need many things to wear down their beak, 'cause it keeps growing.' Heather handed Schelle a twig from a pile which could've come from the garden.

'Can we get a parrot?' Allan asked.

'You should come with us on Sunday,' Fran said to Heather, the timing of her remark felt a little off as though parrots were related to the devil.

'Church? Me?' Heather asked, eyes as wide as a parrot's.

In the rear-view mirror, Fran saw Heather watching their car leave, a discontented expression on her face. The church invite? Or was she sad to see them go? Tires crunching on the gravel of the private driveway, Allan and Jack insistent on the idea of a parrot as a pet, Patricia championing animal rights. Fran listened for the sounds between her children's excited voices. How was it plausible that she couldn't hear traffic? Their place, near to Ferry Road, was assaulted by cars, buses, lorries, ambulances and ice cream vans. They weren't that far as the crow flew, yet this was another world: like the crow had learnt the trick of interdimensional travel.

'Settle down,' she told the kids. And caressed Hector's arm as he laid his hand across the gearstick.

'Lucky, Heather, hey,' he said.

She became aware of a taste like pennies in her mouth. 'Aye, lucky,' she said and sent a silent prayer to God not to covet her neighbour's house and to hold thankfulness in her heart. What was positive for Heather was positive for all of them. Heather was right to be surprised about being invited to church. It was Fran that needed to settle her soul.

Chapter 4

November 2017

Heather hadn't been honest with Irvin at the beginning about being a writer; she had been frustrated since childhood by her inability to capture what she wanted on the page. By the autumn he hadn't fired her, yet: despite her hardly picking up a duster. It turned out it was companionship he wanted, and someone to be there in the afternoons to appease his family so they left him alone.

On her days off, she haunted the library. She read of other lives doing interesting things as a substitute for being unable to do them herself. It had to do while she lived on a cleaning salary; until the publishing world did more than send rejection letters.

Libraries are spaces for dreaming. Where the shelves of the library span infinite worlds, as vast as the imaginations of their readers.

Heather extended her palms over the spines. Eyes closed, her fingers expanded to brush overprotective plastic covers, firm hardbacks, cracked backbones. Until an interesting ridge, suggestive of multiple reads, caught the pad of her pinkie and she plucked it out. Ignoring the description, separating the covers, flicking her thumb over the book's edges and lowering her nose, eyes still shut. Each book preserves a scent: the yellow vanilla of a 1980's paperback, the arid tang of recycled wood, the gummy fluidity of a newer book's adhesives.

Some of these smells are caused by the manufacturing process, others by changes in chemical composition over time: the breakdown of cellulose and lignin which allow plant cells

41

to remain rigid and strong.

Cologne gave away the presence of a man who, by the floor's creak, had taken a step back to allow her to progress in front of him, across pliant spines. To an external observer she wondered if her behaviour looked odd. Heather shifted perspective to observe herself from the outside: a brown and grey haired, five-foot one lady, with scraggy split ends in comfortable jeans and a well-fitted coat. A deceptive complexion from spending too much time indoors, so perhaps she's older than she appears, more forty than thirty. The woman flicks through books with her eyes shut and moves on, ignoring those around her which either takes confidence or a contained sense of self. Flicking the pages, wiggling the book back into its cradle, selecting another until a scent tickles her nose. What is it? Woody thyme? She held the book reverently. This one. She's returned to herself.

From her experience paper can be sugary, woody or surprising. People too but it's easier to categorise the characters of books. For instance, the sweet marzipan chemicals of blue biro on her writer's pad; a consequence of the polyethylene glycol solvent that allows the ink to flow smoothly across the surface of a ball bearing.

'This is a fab one,' Wendy the librarian said. Heather barely heard her; her mind caught up in how to describe the thump of an old library stamp. At the Central Library it's still probable to obtain one from Wendy in the front page of each book. A physical reminder of all the people who held this book, and would, before and after her.

Heather ordered a slice of walnut and coffee cake and a smoky oolong tea in the National Library café, across the road, to read and write the afternoon away.

She wanted her books to be on the shelves of the library one day. A thought niggled in the back of her mind: Irvin writes. If she's ever going to ask anyone for help, this is the chance.

Her first meeting with Irvin was the first and only time she got caught jotting imaginings down. But he had remembered;

this week he had given her a journal for her birthday.

'I can't accept this,' she'd said, already sniffing the pages.

'Surely not because you think it is a bribe for sexual favours.' He had wiggled his eyebrows. So preposterous and purposefully sexist she'd giggled, small whoops escaping her like a train's whistle.

'Think of it as a reward for all your demanding work. An outward sign that I am proud of you for returning to higher education.'

'Term's just started. I might fail the access module.'

The skin on her arms and chest puckered like featherless poultry, as the colours of the room, including Irvin's concerned brown eyes, had brightened. Her body had stiffened at the thought: failure. Sharp jabs had run up her hamstrings, prickles darted in the soles of her feet, reminding her of the worst pain she'd ever felt when she was eight.

∞∞∞

All eight-year-olds rapidly discover that adults block their way by indicating what is safe from what isn't. In their option. Heather grinned at Fran's face. She'd negotiated the zigzagging streets and crossings on her own to knock on Fran's door.

'Ma went shopping. We've an hour.' Her high-pitch, out-of-breath voice sounded excited to her own ears.

Fran half closed the door. 'You'll get in trouble.'

'She'll never ken if I'm back before.'

Fran shrugged. 'You want to see me dollhouse?'

The dollhouse was a bit of wooden flooring with a plastic Barbie bed. Fran had arranged her dolls as if they were dancing. 'It's a bedroom ballroom.'

Fran played a CD, and they danced and invented routines and pretended to be pop stars to Michael Jackson, Sonja, Five Star, Blondie, Madonna, and Rick Astley. Heather lost track of the time and had to run, skidding across leaves and puddles, intending to run around the side, climb over the garden fence and act casual.

Uncle and Aunty Noursair flung open the door the moment Heather's foot was on the driveway. Oh boy, Ma must have called them. She ducked their angry arms.

'You will behave!' Her uncle dragged her inside the house like she was a piece of furniture to be repaired and reupholstered. Heather struggled, bit down on his hand as it shifted over her mouth to silence her yells and ran up the stairs. Her legs lacked stride but she propelled herself up in leaps of two at a time.

'Little bitch, did you see what she did?'

'Ma! Ma!'

The room was empty, the bed neatly made.

The creaky top step gave her uncle away. Heather ran into the corner as Uncle's hands formed fists. 'I'll show you what happens to misbehaving little girls.'

'I want to see her! Ma?'

'My sister is dead, selfish girl.'

The ticking of her heart stopped. Her breath stopped. Time folded and engulfed her. Uncle's fists dropped. He stifled a groan and packed her into his car. Strapped her in. The car's engine sounded muted; birds in the birch outside Uncle and Aunty's house were muted. Any moment now they would notice that her heart had stopped. That she wasn't here. They put a plate of food in front of her and took it away. They left her pressing her face into a strange smelling pillow in a strange room.

Heather wraps herself in the citron-scented sheets, wiping her nose on them. It's hard to breathe but it muffles the voices through the wall. She thinks of Christmases, when laughter through the brickwork of this same house soothed her to sleep, though the occasional creak from the landing woke her and Maither poked her head in the room. Now the voices are raised. She gives up, flinging back the covers. The heating in this house is too high. She gets up and tries to turn off the radiator but the valve refuses to budge. She rests her head against the hot metal, smelling paint, pennies and her own sweat. Tears drip off her nose and down the steel ridges it's pressed against.

'No one will remember her, Phyllis. She had a future. Then … she kept the bairn.'

The implication that it, Heather, was a bad choice hung in the air; she holds her breath.

'Why does it matter, Harry?'

Uncle Harry's consonants are as sharp as lemons. 'Kept the bairn and became a canteen lady.'

Kept. An odd choice of word. After Heather had her sixth birthday, she'd directly asked Maither about her absent Da, and her maither had given a soft smile and stroked Heather's hair. 'He wanted to be with me more than I wanted to be with him,' she said.

'Will I ever meet him?'

Helen's face twisted from her eyebrows to her chin, Heather didn't understand why. Helen replied, 'No. He wasn't desirable for us to be around.' Maither had hugged her until Heather squirmed to be free. Maither had said she'd never meet him, so Heather never asked again. She would have at some point. Now the possibility had been taken away, until, that is, Uncle Harry and Aunt Phyllis's words revealed that they knew her da. Heather returned to lie on the bed, letting the remarks swirl around her.

'My sister could have completed her nursing qualification. Then she had this child. His child.'

Heather's heart sped up, knocking against her consciousness. See, I wasn't wanted, wasn't planned.

Aunt Phyllis said, 'I can't imagine how devastating it must have been for her to look into her own child's face.'

Something didn't feel right. First, they'd been disapproving of Maither's choice, how they did not like her da, or to be reminded of him through her features. Heather traced her chin, cheeks, nose, and hair with her fingertips. All like her mum. No wonder they detested her. Feeling the arc of her eyeball she compressed her eyelids gently. Da was here, and here, she tugged the lobes of her ears.

'What good,' Harry spat out, 'is she doing in the world other than creating a martyr of my sister? She died alone. Forgotten. A wasted life.'

Wasted, the opposite of … Heather played the game she had learnt at school … valuable.

'I wish she had not told me the whole story.'

'Perhaps if you tell me,' Phyllis said.

Heather propped herself up on her elbows. Their voices had fallen. She strained to hear every word.

'Not much to tell. The man had a knife. Helen was too scared to make a sound in case her flatmate also got raped.'

Raped, Heather filed away that information to look up later in the Oxford English Dictionary on her Uncle's bookshelf.

Rape: forcing another person to have sexual intercourse with the offender against their will.

Sexual intercourse: sexual contact between individuals involving penetration, especially the insertion of a man's erect penis into a woman's vagina.

Vagina: the muscular tube leading from the external genitals to the cervix of the uterus in women and most female mammals.

Cervix: The narrow passage forming the lower end of the uterus.

Uterus: The organ in the lower body of a woman or female mammal where offspring are conceived and in which they gestate before birth; the womb.

'How did he get in?' Phyllis asked.

'Some problem with the door jamming. She tried to

convince him otherwise. Said she screamed inside the whole time. Who says that to her own brother? Though she was pretty out of it when I showed up at the hospital.'

Maither had been attacked by a trespasser. Looking back, Maither disliked being outside after sunset in winter. She'd joked she was a sun lover but avoided getting a tan. She disliked horrors or thrillers. She disliked strangers brushing against her during the Edinburgh festival. Heather didn't doubt her maither loved her. Now it was too late to ask, how did you do it? Why raise me and not put me up for adoption or terminate the pregnancy? Religion wasn't her thing. A half-formed memory swirled back, 'When I held you for the first time, I knew I'd never let go. No matter what the rest of the world said.'

She'd prove her aunt and uncle wrong and make up for the actions of a da that took on the appearance of a sketched outline in her imagination. The colour of his hair and skin, the strength of his laugh, what made him angry or happy, every aspect of him unknown.

She wouldn't waste her life, Heather swore for Maither's sake.

That hadn't been the worst bit. The worst bit was Aunty dropping her at school the next day. Heather's stomach had tilted and swirled all the way to school in Aunty's pine-scented car as the woman said nasty things about transferring schools because this was too much of a drive in the morning, adding fifteen minutes to her usual commute. Heather had chewed her cheek and fretted about how she could answer the usual question, 'How was your weekend?', when Fran and Hector asked. Why were her uncle and aunty making her go to school at all? No doubt, some self-reliant crap they'd read in a parenting manual such as 'routine is beneficial'.

Heather doubled over her shoes – don't throw up – staring at her murky outline in the high-gloss finish of her leather shoes. What if this playground didn't exist but was merely a cracked reflection in a child's shoe? As her brain sought relief in story, an ominous form bloomed on the leather with its arms outspread. Ma?

Fran skipped up to her. 'Hey, Thistle!'

Heather swallowed a mouthful of bitter saliva. Would she forever search for Ma in every unexplained movement and shadow? Last night it had been the bushes outside the house, and the shadow of tree branches on the bedroom wall. She waited for Fran to ask the usual question, and readied herself for the tears that hadn't stopped all night.

Fran slapped her on the back, 'You're it!'

Fran ran into the school.

Heather watched Fran's Dutch braids through the school gates. She'd been so worried how to reply she hadn't considered that no one would ask. At reception, morning break, lunch, afternoon break, in every class. Not one person asked. Her uncle and aunty must have told the headmistress and asked the teachers to watch out for her. They'd done that for Alice last year when her da was in a car crash. Heather stared forward in each class, experimentally moving her limbs now and then; moving was like swimming through thick treacle – which made no sense as you couldn't breathe treacle. Though Ma had sworn by a teaspoon after breakfast to raise her iron levels, and Heather had caught her more than once stirring it into a bowl of porridge.

After school, as the bell chased them out into the sunshine, Hector went on about trains. He'd seen a new one with his da that weekend. Fran obsessed about a recent music band during Hector's pauses. Hector could be clueless much of the time; Fran was more observant. Of course, Fran didn't know that while Heather had snuck to her house, Ma had felt sick and returned home seeking Heather, but Heather – selfishly – had been with Fran.

Heather had been prepared for silence and sympathy, not life continuing as it had yesterday.

'What's with you today?' Fran asked. 'You're not listening.'

The tears returned. Crying all night had done nothing but

make the corners of her eyes ache and now they ached even more.

'What happened, Heather?' Hector asked.

Fran crossed her arms. 'There, there, you brought it on yourself. I said you would. Heather snuck into my place when her ma went out.'

'Awesome.' Hector grinned, yet frowned as Heather kept crying.

'Not if she got in this much trouble. What did your ma say?' Fran asked. 'Ms Salt gave me the worst homework for—'

'Shut it, you idiot,' Hector said. 'Can't you see she's upset?'

Heather managed two words, 'Ma. Dead.'

'Wha!' Fran's crossed arms dropped to her sides.

'That's not helping, Fran.' Hector gently stroked Heather's back.

If Heather didn't understand how this happened, how could anyone else? The St Christopher around her neck, a gift from Maither, rubbed awkwardly against her neck. Why would God take the one person she had in this world?

'Why'd they send you to school?' Fran asked. 'If anything justifies a day off this is it. It's Uncle and Aunt Nose-hair, right? I bet they had no inkling what to do with you.' Fran turned to Hector confidentially, 'They own a poddle.'

'I think you mean poodle.'

'I know that numbskull. How pointless is that.'

'Owning a dog or a poodle?' he asked.

'You should be comforting Heather not asking me silly questions.'

Heather floated away from their conversation. When she was gone from her body, would people still be boiling water for cuppas and hanging out the washing? What if she hadn't gone to Fran's? Wait if Ma had told Heather she was sick? Mayhap if she'd been present, maybe …

'I don't know what to say to someone whose mum died,' Hector said.

Fran growled like a mother bear. 'Well, that was a thought

best kept in your head.'

'Owch,' Hector said. 'Why are you picking a fight?'

Fran scowled. 'Straight talking's not fighting.'

'I'll be okay. Not right now, but I will be,' Heather said.

'You don't have to be brave, Thistle, it's your ma.' Fran pressed Heather's head into her shoulder.

Heather whimpered, and the whimpers became rolling sobs that assailed her ribs.

Fran whispered a prayer as she rocked her, 'Hail Mary, full of grace, the lord is with thee … pray for us sisters, now and at the hour of our death. Amen.'

'Sinners, not sisters.'

'It doesn't matter, Hector!'

The normality of their arguing soothed Heather into a state of numbness. Hector hugged Heather over Fran's embrace. It was more than her aunty and uncle had done. She promised to never forget that they were there for her in her hour of need.

Now, in Irvin's study, as he scoffed and wiggled his expressive eyebrows, Heather rubbed her arms to chase the goose bumps away. She was no longer a scared eight-year-old girl, and over the years her writing skills had improved. Still. Whenever she raised writing Fran said either 'drop it' or 'writing makes you miserable'. The only person on her side with this was Irvin.

'Fail? Nonsense! Not with my tutoring. Every assignment, you run it by me first. Every text. We will discuss before you even start writing your thoughts down.'

'I can't take up—'

'—the time of a dying man. Nonsense!'

Yes. Perhaps. Why not? She could do this. And Fran didn't need to know.

'As a Doctor of Letters, I would prescribe … Maya Angelou. "You may trod me in the very dirt. But still, like dust, I'll rise".' He drew a book from the shelf: *And Still I Rise*. 'Read these.'

'I'm not knowledgeable about poetry.'

'Read it.'

Open University, she told herself, not a proper university akin to world renowned St Andrews. The benefit being the lack of formal entry requirements as a barrier. She could do an open degree. By correspondence, they used to call it. Now everything was digitalised online, even the reading list. In three years, if she studied every spare moment, she could complete the course in three years, the equivalent of fulltime. No point hanging about, as Irvin said.

Irvin interrupted her thoughts, 'At least tell me what genre you're writing.'

'No.'

Irvin sighed, his eyebrows taking a downward tilt, mirroring his mouth.

'But thank you for the encouragement.'

He chuckled. 'If your protagonists are as evasive as you that's going to be one spectacular first book.'

His locution reminded her she was forty, a failed author.

'Hey.' He shook her shoulder. 'George Eliot, Anna Sewell, Maya Angelou and Raymond Chandler published a first novel after forty.'

'Margaret Atwood, James Joyce, Mary Shelley. Before they were twenty-five.'

'Admittedly, there has to be a bell curve for published age with most falling,' he dropped into his armchair as if to emphasise his point, 'in their thirties and forties, I am sure.'

'Speculation.'

'Effective, you used that word exactly right!'

'Bampot. Know that one?'

'Back to the point though, writing requires life experience. I never used to think so and then I got into poetry.'

Heather stared at the cover of the poetry book in her hands, leaning on the journal he'd given her. So life must be crushed and mashed by the paper press of life in order to make yet more paper?

'Like dust, I rise,' Irvin said.

'Thanks, Freud.'

'Ummm,' He wriggled his brows. 'Tell me about your papa.'

Heather's tear ducts prickled.

'Ah, unsurprisingly I put my foot in it. Sorry, Heather.'

She was so used to Fran brushing off feelings like a duck shakes the rain off, she didn't know how to respond to someone acknowledging they'd put their foot in it. She'd never suspected her friendship with Fran was so lopsided until Irvin. At night, she tried to tell herself that she hadn't told Fran about Open University because her friend hadn't been supportive in recent years about her writing dreams, and, in general, mocked those with a university education instead of one from the university of life. Fran's attitude was so negative about these two subjects that the thought of mentioning her course made her elbows shake as much as the first time a horse had towered above her on a city road, shaking its muzzle, all lips and incisors.

Fran had been there for her whenever she'd needed support. Heather clung to these memories. It was hard to pinpoint one exact circumstance because there were so many. And in Fran's local community too, an accumulation of voluntary work for the church nursery, Sunday school, Christmas boxes for refugee children, and elderly befriender for the City of Edinburgh Social Work Department. Her biggest act being to try to save Scott, which she sometimes laughed, bitterly, would count against her as her biggest failure at the gates of heaven.

Those first months at primary school, Fran hadn't gone out of her way to make friends or enemies. Her innate tendency appeared, at first, to sit and stare; assessing the world and where she should slot into it. Hector suggested they conduct a psychological evaluation on Fran as a science experiment, being halfway through that type of book. Fran after a period of unknown observation answered all of Hector's questions, such as 'Do you prefer to work alone or in a group?', 'Have you ever told a lie?', 'Do you often have a desire to get even with others?'

Hector seemed confident that Fran came out as practically minded in various personality tests: the Myers-Briggs, Minnesota-Multiphasic and the Reiss Motivation Profile. Heather couldn't have told one test apart from another.

Meanwhile, Fran joined in with Hector's odd compulsion to test the things out from his odd selection of reading materials by sourcing all kinds of things for the "experiments" they could try.

After three months of Hector's odd and rather awkward questioning technique, Fran's response to an inkblot test had been, 'Enough already. I'm not a psycho, okay? You writing a book on how to psychoanalyse your friends?'

'You're not interested in the results then?' Hector asked.

'Keep talking.'

Hector said, 'You have a powerful desire for self-reliance and a predictable environment, a low desire for influence and acceptance. You're quick to anger, and despite appearances,' he looked over her punky hair, 'cool down quickly.'

'I was curious,' Fran said. 'I thought I'd be conkers.'

Hector concluded with a thumbs up, which made her double over laughing, and by that time the three of them were friends.

Chapter 5

May 2019

Not paying attention to the sermon that Sunday morning, Fran eyeballed Jesus on the cross, and sniffed. Carpet cleaner hung in the air. As much as she wanted to sterilise the association with the old church – Dougie's church – she couldn't ignore its chemical reek: of incense impregnating the fabric of the wooden benches, of vanilla candles, of the beliefs and odours of the thousands of people that had walked these stones before this congregation. Yet one chemical association took her back to those vulnerable days when adults held power over her.

Possibly because her first church experiences involved Dougie slapping her knees when she swung her feet between the gap between their pew and the one in front. The service was unfollowable due to the priest's weird words delivered in an unnatural, deadpan, manner. The best bit of the experience was private prayer time. Then Dougie zipped his face tightly closed and muttered under his breath for forgiveness. He needed a lot of forgiving.

Rather than bow her head in prayer, Fran would enjoy the rare freedom to stare at people and try to guess what they were praying about. Who also hit their kids at home? Who cursed at their neighbours? Drank too much and did a shit on a neighbour's front step?

Some would clutch their interlaced palms against their heart: lips moved, palms kissed, armpit-stained shirts. As far as she could see, they all had something to feel guilty about.

Silence here was different from pauses in regular life.

Silence then could be soothing, rather than tense and apprehensive. A cough hit a wall of divine prayer; a sneeze naturally stifled instead of letting rip. Most fascinating of all was the way Dougie changed – all politeness, please and thank you, to calling his fellow churchgoers names behind their back as if female body parts were an insult. How can a person who goes to church want to beat up on other people? To all her observations Dougie hated other people. So why then sit amongst them every seven days? Fran pondered this complexity week after week, pressing her fingers against the bruises on her skin, watching them slowly fade and new ones take their places. She never did anything right.

Sitting next to her children, Fran found herself watching the congregation. Adults shifting in creaking pews, bright-eyed children crawling underneath. Attention locked on the priest, raised to the cross or the stained glass, or cast down at their folded hands. As she took in these details, she planned how to exit the church with minimum contact. The key was to get out while people were distracted with the tea and cake. These thoughts led her to become self-aware. This soul cleansing time wasted with pettiness.

Fran stared at Jesus crucified above her and tried to connect to that voice within connected to God. Her own personal private line: I'm sorry. I'm grateful. I'm lost. Because I'm jealous of my best pal and I don't know how to shake it.

Listening for a reply: none came. Fran stifled a sigh and blinked her lids open as her belly rumbled. Her punishment for skipping breakfast so she could feast on the Sunday roast.

They'd arrived, as usual, at the last minute to sit, strategically, at the end of a row near the back. In this way Fran avoided being greeted by fellow churchgoers as they took their seats. Families slotted into their usual spot with their usual conversations week after week. Fran was of the mind that it was sufficient to nod politely after each mass and ferry the kids to the exit. Occasionally she got caught by individuals in the community who took it upon themselves to be welcoming:

volunteering in the church to hand out leaflets, speaking to different people after each service, baking cakes, giving off an aura of sickening cheer and helpfulness.

Today she's so damned hungry the cake is tempting. The kids whispered, 'Carrot cake!' to one another on the way in. Cake, carrots, cake, her brain says – it's supposed to be communing with God.

It's not that she doesn't want to be part of the church; it's tricky to juggle work shifts and everything else. She used to help with the Sunday school but it's not realistic right now. She wants to be happy for Heather. Of course, she's happy for Heather as any mate would be. And she has many things Heather doesn't have: her faith in God, a husband and children, and the financial stability of a second household income. That's why it should have been her that got the house, to put a permanent home over the kids' heads. Houses in Edinburgh were too expensive, and the bank didn't consider her cleaner's income to be adequate. They'd been stuck renting while Heather also benefited from Irvin's money. A worm of jealousy had hatched.

Sometimes, she doubts God knows what he is doing heaping extra emotional burdens on her when she'd be at her best unburdened so as to help in the church community.

'God knows what he's doing,' the priest said, as if He'd read her thoughts and was speaking through him. 'We need to trust him. At the same time, maintaining our community is our responsibility. So I'm going to remind us all about the ingredients of a community. One: awareness. To keep our eyes and ears open to the people around us to see how we might help them. Two: kindness. To try to show as many people as possible love, without expecting anything in return.'

Watching other churchgoers nodding their heads, a disconnect yawned between herself and the congregation. Not to her faith. Not to God. To these folks.

'Three: humility. It's wholesome to be self-reliant without turning away from the benevolent will of others, as without offering ourselves to God and to our community there's a tendency to look inward instead of connecting.

'Being a part of community is the spiritual duty of every believer. Therefore, during tea and cake today I'd ask each of you to converse with three new people, or those you don't usually encounter.'

Fran inwardly groaned. Sorry God, but you're testing me today.

'Let us try to "be the church" in the community – every day.'

The chaplain's right. Faith is a way of life, not showing up for mass each Sunday. The challenge is fitting that priority into life when the rest of it could be so draining.

'God bless.'

Folk started to move. Fran jumped into the usual routine of herding the kids up the still unobstructed aisle from the chapel to the entrance hall. She could hear birdsong as the sun tried to break through the clouds outside.

'Cake mum!' Jack, Allan and Patricia pulled her away from the exit to the tables of tea and cake laid out in the community hall opposite. So close.

'Dave,' an elderly man introduced himself. 'My wife, Edith. Our neighbours made the cake this week.' As Edith checked that each of Fran's children got a slice, Dave offered Fran a cup of tea, wobbling in its saucer. 'Nice to see you stayed today,' he said. 'Didn't you used to help out with the food bank?'

'The crèche, before I had my three.'

This was the thing about church conversations – or with such a close-knit community, like the playground – she found herself constantly trying to hide the details of her life. Today she misdirected and asked Dave and Edith about their kids and gulped down her non-sugared tea because going for the sugar would put her in danger of mumsy conversations by the look of the group gathering there.

Yet this strategy didn't prevent her being cornered by a younger mum by the community board full of fliers for yoga classes, piano lessons, jumble sales, film nights, choir Wednesday, private counselling, blood donations, food donations and community seminars on local history topics. The woman shoved her bairn in Fran's arms, the minute Fran put her cup and saucer down, so that she could eat a slice of cake.

'I'm Steph, that's Fiona.'

'Mm-hmm,' Fran said, eyeing the cake that was supposed to be hers disappearing into Steph's mouth. The bairn attempted to bite her chin with a moist and gumless mouth.

'I wish I had the time to get to know people more,' Steph said. 'This one's demanding. Plus, I breed cats, the kittens can be a handful.'

White hairs clung to Fran's knee-length cardigan. Fran muttered something about being 'allergic to cats' as she handed the baby back to wrest the hairs off her clothing and called the kids to follow her out – they stuffed another helping of cake in their mouths on the way. Never got a slice herself. Thanks a bunch, God.

∞∞∞

Fran arrived late in Morningside on Sunday afternoon. 'A toy found its way into the toilet. Soaked the hallway carpet.' She peeled a piece of toilet paper off her skirt. 'Must borrow a carpet cleaner.'

Heather grabbed one elbow. 'Don't mention it to James. Borrow the cleaner from work.'

Fran broke away from Heather's touch by sidestepping a bicycle chained to a lamppost. And asked herself if borrowing the machine was permissible in the eyes of God; given her financial circumstances, and how much everyone disliked James who didn't work for his extra pay grade? Justifiable after all the radiators she'd dusted behind, chaffing her knees. 'Let's go to The Thrift,' Fran said.

To a soundtrack of cars and buses, under a Drummond grey tartan sky, the all too brief winter light highlighted the sandstone buildings like carrots in a Scotch broth. Folk scurried by painted shopfronts as if everyone had left the hairdresser today with a contrasting style. Doggies of all pelts and heights sported fashion accessories, designating this area of town as 'a cut above'.

Above Pilton at any rate.

She may be an outsider here, and at the church and at the school but at least she and Heather had each other's back. 'What's new?' she asked Heather.

Heather blinked, too slowly as if – Fran reflected – she had been daydreaming, and pulled at her earlobe to remain in the present. 'Not much. Did Hector's bulbs grow?'

'Shouldn't you shop in boutiques now?' Fran asked, as they hastily explored the rails before the store shut. 'What with Irvin's money ...' The words came out stilted, unnatural, the real question being: Did he leave you money as well as the house?

Heather blushed like a coffee stain spreading across a paper towel, in patches. A sure sign of some inner thought unshared.

And that slow blink again before she spoke, 'Sterile, over-priced shops with three railings? No, thanks.'

'Same here.' Fran pointed to dried food stains on her coat: tomato sauce at war with peanut butter. 'Parenting and designer wear equals Irn-Bru disaster. Dry clean only is about as useful as octopus arsehole soup to a working mum.'

Heather chortled. 'Octopus arsehole soup!'

The volunteer at the store told them the shop was closing.

'I know the snowdrops did well,' Heather said, turning towards the door. 'I was wondering about the daffodils.'

'Grew in bucket loads.' Fran rubbed her left calf muscle and grimaced as they exited the shop, wondering why Heather was so obsessed with their flowers. 'I need the lavvy. Let's pop into that café.'

If Heather had noticed Fran didn't buy much, she didn't say. Posh neighbourhood ladies drove the prices up. If Fran wasn't worrying if the kids' shoes would fit, there was the dilemma about heating and whether they could put on another jumper or should put the heating on, or whether to invest in new thermals because the old ones were practically holes connected by thread. Two incomes didn't stretch that far paying rent, feeding, and clothing three kids.

From the café window Fran and Heather were as snug as two slaters in a compost heap. They watched several families heading to the park. Families and bicycles competed on the pedestrian and cycleway paths beneath the trees.

Fran counted pennies onto the table. 'Let's share a brownie; could use the sugar.'

'Hector still trying to lose some pounds?'

The grinding of the coffee machine interrupted their conversation. Then Fran said, 'He's more obsessed with politics. Given the Brexit referendum coupled with the 2017 general election, he expects another vote will be pushed for ahead of 2020, 'cause MPs aren't backing Theresa May.'

Heather hadn't made a move to order, so Fran waved at the lady and mouthed the command 'choc-o-late brow-nie'. The girl behind the counter pointed to the chocolate cake. 'A brownie!' Fran fought the urge to cry, though it wasn't like she was keeping secrets from the sugar police. Must be hormonal, she told herself.

'Most of our lives we've lived under a Conservative parliament,' Heather said, making a face as if she'd learnt that sugar was contraband and they'd have to use salt as a substitute. She tallied the names on her fingers, 'Thatcher, Major, Cameron, May. Four Conservative prime ministers.'

'Country's going to the dogs, as Ma used to say.' Fran slumped, shoulders scooped, feeling her belly bulge forward. She tugged her jumper over her tummy. 'When Hector and I married, Labour's Blair had just won, ninety-seven wasn't it?' Fran asked, slicing the chocolate brownie in half and jamming it in her mouth. 'That's a lot of shit under the bridge.'

'Maither's death,' Heather said. 'Sc—'

'Jack being born prematurely. Hector's parents.'

'Irvin's death,' Heather added.

The brownie stuck in Fran's throat. 'My ma too,' she said. Hector's grief was newer than hers, even if she'd barely had time to process that Ma had gone before Hector's parents passed away.

'No weddings, but four funerals this past year.' Heather gestured to Fran to finish the remainder of the brownie.

Fran stared at the rich chocolatey goodness on the plate. She shouldn't. Really. Every scrap of food went to her belly these days, and she's already eaten about half a chicken with roast tatties and parsnips, carrots, sprouts and a bucket-load of gravy. 'Life dumps crap,' she said.

While Fran liked to display photos of the kids, she hid the ones of herself: reminders of her failure to become a model. Working mothers with a baby pooch didn't get to be models.

'Aye, life dumps crap. Sometimes it drops a house,' Heather said.

For *you*, was Fran's inner response to Heather's optimism. The one blessing this entire year: the house. It couldn't have been for us … Her stomach writhed. She shook its mixed bag of jealousy and frustration trying to unearth empathy. Heather hadn't asked about her life, only Hector's damn flowers. She'd three kids, no grandparents to provide childcare and if her back didn't ache, her feet or calves were happy to protest about their misuse.

Fran closed a fist around her cross. Should she say anything? Be honest, Fran, appeared to be God's answer today. Fran said, 'Heather, I listen to all your complaints. When do I get to go on about my life?'

'Anytime, Fran. When I share things about my life, that's an opportunity to share your own.'

Heather's response threw her. Sure, even if Heather didn't ask questions, what stopped Fran from sharing her grievances? Everything did. There was so much to do day-to-day. 'You only have yourself to think of. I've four other people, plus you. Forget about myself sometimes.'

Heather gazed at her. Fran couldn't shake the feeling that she wasn't listening, and was more gazing through her than paying attention. 'Do you miss Irvin?' Fran asked. It was a deliberate attempt to get a reaction.

Heather's sharp inhale reminded Fran of when they'd got their ears pierced. Heather drew her hands over her face. 'You're so lucky, Fran. You have a wonderful family.'

Again, the deflection away from Heather's relationship and feelings for Irvin. 'I don't need luck. I've faith,' she said.

'It can't be easy to find time for yourself. Want me to watch the kids one night?' Heather asked. 'Hector and I could play Monopoly, so you can do something for yourself.'

Fran pressed her lips together. Hector was capable of watching the kids alone ... why would Heather have to be there? Didn't she wanted all three of them to hang out anymore? 'Any other woman would be nervous having her husband hang out with a single woman.'

'Me and Hector? Hector, adores you.'

'I've three children to prove it. And this,' Fran prodded her belly.

'Seems like so long ago, 1999. Remember shopping for your wedding dress?' Heather asked.

'You were in a mood that day,' Fran said. At the time she'd known why but tried to ignore what threatened to drive a wedge between them. She'd asked Heather whether it would be okay if she dated Hector and that had been Heather's opportunity to say no.

'Aye. You were in a rotten mood,' Fran repeated, ready to pick a fight today.

'Was I? Remember the window display?' Heather asked. 'What a dress.'

∞ ∞ ∞

Several wedding dress windows flaunted their importance as they ducked in and out of charity shops that afternoon, in September 1999. If Heather had pangs of regret, it was only because she wanted what they had and wanted to be happy for them.

'What a dress' being an understatement. A flouncy skirt, more of a monster than a gown, had engulfed the other frocks in the window of the bridal shop. It must have eaten the others to have grown this immense. Heather pictured Hector in church, music commencing, guests standing, Fran's entrance in The Dress, guests running and screaming as if pursued by a slow-moving marshmallow …

Fran elbowed Heather out of the way. 'See the layered skirt? The way it bunches at the front and sides? I looove it. That's the one.' She tapped a nail against the glass. The wind blew her ciggie smoke into Heather's face. Heather purposefully coughed, waving an arm in the air to dissipate the smoke.

'Sorry, pal,' Fran shifted the ciggie into her other hand.

Fran's maither, Donna, slapped a worn hand to the glass. A faint waft of school meals still followed her around after all these years. It struck Heather how Fran and her mother aged alike as the years passed: work-worn hands, trouble-worn faces. 'Bonnie, the different colours … Fran, is that ivory at the top and white at the bottom?' Donna and her daughter were alike – sharp with their tongue, yet loving – lean in body type except after three pregnancies around the belly area.

Heather shifted from foot to foot. Let's play a game: how long can one hold a smile before it cracks? Her lips wobbled and she forced them wider.

'Don't mark the glass!' Fran batted Donna's hand away from the window. 'I want to try that one.' Fran prodded the window.

A fingerprint remained as evidence.

While Fran stamped on her ciggie and rang the security bell, Heather squinted at the dress and tried to see what they could. Sensibility won out. No one could look attractive in a fashion disaster of such gigantic proportions.

The bridal sales assistant – her sable-coloured hair in an off-centre ponytail – inspected Fran, Donna and Heather from her desk and buzzed them in. 'Can I help you, ladies? My name is Fiona. You must be Fran.'

Fran nodded. 'I want to try the dress in the window.'

'Certainly.' Fiona's confident steps led them around the cramped interior. 'You might find the contours of each dress differs once on. I'll leave a rail here for you to pick out some options.'

The interior of the shop bulged back-to-back with fabric that suggested actions such as flouncing and prancing. It had that wardrobe smell: washed textiles and a faint perfume. Not as strong as Lush though, which could trigger nausea or a migraine in Heather by walking past their handmade cosmetics shop. Heather approached a railing of silk dresses with a faint odour of mulberry, the sequinned rack next to it smelled not unfamiliar to plastic Tupperware – of the chemicals that clung to the synthetic fibres and jewels.

'Textile claustrophobia,' Heather whispered, under her breath. Whispered was a word that dress designers used to describe how fabric rustled. Flammable also came to mind, in a different context.

Fran pulled a face at the sales assistant. 'I want that one in the window, Fiona.'

'That's a strapless asymmetrical bodice, white taffeta underskirt with ivory silk and a bunched overskirt. Have you tried on assorted styles elsewhere?'

'Nah.' Fran crossed her arms and gave Donna and Heather a 'what's-with-her?' expression.

'Is this the mother of the bride?' Fiona asked.

Donna beamed.

'Welcome, madame. You must be thrilled to see your daughter in some dresses. What time of year will the joyous occasion be?'

'Don't know.' Fran ran her tongue around her mouth which gave the impression of a mouth full of marbles. She always did that when she felt as if people were being uppity with her.

'That's no problem. Where are you getting married?'

'Don't know. See,' Fran said, 'I want to try on dresses. That's all.'

'Of course, miss. Feel free to consider a range of silhouettes, while I fetch the one you have already picked out: fishtail cuts are on this side, princess, here, A-lines, modified A-line, ballgown, snug fitting, vintage. Have an exploration and choose about eight to slide on the rail, here.' Fiona vanished through a door at the back of the shop. Leaving a trail of jasmine in the air.

'I'm surprised she didn't lock us in, snooty bitch,' Fran said.

'She seems nice.' Donna waved her arms in the air like a fairy godmother. 'Let's pick some dresses!'

They leapt amongst the garments like synchronised divers, with a sparkle of Swarovski crystals, fake pearl and a splash of taffeta and organza. The skirts crammed against one another reminded Heather of her old flower press; thin cardboard pieces with paper in between that she tightened by screwing down metal bolts.

Heather checked her hands for stains then caressed some lace. It's only fabric, be it the fabric that she's marrying the man she loved in. No, no, no, imagine … flowers. Yes flowers. The flower press she'd had that she and Fran had filled for hours.

'These dresses remind me of pressed flowers.'

'Odd thing to say.'

Heather's smile shattered. 'Lace, or no lace?' she asked.

'Urgh! No lace! Don't you know me at all?' Fran hung an embellished princess skirt on the rail; silver beads reinforced floral designs on the bodice.

Heather yanked at a skirt or two. The next row to her consisted of heavily sequinned fabric. 'Do you want sparkles, Fran?'

Fran flung her arms wide. 'I want to be the most beautiful woman in the world. How's that credible without glitz?'

'These dresses are heavy,' Heather muttered. A bride in one of these, too close to a lake of water … oh, no, no, no you love Fran. You love Hector. You're glad for them. Pissed he preferred her, yes, but it's time to get over that.

'Like or loathe, Fran?' Donna tugged out a tulle meringue. Its waist swathed with a gigantic satin ribbon.

'Love it. Heather, cheer up would you. We're not funeral shopping.'

Fiona returned from the back with the dress Fran and her mother had ogled in the window. 'Are you ready to try a few dresses on, and make your mum cry?' Fiona asked.

'Yes!' Fran pranced behind a curtained section of the shop to change with the assistance of Fiona. Fran didn't prance. She wasn't girly-girly by any means. Put a woman in a wedding dress shop and she goes radge.

'I'm ready!' Fran burst out; her breasts enhanced by two massive cone-like structures. Heather tried to suppress a burst of laughter and failed, even with a hand over her mouth.

'These points are wonderfully Madonna.' Fran shook her chest, her pyramid breasts wobbled, and the edges of the top slipped off her skinny shoulders. 'What do you think?'

'Gorgeous.' Donna beamed. 'You'd be gorgeous in anything, Fran. Wouldn't she Heather?'

'Heather? Ah, I see.' Fran clamped her lips together.

The dress was hysterical. A child's embroidery project gone wrong. The neckline moved like a sentient zipper; zigzagging across one shoulder then down to the V between Fran's traffic cone breasts; while the layered skirt gave off an overstuffed vibe.

'Sorry, sorry, it's the shape putting me off. The colours suit you. Whatever makes you happy.'

Over the next hour, A-lined and mermaid tails came and went with frowns, gentle suggestions and laughter.

'Definitely the first one.' Fran wavered between the cone-breast monstrosity and a flouncy number Fiona had picked out.

'This is the one!' Donna insisted.

'Don't feel pressured, Fran. You can try your favourites again. Anytime,' Fiona said.

Fiona acted like the best friend and Heather an onlooker. 'I think, I think …' Heads turned towards her. 'It's important to choose what you relish, ain't it?' she asked.

'I know what I want,' Fran said. She and the shopkeeper vanished into the changing room, and Fran emerged with a V-neck, shoulderless, tulle ballgown with jewelled flowers decorating the skirt, that she hadn't tried on before. 'I was fooling. This is the one.'

For a non-glowy type of person Fran was … was … glow-ish. The dress was all skirt. Highly impractical to pee in. Fiona had tied a satin ribbon around Fran's waist, and fetched a tiara from the accessory display.

Donna dabbed her mascara. 'My bairn is a princess.'

Fran lifted the skirt to display her practise flats. 'I'll get this thing off an' let's go out on the skite.'

One version of hell is wedding planning with one's best friend when she's marrying your other best friend.

'Can't remember my mood that day,' Heather said. 'Me and fancy shops … not an auspicious combination. Your final choice was perfect.'

'Aye,' Fran said. 'Got to get back. Plans with Hector and the kids.'

Heather opened her purse, put a note on the table to pay her uneaten half of the brownie and extracted a ticket. 'I'm off to the King's Theatre.'

'Why?' Fran asked.

'To see a play.'

'I mean why bother?'

'To try new things.'

'Well there's my bus. Cheerio.'

'See you tomorrow.' Heather waved.

Fran did not wave back. She scowled at the King's Theatre as the bus paused, then rumbled up Lothian Road. Chinese food clung to the man sat next to her; she breathed in the taste. Rain began to drum on the window in time to the bus engine's bumping in and out of potholes. Theatre tickets. All right for some. Not that she'd want to spend two hours of her life watching dreamers prance about the stage in weird costumes wittering about hope and opportunity. Nonsense. Plus, she got plenty of preaching about redemption at church. Heather could enjoy her fancy house, her fancy new life. Now that her life was so fabulous she could make other pals. Quality people who bought annual National Trust memberships to visit fancy houses.

Before she'd believed that, despite being an outsider at the church and at the school, at least she had Heather. Now their relationship was in question. Delving deeper, facts she'd rather drown bubbled to the surface: once Hector had admired Heather. It had been an infatuation. One Heather didn't return. Though things had been awkward when Fran and Hector started dating. Ever since then, no, before then, to be fair, as Heather had always avoided serious relationships, in general, as if the loss of her ma cut too deep. She also avoided new friendships for the same reason. Irvin … a friend or a lover? Despite Fran's probing Heather never mentioned him in a romantic way. And if you were infatuated with a person, in her experience, it was hard not to bore everyone around you about them. It was silly. The only man Heather ever prattled about was Hector. Heather couldn't have been carrying a secret flame for her husband all these years. Could she? And where exactly did Irvin fit in?

Oh, come on, she told herself, Heather is your oldest pal. It was worth investing the effort to overcome her jealousy and patch things up better than ever.

By the time the bus got her home, Fran decided that next weekend they'd do their usual Sunday roast with the family and Heather, and have a discussion.

Chapter 6

May 2019

Next Sunday morning, Heather ensconced some favoured photographs in the kitchen. The largest was of their trio in a single embrace when they were eighteen, before Fran started dating Hector. Fran had chopped her hair painfully sparse that summer with a pair of scissors and as the strands grew back they exploded at odd angles – more Alek Wek than Twiggy. Hector had been trying to grow a beard, but the hair had grown in wispy and interspersed. More mad hatterish than masculine. Lastly, Heather had been going through a stripy top phase that did her curves no favours. Next to the photo of the three of them, she'd placed one of her and Fran blowing bubbles at age seven and another of Hector and their three children: Trish, Allan and Jack. Allan had the characteristics of his father at that age, and was as inquisitive.

The phone rang. 'Knock, knock,' Fran said.

'Who's there?'

'Seriously, knock, knock.' Fists pounded against the front of the house. Heather heard the kids' voices:

'Can I?' Allan said.

'No,' Fran said.

'Can I?' asked Jack.

The two boys were shoving one another away from the Tibetan bell, all elbows and Chinese burns.

'Morning!' Fran said.

'Morn-ing!' cuckooed the kids.

Fran squeezed her. 'Hi, Heather. Still in your jammies, I see.'

'Jammies!' Jack laughed, embracing her leg and biting the

fabric, while Trish groaned; a gesture that was ill-suited to the tiny rainbows dancing across the legs visible below her coat. 'Ma said we were too much of a handful to dress before coming. We're having a jammies day.'

'That's not technically true because I've a change of clothes for everyone,' Hector said. He stood at the back with a large rucksack and smudges of what might have been honey on his glasses.

'Inside,' Fran barked. 'Try not to break anything.'

'Can we see the parrot?' Jack asked.

'I'm hungry,' Allan said. 'Aunty Heather, can you cook us pancakes, please?'

'Pancakes!' Fran rustled his hair, making Allan squirm. 'Since when do we eat them for breakfast?'

Hector gave Heather a hug and a look that said: I was woken by three bairns jumping on the bed, don't judge the state of my glasses. He embraced her in a waft of fabric cleaner and roast chicken. Heather breathed it in and, reluctantly, let him go.

Fran pulled a face. 'In this family, we eat porridge,' she said. 'End of argument.'

'I don't think I've any porridge,' Heather said as they invaded her kitchen. 'It will have to be scrambled eggs.'

Hector tickled Allan's ribs as he went in for a playful punch; aye, watching Jack fling his head back he was so much like Hector that the memories curled themselves round her heart, along with the knowledge that she loved him still. Albeit in an altered way: not as a paramour, Irvin treasured such words: paramour and inamorata. She guessed they meant something similar: to be enamoured.

'Why are you here?' she asked Fran, since she'd expected to see them after church.

Fran yawned in a way that would scare a lion. 'Make us a cuppa. We get no time at all for lounging in on a Sunday with this lot.'

Shit, they entered the kitchen where she'd left an Open University course brochure on the countertop. Swiping it into a draw, act casual she soothed herself, while Fran and Hector settled around the side of the kitchen island where four stools stood. On the other side of the island was extra storage – the draw where she'd hidden the incriminating course work – and a dishwasher.

'Duck-egg, nice colour,' Hector said.

'Bit posh.' Fran tapped her fingers against the granite surface and pulled a face at Heather's photo display.

Heather dug hardened sleep from the corner of one eye, and tried to look casual as her heartbeat slackened.

'Are we disturbing you?' Fran asked. 'Allan, put down the egg whisk, utensils are not for playing pirate with. Jack, put the … thingy down. What *is* that?'

'An apple corer, I think. Though it also makes an excellent, um, periscope?' Heather made a guess from the sonar pings Jack emitted.

'Well la-di-da, that fella had utensils didn't he. Where's the tea?'

'He had a fancy coffee machine and all,' Hector said, getting up to examine the machine. 'Does this grind the beans?'

Fran's fingers stilled. 'I don't drink coffee.'

Heather filled the kettle. 'We know that. Irvin didn't when he was fitting out *his* kitchen.'

Hector laughed. Fran didn't.

Don't read anything into it, Heather cautioned herself. She put Fran's finding fault with everything down to self-doubt influencing her perceptions. A result of the paranoia quickly following being caught out with her university papers.

Heather asked, 'Church closed?'

Fran nodded. 'Bust pipe. There'll be a service later.'

Hector said, 'Since it's part of our routine, to spend some time together on Sunday, and your new place's further, I thought we could switch it up a bit.'

'Be more convenient for you to come to ours,' Fran said. 'Have you started to unpack at all? These boxes haven't moved.'

'I only moved last Friday, Fran.'

Heather grabbed the egg box, stuck six slices of wholemeal into the toaster and fished in the tea cupboard for the Earl Grey Hector preferred, stashed behind tins of jasmine tea and gunpowder green.

In the light from the large windows, Trish continued to lay out the contents of one draw onto the worktop: mixing spoons, ladles and spatulas.

'Once we've carefully put back all of Heather's kitchen implements and uncovered where the tea is hidden, what will we do today kids?' Fran asked.

Jack stopped picking his nose. 'Parrot training.'

Trish said, 'I don't know.'

'Does the park have dinosaurs?' Allan asked.

Heather watched Fran peer up at the sky through the kitchen window; there was a space as vast between them today. One blue sky in an endless parade of grey ones. 'The weather's not pissing down we shouldn't waste it. Where's me tea?'

'It's coming.' Listening to their conversation Heather whisked the eggs. The kids were the centre of attention at Fran and Hector's. She spent her spare hours drafting unpublished stories; while they sacrificed sanity to bring up their kids. It made her efforts at life seem futile. Of course, studying for her degree without Irvin's guidance raised doubts in her about her writing ability.

'Coming to the park?' Fran asked. 'Wearing jammies is optional.'

Heather shovelled the eggs onto the toast and fetched the tomato ketchup. The kids dug in.

Fran smiled at the photos on the kitchen countertop, her earlier scowl gone now she had a mug in her hand. 'I remember this one; I looked fair with spikey hair.'

'I think you look wonderful now, little penguin.' Hector kissed Fran's neck.

Heather pushed aside the frisson of arousal that swept up her neck. 'I was up last night. Mostly sorting Irvin's stuff, so I could put my things away.'

'That's what's in those bags?' Fran asked, referring to the black bags heaped in the corridor.

'I dredged up a nice parka. Rest's for charity. Check out the cashmere sweaters. Too large for me. Perhaps for Hector?'

'Cashmere's impractical for washing.'

'Nonsense, wash it in the delicate cycle.'

'We can take it in the car for you,' Hector said.

'Sure, go ahead.'

Fran added, 'To the shop.'

'Sure, might be something for you, Hector. If you want it.'

'Maybe. Not that we're a charity.' Fran put an end to that topic, like loppers closing with a swoosh on a robust rose stem.

'Won't hurt to look,' Hector said.

'I should continue to unpack.' Heather placed the kids' empty plates in the sink and made up her mind to go with them the next instant, to erase the negative pressure between them.

Fran flapped a hand dismissively. 'Plenty of time for that. Come with. Get some fresh air. We worry about you, Hector and me. Come on head down, arse up!'

'We can help unpack, Aunty Heather,' Trish said. She'd placed the kitchen implements back in the drawer after gobbling up her breakfast.

'Maybe later, Patch,' Fran said.

'Patch is a name for a baby!'

'Sorry, darling.'

'I think,' Hector said, 'that Aunty Heather needs some fresh air and distraction from unpacking. Unpacking is for rainy days.'

'What's dis-traction?' Jack asked.

'That's you lot,' Fran said.

'Why?'

''Cause we're annoying. Aunty Heather, do you have a trampoline?' Allan asked.

'Nah, sorry.'

'I can mow the lawn sometime, if you like,' Hector offered.

'Thanks, Hector. A guy comes to do it.'

Fran tutted. 'Though Hector says "mow", what he means is butchering the grass. If you want bare, uneven patches, he's your man.'

'I'll get the kids changed,' Hector said, and grabbed his rucksack almost striking a figurine of a Chinese man fishing. 'Before you exchange me for a fit young gardener.'

'That was harsh, Fran,' Heather said.

'It's called banter. He can give as good. How's your writing? You were writing before we dropped in?'

Fran had mistaken the brochure for a notebook. Heather sipped her warm drink and released a long, slow breath. 'My brain keeps circling round to the fact that maybe I'm not a writer. How am I supposed to do it without an education?'

'You read. That's education – ain't it?'

'Should've got my degree.'

'Can't you do it with Irvin's money?'

There was a turnaround. Fran had been unsupportive about her writing when tossing around her own business concept. If she wanted to tell Fran, now was the time.

'Waste of money, though, if you ask me.'

Ah, there it was. The dependable anti-education Fran, she who'd said that the university of life is a thousand times more relevant.

In the garden young birds were learning to fly. The gutter that horizontally skirted the building close to the kitchen and the tree opposite formed the hatchlings' training school. They made haphazard zigzags from one to the other, occasionally passing close to the windows. Fran was right, despite their fears every chick had to learn to fly eventually.

'It's about self-education now,' Heather said, to get them off the subject of university study. 'There's tons accessible via the internet … I'm struggling.'

'Then don't write.'

'I can't do that either. Every thought comes back to writing.'

'Then write.'

'Aye.'

A corpulent butterfly, more moth-like, flapped upwards from the flower beds but evaded the open window and the looping hatchlings. Heather tried to take it all in, the dream kitchen, the sweep of the garden sheltered by tree branches and the birds' feathers as they prepared to swoop again. How blissful it would be to lose all sense of time – Monday to Friday, nine to five – and just be. Why couldn't she be content with this house and Irvin's generous income? What was wrong with her that she had to reach for more? Part of it is that Irvin believed in her. He'd started her on this path, so to not finish wouldn't be just her own failure.

'Least we got jobs,' Fran said.

'I need to devote more time to writing. Yet everything seems written. Tracey Chevalier for stories of friendship, Maggie O'Farrell for atmosphere, and Isabel Allende for magical-realism.'

Fran's frown indicated that these names meant nothing to her because spending time reading a book was for people who didn't have families. 'Nice for those that can,' Fran said.

'Guess so.'

Their conversation was punctuated by a squirrel's alarm call as it flicked its tail and barked at a neighbour's cat. The cat scooted after the squirrel into next door's garden, and the hatchlings resumed their flight training.

'It's true that life doesn't work to plan,' Heather said.

'What's the expression: life is what happens when you're trying to plan it out?'

'Trust me to take the long way round. Took about twenty years to figure that out.'

'And now?'

'I'm lost, Fran. I used to be sure a book deal was within reach and scribbled every breaktime, every lunchtime, and wrote every afternoon after work. What happened?'

And, Heather asked herself, what if I'm one of those people

who only think they can write?

Fran raised and lowered her shoulders as though she'd spent her life running uphill to be told, you should have been running in the other direction. 'I don't have any of the answers, Heather. I'm a forty-year-old woman, with three kids, renting a house and cleaning for a living. Hardly a poster advert for following dreams.'

'Why shouldn't dreams be capacious?'

Fran snorted. 'What does that even mean?'

'I'm being serious.' Despite her words, being a writer was an aspirational task. And Heather wasn't content with writing and self-publishing for an audience of none.

Fran fingered the cross at her neck. 'Keep your life free from love of money and be content with what you have, for he has said, "I won't forsake you". I find comfort in my faith. Your faith, your reason for being, is writing. Don't lose that.'

Hector and the kids stampeded down the stairs. 'Ready!' Hector said.

'Ready!' cuckooed the kids.

'Coming with?' Fran asked.

'Sure.'

'Aunty Heather's coming in her jammies!' shrieked Allan.

Part 2

Ale sellers shouldn't be tale tellers

Chapter 7

June 2019

Fran hummed a tune from church as she hoovered upstairs: today was the day she was going to show Hector her business proposal. Excitement ran in ripples across her skin. *Aye! A professional businesswoman. Almost. Like those women in her magazines? Pah! Unlikely.*

'That's my shoelace ... how on earth?' Fran tugged the frayed lace from the Hoover's nozzle, then scrunched it into a jean pocket.

The fishing game again, with her shoelace no less; my, how glamorous a life a businesswoman leads.

Fran bumped the juddering Hoover against the cupboard drawer between the beds in Allan and Jack's room. Heather often compared Fran's antique Hoover to a camel because it spat out a dusty reek as fast as Fran could rake its bristled tongue across the shabby carpet, eager to chew up marbles and plastic soldiers. At least the boys had slung their shared toys in the drawer, for Patricia had decorated her bedroom floor with spare magazines from school pals Isla and Jessica. Fran scooped the perfumed magazines into her arms and dumped them on the second-hand coffee table that doubled as a desk. She raced the Hoover to the finish line – the discoloured hall carpet – and opened the windows a crack. As she lugged the machine downstairs, Fran noted Hector's work shoes tossed beside the shoe rack in the entranceway, beneath the dent in the plasterwork where Hector had scraped the kitchen table when her parents bought it as a wedding present.

'Hector? You home?'

His coat wasn't on its peg: it was on the settee. Work bag discarded in the doorway between the lounge and the kitchen. 'Thinks me got nothing better to do than tidy up after your lazy arse?'

When they were first married, he'd always give her a kiss arriving or leaving. Shouldn't have let things slip; a kiss on the cheek is the minimum she should expect day-to-day.

She followed the trail of crumbs ... Hector had sprinkled coffee grounds and bourbon biscuit crumbs, beside a coffee-stained mug. The kitchen clock read 3 p.m., in half an hour she'd have to go to collect Allan and Jack. She dumped the mug into the sink. 'God helps those who help themselves.'

The back door swung on its hinges. There he was. Digging in the garden in his work suit.

'What. The. Hell?' she asked. If he thought she would scrub the dirt out of those kneecaps, he better think again.

Hector swore at the flower bed. He came here when his head needed clearing. 'Calm mind; inner strength,' as her ma used to say. *Find out why he's acting like a dolt before tearing him a new one. 10, 9, 8 ...*

'Bad day?'

'Brilliant.' Hector stabbed the trowel into the ground and levered a primrose from the peaty soil, even though he'd been the one who'd selected the flowers in the first place.

'That's a primrose.'

'Holy shit.' He jammed the plant back into the soil and attacked a dandelion. This didn't look like a good day to be sharing her business plan.

'Out with it.'

'They fired me. Called it "redundancy", but it's the same fucking thing, ain't it.'

The wind whisked the husks of last year's leaves around the side of the house and across the felt baffies protecting her feet. 'Leaving money?'

'Eleven weeks statutory redundancy for twenty-two years of service. Twenty-two years of bullshit, more like. And it'll take longer than eleven weeks to find a job. The market's rough.'

She worked it out on her fingers with mounting dread. But that's nothing … less than three months' pay. A fine mist dampened her hair and his glasses, enough to cloud the vision, but not sufficient to get you wet. A good thing she'd long brought in the washing. 'Still, put two pennies in a purse and they will creep together – with my salary it should stretch a bit longer.'

'Super,' he hissed a breath through his teeth, 'more *fucking* supermarket own-brand baked beans.'

'They're not that abominable.'

This was wrong, very. Not about the baked beans: the timing. The business plan had counted on Hector's salary to keep them going while she got started. Typical. It was never going to happen. Of course not. Life certainly held its down moments, and here she'd begun to think that the worst was over; better not to take that for granted.

'We shouldn't have to struggle with this shit,' Hector said. 'Years I worked through my lunch for those bastards, and they let me go like that.' He clicked his soiled fingers and hurled the trowel across the grass. It skimmed across the damp surface to land in a pile of leaves. 'Those *arsehole* CEOs with their hundred thousand-pound salaries. Nobs who think we should be grateful for a one per cent pay rise. They don't know what it's like to live on chicken feed.' Hector rolled his eyes as if praying, or swearing, at the big man up there on his padded cushion. 'We'll never get on the property ladder now. Good God, Fran. I'm sick of struggling to get by.'

She also raised her eyes to the thick clouds, hoping God would grant a bit of sun this week. 'Still, this could be a chance to get into something better, aye?'

Hanging his head low, he dug his fingers under the soil to hide his shaking fists. 'I feel like a battery hen about to get the chop.'

'No, no, no, sweetie.' She knelt beside him, took his head in her hands, eased it on to her shoulder. The wet grass soaked through her jeans.

'I'm a fuck up,' he said, his cheeks humid on her neck.

'No, they're the fuck ups. First thing's first, work on your CV, draft a cover letter. You know the drill.'

'Too well. Since they chose Mick, for the promotion, I've been applying for other jobs – and nada.'

She stroked his greasy hair, which smelt of French fries.

'Now there's more at stake, it might be the kick up the arse you need.'

He pulled away.

'You know what I mean. Come inside, it's damp.' She brushed a leaf from her jeans. Being pissed at him wasn't fair, because he didn't know about her plans, and she couldn't bring up the proposal now; best to form a game plan with Heather. If costs were kept minimal perhaps a few regular clients could bring in decent cash in the afternoons after work to get started. Heather might even want to work with her. That thought was followed by another: Heather didn't need to work. Their circumstances were different.

'I'll be in. In a minute.'

Times like this made you question your faith. Sure, He only threw at you what you could handle, did He? Who did this omnipotent being think He was to mess up her plans like this?

She returned to her hoovering: on the bright side, someone would be home to help with this sort of thing now.

'He just walked in?' Fran let her mouth fall open. An exaggerated what-the-fuck movement. Her knuckles whitening around the phone. Her accounts forgotten.

Anticipating it would take at least six months for Hector to find a new position, Fran had added everything up the afternoon after Hector had told her he had lost his job.

Fran's world shrunk to the size of a spreadsheet.

Cuts would have to be made, as expected, to make it through to month seven; assuming they were living on her cleaning salary and Hector's redundancy. What they had would go further if she transferred their TV, Internet and phone to a basic phone plan, and economised on own-brand items at the supermarket. Clothes, coffees with Heather, the children's swimming lessons, would have to stop. And Fran could use what she and Hector had managed to put aside for their holiday fund which tended to be used for emergencies rather than the wished-for caravan holiday at Silver Sands where her parents used to take her when she was seven.

The seventh month was trickier. If it got to that stage and Hector hadn't new work, they might need to sell the car and walk and cycle as an alternative to taking the bus.

Heather had phoned as Fran was pondering what else could get them to month eight. Hector was drafting a list of potential jobs; chewing the end of his pen – when not rattling it against the top of his laptop. This was an improvement, as some days he went to bed earlier and earlier, despite the sun setting later throughout the summer.

Heather recounted to Fran what had happened, and as she did so Fran squeezed her lips together until they blanched.

It had been two months since Heather moved in, and she hadn't got used to the silence and the shadows of Irvin's house. A tell-tale heart of a knock drummed on the door. Rat-a-tat. As if under the welcome mat beneath the lintel a concealed body was impatient to rise. Rat-a-tat. Rat-a-tat. Heather smoothed the goosebumps on her arms and flicked on the porch light:

highlighting Brother Baneshanks' hat as he skulked on the front step haloed by a ghostly mist.

Baneshanks pulled his curved fist away from the door, stepping back with a grimace at the brightness.

Heather was tempted to ring Irvin's bell to scare away the menacing spirit of his brother.

He was wearing the same coat that he'd worn for the funeral; a tobacco scent clung to the fabric. 'Mèirleach,' he drawled, calling her a thief to her face.

'Mr Peters, I—'

'I'm here for my things.' He swept through her, halted at the cardboard boxes she'd been emptying and refilling since moving in, and snorted. She'd strained her back stacking a neat pile to one side of the hallway marked with the names of Irvin's family.

'I know it's taken a while.' She rested her hand on the nearest carton. 'The items Irvin wanted his family to have are all here. The solicitor left instructions.'

'The person who oversees a will is called an executor.'

Crivvens. If he reacted that way to one word how would he react if she'd written Baneshanks in place of his real name?

'You're precise about one thing, we're his family.' He grabbed a box and tore it open to verify the contents. 'Me, and my children, and their children, and our cousins. Not. You.'

'Look here—'

'Whatever trickery you used to get this place ...' He brandished a fist. 'I have a lawyer checking the paperwork.'

At least he said *a* lawyer and not *his* lawyer as if he was in the habit of suing people.

'I can understand that. I'm a stranger,' she said.

'Exactly!' He hurdled her words like an affirmation of his right to all of Irvin's possessions. Including, no doubt, the house. Yet if he was family, how come he hadn't visited in those final months, or that final year? She captured her tongue between her upper and lower incisors to prevent any misguided utterance from slinking out.

'I'll take all these containers now.'

'I'm not sure that—'

'Budge.' He jabbed his jaw forward, the upper and lower bones out of alignment like he was a cow in mid-chew.

Heather 'budged'. Not towards the front step which bore the risk of being locked out but to the boxes she'd been folding flat in the front room, which Irvin had called the drawing room, as he ferried boxes to his car; knick-knacks Irvin had indicated with coloured stickers for certain people. She'd found it morbid at the time to help him colour-code his possessions. Yet it had made the final organisation easier – not emotionally easier as removing these items would not erase him from her memory. Not accepting the house; the gift balanced uneasily on her bones. The house was plenty. More than. The desire not to forget. He'd given her so much. Too much. And most of the objects sellotaped into packages was junk. Tacky religious ornaments brought back from his travels, a collection of stereotypes from Africa to Asia.

He'd given her something more precious than paraphernalia: approbation.

'Do you have everything?' she asked.

The door slammed leaving a faint trace of the cypress scent of his aftershave in the hallway, amongst the piles and piles of books – part of Irvin's legacy to her that remained untouched.

'There's no speaking to some folk,' she whispered to the empty house, then shuffled in her baffies to Irvin's gramophone to find comfort in the voice of Ella Fitzgerald, 'Into each life some rain must fall …'

A banging protest resounded on the front door, Brother Baneshanks demanding she relinquish the gramophone because 'it was a family heirloom'. The machine wasn't on any list the executor had given her, a list she'd prudently reviewed.

Screw you! – Heather channelled Fran. And flicked the porch light off. He lurked in the shadows, the mist had dispelled, and he was framed by a sky pinpricked with unfathomable stars.

None of the neighbours' lights were on, and Heather didn't

dare look outside again in case he was blocking the driveway with a glare resembling old Baneshanks himself, collector of departed souls. At moments comparable to this her ma would give a hiccup of a laugh, shaking off the 'bad vibes' and say, someone's dancing over my grave. Which used to be funny, until she's lying in a grave and no one is dancing.

If she were to lose the house, Heather reflected, it would be another failure on top of a disappointing life. Unquestionably, cleaning wasn't the bright future her ma had in mind when she taught Heather how to read: huddled in a single bed over the dark winter months, until the swimming letters on the page transformed, like larvae, into fluttering Hs and Ms and Es in Heather's imagination, and she began to cobble together pages of her own which Ma first listened to, then helped her write down and polish. 'One day, you'll release these butterflies into the world, Heather,' Ma had told her.

She'd tried to please, as a child and now: writing every afternoon after work without success. The stories, the novels, the embarrassing attempts at poetry, the other worlds she'd dreamt up lay on old storage devices that weren't compatible anymore with current technology. Each one rejected by agents in turn. A ladder of failures, until the butterfly wings stilled in her mind, desiccated.

She was as undeserving of the stories that had come to her at all hours as she was unworthy of this house. Too much generosity on Irvin's part. Baneshanks had called her a thief, and he was dead-on there.

Heather slumped on the settee and reached for the phone. Fran would not believe the nerve of …

'That man!' Fran completed the phrase. 'He's as welcome as water in a holed ship.'

'He scared me. It's silly.'

'He shouldn't have forced his way in when you're alone in the house. Should I come round?'

'No, no. He's gone now. Thanks, Fran.'

Fran waited for Heather to ask what was new, so she could

tell her about Hector's news. Misery. Company. All that.

'It made me think about my horrid uncle and aunty,' Heather said.

Fran crossed herself. It was impossible to forget the day Heather should have been at home but went to Fran's because she was eight and rebellious. Neither of them could have guessed Heather's ma would die that day.

'You praying, Fran?'

'Aye.' Here was an opening, a gulf to be filled with endearments to make Heather feel blameless for, according to Baneshanks, 'filching the family home'; but Fran didn't feel up to the role today, there were serious financial problems to think through on her end of the line. Heather, obviously, didn't care enough to reciprocate and ask how Fran was doing.

Heather sensed her detachment for she said, 'Sorry for bothering you. I know evenings are the only time you and Hector get alone.'

'No bother. Night.' Fran hung up. This was her family time. The truth was, if she could admit it to herself, that she'd almost thanked God about the house being under threat. A horrible thought to wish on a pal. A pal she'd hung up on, sure, but that was to spare Heather from any harsh words on her part. She needed time to process this lousy dream.

Fran let her body fall heavily onto the settee, next to Hector, and picked up her scribblings, frowning at the numbers – these were accurate?

'What did Heather say about the redundancy?' Hector asked.

'I didn't tell her. Irvin's brother turned up at her house and freaked her out.'

Hector stood up. 'I should go round.'

'No need, he's gone now, and I'll tell her another time.'

'Yes, but you know how she retreats like a clam when any conflict arises.'

'She's okay, Hector. She knows we're only a call away. Everything's fine.'

Hector glanced at the phone as if he didn't quite believe her. There was no sense mollycoddling Heather, she needed to get used to the new house, get used to living further away from them, get used to this new independence. And it wasn't like she hadn't developed the habit of retreating from them whenever she needed some space and alone time to write. Though it was just like Hector, sweet guy, to want to crosscheck.

Fran held out the phone. 'Call her back, if you like,' her words came out softly, the way Hector always managed to coax out her softer side.

'No, I'd let it slip about the redundancy. Unless you want me to tell her?'

'I can do it at work. In person.'

'Aye, that's better.'

Fran stroked Hector's hair as he relaxed into the sofa. 'You're a good man, Hector,' she said.

'I thought you married me for my body?' he asked with a wink.

Chapter 8

July 2019

Damp sheep, damp dogs, damp socks. Pretty much summer in Scotland. The rain-damp scent of lavender welcomed Fran as she jimmied her key until the front door cooperated. She could hear the kids playing in the back garden. Feet scuffing their plastic ball. 'Goal!', 'Chance, more like.' For once in the summer holidays, Fran didn't have to worry about where to put the kids since Hector was home. Entering, glad to be able to finally relax, she kicked off her shoes, placed them side-by-side, hung her coat, and padded into the lounge to collapse on the settee and rub her aching arches. Feet half swung up towards the coffee table Fran swung them down again; custard cream crumbs mottled its gouged oval top and an empty packet of Jacob's Cream Crackers obscured Hector's discarded notepads and pens. She read a page: national wealth management firm, valuations, record keeping, pension or retirement planning experience, audit trail … yawn.

The kettle bubbled from the kitchen.

'Bring me a cuppa would you, sweetie?' Fran called.

The glug of pouring water was his reply. The ding-ding of a spoon as he stirred in the sugar, then he thumped across the kitchen floor.

'Ahh.' She massaged the ache in her lower back and her fingers ached for a ciggie.

He scratched his stubbled jawline. 'I'll clean this up.' He waved a hand at the mess.

'Too right you will.' She slurped her cuppa, the bitterness soaking into her tongue, and let her head fall back on the headrest.

'We need to stock up on food,' he said.

'Aye, next Monday.'

He tapped his foot against a table leg. 'There's not much for the kids' tea.'

'There's macaroni pies, tins of baked beans, bread, eggs.'

His foot stilled. 'I, we, ate it.'

She lifted her head. 'Whoa, you ate *all* of it?'

'Fuel for job hunting? Plus, we're all home for lunch these days.'

He tried – the evidence was right here on the table. Remain. Calm. Be. Supportive. 'How many applications did you fill in today?'

He slapped his thigh, with the aspect of a Scottish fisherman who's scored the biggest catch of his life. 'Ten. I'll have tons of interviews shortly. You'll see.'

'Sure. So … for tonight, we've no food in the house?'

He shrugged. 'I'll go to the shops after my tea.'

'Don't you get it, you've eaten it. That was meant to last us all week, and you're fucking sitting here eating all the biscuits and getting obese!' Fuck taking it easy, Fran thought. Anyhow, a bit late now; she'd said what she was thinking, tense with financial responsibility and foreboding. Her horoscope today said, *anticipate the unforeseen.*

'I'm not obese.'

'No, sorry, sorry. I'm as jumpy as a bag of frogs today. It don't matter. Ignore me. What'll we feed them tonight?'

'I think there's some Cup-a-Soup at the back of the cupboard. If we're out of dosh I'll go to the food bank tomorrow, sign us up.'

She slammed the mug on the table. 'My kids ain't eating from no food bank.'

'Fran, we've got no choice.' He leant forward and, with a sleeve, mopped a spot of tea off one notepad. A sleeve she'd have to clean as he kept forgetting to load the machine, as he also, conveniently, forgot to empty the rubbish bin. Clearly, she couldn't trust him at home on his own all day.

'Your bum's out the window,' she said.

'Nonsense. This is reality. Your wages don't stretch far enough, and my redundancy has been eaten up by the rent. We need help.'

She bit the inside of her cheek. 10, 9, 8 … she could try … 7, 6, 5 … even if the numpty didn't think she might like a custard cream … 4, 3, 2, 1. Her stomach gurgled. 'We don't need any charity.' She picked up her mug: better a warm tea than nought. She'd have to plan a shop before the weekend to stock up for their weekly Sunday roast with Heather.

'Aye, we do. We're living on the breadline,' he said.

'No, we don't! We – If you didn't eat through my hard-earned groceries!' She slammed her hand across the whoop of rage that leapt from her mouth. It faded into a wail. 'I don't want to fucking bring up my kids in poverty, Hector. I had to deal with that shit growing up.'

'Our kids, that I've been entertaining all day.'

'Now they're our kids? Now that you've eaten us out of house and home and are jobless.'

A look crossed his face, more painful to her than the one he'd worn in the garden that first day he'd been let go.

'Sorry, that was harsh. I'm exhausted.'

'It's not poverty, Fran. It's called social exclusion. The system's against us. The British economy can improve, but we're stuck on a cleaner's salary. I mean … I don't mean that's a rotten thing.'

Her stomach rumbled another protest. Things couldn't go on like this, on her ratty salary. Not if it meant they raised their voices at one another.

'I'll phone Citizen's Advice tomorrow,' Hector said. 'Ask if we can qualify for more benefits.'

She wiped a hand across her face. 'You can't. The phone bill hasn't been paid.'

'I'll go to their office then,' he said. He must have seen her wriggling her swollen toes, for he patted his lap. 'Give them here.'

She swung up her legs – it was amazing how calming a pair of large warm hands could feel after withstanding being on her feet all day.

'I'm sorry, Fran. This is tough on you. But I'll get a job soon. I've applied for everything going. It would be taxing to find a job that I haven't applied for today.'

She fingered the cross at her neck. Please, God, make it be soon. If you're listening. Are you?

Three months into Hector's redundancy and they were struggling to stay on budget: she'd snuck, pragmatically, around the house last night, when Hector and the kids slept, and put aside things she could sell if they hit the sixth month mark. Hector hadn't touched his dumb-bells since Patricia had been born; there was a first-generation Kindle, an iPad that she only used to watch her shows during Hector's rugby; a few lamps she'd put in the attic when Jack had started to pull himself to standing as a toddler; a rarely used toasty maker and a bread maker. She wouldn't need to touch her jewellery, including the wedding and engagement ring she'd inherited from her gran. Extra clothes could also be sold online before cancelling their Internet subscription.

She'd considered a second job but until he started acting like himself … she needed to be sure he could responsibility watch the kids for longer hours.

And Heather didn't care enough to ask. Until she did Fran decided not to say a thing.

Want to know what it's like to live like me?, she thought as Hector switched on the news, *Blair, Major, Brown, May, current twat-head?* It's hard. Only folk with money say there're things more important than digits in the bank. That's crap, it isn't true. It's enough to make you doubt your faith.

One Sunday, nostrils filled with the honey scent of roses from her new street instead of swirls of flies on fresh dog poo from her old street, Heather travelled to her old neighbourhood for lunch with Fran, Hector and the kids. From her new place, this involved a shortcut through the Water of Leith Walkway where Heather spied minnows and graylings in the river, her vision partially obscured by a scattering of jewels as the light caught the raindrops. The flow was turbulent. A scrawny heron hunted on the far bank also gazing at the fish darting in the water. She kept them company, trudged up the steps up to the grounds of the Modern Art Gallery and crossed the road to pass Building Two – what used to be called The Dean. She skirted the borders of Dean Cemetery to catch the 47 bus from Learmouth Terrace.

'Watch where you're going,' a pedestrian snapped, as Heather bumped into their shoulder while trying to avoid their eye-height umbrella at the bus stop. For a moment, Heather thought of Mrs Merkle. Every street has an elderly person who confiscates balls and speaks their mind. Sometimes they're known as the old bat, sometimes the child eater. Fran even had one on her street growing up. When they played tennis on warm, or possibly mild, summer nights – though in her memories they were always inviting and carefree – her name had been Mrs Merkle. Mrs Merkle – or Old Bat – from their experience loved nothing better than to point out faults in demeanour and confiscate wayward toys. One day their ragged tennis ball had ricocheted off a lamppost and rolled up the path to her door.

'Quick! Before Old Bat spots us!' Fran vaulted, as she spoke, over the gate and raced to retrieve it. Then stood on the path staring into the window. 'She's waving a fist at me. Her leg's in a cast.' Fran said and skipped the last five paces to the door and rang the bell. The sound of a lot of huffing and puffing came down the corridor, excruciatingly slow. Heather felt a sudden urge to pee and crossed her legs.

Bent over by age, Mrs Merkle, scowled across at them. 'Your backhand needs work. The street isn't a tennis court, in lieu of a babysitter.'

'Mrs Merkle, do you need anything?' Fran asked.

'Why – I – certainly not!' Mrs Merkle took in the grimy ball in Fran's grubby fingers, and the neutrally polite look on Fran's face, and Heather crossed legs. 'Well, I am short of a pint of milk. Blasted electrician doesn't know how tea should be drunk.'

Fran fetched the milk and accepted fifty pence in return; though it was too much, a fact that Mrs Merkle told them followed by her expectation of another pint on Tuesday.

The next day as they were passing, Fran said, 'Let's go check on Mrs Merkle. She'll be in that cast for weeks and weeks.' And for weeks and weeks they checked on Mrs Merkle once a day and took her groceries as requested. Once, they even went inside: after wiping their feet, and taking off their shoes, and under strict orders not to touch anything with their grubby hands.

As Heather tried to ignore the queasy feeling the glassy eyes of Mrs Merkel's doll collection gave her, Fran said, 'Don't you usually make apple sauce this time of year?'

'No business of yours.'

Apples dotted the back lawn, rotting on the grass.

'We can collect the fruit for you.'

'And wash it, peel it, chop it, and boil it,' Mrs Merkle instructed.

That was how they ended up taking a warm jar each home. Heather's ma gave a satisfied smile and dipped a finger in the warm mixture. 'This is a good thing you're doing, darling. That Fran's a kind lass.'

Heather learnt later from Fran that she got scolded for being late to tea. Yet Fran, Heather thought was a better person than her because she did stuff while Heather fretted and worried about the possibility of interacting with others. Heather tried with all her might not to cause ripples in the calm pond of her life. While Fran acted. Reached out. Like that time with Carlisle – the pigeon.

He'd been hopping about outside the local food cooperative; one wing neatly folded, and the other outstretched and drooping.

'Cat's almost got him, for sure,' Fran said, bending down to inspect the damage. 'Found one in the garden last month and Dougie – anyway, what he needs is a place to recover. But I can't take him back to mine.'

'Me neither, Auntie and Uncle ran over the tail of next-door's cat and didn't even care.'

'That leaves Hector.' Fran scooped up the pigeon, holding its good wing against its body, and folding the injured wing carefully in the same manner.

'What he needs is a warm cardboard box and a blanket,' Hector said. 'Birds are calmer when wrapped in something.'

Garages, as well as being awesome to conduct science experiments, are wonderful places to stash injured pigeons. Hector was disappointed when five weeks later he released the pigeon to test its sense of direction and it did not find its way home – not to his place at any rate.

Heather smiled at the memory as she hopped off the bus. Fran and Hector's place was about a ten-minute walk from Boswell Parkway where Granddad had once told her the store was called the Provident. A milkman by trade, he used to deliver glass bottles of milk in the area, and reminisced, many a time, about how he had to manoeuvre his cart around rubble after the storm of 1968. Granddad had visited her after Ma's death, just to natter. He told her about licorice whorls as large as the palm of your hand for a penny. He told her he used to munch on pan loaves wrapped in thick, waxed paper. That the smell of fresh bread used to roll down the street, combined with the aroma of milk and cream. Warm from the cow, he said, and she'd believed him at the time.

Heather shared what she could recall of her granddad's stories with Hector and Fran over the usual roast beef, tatties, sprouts and carrots swimming in gravy.

At one point, St Cuthbert's milk carts were drawn by horses, some still around in the 1980s, with men leading the carts stacked high with plastic crates full of clinking milk bottles. But before that, Granddad had described something like bookshelves on the cart with slots for the milk crates. Heather got confused about whether Granddad drove a horse cart, or his father, or his father's father. Or if they even came out as far as Granton and Pilton. Though how else would people have got their milk back then? Walked to the nearest farm themselves on the outskirts of the city?

After tea, Hector mowed the lawn while Heather and Fran sat on the grass to observe the kids bounding on the trampoline.

Fran's home always smelled faintly of marigold furniture polish, mixed with a lavender scent that blew in from the bushes outside. Today the air hung heavy with grass. Hector's nose was watering as he leaned into the mower.

'Ma! Look at me! Ma!' Allan bounced as high as the rim of the net on the trampoline. Trish alternated between star jumps, seat drops, and twists. While Jack favoured 180s and 360s.

Fran groaned and patted her belly. More compact than the last time they'd met. 'I only have to think about jumping on that contraption and I've to run to the bathroom.' She waved at the kids and reclined on the grass, kissing smoke circles into the air.

Heather fingered the rim of her orange juice.

'The old plumbing needs a clean out,' Fran said, followed by a chain of pale circles.

It could be a statement about Fran and Hector's sex life. There was an unspoken tension in Fran, had been for about the last three months. A tension unspeakable because if Fran and Hector didn't work out, in the long run, how would this three-way friendship work? Would she have to choose one side over the other. Whose would she choose? She'd been friends with Hector first, Fran second. Did that mean Hector had to come first, or was a women's bond more unbreakable? Too many possibilities, too much strong emotion, Heather pushed it away and tried to focus on her friend in the current moment.

Heather was about to ask, what's up?, or perhaps change the subject, when Hector manoeuvred the mower around the bumpy patch of lawn the noise of the motor rupturing any possibility of conversation. Killed a tulip (on its anyway). A patch of daisies also. 'Hector, are we in the way?' Heather shouted above the hum of the machine.

He turned, his slight beer belly poking out of his T-shirt. A bug smeared across one glass lens. 'Nah, I'll mow around you. Make a feature of it, like a crime scene.'

'Fuck's sake,' said Fran, under her breath.

'We should move, no?' Heather asked Fran.

'I'm not fucking moving. He doesn't have to be mowing the lawn this exact second.'

The buzz of the lawnmower severed that conversation. Fishing around for a distracting topic once the mower was a safe distance away attacking the grass under the trees, Heather said, 'Finally took down my shed yesterday. Deconstructing a shed is challenging.'

Fran continued to play with her ciggie, seeing Heather's eye rest on it for a moment then flick self-consciously away. Aye, she'd promised to give up and coughed guiltily about it now.

'Are you—?' at a jerk of Fran's hand, Heather changed direction, 'The door was easy,' Heather continued seamlessly. 'It took me a half hour to get the window off without breaking it. Some of the boards cracked on the roof when I tried to lever them up. I finally took the roof off by bashing it with a hammer from the inside.'

'Um-hum.'

'Now I'm thinking the old shed was solid. It could've lasted another ten years. It was the wood foundation that was rotten, not the shed.'

Fran blew a ball of smoke and re-inhaled it. 'What for?'

She could be blunt sometimes, but Heather was used to it

enough to know that when Fran was ready to vent, she'd vent, there wouldn't be any stopping her, like there was no rushing her now. There were things she'd never told Fran either, such as her conception as an unwanted baby, never made to feel unwanted, or unloved, not by her ma at any rate. That came later from her aunty and uncle.

For a moment Heather watched Jack trying to find his footing on the shaking trampoline. He said something to the others and they moved, watching as Jack did a forward roll. She missed Fran's question. 'Huh?' Heather asked.

'Why pull down the shed? I could've sent Hector. He likes to destroy things in the garden.'

'That's all right. It's finished.'

'Hector could have saved you the hassle.'

As Hector thrust the lawnmower into the shed, they could hear Trish making Allan and Jack giggle with her impression of an Irish accent. Allan tried a German one but got stuck on his s's.

Fran said, 'Allan, use v's and z's for a German accent. Like this: Heaver enjoys deztroying vings ... vell Frauline, is vis the zame attitude you 'ave towards relationzhips?'

Jack flopped to the floor of the trampoline, laughing.

'Ha, see Mummy can be as funny as Daddy.' She lay down with a contented smile.

'Why can't I enjoy DIY?' Heather asked. 'Aye, it takes longer than if Hector did it, that doesn't mean I can't finish the job myself.'

Fran pursed her lips. 'That sounds like something a feminist would say. That attitude of I-can-do-it-as-well-as-a-man. It's silly, ain't it? 'cause a man can't give birth, and a woman can't pee up a wall – not without wetting her skirt at any rate.'

Heather lay on the grass, cupping her nape in her hands. 'That's one way of seeing it.'

'What's another?' Fran asked.

'Ma! Pat kicked me!'

'It was an accident,' Trish said. Allan and Trish started

to wrestle on the trampoline. Jack vaulted off like an uncoordinated bouncy ball and raced to Fran for a hug.

'Well, women carry the bairn, but an egg requires fertilisation.'

'A man can't lay a bairn. I mean—' Fran gave a smoker's cough. 'You know what I mean.'

'Was I an egg inside of you?' Jack asked.

'You were,' Fran said. 'You grew in my tummy.'

'Your example proves that women can do something men can't. Not the other way around.'

'Women can't fertilise an egg.'

Jack asked, 'How did I get in your tummy?'

'God put you there.'

'How?'

'Mummy and Daddy prayed for you, and God answered our prayers.'

Heather sprawled on the grass and called herself a coward; she'd never told Fran and Hector about the rape … now it had been a secret held too long.

Fran's answer satisfied him because Jack nodded and raced back to join his brother and sister.

'Women can fertilise an egg if they buy sperm,' Heather said, 'but not biologically, no. A man still cannot lay an egg.'

Fran chuckled. 'You're a strange one.'

'I thought I was, you know, average.'

Knots, like the ridges of wrinkled crust fungus, raised on Fran's forehead. 'Heather, you're also generous, feel too much, yes, but you stand up for people and what you believe in. You've courage.'

Fran was in a charitable mood with that compliment. Must be the nicotine working its magic for she had been glum at home and at work for months. Courage, sure, that's why 'imposter' echoed through her mind every time she turned the key in the door of her new place, and peered outside, opening the door, expecting Brother Baneshanks to return with his lawyer and a couple of police with a request to vacate the property.

Heather stared into the blue, no azure, sky. A helicopter hummed overhead; the looping rows of flats and houses, trees, roads and parks, must be impressive from above. 'I used to have courage. Remember when we met?'

'Aye, thanks to Alex Simons in the school canteen.'

'You thought he was bonnie.'

'All the girls did.'

He was handsome, Heather recalled, in a boyish unshaved way. Shame he had such an ugly personality. As Heather flexed her hand and watched the kids on the trampoline PE lessons came to mind. The torture of the week where the sports teacher pointed out their physical weaknesses and made them dress inappropriately for the weather. Heather often pondered why they did sports outside in autumn and the lasses were forced to wear skirts.

'My theory,' Fran had said, 'Is that the sports teacher is a sadist.'

'What's a sadist?' Heather asked.

'Someone who likes to look up girls' skirts while their legs are glacial.'

Glacial being their current favourite word after learning it in geography last week.

Heather shivered as the glacial autumn air teased its way up her legs, raising their fine hairs. Dreaded team sports with pleated skirts and navy knickers for the lasses, and navy shorts for the lads. Scant skirts and pre-adolescent girls … what were the teachers thinking? Fran was right – about Sir being a sadist.

'Irvin.'

'Paul.'

'Simon.'

Heather shifted her weight from sneaker to sneaker as she waited to be picked.

'Fran.'

'Beth.'

'Sarah.'

'Hector.'

'Yes!' Hector punched the air causing his glasses to slip off his nose.

Florence sighed, shifting on her crutches and gave Heather a sympathetic wince. 'It would be jolly not to be the last to be picked, every time.'

'At least you get picked last because of your cast. I simply suck at sports.'

'Florence.'

Florence laughed. 'Sorry, Heather.' Florence limped to join her team.

'Heather.'

'Whoo-ooo, you're on my team!' Fran gave her a hug.

'Lesbo!' Alex called.

'Shut up, Alex!'

'Language, Fran,' said Mr Noel, the sports teacher.

'What about *his* language?' Fran asked.

Her comment was ignored.

'Just 'cause he's the new golden child at sports,' Fran muttered.

'That was a cool film,' Heather said. 'My mum loves that movie. Let's pretend that PE is like the trial that Eddie Murphy has to do in the film.'

'What are you wittering on about?'

'The movie you watched at my place. Don't drop the water?'

'Right. Aye. Don't drop the water.' Fran grinned.

'Cease blathering girls and grab your sticks,' Mr Noel said.

Fran grabbed two hockey sticks and chucked one to Heather. Heather missed, of course, and it clattered to the ground. As Heather's hands touched the dangerous curve of wood she said, 'I hate hockey most of all. Surely this is more of a weapon than sports equipment.'

A brush of air swept up the back of her skirt.

'Alex!' Fran screeched.

Alex had his stick hooked under Heather's skirt, showing her navy knickers to the entire class. Heather's blood didn't boil, it evaporated along with her common sense, and she heard herself growl a warning like an uneasy dog. Alex shuffled back. His smirk only wavered when Heather's fist met it.

For a moment the world folded around her bunched digits, dough-like, preserving the open-eyed look on Alex's face, Fran's half-gaping half-grinning mouth before she whooped for joy, the lads' scowls, the lasses' laughter, and Mr Noel's look of disapproval.

'Sadist!' Heather hissed into Alex's reeling face.

Mr Noel's frown deepened. 'Headmaster's office. Now.'

Ma had come to her defence that day, saying any lass had a right to defend herself from perverts such as sadists.

Heather opened and closed her hand, the back covered in the small criss-crossing lines of age. Green veins visibly threaded through her skin. And her legs, if she dared inspect them, would be a wriggly mess of mauve veins, crawling to the surface.

'Gosh,' Fran said. 'Remember when you punched Alex in the face? That was awesome. Fearless.'

'I feel like I had courage … once. Then I realised life's limitations.'

'Huh?'

'I'm bringing up the fact that life isn't fair, Fran.' Heather hugged her knees. 'If it was then everyone would have enough to get by.'

'Not that you ever ask.'

Was that a warning in Fran's voice? A suggestion that something was not quite right?

'Pardon?' Heather asked. If anything was going on Fran would tell her, eventually.

'We have enough, don't we?' Fran asked. 'Some of us more than others.'

'To survive. I feel like there should be more to it than getting by. Don't you?'

'A higher minimum wage,' Fran said, with conviction. Yes,

she must have a bee up her backside about their pay rate. A weight that had been lifted off Heather's shoulders thanks to Irvin's generosity. He had left her a bank account as well as the house and his family weren't happy about it. Night and day Heather expected a letter from Brother Baneshanks' lawyer on the doorstep to contest the will.

'It's not only about finance,' Heather added. 'It's about access to things. Like art, right. The government decided in the nineties that art would be available to the public. We sometimes forget that is why we can go to the National Gallery and the Modern Gallery for free.'

'And did you find the meaning of life?'

There it was again, an unnecessary edge to Fran's voice, a way of guilt tripping her, perhaps; though, why was the enigma. Heather decided to ignore it. Fran customarily blurted out anything that bothered her, eventually. Better wait than play a guessing game.

'Funny,' Heather said.

Fran's forehead ceased up, as if annoyed Heather wouldn't spar with her today.

'You should come with me some time with the kids,' Heather suggested.

'Families don't go to art galleries, Heather.'

Heather recalled the painting that she'd wanted to tell Fran about. A simple image of a wave about to crash, like someone had suspended time to catch a moment of anticipation. She opened her mouth to tell Fran about it, Hector collapsed onto their patch of unmown grass, emerald strands on his sweaty skin; and Fran, despite her earlier streak of hostility, with a suggestive smile clicked her fingers above a smoke ring, reshaping her smoke circle into a heart.

Chapter 9

July 2019

Following an afternoon shower in late-July, an orange and black Small Tortoiseshell butterfly mistook their lounge for a flower bed. It fluttered from the curtains to the wall, to the mantlepiece, to a framed photograph of Edinburgh Castle from Calton Hill, to the floral lampshade. Hector moved in overexaggerated arches of the arms, entertaining Jack, aping around. It became a game, Hector inexpertly loping after, and missing, the butterfly. Jack's shrill giggles shadowing him, like Tinkerbell, around the room. Fran leaned on the door frame shaking her head. Her husband, for a moment he was back in the gleam of his eyes, shot her pleased winks; until, giving up on the game, this untouchable calm creature evaded him for real. His hoots switched into chimpanzee-like snarls.

Jack gasped as Hector's palms smashed together. Hector wrinkled his nose. His palms unpeeled revealing a mashed abdomen, the butterfly's crushed wings and antennae. Wee Jack fled upstairs.

Fran, as she went to check on Jack, remembered that the foundations of one's daily life were as fragile as a butterfly; it's security an illusion. She'd learnt that long ago, thanks to her step-da: Dougie.

The first blow had been the worst. Unexpected. Fran had been around sixteen, on the lounge floor, splayed on her stomach, frowning at her maths homework. Ma – 'Donna, my bella Donna' as Dougie sometimes sang – prepared bolognaise in the kitchen. Scott – ten years old – played with a plastic wrestling figure of Hulk Hogan. Dougie had been off the booze for about six months. Their lives had taken on a new routine, especially at weekends when Dougie would lob or strike a ball with them in the street, tell them dirty jokes (that they weren't to share with their ma), devote family time to competing at Monopoly followed by *Gladiator* on the telly, a sports entertainment show which pitched everyday people against athletes.

He'd been playing snooker at the Anchor Inn. He entered looking sober enough. His character was slippery. If you ever asked the name of a bird in the garden, Robin, Blackcap, bluethroat, he could identify every bird in the sky, yet not a thought about being a decent human being to animals or humans alike: he'd fill his own belly before yours, even if there weren't enough to go around, and was never in the wrong – in his mind – not about one misinformed fact.

Dougie skipped over Fran, ruffled Scott's hair, pawed Donna in the kitchen. Just visible through the doorway. His hands up her skirt. Then he returned to the lounge and ordered them to the kitchen table. As Scott went, Fran peeked at Donna who hadn't called them yet, and didn't like them in the kitchen till she was ready.

Dougie grabbed a fist of Fran's hair, forcing her to stand. 'Not a good enough Da for you, you runt?'

Donna turned, holding the spoon, dripping sauce on the lino. 'Tea's ready.'

'Coming, darling.'

Donna turned away.

He sneered at Fran. Stretched his calloused fingers under Fran's jaw and lifted her off the ground, scrutinising her: sick bastard, wanted a reaction. As his fetid breath caught at the back of her throat, she could feel her toes leaving the carpet. She gagged. Abruptly, Dougie let her go. He stood in the sauce on the kitchen floor, swore, and punched Donna in the stomach. To stop the tears coming, Fran dug her thumbs into the flesh of her index fingers.

The sight of algebra or the smell of pasta sauce always made

Fran want to vomit after that.

It started a trend of petty conflicts between him and them – Fran and Scott. Behind Donna's back, he targeted Fran with pinches on her thighs. His beefy fingers left bruises. Scott wanted them to tattle, but Fran was scared to in case it made things worse. She couldn't figure out what she'd done wrong. If they could resolve the problem then things would improve.

The day he booted Scott in the leg making him wail was that step too far. The problem – the putrid core of their family – was Dougie. Fran put some clothing in her school bag for her and Scott. They didn't have much. Didn't need much. The next day when they'd ordinarily stroll home together, Fran told Scott they weren't going to live there any longer because Dougie was a depraved man who would continue to hurt them. She'd brought Scott's favourite toy, so he wouldn't miss it.

Fran enfolded Jack in her embrace. He was a sensitive wee lad, like her brother Scott. Ma had confessed to Fran that through having a child, you realise how much of the world is out of your control. Parenthood introduces new fears into one's life: first the fear of pregnancy or the fear one will fail to get pregnant; the fear something will be wrong with the bairn before its birth; survival of the birth; and then, even worse, survival out there with stairs, water, fire, knives, strangers, pandemics – it's a miracle any of us live at all. Still, with all this explained, Fran hadn't truly understood that the fear of losing one's children extends beyond the physical to the emotional: their first shrug and pull away from you, their exasperated glances, their will for independence. Friends did that too of course, a gradual forgetfulness, until you could scarcely remember who they were. She could hardly follow Heather's thoughts these days as her best pal explored new things and left her behind.

Fran once watched an episode of *Grey's Anatomy*, a medical drama, which compared parenthood to being sucked dry until only a husk remained. Humorous and only part truth. Certainly, in terms of time and effort. The role against all fears to protect one's child could overwhelm you, if you let it.

Later in bed, with Hector's sock over one fist, Fran lay the fabric, fraying sides together, and criss-crossed a series of darning stitches over the rend. Hector reread a book on finance, clicking his tongue whenever he came across a badly written paragraph.

Fran said, 'Darning socks in bed wasn't what I imagined married life would be.'

'We were tadpoles when we got together.'

'Not *that* young.'

'It didn't feel like it at the time, but 19 is young. And 21 is an uninformed period to get married.'

'Hum,' Fran agreed. They'd grown up together, changing immensely throughout their twenties. Most of the other couples they hung out with were on their second marriages.

'Regretting your decision?' Hector asked.

'Never. A man that doesn't snore is a rare find.' That was a lie, for Hector did snore –when he had a cold.

'And a woman that doesn't yell is – I won't end that sentence.'

'I don't see the comparison.'

'Aye. Heather would have thrown a feminist pass at me if I'd tried that on her.'

Fran barely followed the Rugby analogy but let it go. 'She used an expression the other day that I didn't follow.'

Hector turned a page of his book. 'Hmm?'

'Imagined Sisterhood. Any idea?'

'None.'

Fran pulled the end of the thread, which drew the hole closed, then double backstitched to hold the end in place, cut the thread. 'Heather has thoughts that leave me behind.'

'Aren't you happy for her?'

'Of course. Why ask?'

'Because of the way you comment sometimes.' Hector removed his glasses and rubbed the spot below his eyebrows.

'In an unchristian way, I suppose.' She bit her tongue, too late, she'd spoken her mind again.

'It's not a judgement, Fran. You're annoyed with her, aren't you?'

'I think she lied to me.'

'About what?'

'Irvin. She said they didn't have anything but a professional relationship.'

'I can follow what you're thinking … why did he leave her the house?'

'Right enough.'

Hector slammed his book shut, placed it carefully on the bedside cabinet and knocked his glasses to the floor. 'People don't act how we expect. Heather might not know the reason herself. It was more about his family than about her. From what you've told me they weren't there for him while Heather was.'

'He was paying her, that's different. When family is sick you go.'

'Not everyone can handle death. Remember how Heather was after her mum died, she was crushed. Not everyone has our faith, Fran.'

She laid the sock and scissors and thread on her bedside cabinet, and switched off the light. 'Heather's just so …'

'She's hurting, healing. Gone into one of her retreats. She'll surface in time. Let's be happy for her. Unconditionally.'

'I'm happy for her,' Fran said. Aware that as she lay in their rough bedsheets in a rented house Heather was presumably snuggled in brushed cotton.

'Jealous too, I bet.'

'She's self-centred. Not asked about us at all. Not even about you.'

'You know Heather. She retreats into fantasy ... it's not her best characteristic, but she's had a lot on, so have we. After a bit of time to settle herself, talk to her, Fran. If anything, she should be jealous of what we have.' Hector tickled her neck with his breath.

'Wrath is cruel, anger is overwhelming, but who can stand before jealousy ...' Fran stroked the cross at her neck, warm from her body heat.

'What did you imagine about married life?' asked Hector, propping himself up on one elbow.

'A mortgage on a house with a nice garden, a cat and unlimited sex.'

'Glad to hear I satisfied one of the three. Also, we could get a cat.'

'Let's see how things go.'

'That's my cue.' He shimmied his fingers under her nighty and blew raspberries on her neck.

She chortled. 'Get off with you, wet frog!'

'If you kiss princes they turn into frogs, correct?'

'Other way around, Charming.'

'Then kiss me quick.'

Chapter 10

It would be a relief when Jack and Allan moved to the same secondary school as Patricia. But then again, the parents would move too. Fran would try to encourage Patricia – who walked most days with the twins, Isla and Jessica, and their mum, Corrinne – to walk her brothers home. Fran entered the school playground and nodded to Beth and Miss Reed from the Parent Council. Only kind-hearted gossip circulated about the kids' favourite teacher: Miss Reed. On the other hand, a rumour travelled from mouth to mouth that Beth was, horror of all horrors, a single working mum. This notion had been batted about the parents since Sylvia had overheard an argument between Max's parents about a potential separation. The gossips of the playground; that is to say, Emma and Sarah headed by queen bee Sylvia had been discouraged by Beth's defensive tactics. But then, Sylvia doesn't know any better, Fran reflected; she's like a child parroting the political perspective of their parents, whatever gossip she hears she repeats it as fact instead of fiction.

Today, Sylvia, Emma and Sarah huddled in their stay-at-home triangle on the fenced-in tarmac against a wind strong enough to dehorn cattle. What was their problem with Beth? It might be as simple as envy. Women being the worst critics of other women. Beth's attractive and thoughtful nature was a threat to the others' social obsession: to find a man and keep him as if there weren't plenty of single mums nowadays. The adult playground was split between the opinion Beth deserved the separation and didn't, which said more about parent politics than any right to privacy that was being defended. Intense, sinister underbellies were no longer restricted to the black market but caused parental divisions at Scottish primary schools.

Fran cautiously approached the triangle, centre-front, before the metallic gate where the children would file through one at a time and combine on the playground to form a cacophony of flapping coats, scuffed knees and discarded lunch boxes. Sylvia flicked her blond hair, darker at the roots, and turned her voluptuous face towards Fran – the type of face that spoke of silk sheets and scented massages.

Fran tried to evade getting too close but was defeated by a child with a bloody nose. Miss Reed pushed past to offer a hankie from her sleeve and Fran found herself forming a star with Sylvia and the queen's ladies of the court: Sarah holding Baby Gemma; Emma with a shaggy grey puppy on a lead; plus Dorota, the new Polish mum whose serious eyes were downcast as her hands twisted around the handles of a reusable Sainsbury's shopping bag. More foreigners, taking British jobs.

Sylvia was in competitive mid-rant: '... and he had the nerve to say I did nothing. So, I said, iron your own damn shirts.'

'No!' Emma said and 'Naughty dog!' to the puppy hitching its front paws on Fran's stomach. 'Puppy' was a loose term as the Scottish deerhound was already the size of a miniature horse.

'It's fine,' Fran said, though Emma could likely tell from her tone that she didn't like dogs who enthusiastically said hello by leaving paw prints on the front of her coat.

Emma didn't notice as she shared a rare titbit from her life which simultaneously avoided any detail, 'With us, it's the lack of us time.'

Not to be outdone Sarah said, 'My husband's fortunate when he doesn't get a plate resembling a smiley face.'

Sarah was the kind of person who'd moan about no one taking her food intolerance seriously after inviting folk to tea without asking if they didn't, or couldn't, eat anything.

In contrast, Emma was reluctant to express an opinion. She filled silences with smiles, so that the conversation could hang, awkwardly, in the air.

Sylvia shot a sidewards glance at Beth and caught Fran's eyes. 'Imagine trying to manage kids and career,' Sylvia said. 'I wouldn't wish to promote being a supermum. So much pressure.'

Because Fran collected Jack they assumed she was also a stay-at-home mum. She wasn't about to reveal otherwise.

The others nodded reminiscent of a set of bobblehead dogs, with the exemption of Dorota who bore a frown of concentration. Fran wasn't sure what her English level was. Last week Sylvia had said, 'These foreign mums should make more of an effort.' Not that there were many, Pilton being predominantly white working class which drove the middle-class mums (Sylvia, Emma and Sarah) together. Parents that came from outside Scotland were mostly Polish, a smattering of Chinese, three Syrian families, two French, and one Moroccan household.

Sylvia's eyes gave a sideward look at Dorota. 'Such first world problems, I know.' Sylvia pulled a face.

What would she know? Mrs married-to-an-expert-in-Cyber-and-Information-Security with the financial security that job entailed couldn't comprehend Fran's problems – all the more imperative to keep Hector's redundancy secret. Why's it that the poor should be pious and the rich can say whatever they damned please? A test to be sure. Fran chewed the inside of her cheek and spotted Nike as she limped across the road, her foot in a cast.

Each year, Fran observed incoming and established parents circling one another to identify by accent, vocabulary and education whether they occupied the correct place on the social ladder. Sylvia blanked Fran's neighbour Nike once, by asking, 'Do I know you?', two years ago when Nike was trying to request a play date for her son. After that Nike started listening to music rather than interact with the other parents.

A tell-tale tightening of Sylvia's mouth caused the others to glance up and then glance away. Nike limped by their group, her music blasting her ears.

Being a neighbour, Fran received regular updates of Nike's state of health. Last week constipation was suspected bowel cancer, last month the flu was lung disease, the month before that a bit of tiredness was Lupus, the month before migraines became a symptom of brain cancer. Did a word exist for the fear of being well? Cherophobia came to mind. No, that was an irrational fear that being happy will lead to something ghastly happening. Easy to feel superior to a woman like that, according to Sylvia. Yet, Nike had a good reason for being stressed: her hubby was a soldier in Iraq.

The queen bee displayed a frozen façade of intimacy towards Dorota. 'Housework is real work, don't you agree?'

The chatter lulled. Dorota pinned near the rattling perimeter fence like a prize specimen. She said, 'It takes much work keeping the bathroom clean in a house of eight.'

'Eight!' Sylvia said. That knowledge would, no doubt, be shared around her sewing circle that evening.

Dorota counted her fingers. 'Mother, father, brother, children' – she tapped five fingers – 'me.'

'S.A.H.D. alert,' Sarah muttered, as David – his freckles and red-gold hair like Mary Queen of Scots' in later age, and thus depicting him as a 'true Scot' – strode towards the group. That was unfair of Sarah considering that David's wife earned a decent living in pharmaceuticals, and they'd made a sensible choice for the man to watch their adopted children.

'What is the meaning of this alert?' Dorota asked Fran.

Fran kept her voice low, she liked David and didn't want him to take offence. 'Stay-at-home dad.'

'Hi, David!' Sylvia and her bees chorused. For a second David's cherub face was facing Fran. His back to the others. He rolled his eyes for her benefit.

'Hello, ladies.'

'How's the adopted darling?' Sylvia said, cooing over the

wriggling bairn with thick, curly hair, and melted chocolate skin to die for.

'We prefer to call the darling by his name. TAA-uw. Meaning lion.'

Tau grabbed a handful of Sylvia's blond straightened locks and yanked.

'Owch! Get it off me!'

David swept back his mop of hair. 'What's the gossip?'

Emma gave a smile that barely reached her cheeks, and pulled back the overeager puppy.

'We don't gossip.' Sarah tittered.

'We do,' Sarah said. 'But who can blame us when at home it's all: when to feed, to change, to do extra laundry.' Sarah soothed Baby Gemma's fine feathered fuzz and yawned.

David nodded. The circles under his eyes also attested to some recent long nights. 'I also have two to juggle now. Alex doesn't like me to use that word: "We don't juggle with children, David." Alex has plenty to lecture me on, but I'm the one at home all day.'

'School traffic is frustrating, isn't it?' Sylvia asked.

'We walk,' Fran said.

'Cycle,' said Emma, gesturing to her bike with its baby carrier.

Sylvia ignored them. 'Jeff double-parked at the drop-off spot again. Can you have a word with him, David? It would be better coming from a fellow dad.'

'Parents like him bring traffic to a standstill,' David said.

Sylvia didn't look like she caught the sarcasm as she gave a preoccupied smile as Beth joined them, straight to business under the pressure of Sylvia's faux greeting, kiss kiss and all that.

'The council approved another Halloween party. We need volunteers to handle the drinks, food and baking.'

'I can pre-order some scones,' David said.

Sylvia addressed Emma, 'Can you bake extra for muffin day? I can't get my cleaner to bake. I even offered to pay extra.'

Emma yawned.

Sylvia turned to Fran. 'Andy asked this morning if Jack and him could have a sleepover. Would today work? Tuesday is swimming, Wednesday is Zumba, Thursday – well you get the idea.'

'Today? I haven't packed any PJs or anything.' Jack frequently wet the bed. At her place, it was one thing but at another house …

'No problem. I can find spare attire.'

Emma and Sarah were distracted by their two Sara's – also demanding a sleepover. David watched the lasses with a faint smile as he fielded Beth's sign-up sheet and his son Sam ran out of the school to greet him, and Dorota was chatting in rapid Polish with another mum. Lucky her being able to use language as a means of escape.

Fran used the distraction to tell Sylvia, in a lowered voice, about Jack's bed-wetting.

'That happens. They're six. I got it covered. I can take him tonight and make up two lunches for tomorrow.'

Fran recalled the plain white bread and salad cream she'd dumped in Jack's lunch box. 'Don't go to too much trouble.'

'How's things at home? Hector has a new position?'

'How do you know that?' she asked, unaware her voice had raised until the group had swivelled towards her, as well as a nearby clan of Asian mums. She'd not mentioned their situation. She clocked Nike's downcast look (incidentally her neighbour). The only parents not staring were the two chittering Polish women. Fran recalled some Polish families had moved back home after the 2016 vote, in spite of the Scottish majority voting against Brexit.

'Things are fine.' The laundry basket had overflowed to be dealt with when she got home. Should she worry? Its presence was a reminder that Hector was going through something he wasn't willing to share.

'You okay, Ma?' Allan asked. He and Jack were standing beside her.

'Course. Jack, want to sleepover at Andy's tonight?'

'Yes! Can I?'

'Course. I'll pick you up from school tomorrow.'

Allan babbled about his day as they crossed the street. Rumbling cars blocked the street, the sycamores that had grown year-on-year as the kids had grown out of pairs of shoes sported black spots. She'd walked across the road, and along to the park, with each of her children as toddlers, their hand in hers. Before that, she and Heather had walked a similar route as kids. Life continuously pushing on. Hector, of course, still grieved for the loss of his parents the previous year, but it had only been a half year before that since Fran had lost her ma. Which now didn't seem to matter as Hector's grief took precedence. Mean thought, sorry God. Fran addressed him internally. It's hard, you know? Especially with Heather's lack of support. I'm losing her and it's not like I have any pals amongst those backstabbing parents or at church. Course you know that. How's things with all the demands you are certainly getting at present? She wouldn't add to them. We're okay. Thank you for everyday that we are okay. She promised to think more charitably about Sylvia and listen to her son before he grew too independent to share his life with her.

The next day, Fran collected Jack and Allan still fuming about Nike informing Sylvia of their personal lives. God was constantly in a testing frame of mind lately. Allan told them, in excited tones, all about the sleepover as they headed for the park – she should have been paying better attention to her son, rather than worrying about what Sylvia knew about their lives via their neighbour. Did she know, for instance, that Fran wasn't a stay-at-home mum?

'We ate pizza with pepperoni and chips, and had a bath, and played with Andy's action figures in the bath, and I wore Andy's pyjamas and a nappy—'

Allan opened his mouth to comment on his brother's use of the word nappy. Fran distracted him with a football card she'd discovered marking a page in the newspaper at work.

'—and we watched a cartoon and sang karaoke and—'

As Jack didn't say he was bothered by the nappy Fran didn't pry further. It wasn't uncommon for some parents to use pull-ups with their kids at this age.

Fran listened as Jack relayed they'd eaten porridge and blue Benny's for breakfast.

'Blueberries?'

'Yes, those ones.'

Posh that. Blueberries for breakfast. The price of them was enough to make her eyes water. Fran stroked her stomach, as her belly shrunk, somehow her worm of jealousy was growing fatter and spreading from Heather to all others who had more than she did: most of Edinburgh's half a million inhabitants.

On the way to the park, Jack and Allan scuffled under a row of sycamores providing shade from the summer sun. The boys kicked immature acorns, knocked from the trees by the high winds, while chanting their times tables. A collection of fast-food wrappers and takeaway boxes circled their feet. Despite their school's, their city's, and their country's drive towards zero waste, crisp packets stuck to fences and aluminium cans decorated hedges. Asking people to care about waste when they were trying to feed their kids each day ... well, in this neighbourhood, you might as well ask, 'can you go four miles out of your way to the nearest zero waste shop, spend extra on your weekly food bill for a seasonal veg box, and find the time to make your own natural beauty products?' The answer, of course, would be no. The middle-class mums, like Sylvia, at the school didn't get it.

'And for breakfast, she made me a ploughman's sandwich, a juice box and an apple. Can I sleep over again?'

'If Sylvia doesn't mind.'

'She's awesome. She won't mind.'

'By awesome do you mean she let you play video games?'

Jack paused, half shook his head, a delaying tactic if Fran ever saw one. He said, 'Yes, but not the violent one like last time.'

Right, a new violent one she assumed. Why didn't parents check the rating of those terrible games?

'What's it called?' she asked. It was hard not to let the disapproval show in her voice, as it was hard to not let Jack's use of the word 'awesome' cut her to the core.

'You won't know it.'

'Try me.'

'It had creative in the title.'

'Fortnight Creative?'

'Um …'

If that had been the one, it not only had an age rating of twelve but was a platform where players could create anything they want on an island, including battle arenas. More fighting. All these multiplayer scenarios emphasised shooting people. Whatever happened to finding your way through mazes using role-play and object finding skills, or sending a ball pinging back and forth across the screen in a frustrating game of Pong?

'You know I don't mind games,' Fran said. 'Age appropriate ones.'

'Everyone plays that game, Ma,' Allan said.

After the boys had run off some energy in the park playground under a patchy sky, they reached home as the sky clouded over.

'Please don't blab to Andy's ma or I won't be allowed to visit again,' Jack said.

'You're only allowed to visit if I let you.'

'That's not fair!'

Nike next door caught an eyeful of Jack storming into the house. That was just fiddley foodle – to laugh at the fiddle-faddle of it all.

Fran waved and closed the door.

Hector had been brilliant in the summer holidays with the kids and the house. Now he was letting things slide. In the kitchen, dishes cluttered the sink and the smell of the bin bag made her gag; its greasy scent had attracted ants from the garden. They circled the bin and marched out the rear door. Doing whatever ants did.

Their bedroom smelled rank. It didn't help that the stale air reminded Fran of when Patricia last brought home the flu. She tugged the curtains open to let in some fresh glacial air and sniffed the frosty wind. Perhaps it would snow – a glitch in the seasons – before the temperature rose again. The kids would be delighted and return cold and eat, while she would be coming up with excuses not to put the heating on. A warm bath, several jumpers and hot chocolate should do the trick. Fran hoped this was a momentary dip in the mild start of autumn temperatures. With the curtains open, the light highlighted the dust over the built-in wardrobe mirror, the tousled bed, the dented, pre-loved bedside cabinets, and one broken lamp. Dirty pants, trousers and jumpers lay where they were discarded by Hector on the floor, socks and shirts drooped over the stand where she used to put on her make-up. Back when she could be bothered.

Hector groaned from the bed.

'I don't know how to pull you out of it,' she said. 'You need to shower.'

He pulled the polyester stuffed duvet over his head.

'Seriously, you're clatty.' She pinched her nose. 'How can I sleep with this mess …? I need all the sleep I can get working extra shifts … Have you even left the house today?'

Fran had to remind herself of the geeky youth with his animated hands. That Hector was hard to remember, left somewhere between now and the moment in the Central Library by the biography section where they'd stolen their first kiss.

His reply was muffled.

'So now I have to tell you to speak up, like the kids.'

He poked a gap large enough for his mouth in the duvet. 'I've to go to the jobcentre tomorrow.'

'Right, right, and a letter came for the Council Tax. Positive news for once.'

An eye appeared in the hole he'd created.

'We have a low, whatsit discount,' she said.

'Income.'

'Yes, low-income discount. We can split the payments, but still have to find the dosh for it. Guess we'll find out tomorrow.'

'We've reached the limit. I'm unemployable.'

'You're not.'

He pulled the duvet back over himself.

She flung a dirty sock to one side and sat on the bed. Then laid one arm over the other, to rub her elbows and calm herself down. There must be some way she could get through to him. 'Look, this lack of showering paired with overeating isn't helping. I mean, indulging yourself don't help me buy food, and makes your mood swings worse.'

'I'm fine.'

'You're a chancer. You haven't shampooed. Haven't shaved. Haven't been applying for more jobs.' She grabbed a corner of the rank duvet to jerk it off him, but he wouldn't let it go; it was like fighting with a rat in a bag, an unpleasant image that made her let the duvet go.

'It's pointless.'

'I think you're depressed, sweetie. See the doctor. Perhaps he can write a note for extra assistance on medical grounds.'

'That's all I am to you … a wallet.'

'That's not what I meant.'

'Then lower yourself a peg or two and stop at the food bank.'

'Fuck, I can't say anything right. When will we qualify for more? When we're out on the street?' She began to keen. 'You can do this. You must, 'cause I can't. I can't do it myself. Help me!'

He sniffed under the covers. 'Gonnae no do that!'

'Christ's sake! You bairn!' She punched him through the bedding. He sat up, wide-eyed.

'You punched me!'

'My head's mince. We can't go on like this. Go to the doctor.'

'Motion refused,' He flopped down and rolled under the duvet once more. What could she do if he wouldn't co-operate?

A tap, tapping came from the bedroom door. 'Ma?'

'Yes, Allan?'

'Pat bit me.'

'I DID NOT!'

'YES, YOU DID! Yes, she did.'

'Be right there,' Fran said, squeezing in a quick prayer, 'I lift my eyes to the mountains – where does my help come from? My help comes from the Lord, the maker of heaven and Earth.'

'God's not listening,' Hector muttered. She heard him too as she left the room, but what was the point in replying. He might be right. Still, she was tough, and could get through this with or without anyone else.

Chapter 11

February 1995

Hunger. For many people just a word, for others a gnawing belly pain, the involuntary licking of dry lips, waking crying, an ability to eat anything to ease that ache … no matter how tasteless: wrappers scrounged from bins, cotton wool smeared with make-up residue, cereal packaging. Thoughts plaguing their nights: I could pray … I could borrow … I could beg … I could steal …

Often, Fran remembers living with Scott beneath that old oak prickled with holly in the shelter Hector and Heather had helped them build. Fran remembers how cold the nights had been. The blessed warmth of the school showers. It hadn't been too appalling at first. Plus Hector and Heather helped out. The large bins outback too, where the canteen ladies threw the leftovers. Her stomach kept her awake at night during the school break when it was harder to forage for food. Please, God, she prayed, help me find some food for Scott tomorrow.

Maybe it had been the food, or lack of it, that had made Scott sick, or Dougie's kick to his stomach.

The thing you learn about living on the streets is that hunger eventually goes away over 36 hours with the certainty that the pangs would return worse than before. Scott complained of pain like a mole grazing his insides. When she found food, he only managed a few bites, which meant he lost weight. Mr Feilds asked Fran about the weight loss, and she made up a story about Scott seeing doctors for some stomach thing she didn't understand.

At first, they had been careful to go undetected living in the woods behind the school – not wanting Ma or Dougie to find them. Heather and Hector helped them out by giving an all-clear sign, a tap of the head, outside the school to indicate to Scott and Fran it was safe to sneak around back. They also had to avoid teachers, and snitchers, spotting them traverse the car park beside the bins.

It should have shocked Fran that neither Ma nor Dougie came looking for them. As a child she couldn't understand it, but at the time it eased her internal pressure, wound up tightly like a bobbin thread, at the thought of going back to that house and Dougie's vengeful fists. As a mother, Fran understood this. Donna hadn't wanted them to be near Dougie whose treatment of her had deteriorated without the semblance of family life. Though, at the time Donna was still a dinner lady at the primary school, serving food to kids while forgetting her own.

Well, fuck her. Fran had a plan. She'd created a CV at school in the computer room and would get a job to pay for a flat. Heather said she'd do the same, so they could both look after Scott.

Then Scott got sick.

Fran dragged him to the hospital at night; all the while, he insisted it was hunger, that it would pass.

'Let's go to hospital.'

'We can't. They'll take us back, and he'll kill you!'

'Then we'll go to Eileen's house,' Fran said. Eileen was a lady with a kind face who always wore blue and scratched at her flaking skin as if it never stopped itching. She had four lads and a lass and lived next to the church, and, more importantly, would know what to do. 'We'll get help there.'

Fran verified that Scott wore his hat and scarf and gloves and off they went. It was a three-mile walk to the church. Semi-frozen puddles caught the moonlight and street lights but not the rare sight of stars about the luminous city. They took care not to slide on them where commonly this would be a game – Scott didn't have the energy. One mile in Scott leant on her for support. The glare of the street lighting picked out his pale features. A payphone stood ahead. Its safety glass shattered.

'Sit here,' Fran ordered. She helped him to a low brick wall.

'Don't leave me.' Shallow breathes left his body in sharp outlets of steam.

'I need to get help. There and back. Promise.'

Scott watched her point to the payphone and nodded, his movements slow and painful to watch.

Fran ran to the payphone. It smelled of pee.

Time stretches waiting for an ambulance to arrive. The chewing gum of time. Especially when you are squeezing the hand of someone you love and they're panting between groans. God, she prayed, please, please be listening. I'll do anything if you save him.

'Tell me about what we're going to do this summer,' Scott said.

'Again?'

'Again.'

'Heather and me are going to get jobs. Earn enough to rent a flat for us three. Until my modelling career takes off. And you'll study to become a vet.'

It took longer than usual for him to correct her purposeful mistake.

'Nooo, a pilot,' he said, lips flicking upwards for a few precious seconds. 'And Ma will visit for Sunday lunch.'

'Every Sunday, and Hector too. All the people we want to be in our family.'

His grimace softened into a smile. 'Your kids and my kids playing together.'

Shit, what had she done? Here he on the ground on a freezing night because of her. 'I'm sorry, Scott. So sorry. I thought I could keep you safe, choose what our life was going to be. It's made you sicker than his clouts.'

He squeezed her hand, pulsating softly like the beat of a wee bird's heart. Staring into her eyes as though to convey *you kept your promise, you kept me safe.* But, if that was the case, how come they were on a cold street waiting for an ambulance?

Fran crushed her forehead to his and hugged him close to keep him warm.

The adults arrived, they'd know what to do and everything would be all right. She could feel it in the warm blankets wrapped around them, in their steady voices, in the movement of the ambulance towards safety.

A doctor at the hospital asked if Scott had vomited blood, Fran shook her head while Scott dipped his, he said he'd hid it from Fran as he didn't want her to worry, didn't want her to have to go home. A docile nurse with sweets in her pockets took their information and asked where their parents were. Fran gave Ma's name and address.

The chewing gum of time contracted and events raced ahead. Movement. Motion. A blur in Fran's vision. Scott's eyes sought hers out and gleamed for a moment, emptying out. She squeezed his hand. Squeezed it again. No response.

'He's dead,' a doctor said.

Wait, that can't be true. 'No, no. You're going to fix him. We're going to rent a flat. Scott's going to become a pilot and-and-and …'

A look of pity crossed the nurse's face as if Fran was the one who was dying. She'd tried to change things. Everything was going to be different away from Dougie.

For a moment, the world became a blank page. Where pain is knowing that you are responsible for your brother's death.

No Scott. A gurney's wheels hissed by the room. No Scott. Clanking keys dangled from a man's belt as he paced down the corridor. No Scott. Cheese and onion crisps, the thought came randomly until Fran noted that's what the nurse smelled of. Something within Fran crunched. She sat on the floor and curled into a ball.

Donna arrived. The one who was supposed to take care of them. Fran stood. Braced herself, expected to be hit and hugged close, instead she flinched from Donna's animalistic screaming as Donna gathered Scott's limp body in her embrace. Amongst the indistinguishable words and mewls of her ma, Fran understood enough. Scott was gone because Fran had brought him to the doctor's too late. And Donna had arrived too late to be there for him. Dougie was gone, she'd kicked him out, changed the locks, kept asking Fran, did he touch you? Did he touch you? Not relinquishing Scott's corpse. Until all fell still in the room, the nurse remaining in one corner, her face lowered, yet not leaving them alone for a second.

The nurse maintained eye contact with Fran as her Ma clasped Scott, almost as though trying to silently communicate something her profession did not allow. At the time, Fran had felt only what she could label as guilt; yet the nurse was probably trying to console her.

Sobbing Donna rocked back and forth with Scott in her arms. She eventually glanced to see whether they were still there or she was alone, Fran tried to say with a look of her own what she couldn't yet verbalise: you've let me down too.

Ma stood from the hospital bed, arranged Scott's hair, so it neatly framed his face. Dragging her feet over to Fran she made a similar gesture, stroking Fran's hair, then her cheek. 'I forgive you,' Ma said, then slapped her so hard that it brought tears to Fran's eyes. The nurse moved between them.

Fran opened her mouth. Her voice had been replaced by a hard, dry nut of hunger in her throat. She gagged on her tears and ran from the room, scurried along empty corridors, past the Pharmacy and paused before a door sign: Chapel. Despite the lateness of the hour, or rather the earliness, the door squeaked and swooshed. Someone had left pink carnations on the altar by a simple wooden cross, perhaps the man with the white collar, who was sitting in prayer, hands folded together.

Fran flung herself into a pew and glared at the space in front of her: a simple wooden cross outlined by the dawn light, from the windows at the far end. A pamphlet slid from where she'd pitched herself and glided along the floor. The world imperfectly spun on its orbit, creating weight. Scott had gone ... Fran wasn't sure where she believed he had gone to. Her mind was a carpet bag of emotions: shock, anger (for Scott and for herself, and at Scott), self-pity, pain, each second a different thought flittered into her mind's eye. It was all so confusing.

Leaving her with her thoughts at first, the man sharing the chapel with her eventually unclasped his hands and gave a friendly smile, or a creepy one, it depended on how you took it.

'Hi. I'm the hospital Chaplain, Anthony.' His eyes flicked towards the pamphlet, but give him his due he didn't move to pick it up. Indicating that the person in front of him was a greater priority than any paperwork.

'If I'd prayed, would it have made a difference?' she asked. What she was thinking was did I do something wrong? Did He see me acting out in church and decide not to help?

The chaplain said, 'What was your intention?'

'To help my brother.'

'How did that work out?'

Fran sniffed. 'Your God took him away.'

'There's a story I like to tell of Mary and Martha, friends of Jesus. Do you know it? Their brother became sick while Jesus was travelling, and they sent for him. But Jesus didn't come right away. He was too far. The walk too long. Lazarus died, and the sisters wrestled with thoughts such as *if you had been here, he wouldn't have died.*'

'Did he bring him back?'

'Lazarus had been dead four days by the time Jesus arrived. Jesus said, "I am the resurrection and the life," and they walked to the brother's tomb and Lazarus came out to greet them.' Anthony paused, looking ahead of him to the cross on the altar. Did he see God there, watching them?

Anthony said, 'It's a symbolic story, more than factual. Either way, the sisters had no power over Lazarus's death, only God.'

'I thought he'd be safer with me. If I took control … What was the point if he was always fated to die?'

'People ask that every day and only God has the answer.'

'That's a shit response.'

Anthony chuckled. 'Think of it this way,' he said. 'The Bible says, "God is love". Whatever He puts you through He knows you can handle it. He can and has protected some. Sometimes many. Yet He does not always choose to do what He is able to do.'

'That's a contradiction.'

'It is.'

'So, you're saying, He could have helped but didn't. And only He knows the reason. I could have guessed that.' Fran swung her legs, kicking the wooden pew in front. Dougie claimed to be a believed. Dougie had kicked Scott in the stomach. 'I think churchgoers are hypocrites. How can they listen to sermons on compassion then hurt others?'

'Sounds like you say that from experience.'

'My step-da believes in God. He's a mean man. Goes to church every week.'

'That's … contradictory. God tests us in different ways.'

'It's not fair. Nothing's in our control. Heather lost her ma, me Scott.'

'You've had a rough time.'

'That's life, isn't it?' Fran gave him what she hoped was a sceptical look, a gown-up examination. 'You got one reason why I should keep going to church?'

He considered the cross as if conversing silently with another power. 'To learn to live in acceptance of the loss, not in spite of the loss,' he said.

What did that even mean? How could she accept her step-da beating on them, accept her brother cruelly ripped from her arms, accept her mother slapping her in the face? And all those pointless summer plans when we're lucky if we survive childhood.

'God asks a lot.' Fran decided to rely on herself from now on, and those who had been there for her: Hector and Heather.

'Aye, he asks us to live despite loss, to be compassionate to others, to help our community.'

Still, the point the chaplain made about community was intriguing, even if it was a contradiction again, for as far as

Fran could tell nothing was in their control in this world.

Chapter 12

October 2019

'Hi, Fran. It's Miss Reed. It's the harvest festival this week. I'm sorry to have to ask. Having to have a bit of a phone round. Can you bring anything in?'

'No.'

'Some potatoes even?'

'No,' Fran said. Shit. It was late. Fran yawned. The call had woken her. Hector had temporarily borrowed a mobile from a mate in case of interview calls. Though routinely it was Fran silencing the annoying ringtone from pals of Nick. Predominantly, she went to bed not long after the kids due to having to be up in the early hours for shifts. Though, she hadn't been sleeping, mostly too busy contemplating Heather's news, or rather the news she'd gathered second-hand through her boss.

'Okay, sorry again, for bothering you. See you at school.'

Fran grazed the irritated skin on the back of her hands. The upper layer flaked off. Mocking her with its scaly rash. Even the viscous and repugnant barrier cream provided at the art college hadn't made a difference.

Hector revolved to face away from her as she stumbled back into bed. He hadn't made his appointment at the jobcentre. She'd had to trundle him out of bed to change the sheets after calling the jobcentre to explain depression was a medical disorder.

'You asleep?' Fran asked.

Hector flopped on his back. 'I was.'

A car had splashed through a puddle and doused her shins

on the way back from the chipper as a treat for the kids, at least the chips had remained warm and dry.

'Heather left work. Without telling me,' Fran said, peeling off her jeans.

'Makes sense,' Hector said.

'Makes sense!?'

'Because she has the house now and all that wealth.'

Fran would do the same if the opportunity had been hers like it should have been; except, Fran would have had the grace to tell her best friend beforehand, not sneak about behind her back – as Heather had done. At this point it was becoming unfeasible to see Heather as a friend, let alone her best pal.

'Do you know why I nicknamed her Thistle?' Fran asked.

Hector yawned. 'Because she's resilient.'

'Nah, 'cause she's spikey.' Though, as those letters left her mouth, Fran's tongue prickled.

'Be happy for her.'

'I am!'

'You sound angry …'

Anger's a useful channel to motivate oneself to get out of bed in the morning; she couldn't exactly say that to him right now.

'I'm trying to be compassionate,' she said.

'Doesn't advertise like it.'

'That's 'cause I'm also trying to work through why there's a detachment between us.' Truthfully, with Irvin out of the way the expectation was that the energy could return to normal between them: the wee confidences and the insider jokes. Likely she was making new acquaintances, some of those posh neighbours in her new locality. Well, Fran could do the same plenty of parents at the kids' school were potential pals in the making.

Hector, all limbs, taking up more than a fair share of the bed space ambulated towards her, making her portion of the bed even smaller. He said, 'Because you seem pissed off at her lately.'

'Might be more about me that her. I'm pissed off at everything lately.' Fran pulled the duvet up to her neck and, struggling to turn with the few centimetres of space afforded to her, turned away from him. He was supposed to be on her side, not Heather's.

'You always sound angry. At me. I'm the reason.'

'Aye. No. It's complicated.'

'I should get off my fat arse.'

Fran curved towards him, restraining herself from pushing against his overly warm body to reclaim some breathing space. 'Hector, you're not fat. But the kids and me are concerned about you. I don't want them to smell alcohol on their da and see him in a state. It brings back too many monstrous memories.'

'Oh, God!' Hector folded away from her in the bed. The extra surface area a welcome relief.

Fran scooted towards him, flattened her front against his back and planted an arm around his waist.

'The new jobcentre appointment is tomorrow,' he said. 'I'll get out of bed and shower and shave. I promise.'

'I'll help you.'

She caressed Hector's greasy head. Waiting for him to drift off. How to get herself to sleep was another question. Instead of writhing in bed fretting about what they didn't have, or what might be, she needed to enjoy what they had, she had; not fixate on what she lacked. There was still an awful lot that could be squandered if she let things get on top of them.

The next afternoon, Fran sniffed, blew into a tissue, balancing her umbrella in the other hand as she waited to collect Allan and Jack. Dorota arrived at the school playground, chatting to Laure. Unlike the stereotype of a typical French woman, Laure didn't smoke or wear black polo necks with Audrey Hepburn hair. Instead, she wore jeans over a sunflower yellow waterproof with a brown wool scarf. Laure came across as emotionally stunted, on a first meeting. The genre of person who would rather leave the room than wait for a reply after asking 'are you okay?'. And on subsequent meetings, this abrupt, aloof manner continued. Fran dismissed her as friendship material.

Before Dorota or Laure could greet Fran with other than a smile, Miss Reed intervened with a clipboard. 'Hi ladies, I'm looking for volunteers to bake for the Halloween party after half-term. I know you're busy, it's no problem if you can't help.'

... but I would appreciate it, hung in the air between them along with the trace of smoking wood as a gardener burnt leaves, rekindling memories of toffee apples and sparklers.

Dorota volunteered to bake a cake, while Laure and Fran shifted their gaze towards one another.

'Muffins?' Miss Reed asked Laure.

Laure pouted her lips. 'Non.' That answer was clear.

'We also need help with nativity costumes,' Miss Reed added, turning to Fran whose sewing skills ended with mending holes in socks with irregular stitches.

'Nativity?' Dorota asked.

'Our school play before Christmas. After half-term, the kids will know whether they are an angel, a shepherd, or a sheep. Baa!'

Fran had always been a sheep, once the inn keeper's door, in her day. She dabbed her nose with a tissue, and shifted one foot to prevent the rain soaking through her shoes, and waited for Dorota to volunteer her sewing skills. Dorota clasped her hands and stared at the back of them. It was a shame that she didn't have more confidence in her skills. The language barrier shouldn't be an issue.

'I can't sew or bake,' Fran admitted, recalling Dorota mentioned something about handmaking all her children's clothes. 'Dorota is the one with talent. Unless she can show me how, I can't help there.'

'You can sew?' Miss Reed asked Dorota.

Dorota made a clucking noise with her tongue, which might have indicated reluctance. 'I designed clothing in Poland.'

'Terrific! That would be super useful if you can organise the others.'

'Organise?'

'Be in charge of making sure every child has a costume. Thank you, you're a star!' Miss Reed scribbled a note on her clipboard and held it out for Dorota to add her details.

'Easy, she also has five kids,' Fran said.

'That sounds busy!'

Dorota took the clipboard. 'How does it work?'

'The school gathers donations from parents, or donations of old clothing, and the person in charge decides how to use that to make costumes. We could use a skilful eye.'

'I will help.' Dorota said.

When Miss Reed left, Dorota confided in Fran and Laure, 'I hesitate as I wonder where the cloth comes from. We have no money. Baking is different. I bake much cakes at home.'

Miss Reed hadn't bothered asking Fran for any aid towards the school. Coincidence? Or were the school gossips at work on her and Hector's lives? She'd have run the notion by Heather, except Heather didn't seem inclined to listen to kid-related stuff, as she had no offspring of her own.

Sylvia called from her group over to Dorota, 'Do people shop locally in Poland?'

'At the supermarket, yes.'

'We've been discussing one-use plastic, see, and Sarah saw that in France lots of people still go to the market to purchase their fruit and veggies.'

'With their own bags and wicker baskets,' Sarah added.

Dorota, Laure and Fran amalgamated with Queen Sylvia's group.

'Emma here buys pre-peeled veg, can you envisage it?'

'I dislike chopping,' Emma said.

Sylvia gave a disapproving shake of her head as if Emma was a lost cause. 'I'm doing my bit for zero waste: I'm regrowing celery.' She launched into an explanation without seeing if anyone was interested, Laure and Fran's eyes met and widened.

'Isn't zero waste expensive?' Fran asked. She hadn't the patience for Sylvia and her bees today. Tricky creatures. She hated them as almost as much as she hated wasp stings. Not friendship material either. Who did that leave? Dorota?

'It saves money. For example, we've got a' – she lowered her voice – 'bidet attachment. *Voilà!* No more toilet paper.'

Fran calculated the price of a family pack of cheap toilet paper was less than the outlay of a coffee per week. Compare that, to the one-off initial expense of a new electrical attachment to the toilet, around half a week's worth of shopping? So it would pay for itself after two to three months. Of course, a free alternative would be to hose the kids off. She refrained from suggesting that method.

Miss Reed was now in discussion with Rima, who had explained to Fran last parents' evening her name meant white gazelle in Arabic. Her long-lashed eyes were bunny-like beneath her glasses, but no one could be that cheery and squeaky clean all the time. For a moment, Fran understood the appeal a natter held for Sylvia the nosy parker; it would be comforting to see other people's struggles for a change. Fran reminded herself to send a letter to Heather after work tomorrow, pop round for a natter at Halloween – the only evening this month she would have the time, if Hector took the kids.

Part 3

The chameleon that landed on the kilt

Chapter 13

In the first week of November as the days continued to shorten Fran prearranged to meet Heather at the house Fran still referred to as 'Irvin's house'. Autumn, temperamental from year to year, hit them with a wet spell comprised of mists, downpours and drizzles, in a kaleidoscope of ever-changing patterns. Heather positioned Fran's shoes beneath the radiator, and, as Fran peeled off her wet socks and towelled her damp feet, fetched her some bed socks to borrow. They gravitated towards the kitchen, where Fran switched the kettle on and fetched their usual mugs from Heather's cupboard: one with a Jane Austen quote about people being 'intolerably stupid', hers, the other a Penguin Books mug that stated 'Go away, I'm reading', Heather's. Heather loitered, overseeing every move, as if Fran didn't have the right to regard Irvin's mansion like Heather's previous hovel of a flat.

Fran half-listened absentmindedly stroking the white poppy pinned to her jumper. Heather wittered about Jamaican racism – doubtless her most current reading material. While Fran anticipated the right moment to announce Hector's redundancy. Tell Heather that Hector was made redundant. Simple. That is, it sounded elementary in practise. But when is revealing the inner workings of your life ever easy? Especially the embarrassments you want to suppress from others. Hopefully, Heather would understand six months later why it had been difficult to bring up Hector's lay off around the same time Heather had inherited the house. Fran also had a thing or two to say about Heather not instructing her she was going to quit. Taking into account that Fran had found her the job in the first place.

'Spitting mad's the expression, ain't it?' Fran interrupted. Unable to wait any longer. 'I know you resigned, Heather. That ain't even what makes me mad. You know what did it.'

'The stuff about the Patois lass from school?'

'No.'

'That I should have told you before resigning?'

'Aye, but no.'

Each reply Fran presented chipped further confusion on Heather's face; until her features crumpled unearthing a dazzling vein of torment beneath the undercoat.

She was starting a fight, despite it not being her intention. Fran puffed her cheeks out, to regulate her frustrated breathing, and left Heather to dunk the teabags.

There were plenty of cosy spaces to choose from aside from the kitchen, as Irvin appeared to have placed a few crooks and crannies in each room for sorting through his piles of books. Heaps which Heather hadn't touched. Fran settled on a pair of sunflower yellow armchairs in a nook under the main staircase. It offered a view of the sun-filled garden with its immaculate flower beds. Fran considered matching furniture a sign of inadequate taste or wealth, crude to flaunt either way.

Heather joined her, curling her feet beneath a tartan blanket woven from threads of gold and pink shades, though the heating belched a blaze over Fran, more used to layers of hole-ridden jumpers than the incessant rumble of a boiler. The house was too quiet, no fights over plastic toys, no school bell, no crappy ancient boiler, or lorries rumbling past the window.

Heather waited, waited awhile, then sighed. 'I don't ken what I've said or done.'

Fran suddenly didn't want to be starting this fight. Confronting Heather had been a solid idea until she'd seen Heather's brow furrow in confusion. The only other topic that came to mind, however, related to Hector's obsession with the up-and-coming election, so she leapt in: 'Think Sturgeon's plan to stop universal credit will succeed?' It was a peace offering Heather would either take or reject. Fran's bet was on take because Heather detested arguments. There were times Heather had been there – Jack's hospitalisation as a baby and the death of Fran's ma – but they'd also been times she'd been distant. Since she'd inherited Irvin's house, for instance. Since she'd met that annoying man for that matter.

'Would the replacement be better?' Heather asked.

Fran snorted. 'Not sure they've thought that far.'

'Each person's got to think about their lives ... Except well off-folk, who should think about others' standards of living.'

'Not everyone thinks of others,' Fran said. A jab against Heather at the problems lurking beneath their approachable facade. She'd count to three and come out with the word 'redundant', after that she would be obliged to tell Heather everything.

Nevertheless, Heather, Fran observed, was the type of person to carry others' troubles with her, yet somehow also managed to take up space for herself to recuperate. Fran didn't have that luxury. And there'd been no time to recharge her batteries succeeding Hector's redundancy. Though that wasn't a justification for snapping at her best friend. No, she changed her mind, best not to broach such things when she was in a mood like today.

'I ain't read much,' Fran confessed. 'Hector, being Hector, has given me his opinion. Labour, he says are favourable on paper, but it's hard to trust their promises. Johnson's "getting Brexit done" may send us into another recession. And the Lib Dems ... er, who's in charge?'

'Jo Swinson.'

'Hector says, her party will increase NHS spending. Yet I'm not sure she'd be any good running the country; the way she bad-mouthed Corbyn put me off. Anyway, Lib Dems would also let in ten thousand migrants a year to steal our jobs.'

'Refugees,' Heather said.

'Same thing.'

'Escaping war and persecution is *not* the same as the right to move within Europe. But, Fran, is this what you want to blether about?'

Fran stubbornly pushed on, 'I don't think the Green Party have a clue how to run a country either. So, should we vote SNP?'

'Depends on your stance.'

'Pro-Europe, of course. Don't want those racist ones.'

Heather's reaction was slight. They'd been pals long enough for Fran to notice the slight shift in the muscles connected to the skin over Heather's third eye. 'Why are you ranting at me? You're trying to gall me into an argument on purpose.'

Fran couldn't leave it at that this time. Fran squinted at the clock – made from an LP record – to check there was plenty of time left before collecting Allan and Jack.

'You're supposed to be my friend,' Fran said, wishing to hurt her; but at the same instant wishing she'd never said anything because their companionship was so deep-rooted it hurt to cut the branches of the other. 'If you weren't too caught up in your own shit to care.'

'We're friends,' Heather replied.

'Friends ask how their friends are doing.'

'I ask every day.'

'Fit like, fine, is not asking.' Fran chewed the inside of her cheek. 'You've changed.'

Heather tweaked the blanket over her legs. 'We both have since primary school.'

'Nah, more recently. You've gone snobby, with your house,' Fran said.

'I thought you were happy for me?'

Watching Heather balance her mug of tea on the armrest Fran was tempted to push it over her lap; to, finally, obtain more of a reaction than reasonable banter.

'I was,' Fran said. 'Then you resigned. You took off your watch in the tea room and left it on the table. Henry saw you.'

'Aye, 'cause I'd no need to be up in the morning at 4 a.m. for work. You're annoyed that I left my watch?'

'More that I had to hear the news from Henry and James. You pissed off without a word to me. It's the attitude. You have wealth now, and a demeanour to match.'

The phone rang.

'Don't change much,' Heather said.

'How can you say that? Everything's changed!'

'Like what?' Heather noted the ringing phone. 'We still meet for a cuppa after your work.'

'Omitting you pay each time.'

'Do I? Hadn't noticed. You going to get that phone call?'

'No. See, same as that, regular people notice what they're spending. Take turns paying.'

'We can do that if you want.'

'That's not the point.' Fran stood and cadenced back and forth in front of the LP clock on the wall.

'Anyway, you've given me unlimited roast dinners over the years. What's a few cups of chai?'

'I'm not tallying it up.'

'Seems like you are.'

'Hush your mouth,' Fran said.

'Hush *your* moth, I mean mouth.' Heather exhaled. 'You know, you're as rough as cobblestones sometimes.'

'Away an' boil your head!'

'What's causing all this resentment? It can't be material goods.'

Fran almost threw her cuppa. If only it wouldn't make a mess someone would then have to clean. 'You don't understand.'

'That's 'cause you're not telling me. This, Fran, ain't like you; usually you're a straight talker. Today you're sprinting in circles.'

Fran identified she could be a chatterbox sometimes and bit her tongue. Fine, let Heather say her peace first.

Heather waffled. Fran wasn't listening, her mind kept skipping over the one issue she wanted to tell Heather about and all its accompanying secrets: that Hector had lost his job, was roller coasting in and out of depression, that the burden of carrying her family alone was too much, financially and emotionally. But jealousy and frustration constricted an iron band around her heart.

Her mistake: she'd assumed they had one another's back no matter what. All this time Heather had, had it in for her. She'd replaced her with Irvin, and even now, after his death, refused to close the space between them ... aye, she was, no doubt, embarrassed to be associated with a cleaner now she lived in a more upmarket part of town.

'Unfucking believable!' Fran said.

Aye, now she could see it all too clearly; there was no space in Heather's life for her now, combined with the hurtful words Heather had said about her brother. A deliberate shove by Heather to eject her out of Heather's life.

'Fran, wait.'

There was no way she was about to be cornered and spoken down to again like this. Fran grabbed her shoes and coat and hurried into the rain, putting them on as she hopped barefooted over the sharp gravel. Owch. Owch. The rain misted her hair and clothing – a baptism, she imagined, washing her clean of another disappointment. Served her right for believing in anyone, or anything. *We're done, God. Hear that? Done.*

THISTLE

Fran began complaining the moment she was through the door, about it raining like ropes, about the holes in her shoes, about her damp socks, about her aching feet and cracking hips, about work. A red emergency button flashed to mind. The kind you see on buses, trains or trams, which read 'In case of emergency break'. This hadn't been the first time Heather had been tempted to twist, or push, one and holler – though it was the first time a rising internal pustule tried to force itself out the top of her head.

Heather needed a task to keep her hands occupied, so scurried upstairs. After fetching Fran some clean socks from upstairs she found Fran in the kitchen filling the kettle, making herself at home, so all Heather could do was stand there, plucking at the hangnails on her fingers.

Fran said, 'Remember that Patois lass? Her da was the school jannie.'

Heather grunted. Fran had marched into her home to moan about past grievances? In addition, Fran had made a classist and a racist comment. 'Some words should be dropped from the dictionary,' Heather said.

'What?'

'Patois is derogatory.'

Fran scowled, the ridge between her eyebrows forming and disappearing. 'I ain't high and mighty, pal.'

'It's the word,' Heather said. 'Patois refers to someone of a lower status.'

Why did Fran have to speak that way about migrants? Her parents had retired to the Costa del Sol in Spain. Though, of course, her da had often repeated the sentiments of his father, viewing those who had moved into the old neighbourhood since his last visit with a sniff of disapproval before the rant began. 'They should all be put into a boat and sailed away,' he'd said. A shocking parallel to the MS St. Louis carrying Jews who were denied refuge in Cuba, the US and Canada, returning to Europe where countries accepted a mere three hundred of these survivors.

'Fuck's sake. No one exists of a lower status than us.' Fran jabbed her chest and winced.

Heather became aware of her own pre-menstrual breasts, rubbing against her bra and wondered if Fran's fingernail had skimmed a nipple through her thin work tunic. 'Don't make it right to use the term.'

'Get your stick out your arse. You'll be saying I can't call a blackboard "black" next.'

'Chalkboard.'

The kettle's crescendo rose and fell.

'Bawbag.'

Heather winced. 'It's important to interrogate the language we use, that's all.'

'Why?' Fran asked. She appeared more worn than usual; the white sclera dull, greyish.

Heather spread her palms upwards, the impression of the gesture religious in Fran's presence. 'Words shape the world.'

Fran swore. 'The world was here before humans. Same as when we're gone.'

'I mean, that language shapes our realities,' she tried to explain. 'Words carry social meaning, if you want.'

'I didn't mean Patois in that sense. It's a description. She ain't Scottish.'

'For all you know she's second generation.' The sides of Heather's mouth suck to her teeth. Fran impatiently tapped one foot.

'Then,' Fran said, 'she should fucking learn to speak better.'

Heather shuddered. 'Does every second word have to be fuck?'

'You're judging me, an' I'm not the one in the wrong here. Fuck. I'm gone.'

'Wait, Fran.' Heather put out a hand that grazed Fran's grey cardigan. 'I'm sorry. I dislike that word. Why'd you bring up Abigay?'

'Don't matter.'

'I could use a cuppa,' Heather said. Fran sighed, as soft as a sofa cushion sliding out of place. Before Heather could touch the kettle, Fran poured the water in the mugs, spilling it across the counter and shambled away. Heather made up two mugs. Fran sat, legs splayed, in Irvin's forsythia yellow armchair in the stairwell, and – despite the confusion of surveying Fran make the tea, then abandon her attempt, almost like a child mid-tantrum – Heather positioned Fran's mug within easy reach on the side table.

'Tell me what's up,' Heather said, curling beneath a blanket. The heavy fabric soothed her. Obviously, due to Fran's skittishness, it was best to address this head-on.

'Spitting mad's the expression, ain't it?' Fran repeated her earlier words from the kitchen. 'You're at it.' Fran crossed her arms across her chest. Left her tea to go cold.

As a rule, their silences were comfortable ones. They never argued, so it was hard to commence now.

'This Irvin's chair?' Fran asked, after what felt like fifteen minutes but was probably five.

'Aye,' Heather said. Her unwillingness to engage, this need to redirect questions about Irvin, had opened a wedge between them, a fissure continuing to crack. And she still didn't want to converse about her and Irvin's friendship to Fran in case she let her secret slip about her university degree. 'How's Hector?' Heather asked.

Fran uncrossed and crossed her arms.

Heather cupped her mug in both hands and stared into the steam, counting the seconds.

Fran said, 'I don't think the Green Party have a clue how to run a country.'

One moment there'd been a suggestion of guns about to be blazed across the hallway, a challenge unmet, then the discussion glided limply into politics. Habitually Heather was the one avoiding confrontation, but she had to unravel what Fran was so up-in-the-air about.

Fran continued, 'That scheme to scrap benefits and give everyone a basic income. Why not have a cut-off point by income, 'cause, if everyone gets it, how does that lessen the wage gap?'

'Aye, might push up prices too. But, Fran—'

'Fucking commercialists. Aye,' Fran raised her eyebrows, 'I know the word.'

'Changes *for the people* are good,' Heather said, playing along to try and get them back on track. 'Like Labour's municipalisation of the railways and the Big Six energy companies.'

'When was the last time we went on a train?' asked Fran, shifting the conversation on its rails again.

Heather shrugged. 'We should return to North Berwick some time.'

'The kids would like the train,' Fran said, beginning to smile.

It almost took on the guise of a normal conversation. Heather crossed her legs making herself comfortable. Knowing Fran, however; she still needed time to simmer down. So Heather said, 'Corbyn's also anti-nuclear. A profitable trait for a politician.'

'If only we could vote for the policies we like.'

Heather nodded. 'Vote strategically.'

'How?' Fran asked, as Heather was about to say, 'Tell me what's up with you?'

'Well,' Heather said, 'the SNP won the last time in our constituency ...'

'Course, people are sick of Westminster.'

'This time SNP are predicted to win, again, by a landfall. Pro-Brexit voters will want to join their votes with the Conservatives.'

'So, we should vote SNP to counter them,' Fran said.

'Depends on your stance.'

'Pro-Europe, of course. Don't want those racist ones in charge.'

Fran's refusal to discuss what mattered was beginning to grate. 'Sure, 'cause you're not racist at all.' Heather heard the statement before she could stop it, too sarcastic, too bitter. 'For example ...' she explored, trying to soften the blow.

'You're supposed to be my friend,' Fran said. 'But you've been too caught up in your own shit to care. With your mansion.'

In westerns, both sides were always trying to ambush the other. Why did the mood give the impression that Heather had wandered into a canyon without a map? Heather tried to navigate a way out. 'I thought you were happy for me.'

'I am!'

This was part of the problem. Occasionally, Fran would raise her voice, or screech rather than express what she meant. Fran had never learnt that a deep discussion didn't have to be a screaming match. Often, Heather was guilty of being in her own way, in her own head, her own stories, too much. Today Fran was in the way, so the issue on her mind could be addressed.

'It's not merely myself holding me back –' Heather said '– it's you.'

'Unfucking believable! So help me God if—'

'Don't bring Him into it. Not after Maither, Scott and Irvin.'

Fran's face wobbled, disturbed, but she wasn't enraged. If anything, startled.

'Sorry, Fran, sorry. I just – shit. Fran, wait. That's not what I meant.' Fran clutched her still moist shoes to her chest and marched out barefoot. Hopping on one soggy foot then another, straining to get her shoes on, swearing all the while. Heather reflected that when one door sealed it wasn't always the case that a window opened on new possibilities. She fetched her wellies with the cute cartoon strawberries. She wasn't ready to give up on this friendship yet.

FRAN

It differed from when she and Scott had run away with Dougie screaming, 'I'll kill you!' after them.

Memories weren't always sequential the further back you went: they were far from a neat string of cause and effect. For instance, her step-da hadn't hit her because she'd broken an ornament, or trailed dog poo into the house, his temper could just as well flare poker hot on a 'without a cloud in the sky day' (as Scott called them). One mild February, he swung at Scott, missing his chin, the impact rocking Scott's shoulder. Dougie's work boots caught Scott in the stomach, a flower of smudge bloomed on his red jumper, as Fran leapt between them. Black spots enveloped her in nausea as Dougie's elbow caught her nose.

'He's your son!' she roared as her brain tried to grasp the contradiction of a man who went to church every Sunday, worked hard at the sewage plant, yet drank bitter every other day of the week – sadly, he'd slipped back into the habit.

'That what she say? Bitch! He ain't mine.' Dougie reached for his beer can, shook it, and stumbled to the kitchen for another.

Scott crouched beside her crying. We can change this, Fran decided. We can be anything we want to be. 'Fuck this.'

Instead of the hum of the fridge, Fran's ears zoomed in on a kitchen drawer whip open, knives chiming against each other. The bastard wasn't getting another beer.

Ma's hair was tousled from sleep, mouth in a half-yawn, feet poking through the holes in her slippers. 'What's …?'

'I'll kill you!' Dougie screamed waving a steak knife, wobbling on his feet.

Scott yelped.

Ma intervened, twisting the knife out of his grip as he tottered – the drink, thank Christ for the drink. 'Get out,' Ma said. In her gaunt face was the beginning of an apology: snuffed out as Dougie began threatening her. Ma cowered into herself.

Fran grabbed Scott's hand and sprinted. Dougie had seen the rucksack she'd packed beside the door. Stupid, to leave it there while she'd tried to coax Scott out of sleep to silently follow her down the stairs.

Their idyllic lifestyle, Fran's sarcastic teenage voice told her, would no longer be ruined by two kids cramping their style.

Sometimes, Fran asked herself, first thing before the dawn or last thing ahead of sleep: is this it? This wee life? These folk? This financial situation? Forever struggling … Occasionally a surprise came along, bringing new freshness. A walk in light rain. A decision not to put up with others' shit anymore; even if that other person was the best pal you'd ever had. And then you open your front door, towel-dried, and the problem presents itself again: Heather shaking in the rain, blubbering.

Fran left the door swinging behind her and paced away. She didn't want her here. Their heart-to-heart was done from her perspective.

'I know you resigned, Heather. That ain't what makes me mad. Again, you know what for.' Fran threw her 'friend' a tea towel.

Heather smudged her tears with it instead of drying her hair. The kettle had just boiled, so Fran made them another cuppa; much weaker than Heather's offering in her expensive house with its duck egg walls and fancy flooring. She'd stolen the tea bags from work: if they didn't want her to take toilet paper and tea bags they should pay her a decent wage. The drone of the fridge reminded Fran how uncomfortable a place the kitchen was. The linoleum floor was frigid in the November chill. She made her way back to the worn lounge carpet.

Fran ranted a bit before giving Heather a chance to interject. 'Not all of us had an aunt or uncle to take us in, to shelter us from the abuse of a hideous step-da, with their only option to live on the streets, mid-winter.'

'You weren't alone. Hector and I helped build a shelter. I moved in with you.'

'Aye, 'cause your uncle was *abusive*,' Fran lingered on the word to provoke Heather, 'was he?'

'Mentally, he was abusive. I helped us find a place and pay the rent.'

Fran said, 'I found us the cleaning jobs.' Without those, they couldn't have left school and supported themselves, even if, in their first flea-infested flat, the heating didn't work properly and the lock on the door acted temperamental.

Traffic rattling the sun catcher became the background music to their conversation.

Fran said, 'At least your uncle took you in. The only pleasing thing my step-da did was drink himself into the hospital.'

'I'm sorry for bringing up Scott in that way. I shouldn't have.'

'That's for sure.' Fran turned away from Heather to stare

across at the playground, parents were gathering, it would be time to collect the kids soon. Fran clutched at her abdomen, imagining a fluttering there, remembering the early loss of their first bairn. She'd posthumously named her Donna, after her ma. 'I've made mistakes. Suppose, next you'll be saying I tricked Hector into marriage.'

'What do you think I've done? Slept with Hector?' Heather gave an uncertain laugh, that cut off when Fran didn't join in.

Maybe Heather had. Then again, Fran trusted Hector. He was a principled man. Lately, things between them had shifted. The easy conversations before bed more forced because he kept defending Heather and Fran missed her husband being on her side. Not too much to ask for.

'You'd know if you bothered to ask about our lives,' Fran said. 'Ever since you met that' – she struggled not to be negative about the dead – 'Irvin, ever since then you've been secretive.'

Heather transferred her weight from foot to foot and avoided eye contact.

'I'm not doaty, I know you're holding things back. I knew about Hector all those years ago and selfishly ignored it. Anyway, he had his choice and chose me. No point you being jealous about that now.'

'I'm not jealous of Hector, Fran, I'm ...'

'Sure you are, like I've been mistrustful of that toff you worked for. Did he take advantage of you sexually, or was it a mutual relationship that earned you his mansion?'

'Fran? Heather? Everything okay?' Hector stood in the doorway.

'Bit of a disagreement.' Heather stood up to greet Hector with their customary hug.

'Get your hands off my husband!' Fran flew at Heather. Hector blocked her with one arm. He was protecting her! The other woman! The band around Fran's heart clamped down.

'You've always loved Hector! Don't try to deny it! But you can't have him, so you'll always be alone and I'm glad.'

'Fran!' Hector said, eyes wide, disbelieving.

'I'm glad,' Fran repeated.

Heather dropped her mug on the carpet and ran.

Hector shifted from foot to foot in the shadow of the doorway. 'What did you do that for?'

Fran fetched baking soda and water from the kitchen and coated the tea stain with baking soda, daubed it with a damp cloth. As she rinsed the area with tepid water there was a knock on the door and Hector returned on Heather's heels.

'It's not going to end there,' Heather said, breathlessly, a vein throbbing in her neck.

THISTLE

When Fran opened the door Heather started to bawl. She hated that feeling, you know, when you're worried about others impressions of you, and that they might not be taking your concerns seriously, ignoring that you have feelings about the situation as well as them – if you could find a way to voice them.

Fran's home always smelled faintly of marigold furniture polish, mixed with a lavender scent that blew in from the bushes outside. Now there was a rotten smell, the kitchen bin or a gym bag left too long.

Mugs in hand Heather leant back on the green settee and hugged her knees, leaving her mug on the coffee table, while Fran remained standing, a defensive hand on one hip. An oily scent – fried food? – arose from the fabric. Also the curtains were missing, there was a single hook where there'd been a photograph of the castle, and the bulb above their heads had no lampshade.

Heather took an inhalation to steady herself and began to apologise. She was self-conscious of her tongue caressing the back of her teeth. The dryness of her mouth.

'I knew about your crush on Hector,' Fran said, 'all those years ago and selfishly ignored it. Anyway, he had his choice and chose me. No point you being jealous about that now.'

'I'm not jealous, Fran, I'm …' How to finish that sentence? Yes, she'd previously been envious, but things had changed since Irvin's death, new layers of self-reliance creating a carapace, of sorts, on her skin that she had yet to accept, although she sensed in doing so she was moving away from her best buddy. Yet this space between them could be closed with a confession. Accepting this, Heather opened her mouth —

Fran said, 'You're standing on the same muck as I am, you know. You and your writing dreams. Dreams is all it is. The moon might as well be as far as … the moon. And there's no hope that either of us can leave to find a better place, a better life. Neither of us are worth anything.' Fran moved on to throw unkind accusations at Irvin. She spoke snake-like, such bane dripping from her tongue.

'Now just hold on,' Heather said.

Had she been tricked into a false understanding? Like the miller in the tale of the Handless Maiden who was approached by the devil to trade what stood behind the mill for riches. He thought the devil meant an old apple tree. Not his daughter.

'You can sit there in your fancy house, with your parrot, counting your banknotes—'

'Fran? Heather?' Hector asked from the doorway with sheepish eyes.

'Bit of a disagreement.' Heather stood to greet Hector, his hugs were always warm and comforting.

'Get your hands off my husband!'

Fran flew at her, scratching her neck with her nails. Hector had to block her with one arm. Heather's heart tried to flee her throat.

'You've always loved Hector,' Fran shouted. 'Don't try to deny it. But you can't have him, so you'll always be alone and I'm glad.'

'Fran!' Hector said, eyes goggling behind his glasses.

Across the road, the school bell rang; a signal that catapulted running feet onto the tarmac.

'I'm glad,' Fran repeated.

Heather couldn't, it was too much, a wave of contempt targeted at her. She threw her mug on the carpet and ran outside.

An invisible force stopped her on the front step. No, she couldn't leave it like that … Heather hadn't expected Fran to explode with passion, because she, Heather, was the emotional one who had to back away, take a moment and think over what she wanted to say. Fran on the other hand never confronted her emotions, not her step-da, the death of Scott, or her parents' death. She persevered always facing forward. Ignoring the deeper undercurrents of life. And while Fran went into attack-mode, Heather understood her actions for what they were – that of a wolf backed into a corner. So, it was up to Heather to make the first move to patch things up … or, more accurately, to shield herself against Fran's onslaught for once. Fran couldn't address her in that tone anymore and expect to get away with it.

Heather returned to the lounge and took in Fran on her knees scrubbing the carpet. 'I never got in your way, you selfish cow. You've never missed a chance to rub the husband and brood that I don't have in my face. As if that's all life is.'

Fran stubbornly pushed on, 'Like your dream turned out so well.'

The wind whistled through the PVC window frames in mockery.

'Sure, go ahead and list my other failures. I failed to go to university. I failed to publish anything. I dared to have dreams about life that didn't happen. I know you have regrets, Fran: bairns too soon—'

'I don't regret my bairns. How dare you.'

'—a modelling career that never took off. And, what the hell, I'll say it 'cause you keep baiting where best left alone, you took Hector from me. You craved something and took it. And I let you; to be a decent friend. 'cause friendship is more important to me. While you, you selfish cow, only thought of yourself.'

Yet she knew it wasn't true. She just wanted to hurt Fran as much as she was hurting. The only time Heather could ever accusing Fran of acting over-selfishly was over Hector.

Undulations appeared in Fran's forehead at the expletives 'hell' and 'bitch'.

Heather proffered Hector an apologetic look, he'd formed a decent existence here with Fran and always been kind to her; he'd also been sympathetic enough to remain her friend despite the conflict that sporadically caused with his wife. 'I torture myself, Fran. I don't need keech from you. I've never reproached you, have I? My fault, I should have set limits. So here they are. You will come to me when you're ready to apologise, 'cause I deserve several.'

Fran opened and clasped her mouth.

'You will stop accusing me, even in jest, of trying to steal your husband. 'cause Hector made his choice long ago. You will have conversations with me, and not try to pick fights. Not an extensive list. But before I go, my biggest regret,' Heather continued, 'is I let you put me down, I put our connection and your grief for Scott first and didn't try for university. Sorry, Hector. I didn't want to put you in the middle of this. You know where to find me.' She turned back to Fran. 'So do you.'

'Right in front of me face, bitch!' Fran snarled as she slammed the front door behind her. At once Heather regretted everything she'd mouthed off about. *Oh God, what had she done?*

That night three friends lie in their beds trying to ignore the instructive moon. Its gravity unravels heavy thoughts from the spindle of the soul. Thoughts of friendship … thoughts of things that were said and that shouldn't have been.

Hector gives into the heaviness of his heart first, down, down, into nightmares about two female warriors at war.

Fran, who can smell industrial chemical cleaner on her aging skin, decides that relationships require a good scrub; until a thing isn't worth cleaning or repairing and one has to burn it out and start again.

Heather lists all the past disappointments her relationship with Fran has caused her, followed by the joys that came from knowing a person and being known and accepted in return, then all the mistakes she made towards Fran and wished she could take back. Duck feathers support her head, rustling like straw. If only they wove pillows to place underneath the heart. She hears the last owl and the first robin, the faint vibrations of commuter traffic. Then thinks about the night of Fran and Hector's first date. The one night this disaster could have been averted.

'Is it too tight?' Fran had asked that night, plucking the fabric of the crimson dress. 'I'm glad you went for the black and I went for the red. We'd be twins in the same colour.'

Heather compared her rounded hips in the mirror to Fran's angular pelvis. 'Humph.'

'I hope H. likes it.'

'Don't call him that. His name's Hector.'

'H. said he likes red on me. It's almost a compliment.'

Heather nudged her shoulders back, fiddled with her frizzy hair, abandoned it in a messy bun. 'He said that? When?'

'The time we went for coffee and you didn't make it.'

'I went to the wrong café.' And Heather was still not convinced it wasn't a purposeful miscommunication on Fran's part; selecting a café with two locations and sending her to the wrong address, so Fran could be alone with Hector. 'What else did you chatter about when I wasn't around?'

'H. complimented my red top. First sign of interest he's shown.'

'But it's Hector. I mean, he's practically our brother.'

'To you mayhap.'

Fran observed Heather from the corner of her eyes, and played with her earrings. 'What's that mean?' Heather asked.

'You've been chums since nursery, then I came along.' Fran applied a scarlet outline to her lips and painted the middle ground. She only applied lipstick for dates. This couldn't be a date. It was a night out with friends: Hector and Heather and Fran. Though it was dawning on Heather that the order should be adjusted to Fran and Hector and Heather.

Hector's lips shaped into a 'Wow' as they entered The Stannary with its sticky floors and watered-down cocktails. The music was ear-splitting. Hector yelled in Fran's ear that he couldn't something-something.

Heather ran her eye over others in the pub: due to the usual reluctance of folk to shimmy sober the dance floor was empty at this early hour (10 p.m.); girls giggled over cocktails, guys appeared to hunt out any that separated from the pack; it was too early for detrimental decisions and too late for groups of work colleagues and couples over an intimate pair of wine glasses.

Hector and Fran shouted into one another's ears, a hand on an arm, a tap on the shoulder or cheek. When exactly had Heather been demoted from second to third wheel? The one who doesn't fit? All this time she'd thought of Fran as the one tagging along in their relationship. A sturdy rubber wheel to her rattling wooden one. Hector's was hers. She liked – no, she loved Hector.

Heather sucked half of her watery Moscow Mule down her straw. Slow down, you're drinking too fast, she cautioned herself. She didn't recollect the rest of that night except for Fran and Hector tucking her into bed. Hector had slept on the sofa. Or so he'd said.

They were nineteen. Mature enough to confront or forever hold her tongue; immature enough to be unable to defend her interest in Hector.

Chapter 14

December 2019

Curdled milk clouds flowed across the sky the next afternoon as Fran's final jibe to Heather echoed in Fran's head: 'I'm glad,' she'd said – an obnoxious way to force Heather to react. Fran knew she could be harsh; a legacy of her upbringing. A few Hail Marys and a rereading of The Parable of the Lost Son couldn't make up for the ruthless words she'd attacked not just Heather with but God also.

On her way back from Church, Fran observed her solemn shadow in each iced over puddle. She wasn't scrying for a sign from God today, or hoping an angel feather would fall from the sky: she paused to reflect, as the priest had bidden, on the intricacies of her life with God and with others. Was her active dismissal of God a sign of her disconnect with others? Was selfishness deeply rooted in her life and actions towards her best pal, her neighbourhood, her church community, and the parents she frequently met on the school run? Was she still worthy to call herself a child of the church?

Fran hovered outside her door. Inside Hector had the telly on. Shivering, she lashed out at the clumps of frosted leaves gathered at the front door. Across the street, people with too much time on their hands waved political banners and handed out flyers. The SNP had posted five leaflets through their door, in November, on the run up to the postal vote deadline. No brochures from the other political parties showed a distinct lack of forward planning. And, although Fran had received no word, Hector had letters than he squirrelled away as if she didn't know his secret spot. A glance at the handwriting and the postcode, told her they were from Heather. He hadn't opened any of them yet. Her fingers itched to break the gummy seal of just one of them. Good thing that God was watching to ensure she didn't dare.

The curtains next door twitched. The incentive Fran needed to enter the space where the fight had ended. Hector slouched on the settee in the same shabby trackie he'd worn for a week. 'How's the job hunting?' she asked.

'Aye, no bad, catching the news.' He gestured to the telly with his beer can. 'As a substitute for this fiasco, what we really need is genuine political agency.'

She tried to overlook Hector's beer can, smothering the image of her step-da as it tried to squirm from a place she'd rather not go.

'Extending autonomy to local institutions, devolving decision-making to grassroot projects, cultivating engagement in civic life at the local level.'

'Hum-mm.' Fran angled her head at the smudge of tea soiling the fibres of the carpet.

'Hiding in the fridge!' Hector cracked up. Her countenance must have shown her confusion for he added, 'Did you not see it? This morning, an ITV reporter tried to ambush Johnson for some questions on *Good Morning Britain*. Live TV, right? With Piers Morgan saying, "Give him the full barrel". And they filmed one of Johnson's helpers swearing "Oh, for fuck's sake" while Johnson waddles off with a blue plastic crate.'

'Into a fridge?'

Hector declared, as Fran escaped to the kitchen, 'He was dispensing milk in Leeds.'

Hector's laughter seeped down her throat like melting chocolate after a month's abstinence. She returned to the lounge with baking soda, a tea towel, a bowl of chilly water, and scattered some baking soda over the tea stain.

'What a confusing election,' Hector said.

She sat on her heels snapping the rubber gloves into place. 'How so?'

'Well we have Labour voters, who voted for Brexit, unsure whether to support Labour. Conservative voters who are anti-Brexit incapable of voting Conservative. Not to mention, pro-Brexit supporters who usually vote for the SNP.'

'A lottery of confusion.'

'No, it's clear cut. Likely to win here, the SNPs. Conservatives overall.'

'For certain?' Fran asked.

'We'll know later with the exit poll.'

A cry of 'Bollocks to Brexit!' clamoured from the street.

'Got a front row seat here,' Fran said, scrubbing at the stain.

'Fran, you're damaging the carpet.'

'Hum-mm.'

She'd seen signs stating that 'campaigning inside polling stations is not permitted', but some hopeful anti-Brexit campaigners had rallied at the congested school.

'Aye, Allan and Jack are spectating from upstairs. They've formed their own mini-parliament and will want to know your judgement on whether the NHS will be "on the table" for the post-Brexit trade deal.'

Fran joined him on the settee, waving away an offer of a sip from his beer can. 'Are you educating them on this stuff?'

'It's an historic moment: Brexit vs no-Brexit, Corbyn and Johnson competing for the keys to number 10.'

'I'm glad we postal voted, I'd cringe with that anti-Brexit lot in my face at the polling station, even if I agree with them. I'm surprised anyone is still pro-Brexit. Brexit will worsen the UK's position.'

'Tradewise? No, that's bollocks. That's fear stalking the minds of the rich.'

'Brexit won't go ahead, will it?'

'I think it will. Scotland is a remain majority. Remainism's loud and confrontational politics may have taken over the media, but Conservative supporters have been quietly awaiting their chance to vote. The anti-Brexit supporters are wise to fear the results of this election.'

'Idiocy,' Fran said.

'Nah, it's an exciting time for politics. Because individuals feel like they can stand up against what Eton-educated politicians covet. Take Andrew Adonis's words—'

'Who?'

'He said, anyone who had been to Eton should be banned from holding public office. Pure dead brilliant. We know the system is flawed. Just behold *les gilets jaunes* protests in France. I don't like this inability to debate, the trolling, the attacking people with different opinions. Since when has that been British?' Hector paused from his rant to take a breath.

'We're Scottish.'

'I'm getting another beer, want one?'

'Nah, I'll see how the kids' parliament is shaping up.' She kissed his unshaven cheek.

In the boys' room, Allan was about to tell Jack a story. 'Sit down, Ma. Join the audience.'

Fran took a seat on the floor and Jack cuddled up to her.

'Act one, scene one. A man dies and—'

'How?' Jack asked.

'Hit by a bus. So, he goes to the gates of Heaven, and they look at his life and give him the option of going to heaven or hell.'

'Heaven!' Jack said.

'Heaven seemed nice, the man thought, but they were partying in hell. The man asked the devil, "Is it always like this?" And the devil says, "Yes." So, the man chooses hell. Immediately the music stops, and the party is replaced by huge towers of fire and the smell of burning flesh.'

'Very graphic,' Fran said, with a keek at Jack who was watching his brother enact the story out in rapt attention.

'The man asked, "What happened?", and the devil said, "Yesterday we were campaigning, today you voted, now it's business as usual." The end.'

She listened to what the boys had to say about the December election, and rejoined Hector downstairs. From the toppled bottles under his legs he'd had more than one extra beer.

'How's the future of the country?' he asked.

'According to them it's hell.'

'Well, we'll get an idea with the exit poll results at 10 p.m.'

Hector barely left the settee, other than to fish out a battered paperback from between two cushions. Patricia arrived home, did her homework then joined the boys' game that was re-enacting a milk delivering Boris by now if the sheep and cow noises in the room above were anything to go by. Fran warmed canned spaghetti on toast for tea. And the boys went to bed, while Patricia stayed up to watch the news with them because it was 'educational'.

Hector had a had a habit of resting a book on his lap and holding open the pages with one fist, the index finger pointed to the top of the page. Fran observed him trying to read a book at the same time as watching the news; telly, book, telly, book, his eyeballs bobbed like a plough hitting stones. Aside from the beer, a baked-mud smell emanated from him. It was a scent which she deemed his potters' smell, even though he had no clue how to throw clay on a wheel. He raised his head, telly to book, book to telly, and caught her engrossed in his actions.

'I'm watching you,' she said.

'I can see that.'

'Worth reading?'

'Aye.'

'Should I read it after?'

'Nah, you wouldn't like it. Sci-fi.'

'Neither would Heather then.'

Hector peered at Patricia, who had fallen asleep with her head on Fran's shoulder. 'Call her.'

Fran stared at the faces of one smug politician after the other: no choice seemed ideal. 'I tried. She didn't pick up.'

'I have a feeling *that* apology has to be in person.'

'You been speaking behind my back?'

'No, I haven't been in touch either. I think this is a situation you two have to work out.'

Hector gave pertinent advice. Sufficient time had gone by; she should attempt to ring again.

'Hm, as I thought,' Hector said.

The exit poll results were in; the Conservatives had won overall, though the SNP retained a majority in Scotland.

'Okay, miss. Off to bed,' Fran said, waking Patricia with a gentle brush of her hair.

Chapter 15

December 2019

Everyone slept. It was too quiet. Even with the telly on. And without the kids' demands there was space to worry … not only about keeping her family fed and cosy, but about Hector: his overeating, oversleeping. He'd been sleeping shortly after the kids these days and lying in. He wasn't showering. He was drinking too much. And who could she converse with?, because she couldn't face making a call to her best pal, and her and God weren't on speaking terms.

Fran sighed. She fingered the cross she still wore by habit. It brought more comfort to her than the horoscope she'd read from someone else's newspaper at work: *instead of searching for a compromise, you should stick to your guns and push right back.* She may not have fully forgiven God right now but as a bird knows which way to fly for the winter she could be sure that he had pardoned her.

'Let your compassion meet our needs because we are on the brink.'

She switched the TV off, and went to check on the kids.

Before she reached the top of the stairs, she became aware of the disquieting squeaks Jack made when he was upset. Her feet halted, her back tensed. She flicked the hall light off. From under the door of the boys' room a strip of light betrayed that the boys' bedside lamp was on. She placed her hand on the door handle as a voice shushed, 'Wheesht. Don't worry, Jack.' It was Patricia. 'We can switch your sheets with mine, and I'll put them in the machine tomorrow before Ma sees, like we did the last time.'

Heat ascended Fran's neck, extended across her cheeks.

'It'll be fine, twerp,' Allan said. The mattress springs creaked, and feet thumped to the floor. 'Let's get you out of these wet pyjamas, before a fish mistakes you for a fishbowl.' A drawer opened and slammed shut.

'Sssesh, Allan,' Patricia said.

'What?'

'Be quiet!'

'Nothing's gonna wake Da up.'

'But Ma's downstairs,' Patricia said. 'Here, Jack. Use this.'

Fran held her breath. Towel buffed skin, the sound made when someone steps out of the shower.

'This about Da?' Patricia asked.

Fran leant her forehead against the door, knowing Jack he was nodding or shaking his head.

Patricia said, 'He's been stressed lately about adult things.'

'Scary,' Jack said.

Allan asked, 'Why are you scared of Da? He's, you know, Da.'

Fran released the door handle and dug her nails into her palms – my poor bairn.

'Smells funny.'

'Yeah.' Allan laughed. 'He needs a shower and a change of clothes before his socks grow feet.'

'That's the alcohol,' Patricia said. 'I will tell you, so you know what's going on and don't need to worry. Da's not well. The doctor's call it being depressed. He lost his job and hasn't got a new one. So he's been drinking. Adults drink to forget heinous things. But the doctors know what to call it you see, and so they know how to treat it. After seeing the doctor, Da will get better.'

'He'll be Da again?' Jack asked.

'Sure will,' Allan said, 'and we'll go to the park like we used to with the football, and have picnics on Saturdays.'

'Ice cream!'

'Well, if it's warm, and not so wet as this August, maybe he'll treat us to an ice cream.'

'I heard Ma mention the doctor, so he'll be back to Da soon,'

Patricia said.

Jack mumbled. Fran couldn't make it out through the door.

'The doctor doesn't need to fix you. You're not broken, Jack. It's en-yur-ee-sis which means your body needs to learn to control your bladder, I mean, it's learning. And it will stop when it stops. No problem, as Da used to say.'

Fran hadn't the patience Hector had with bed-wetting. Each of the kids had made a few mistakes. Had she snapped at Jack the last time? Complained she had plenty to do without rewashing the bedsheets? Fran backed away, leaving them to their whispered conversation as cramps jabbed her lower abdomen. Where she would have previously told Hector what she'd overheard, now she padded downstairs, avoided the creaky fifth step, and flicked the kitchen light on. Bit her fist as tears rolled down her wrists. She never cried, rarely cried, but the pretence of strength she outwardly displayed for the kids dispersed when they hurt. She wasn't sure living without fear for one's children was realizable. She'd feared Jack would slip after each bath and crack open his head. That Allan would run out into a car. That Patricia might get in a car with a stranger. Still, no point being overprotective either cause apprehension don't make a thing happen, apprehension kept you up at night with a knot in your lower back. Fran missed Hector's kid-like chortle, his way of dancing disco-style into the kitchen, chasing them all around like a dinosaur. Now her husband slouched in a five-day trackie, never shaved, smelled of cheese or alcohol, and left her to deal with her trepidation alone.

'Ah, Heather. Why can't you call?'

The phone rang.

'Need you to watch the cat again. We're going on holiday next week.'

'Sure, Beth. You know that's never a problem.

'Thank you, you're a God send. You are. It's so important we have this family time. How are things with you?'

'Fine.'

'That's awesome to hear.'

Fran almost asked, 'Do you really want an answer? 'cause you don't usually care'. They were acquaintances at best, brought together by childminding needs.

'How's your husband?' Fran asked. She couldn't remember his name.

'John is fine … he – anyhoo, nothing interesting to report. Thank you again.' Beth hung up.

Fran twirled the mobile in her palms. If the rumours in the adult school playground were true about the divorce, nothing had been confirmed to her by Beth. Anyhoo, she really desired a blather with Heather, not Beth.

Heather was eleven numbers away. Eleven numbers aren't much distance between mates. Except Fran couldn't get past the hateful words she should never have spoken to a pal. Even if Heather's absence was the equivalent of a bowl obstruction; there was a name for that, intestinal … thingy. Her uncle had died from a rupture of his intestines when part of the intestines stopped functioning and the tissue died. Fran threw the mobile against the settee cushions. Fran trembled.

The next day – with an overdue notice for the gas and electric wearing a hole in her pocket – Fran learnt from Dorota and Laure that playground politics had taken a new slant with the upcoming election. Emma had ventured an opinion that she might vote Conservative, and was now standing apart from Queen Sylvia's court with Wai Lan 'call me Winnie' Shum, Rima with the headscarf, and curvaceous curly haired Davinia from London with two wee ones in matching puffer jackets hanging off her kaftan skirts being billowed by the nippy Northern wind.

Sylvia kept her distance from Fran and Emma. Not that

Fran minded. They'd had a falling out after the nappy incident had occurred more than once, and Fran discovered her son had been wearing a nappy instead of a pull-up. Fran tried approaching Emma for childcare help, whose answer was plain: 'Can't manage it.' Sarah had also declined with 'My schedule's full.' Was this refusal about the thing with the nappy? Had Sylvia spoken to the other mums? Forbidding mothers to help one another seemed far-fetched. David was more helpful, 'Sure, I'll ask Alex and find a date that works for the boys' play date.' Though he hadn't got back in touch. Nike, Fred's mum, was an option but Fran didn't request favours from neighbours who knew too much about their home life already. Which left Dorota or Laure, and Laure kept her distance from everyone except Dorota.

Dorota said, 'The word is play date, correct?' Dorota acted as if her English was terrible but it was far from imperfect.

'Aye,' Fran said.

'As Jack and Idzi are friends, come also for a cup of tea. We should get to know one another too.'

'Cheers.' That was kind of Dorota, and tea – oh lucky day! – might come with biscuits.

Dorota handed Fran a sheet of paper with an address carefully printed on it in capital letters. 'We have no phone. You are welcome anytime after school.'

'Cheers.'

Dorota gave her a beaming smile. Should she offer a play date to Laure also? Laure, with a thin-lipped smile indicated that she had no time for watching others' offspring.

Look at her, hanging out with the Frenchies and the Poles. Mum and Dad must be turning in their graves. Granddad too with his stick 'em on a ship back home policy.

At home, Fran went through her list of items to sell. She'd sold most of the bits she'd put aside now, including more of the kids' board games and their Walkie talkies, the lounge curtains and light shade, Hector's dumb-bells, a vintage pub sign, two watercolour beach scenes, a lunch box, an elephant statue, a photograph of the castle, and an Apple iPad. It had been a hard decision to sell the car. Hector had been hopeful until that point, insisting he'd find a job in six months, seven at most. His face, when she'd told him, 'That guy's coming about buying our Hyundai tomorrow morning', was like seeing a mug falling towards the floor and you anticipate it breaking. That moment you think you could've stopped it and instead watch it shatter. He turned away. Facing the bare wall, where the vintage pub sign used to hang.

Then he'd drawn in a deep breath and said, 'Sure, I'll throw a bucket over the car later, then I'll take the bus into town, and when I get a job I can go by bus too. Whatever helps.'

He hadn't mentioned any new job applications since then though he'd badgered her to approach her boss.

'Did you ask your boss for a raise?' Hector asked for the billionth time, as Allan and Jack ran up the stairs, before she'd even a chance to put down her bag.

'Aye,' Fran said, unbuttoning her coat.

'And?'

She shook her head as she collapsed on the settee.

Thudding on the stairs announced Allan's return. 'Ma, can Jack and I watch cartoons?'

'No, darling. Remember, no more TV.'

'Why?'

'Get into your PJs and I'll come and read you a story,' Fran said.

Jack said from outside the bathroom door at the top of the stairs, 'Books are boring, I wanna watch TV!'

'I want to watch TV. No, books are what smart lads read who want to do better in life than their ma, so they can afford to watch television as much as they want when they grow up.'

'Okay.' Allan's footsteps reached the top of the stairs.

Hector swore. 'I can't believe the bastard said no. They've given you nothing but the bare minimum for ten years!'

'They've given me all the extra shifts they have. The rest of the girls are pretty understanding considering Christmas is coming up.'

Patricia came in the front door. 'Ma? Can I go to the pool with Isla and Jess tomorrow?'

Fran checked her wallet. 'I barely have pennies, darling.'

'Their ma invited me as they buy eight sessions and get two free anyway.'

'Well … if their ma doesn't mind.'

'She's outside, I'll ask.'

Jack ran into the lounge and jumped on her knees. 'Mummy, I'm cold.'

'Put on a jumper, darling.'

'I'm not a bampot, I've five jumpers and three pairs of socks on.'

'Then, you're warmer than me aren't you?' Hector said. 'How's about a visit from the tickle monster?'

'Noooo, nooo! Noooo!' As Hector chased Jack around Fran caught a whiff of stale alcohol and tensed, was Jack pretending to be scared or was he the same wee lad who wet the bed last night?

'Hector, have you been drinking?'

'God, I needed one glass of wine.'

'Isla and Jess's ma says they'll be happy to take me tomorrow,' Patricia said.

'Tell her thanks from me.'

'MA, I'M IN MY PJS!' Allan yelled.

Fran levered herself to her feet. 'I'll read Allan and Jack a story and be right back down to make tea for everyone.' Tonight's routine was all topsy-turvy, hopefully they wouldn't expect another book after their meal.

After a feast of tinned spaghetti on toast, Fran did the dishes while Hector tucked the kids into bed. He didn't come back. Part of her didn't want to know why. Crashed out again. Yet he wasn't in their bedroom; his voice came from Patricia's room: 'There, there, ready to tell me what happened?'

It amazed Fran that a bairn arrived immediately creating a family. What's more each had their own inbuilt personality.

All her lot were agreeable, eager to please like Hector. They'd instinctively run to her as children with cuts and scraped knees. Now they gravitated towards Hector because he innately recognised what to say or what not to say.

'There was a competition at school. For a month we've been discussing how to decorate our table for the Christmas meal. Finally, we decided it should be Death by Christmas—'

'Sounds great,' Hector said.

'which basically meant we needed to cram as many decorations as possible onto our table.'

That's why Fran had caught her raiding the Christmas boxes. Fran winced. She'd overreacted when she'd found her daughter had gone up into the attic alone. It weren't like she were an irresponsible gal, but that didn't mean she wasn't at risk of falling through the ceiling and Fran couldn't afford to pay for plastering repairs or have Patricia at home with a broken leg.

'So, we crammed on decorations almost until the table collapsed.'

Hector chuckled.

'Alice,' Patricia continued, 'Alison's friend on another table, had forgotten it was today. Without asking, Alison gave some of our decorations away. I got angry, and Alison said, "We can't leave them with nothing. That's not nice." She's right, but a bit of tinsel would have been better. Not the dancing Santas. Our team made an effort and none of the other tables bothered. Even then it wouldn't have mattered except the other table won the best table prize. They win stuff in all the competitions for baking and art, how could they steal our prize today and not even acknowledge we helped! They took the chocolates for themselves!'

'So, you're greeting because you lost the competition?'

There was a pause, Fran could imagine Patricia shaking her head as she wiped away her tears, the letters on her necklace P-A-T catching the light. 'We were so excited for the disco. Mrs Butterworth brought in Christmas music.'

'I know you're not greeting because the music was ugly.'

Pat gave a half laugh. 'Everyone danced together. Wig! And then that cheesy oldie, Last Christmas, began to play.'

'Wig?'

'Means so good, makes you lose your wig.'

'No one asked you to dance?' Hector asked.

Fran's tummy ached, a hollowed pumpkin. She wanted to stuff her kids back into her belly and protect them from everything this world could spit at them.

'Rory asked. He's the most annoying boy in the class. Rory asked Alice to dance. She said no. Then he asked Alison, and every other girl there. He finally asked me. I said no, but he kept following me about. Even dangled baubles from his ears and said he was the best-dressed guy there.'

'Sounds like he secretly likes you, but didn't want to ask you first.'

'Ugh! Then Alice and Alison started forcing me to dance with him.'

'You're greeting because you were embarrassed?'

Fran leaned against the door, straining to hear in case Patricia had lowered her voice. Eventually, Patricia gave a sigh.

'Well, I kind of do like Rory. He's sweet. But everyone else finds him repulsive. A joke. I would have said yeah had he asked me to dance first, but for him to go around the others like that, and ask me last. Humiliating! I shouted at him that I wouldn't dance with him, to leave me alone. Plus, I fell out with Alison who had said I'd been mean not wanting to help Alice or dance with Rory.'

'So, you're greeting because it's been a frustrating day.'

'I've no idea how to fix things.'

'You know the right thing to do,' Hector said, fantastic phrasing Fran wouldn't have thought of. Her response would have been, 'Who cares about those losers anyway?' She craved a closer relationship to Patricia, but Hector was a better people person. Though Dorota was keen to be pals, so Fran wasn't entirely skill deficient.

'I don't mind apologising to Rory,' Patricia said. 'It's Alice

I can't stand. She puts no effort in and gets praise from the teachers.'

'You're jealous.'

'It's not fair. She's so extra – meaning over the top.'

'You know what Mum would tell you.'

'Life's not fair. That doesn't help, Da. How do you stop being jealous?'

'That's a hard one, might take a lifetime to figure that out. What works for me is to focus on the other person instead of myself. It's easier when they're someone you like, then you can be genuinely happy for them.'

'Like the time Becky, Tim and I were friends, and we both liked Tim, but he chose to go out with Becky instead? I was sad but happy to see them happy.'

'Gosh, you can't be dating yet.'

'Like that, Da? 'cause I could've let my hurt eat me up and instead I—' Patricia's voice stopped as a floorboard creaked under Fran's foot. '—is someone in the corridor?'

Patricia would rather communicate to Hector alone, Fran could appreciate that; still, the rejection snipped like scissors through the paper of her soul.

Chapter 16

December 2019

Dorota lived in a high-rise in Muirhouse. The flats had been renovated late last year due to their squalid conditions, such as damp caused by out-of-date and expensive to run heating systems. It had been in the North Edinburgh News. Over the road, where new council houses would be constructed, redevelopment, in the form of a demolished chipper and grubby buildings, marked business as usual.

Fran had noted the increase for about sixteen years of Polish and Hungarian sounding voices around Muirhouse and Pilton, the doctor's surgery, the school playground. She didn't know why that was the case, why they came here with Edinburgh being such an expensive place to live and raise children.

Escaping the wind coughing rain in her face, Fran's first impression after the lift that smelled of pee was of an orderly flat: one hook per two children in the hallway, shoes placed in a neat line. Sparse but neat. Dorota waved her through to the lounge where five children raced faded-metal cars across the grey carpet, pitted with scrapes and stains and burns – though the bare walls appeared recently whitewashed.

The kids shouted and quarrelled in Polish, and the radio blared from the kitchen. Dorota waved Fran to sit anywhere on the mismatched set of settees facing each other. A rag rug spanned the space between the settees beneath a wooden pallet with bricks for legs. Dorota busied herself in a narrow kitchen separated from the lounge by a couplet of folding doors which were doubled back to keep an eye on the children's chaos.

Jack tarried on the edge of the makeshift racetrack where books served as obstacles that the others swerved or jumped over. As Fran was about to beckon Jack for a cuddle he pulled two handfuls of marbles – that Hector must have given him – from his pockets and arranged the different-sized spheres on the carpet with spaces between them. Dorota's kids sprinted their cars through the marbles.

'Well, look at that,' Fran said.

One boy with a hole in the knees of his jeans faked a rollover, then offered his car to Jack.

Dorota emerged from the kitchen with a scratched metal teapot and two glass tumblers. No biscuits.

Fran picked at a scab on her wrist to distract herself from the disappointment of her gnawing tummy. 'You, er, made your own rug?'

'I made. I made blankets for beds also.'

'That's … creative.'

Dorota slapped her forehead and grinned like a child playing a prank that has been well-received. 'I forget, forgot the cake.'

She took two steps into the kitchen and reversed with two thick slices of a toffee-coloured cake that smelled of warmed banana.

Fran took an oversized bite. She was always starving lately.

Dorota pointed at the curtainless window being flicked with raindrops like a dotty painter. 'For the blankets, I used curtain fabric. I made clothes in Poland.'

'This banana bread is delicious.'

Dorota took a moment to pluck a boy off a tilting chair, and returned to Fran with her signature beaming smile. 'Grandmother's recipe.'

Fran regarded Dorota's apron. Dorota's quick, long-lashed eyes caught her. 'I designed. This print represents the legend of Janosik – our Polish Robin Hood.'

Dorota went to dislodge a marble from between one boy's curious teeth.

Fran peeped at Jack. He was attempting to repeat a Polish

word faster and faster.

Dorota translated for her, 'He says *Szybciej*, meaning faster. I am glad for your visit, Fran. Other mums are distant here.'

Fran swallowed her mouthful to say, 'They're reserved, at first. Until your kids make friends with theirs.' So gratifying to be exchanging advise with another mum, Fran being the expert for once in a field that didn't involve how to banish grass stains from boys' trousers.

'Reserved describes the British well.'

'Avoid Sylvia if you can.'

'Why I must avoid?'

Fran twisted her plate between two hands to think about it for a second. 'She yaks too much.'

'Being a chatterbox is not a fault. Unless to the point your husband falls asleep!'

Fran laughed. 'I meant about others' lives. A bit of a gossip. I've never connected to that lot, I'm a working mum. I feel out of place.'

'I thank you for your suggestion. The Polish are less reserved. Harder to make friends here. Lucky, I have a belly of kids to fill my hours. Severyn he has twelve years, Angelika she has ten years, Andrzej eight, Idzi has six, Klimek four.'

'Gosh, four kids at primary school at the same time.'

'A large household keeps a woman out of trouble.'

Fran excused herself to use the toilet. Two bedrooms led off the hall. With Dorota's brother and her husband living in the same flat, that meant they were a family of eight in a two-bed – even in a progressive city like Edinburgh.

Fran and Dorota discovered that her two eldest children went to the same school as Patricia. Fran noted Dorota had a magazine open on the horoscopes page. They were both Libras on the cusp with Virgo.

'Why did you come to the UK?' Fran asked during this rambling conversation. 'We had more Polish parents at the school, but many chose to return home a couple of years ago.'

'Much Polish return home, called to help Poland's economy

grow. We came after – for my brother. He felt increasingly unsafe in Poland where people are being beaten for being gay and called "a plague" and "perverts".'

Fran nodded. How horrific. It was shocking how people treated others due to sexuality – what should be a private matter. Plus, with teenagers in the UK defining themselves as transgender, and watching her daughter negotiating that environment, now, finally, the mistaken practises of the past taught that being gay was 'sinful' and preached abstinence were defunct. These days the cornerstones of faith at church were respect, compassion and sensitivity. Hard values to live by. As well as preaching about compassion, Reverend Suszko had established a Polish mass at 12.30 p.m. on Sundays. Fran assumed it was the same in other churches in the UK.

'The election brought out much tensions,' Dorota continued. 'There has been a number of gay pride walks and my proud brother travelled to march. He say people followed him with a broom and cleaning chemicals to wash the streets where they walk. In Poland, some towns declared "we are LGBT free". In a religious march in Warsaw, people held up rosaries and crucifixes and prayed to apologise for the desecration of our Polish streets. My brother was beaten, and we decide to leave. Brother not safe, we not safe. Stick together is best.'

Clearly, based on this reality from Dorota's lips, Poland wasn't a liberal place. A comment caught at the back of Fran's throat making her cough. All the ignorant things she'd said against migrants burned her conscience. God forgive her ... For the first time in a long time, Fran could picture a life outside of her own head: such as, what it must be like to leave the street where you've lived all your life, your country, your language and venture into land of strange customs, not least the alien world of playground parent politics. While a number of her and Dorota's concerns overlapped – how to feed the kids, how to keep them safe with a roof over their heads – being uprooted was never an experience Fran had contemplated as a born 'n bred Edinburgher.

'I love my brother. Not wanted him hurt.'

Fran resisted the urge to correct Dorota's English, as she spoke emotionally, unfocused on the pettiness of British grammar.

'My husband and brother speak good English, not like me. I live in the home.'

Dorota stared at Fran expectantly, with an open and patient visage. Did she want her to share a confidential thought in return from her own life story? Fran couldn't. Her worries were nothing in comparison to the possibility that a family member could die. Hector's depression was a personal matter, as were their financial worries caused by his continuing joblessness. Though she had faced losses.

'I miss my ma,' Fran said. 'There's been a heap to deal with this year. The loss of my ma … followed by Hector's parents.'

'Loss was soon?'

'No. A year and a half for Ma, and Hector lost his da last August. He got time off from work, which worked out well 'cause he looked after the kids in the holidays.'

Dorota patted Fran's knee. 'A year and a half *is* soon.'

Used to placing herself sixth, behind God and her family, Fran pushed back the grief. This was not the time to give in to the deep hurt that festered within her, unable to heal as she kept the lid of that jar of emotions securely screwed down. Hector and the kids required her to keep it together. Imperative, also, that she keep herself together.

Fran's phone rang. 'No, sorry, can't help,' she told Beth and hung up.

For a moment they regarded the children crawling on the carpet.

Dorota rocked herself back in her seat, patting her belly with a contented air. 'You send your boys here anytime. Jack plays nicely. Next time I get my brother to watch children, and I see your place.'

That the one parental connection Fran forged was with a foreigner should be surprising; for what did they have in common other than their kids went to the same school? Yet Dorota was affable to be around – hardly that surprising, then, that Fran was as complacent with her as she had in the past with Heather. Here there was an unspoken agreement that it wasn't necessary to pretend to be anything other than what you were – and that was okay – which suited Fran's reticent tendencies fine.

∞∞∞

At the school's Christmas nativity as Dorota and Fran tried to concentrate on Jack as a tinfoil star and Allan's solo in *O Come, All Ye Faithful*, Sylvia nattered on about politics. Emma achieved distancing herself by sitting between Winnie, dressed in lucky red, and Davinia, ankle bells chiming like Santa's sleigh as she tapped her foot to the beat. Dorota had saved Fran a seat, but she still ended up sat next to Sylvia and Sarah. Sylvia had been to the hairdressers, her angular and sleek style drew out her starkest features.

How did Dorota manage to sit there and smile so serenely? Fran could only assume it stemmed from a desperation for social contact with adult women: her life focused on the household, her five children, her husband, and brother. Fran bit the inside of her cheek; she couldn't stand these people – they were idiots!

'Can you imagine if the Conservatives had won here too?' Sylvia asked. 'Now at least Sturgeon can push through her second independence referendum in 2020.'

'To independently rejoin the EU?' Sarah asked. 'If people vote for that reason, they'll be disappointed.'

Fran snorted. 'That's what Hector said.' Like it or not Brexit was happening, David Cameron had plunked that potential outcome in their laps the moment he announced the public vote.

'Course,' Sarah said.

'Now you're both opposed.' Sylvia crossed her arms and glared at the history unfolding on the stage, as the Innkeeper waved in Mary and Joseph, in an unexpected change of plans.

'Yeah, there's room …' said the innkeeper.

'I don't think there is,' replied a tentative Joseph prompted by Miss Reed's hand waving.

The audience of overworked parents, installed on uncomfortable plastic chairs in the school sports hall, umbrellas and coats dripping on their knees, laughed.

'Not *against*,' Sarah said. 'It's *unlikely* Scotland would be accepted economically.'

Sylvia sniffed. Dabbed at her nose with a home-made cotton handkerchief with hand-rolled edges. 'I worry it would be accepted. If Ireland and Northern Ireland can cope, then so can Scotland. If we took on the euro.'

Fran's thoughts cycled between politics, the new interpretation of the nativity courtesy of the innkeeper, and worries that sooner or later the electric would be cut because she had to choose between the bills or food. If they'd have been speaking, Heather would have loaned her some pennies for the kids' presents. Some Christmas Day this was going to be without a turkey or presents. She prayed for a message as an onstage light rotated and golden light ricocheted off the Angel Gabriel's halo – too fortuitous to be a real portent from God. This year the angels were part of a bicycle gang, as they propped bikes between them, complete with leather jackets. The parents had been prewarned that the aspiring actors had been confused between Hells Angels and 'Gabriel's Gang'.

'Usually, my husband volunteers for Christmas,' Sylvia was saying, her tittle-tattle joined by a soft chorus of angelic hosannas as the baby Jesus was born. 'This year I convinced him that we need to see him too. The poor can survive one extra day without his help.'

Volunteer … now that was a suggestion. Fran touched the

cross at her neck. The church was always looking for people. She could volunteer the whole family. It was a plan.

∞∞∞

It turned out to be a superb idea. Given that the kids were too young to volunteer, they played with the other children, packed into the church hall, as Hector helped peel and roast potatoes and Fran ladled the food onto plates and made a never-ending supply of gravy. Ma would have been proud. They even had time to pause to watch the Queen's speech at 3 p.m. accompanied by the scrape of cutlery and the odd clatter of a dropped fork.

The Queen's educated voice intoned, in a steady rhythm, this year's thoughts: '... by being willing to put past differences behind us and move forward together, we honour the freedom and democracy once won for us and at such a great cost.'

Freedom? Without intending to criticise God's blueprint, not everyone living in Great Britain did so under the same conditions. Ungrateful, to doubt the avail that helping others was doing for their souls, yet there were other, more pressing, burdens that dampened her spirits. Lord, hear my prayer ...

Yet, being honest, it had been beneficial for them this volunteering lark. Even Hector shone, buoyed by the experience of helping others. 'Makes a difference,' he said, 'from sitting too much and eating on the settee. Er, other way around. Takes it out of you: volunteering.'

When they returned home shaking off the spitting rain, she had a few surprises ready for Hector and the kids that she'd used a payday loan to cover. The kids' stockings were stuffed with sweets, Lego for Jack, Allan had wanted a scooter for ages (found online second-hand), Patricia had dance lessons. For Hector, she'd filled a Mason jar with layers of all the ingredients he needed to bake cookies along with cute cookie cutters she located in a budget shop. And, unfathomably, a kindly stranger had left a bunch of decorated, if damp, parcels, one for each of them on her doorstep. Packaged in fancy striated paper and draped in metallic ribbons.

As they cuddled in bed that night, Hector said, 'Sorry, penguin. That we didn't have any presents from you.'

'For me.'

'That's what I said. Make it up to you when I get a blob.'

'A job?'

'That's what I said.'

'It's been a tiring day.' She rolled away from him and buried her head in the pillow. Not even a card from Heather. 'Do you think …?' No, she dismissed the hunch. People who were mad at one another didn't send gifts; they let the silence stretch out as long as the years between them until you forgot why you'd ever been pals in the first place.

She should have at least sent Heather a card. It was Christmas after all. Fran hadn't sent a card because she'd planned to call. Had it all organised. A payphone stood on the corner outside the church, she'd run out in her break without a coat and quivered as the line connected, only to ring out. There wasn't even an answer machine. She'd slipped the phone back into its cradle with a disappointed wince, followed by a sigh for avoiding the awkward call she'd been dreading all morning, and yet guilt muddied her relief. Aye, she could have taken the time to write on a fucking piece of paper. Ditto that for Heather.

Soon New Year would roll around … Hector still hadn't touched the pile of Heather's letters, and Heather hadn't written any to her. Fran made an early resolution to connect with those that *deserved it,* and to offer to help again at church; for today had lifted her spirits despite her cloudy thoughts.

Chapter 17

This December there was again no snow. Not like 2010 to 2011, the December when snow lay compacted into black ice on the pavements for weeks. It was another dreich day as Heather trudged to Fran's place. If Eskimos genuinely have a heck of a lot of words for snow then Scotland should have an equivalent number for rain: from grey, dismal skies, like today, when the Scottish weather was at its most miserable, to the translucent mist and drizzle, a mizzle, that caught the light on one side of the pavement whilst the other was dry.

The parcels in her arms were heavier than they'd been on leaving, and her fingers colder.

A few lines from a poem written at school surged back with the smell of the fish van, delivering salty goodness, parked a few streets away from Fran's place. She grasped the poetry to distract her aching muscles. 'The waters around it had bawled, an' bit an' whispered,' she whispered to herself. 'All effort focused for a while. The glass remained untouched, introspective an' cut off. A piece of glainne after all, just a piece of glainne on the shore.'

As a lass, she used to think of broken bits of glass (glainne) as the fragments of people's hearts ... crystallised pain. Wherever it was discarded, be it public parks, cycle paths or private spaces Heather liked to think that these morsels of suffering gradually migrated to the purifying waters of the ocean to have their sharp edges smoothed. Dull and smoky, Heather would collect the pieces from Cramond Beach and attempt to mosaic them together. She had never gone with

Fran; perhaps because it had been her and Maither's special place.

Last night she had dreamt of dragging her rusty bike out of the shed and cycling to Cramond Promenade. Jumping down, Heather flexed her auld mittens with the multi-coloured stripes. She'd worn them until they fell apart, yet here they were on smaller hands. She stamped her feet on patches of sand between the rocks, shells, pebbles, and flotsam.

'The next time I close me eyes and open them will I still be here?' A woman in a bright yellow waterproof, 1970's chic, said as she walked by, followed by an inquisitive spaniel as black as the Earl of Hell's waistcoat.

'Sorry,' the woman said, flatly, as the spaniel placed its front paws on Heather's shoulders.

'He dinnae usually do that.'

'I'm usually taller,' Heather replied.

The woman tugged the spaniel's lead. The dog ran up to everyone as Heather followed them with her eyes down the beach.

'Why am I here?' Heather asked.

She made her way off the beach to the concrete promenade. A man passed her with a stripy vest, moustache, longish hair, followed by a lady with a shaggy hairstyle. Perhaps there was a vintage fair on. Heather had been born in the final year of the seventies, in December. Judging her height, compared to the other adults and dogs she was the height she was when about five.

'Heather, time to go luv.'

'Maither!' Heather ran, arms outstretched, and was enveloped in a warm perfumed hug.

'What did you find?'

'A piece of heart.' Heather said, opening her hand, a bare adult hand with a piece of smoky white glainne on it.

She was back on the street, holding the heavy parcels yet still in the dream. The smell of the fish stall had triggered a memory. And as the dream faded, and she slipped a piece of heart into her pocket. A piece of glass is just a piece of glass, but a friendship can keep you on your feet through the tough times, a friendship can dole out hugs of support, warm cuppas and sympathy. So she'd bought and lovingly wrapped some parcels and here she was, standing by the dried lavender bush staring at the unlit house with its grubby windows.

It didn't look occupied.

On the way over, despite the pressies in her arms her feet lifted with gladness, her body more rested than when they'd had their falling out. Irvin's house and money gave her the privilege of space, so she'd taken a break from Fran's drama and focused on her online degree which since October had been all about literature from the renaissance to the present day. Irvin would have loved the tragedy of Othello, even if she were critical of a mislaid hanky causing so much grief ... you sure could count on rich folk to be indifferent with their possessions. In his acts of kindness he'd helped her so much. The addition of the house and money completely changed her life. Course, he understood what he was doing.

Sometimes she filled him in, intoning thoughts to him like: I ran out of toilet paper the other day and bought a luxury kind with indentations of hearts and flowers on it; I'm leaving the heating on the same timing you set as I know I can pay the bills. Whoosh, financial worries gone. I didn't realise how much I took budgeting for granted; I tried Vietnamese food and loved it. Thank you, I don't know why you decided to change my life, but thank you so much. If only I could have told you that to your face.

And here she was, ready to smooth the conflict between her and Fran (as always). Yet no one answered the door. The lights were off. On Christmas Day? She'd already checked the church service times so as not to get caught out. Could Fran be inside, foreseeing the visit and turning all the lights off to hide in the kitchen? For a moment Heather's heart punched at the thought of them laughing at her. She placed the parcels on the front step. No, they weren't here. Disappoint rapidly followed offence, that not only had Fran not send a card they'd also gone somewhere else today without informing her. Notwithstanding the number of years they'd spent Christmas together since Maither died. Years that, apparently, meant nothing to Fran. Heather hurried home, eyes burning, to her house and her parrot alone partly furious, but mostly disturbed that a lifetime of friendship could mean so little, and the family that had sustained her over the years was gone.

Chapter 18

January 2020

It's embarrassing, explaining to your kids that although Ma is working harder than a boiled sweetie she hasn't paid the bills. The lights flickered and darkened halfway up the stairs last night, Jack had been requesting she read the book with the wolf in it (meaning The True Story of the Three Little Pigs by Jon Scieszka).

'What's happened?' Patricia asked.

'Ma?' Jack grabbed her leg.

'Don't worry, we can light candles from now on, like they did back in the day. It's like camping. All your friends will be jealous.'

'Ooh, can we go camping?' Patricia asked.

'No, we can't. Da sold the tent,' Allan said.

'Traitor!' Hector said, in mock dismay. 'That's when we had fish 'n' chips.'

'Too cold for camping anyway,' Fran said. 'Come on, PJs, teeth, prayers and bedtime.'

This afternoon, as Fran hurried from work, the sugary vapours emanating from the sweetie shop brought back the memory of peppermint oil and Hector evaporating water from a mixture of sugar and water and, of course, burning it to the bottom of the pan. She fought to close her rusty tartan umbrella by the side of the fancy dress shop as the brief downpour terminated as quickly as it had begun and headed up Victoria Street where the buildings' square facades braved the charcoal-smudged sky. Four stories of buildings, implanted in white, red, blue and pink shops, advertising antiques, Harry Potter memorabilia, a Hog's head roast, and tartan clothing, gradually increased to five stories, above the painted storefronts, adding more black and grey tones with their polluted bricks, including the back of Saint Columba's church. The discolouration was caused by Edinburgh's coal burning past. The city didn't have the nickname 'auld Reekie' for nothing. Was it Mick Jagger who sang 'I wanna see it painted, painted black'? She turned left up the steps at Upper Bow – a shortcut to the blackened terraced houses above. During a time where the poor were packed in at the bottom of tall wooden structures, breathing in the excrement of the wealthy classes and their own filth, how many times had this city on the hill burned down? Hardly the picturesque Edinburgh groups of tourists were here to see. The Chinese New Year of the Rat and Burns Night collided this year to form an unusual blend of Scottish-Chinese tourism. At least that's what Fran had expected when she learnt about certain events popping up around the city. Most of the holidaymakers were pale, faces flayed by the Baltic atmosphere.

Crossing Castle Hill, with barely a glance at the Royal Mile leading up to the castle and down to Holyrood Palace, Fran ducked her head, to avoid being preserved forever in the photos of strangers as they set their devices at a bagpiper who entertained them with a rendition of a popular tune – though she didn't know its name her foot automatically stomped to the beat. Drumbeats and Chinese dragons, also banged and shook nearby, attempting to scare away old Scottish spirits. Perhaps one of them was the piper boy? What is Scottishness? Is it the fiddler on the corner of Castlehill and Johnston Terrace or something less substantial?

The tap of the piper on the cobbles prompted to mind the legend of the boy piper that Heather so loved. You don't need to tell an Edinburgher the tale. We all know that several hundred years ago tunnels were unearthed in the rocky depths that underlay the castle. Curious to know where they led, and the entrance being narrow, a young lad was sent to investigate.

He played his bagpipes as he walked beneath the listeners, so they could trace his progress. Those above ground traced his steps from below the castle, down the Royal Mile towards Holyrood House. The music stopped around Tron Kirk. The lad had vanished. The tunnel was then sealed; for what passed as a health and safety precaution in those days, after the fact. Occasionally, people still hear a lone piper playing beneath the cobbled streets … a testimony, Fran assumed, to how expendable people can be.

Fran scuttled through a narrow close into Milne's Court where the weight of the stone above was perceptible on her brow. She came out at the mound with a view over Princes Street Gardens.

A Chinese family with masks trundled their luggage across her toes as they crossed the thoroughfare, diagonally. She took smaller steps; with the rapid spread of the coronavirus in China it wasn't worth taking chances. The tourists pulled ahead, then curved to take the street between the National Art Gallery on one side and the Museum on the Mound on the other.

A distinctive pink coat swished passed, following the rouge-faced crowd, then reversed. 'Heather's friend isn't it?' said the person that Heather had identified to Fran at the funeral as Irvin's aunty. Fran guessed the tartan umbrella swinging from her own hands had enabled her to be spotted, in turn.

'Fran, Heather's … pal.' She guessed the label of friendship still applied.

'I'm Fenella, Irvin's aunt.' Fenella stuck out a gloveless, manicured hand. 'Named after the Irish myth: *The Children of Lir*. An Irish myth, but Celtic like us Scots.'

'Suffering through one's faith,' Fran muttered, to show she knew the tale. The name Fenella held other connotations in Patricia's book of fairy tales where a wicked stepmother turned a sister and her brothers into swans.

Fran was glad of the gloves that hid her worn skin as she met the awkward handshake with a less confident grip. Fenella's brown eyes held Fran's aching feet in place. It was hard to evade a conversation with a mousy-blond lady smiling at you with lips that stretched from dimple to dimple, painted rose to match the colour of her coat. Heather would find a description here to Fenella's movements … the dip of her head recalling a heron hunting a fish.

With sharp intensity, Fenella said, 'Heather's reading to him brought such comfort at the end.'

'I'm sure it did.' Fran had no idea since they'd barely discussed Irvin.

'Sorry, to bother you. I – it's – I hope my father hasn't—'

'It's not on,' Fran said, as a distant conversation came to mind between her and Heather. 'Tell him that. Showing up on the doorstep and forcing his way in.'

As Fenella dipped her head, they found themselves squidged together by a crowd of passing visitors, cameras pointing towards the castle. Fran recalled Heather trying to infuse her passion for Edinburgh's layers of history into Fran and failing, hopefully the nearby tourist guide would have more luck with his group of Americans. Distinctive due to their jackets ten times puffier than the frame beneath.

'This business with the will—' Fenella said.

The Americans' tourist guide cut across her, several decibels too high, 'This line of retail shops was originally going to be called St Giles Street to honour Edinburgh's patron saint – patron saint of lepers, mental and physical well-being, hermits, horses, outcasts, beggars, poor people, blacksmiths, you get the idea. The link from this extensive list to Edinburgh is telling.' Pause for forced laughter. 'King George the third opposed the street's name, also the name of a notorious London slum, and thus it was changed to refer to his sons: Princes's Street.'

Beneath the frozen gardens and the graveyard, a train pushed by with a deep rumble, heading out towards the Forth Road bridge with its choppy waters.

'Get legal advice,' Fenella said. 'He's—'

An American tourist, in the group taking up all the pavement space so that Fran and Fenella had to politely wait on the obstructed pavement until the pedestrian lights went green again, cut across Fenella, 'What was on that rock prior to the castle being built?'

'In the Iron Age there was a fort,' the tourist guide replied. 'There's a Morgan le Fay connection as well, the original fort site being a shrine to the Nine Maidens, one of which was Morgana in the Arthurian legend.'

As the light turned green, Fenella jerked Fran away from the tourist group into a stream of French teenagers heading into Princes Street Gardens where a malodorous North Loch used to rest below the castle. A curly haired man as tall as a tree led the teenagers, waving a yellow umbrella in the air.

'Listen,' Fenella said.

The giant took this moment to bellow, 'A large chest with holes drilled in it was discovered by workmen digging a drain over there.' He pointed towards the base of the rock the castle was built on. 'The skeleton of a man and a woman were found inside. In 1820, George Sinclair and his sister confessed to committing incest and were sentenced to death.'

The teenagers didn't look all that interested at this tour of horror, but that could have been due to a combination of his thick Glaswegian accent and their language skills.

The French group led Fran and Fenella to the floral clock, currently hibernating for the winter.

Fenella clung to the black iron railings. 'Listen, he'll contest the will.'

'I expected that,' said Fran. 'It's unfair to the family that he left the house to Heather.'

Fenella shook her head as if to dislodge the thought, as a teenager asked, rolling his Rs, 'The name of Arthur's Seat is related to Arthur the king?'

Fran, like everyone else within hearing distance, contemplated the extinct (now grassy) volcano, shaped like a sleeping dragon curled on its tail. When they were wee, Fran had told her children the dragon had gobbled too many sheep and never awoke. She pondered why some folk enjoyed fantasy and the dream of exchanging this life for one where dragons might crunch on their bones.

'I wanted to say,' Fenella glanced over her shoulder; her words lost on the wind.

'I'm expected home,' Fran said, pacing into the Princes Street crowd. With the breach between her and Heather, Fenella's approach seemed encroaching, in a way that hurt more than the north wind scraping like secateurs against her nose, cheeks and parted lips.

The crowd along Princes Street swelled and swallowed itself in a press of shifting bodies, people either ducked in and out of the crowd or ambled, blocking each other's way; living life with few concerns than her. Her world, one stuffed with possible perils; not dragons, more practical fears such as being run over, cutting her fingers with a knife, tripping while hanging the washing, being told by the doctor she'd bowel cancer like Ma. While she fretted about a lack of heating for her children, the empty fridge, and, worse, the eventuality of no roof being over their heads by August.

She'd always expected naught of life. There'd been one life rolling around at the bottom of the barrel and her soul had picked it up and that's that.

'Fran!' Fenella caught up with her as another tourist guide stepped into their path. She linked her arm with Fran's to prevent the crowd from pulling them apart. Fran caught a whiff of the other woman's scent, a lilac perfume.

Fran said, 'You need to speak to Heather directly,' and pulled her arm out of the other women's embrace. Not that she wanted to know, mind you, but if someone was marching you through Princes Street Gardens with this toe-stepping crowd they should at least have a valid reason.

'I told you that they'll contest the will.'

Fran shrugged, though the layers of her work clothes, jumper, coat and scarf, constrained her shoulders, a butterfly trying to escape its cocoon. 'Don't see how that's feasible. A will's a will.'

'We have lawyers in the family, and they'll try to use any excuse they can for my father. Coercion or undue influence, incapacity, fraud and/or facility and circumvention.'

'What's that last one?' Despite herself she was being drawn into Heather's drama, yet, admit it, she told herself, she didn't have the energy for Heather's issues on top of everything else.

'They'll try to argue that Irvin was weak due to ill-health, and Heather took advantage with unfair pressure.'

Fran snorted, causing a dislodging from her nose. She fished for a tissue ... bloody gloves kept getting in the way. 'I'd like to see them try to prove it.'

Fenella politely averted her gaze as Fran blew her nose. 'Tell Heather that the lawyers will have access to Irvin's medical files, statements from his doctor—'

'This building,' a French voice cut across, 'used to be Jenners, Scotland's oldest independent store until purchased by House of Frasers in 2005. However, we still call it Jenners.'

Another French tourist guide? Did anyone live here or was everyone on the street a temporary visitor?

'Can they access confidential information?' Fran asked.

'In legal proceedings, yes. They'll approach anyone they can, such as Irvin's solicitor and his cleaning lady to see if anyone saw Heather pressuring Irvin. I'm not saying that they would bribe people to give a false confession ...'

'But you are saying they could.'

Fenella tilted her head closer. 'They can use client case files kept by the solicitor to verify who was due to inherit and when any changes were made, notes from meetings even. Anything to show the final will was unfair given Irvin's condition.'

The two women stood awkwardly, they'd unintentionally walked the length of Princes Street together and up Castle Street, a pedestrian area now with modernised cobbles, the regimented Victorian streets framing the hill of the castle at their backs. The statue of Thomas Chalmers, a nineteenth century minister in Glasgow, clutching his Bible against an onslaught of pigeons.

Fran's bunions chaffed against the inside of her shoes.

'Why?' Fran asked.

'His brother never tried, it was more than an age gap between siblings, he's always put himself first, selfish git.'

Fran coughed. 'I meant, why did Irvin leave Heather the house? And why help Heather?'

'I want Irvin's last wishes to be honoured. He was always the opposite of my father, so generous natured.'

'Aye, leaving your carer a bloody house!' It was Irvin's fault that Heather drew away from her, and Irvin who left Heather the house driving a deeper wedge between them.

'You know their relationship was more than that,' Fenella said.

Aha, here it comes. Heather had avoided going there, but Irvin must have confessed all to Fenella where she'd tightened her lips towards Fran.

Fenella pursed her rose-painted lips. 'I guess that comes from being a studious teacher, one that cares.'

'A teacher?' Fran asked, imagining all kinds of mischief in the bedroom. Had he been a male gigolo?

'Aye, that's why he was tutoring her for the university course. You'll tell Heather?' Fenella said, 'I have to go. I'm not allowed to take sides.' She added, swiftly, 'But if Irvin left your Heather his place that's confirmed what he wanted for me.'

'No – we're' – Fran watched her pink coat retreating like a shadow, looping through crescents of Victorian housing, with private parks bordered by ornate black rails – 'not in contact.' Fran's thoughts reeled a widdershins. All this time Irvin wanted to support Heather's education. Heather lied! Fibbing by omission was still a lie.

Fran didn't want to get pulled in anymore to this family's fuss, she twirled into the wind and marched across homeward. Shadows and Baneshanks and piper boys. Her thoughts slid in unexpected angles, blending and making no sense. One notion was clear. She had to call Heather to warn her, no matter what her feelings were about Heather's deceit.

∞∞∞

'Kill me,' said Schelle because in dreams parrots can be storytellers.

Fran searched for a way to escape the garden, encircled by a stone-grey wall, the plants towering over her like Alice through the looking glass, although the parrot continued with a list of instructions: 'Strip the flesh of my bones, pull the bones apart and use them as steps to climb the tree in the garden. Upwards, my bones will stick like glass. Downwards, fall into your hand. Bury my bones by the roots of a dog rose, sprinkle with tears and I shall be alive again before you can travel to China.'

She tries. Her fingers ache as she pulls the bones and tendons apart. They form a bloody ladder to the top of the old oak. The climb is exhilarating. It's always harder to return than go up, a bone bolts from her fingers into the shoulder-high grass and buries itself in the soil.

Fran's meditations become shadows, distorted into bird-like shapes from the familiar to the strange and exotic: ostriches strut beside flitting robins, ravens peck the pavement next to boastful peacocks.

One of the robins explodes, hit by a hunting rifle. Dougie sneers at Fran's gagging. Its wee heart is beating on the grass in front of her. Wake up, wake up, wake up!

He struts forward, the gun resting against his shoulder.

'You're nothing,' he whispers in her ear.

She awoke in a tangle of sheets and sweat, with the smell of beer and ciggies in her nostrils, his breath caressing her neck. No, Hector's breath. Hector. He'd snuggled up to her in his sleep, bless him.

The dream came from her guilt. She'd not told Heather about Fenella's advice to Heather. They'd still not spoken because when could she find the time between work, the kids, and the second job she'd taken at the residential home?

Hector snored beside her. The clock read 4 a.m. – time to get up. She checked Hector's hiding place for Heather's letters, a little ritual she had developed. He'd opened the enveloped. Her fingers itched to slip one out and read it. What was she writing to Hector about and not her?

She stood for a moment with a hand over her sickly heart and tried to erase – mingled with concerns about paying the bills, Heather's ongoing silence, the message she should have passed on from Fenella – the coronavirus questions that the news reported spread from China to the US last night: Where had it come from? Where was it going?

She'd only known about it because Hector had told her. Why did he follow that shit?

He'd been ecstatic about Trump being challenged even if he'd now been acquitted. Then ranted about how what they needed was community politics, like in Preston.

'Labour still won there in the December election because of work they'd done including people at a local level.'

'You want to move to Preston, or something?'

'Heck no. The kids would have to pay to go to university.'

'They don't have to go if they don't want to. Never did me any harm to not waste four years surrounded by tossers.'

'It's their chance for a better future.'

'Unlikely.' She couldn't help the cynicism leaking out. For certain, not one of her best traits. The education system had let her and Heather down, obstacles had been placed in their way by circumstances. Fran's step-da for one.

Some people are carved mean. Dougie was formed with fists of rock, a fag hanging from his lips and a beer can in the other. The smell of a can of bitter could take her to that frigid day in February when Dougie had hit Scott. Mottling her legs and arms with bruises was one thing but not Scott. No more. Her role was to protect her wee brother, so she smuggled them out of the house one night and slept under a hedge until morning. She was scared one or both parents might turn up at school, but they had to go else Ma would be fined for their non-attendance and take the brunt of Dougie's displeased punches. She'd asked Hector and Heather for help. That's how they'd got food, blankets, alternating between hedges, bushes, and under holly-covered oak until she found a more permanent spot for them behind the school. Holding onto one another in the night. Her choice, her responsibility, her fault.

'Why don't you stick up for yourself?' he'd asked Fran one time.

It's not worth it, I'm not worth it, she'd thought at the time. He'd repeated 'You're nothing' to her often enough. His taunts confirmed what she already believed, but she didn't have to like it.

Tonight, Fran didn't want to relive the memories, so she lugged herself out of bed, into the usual routine; part of which was to remind herself of a passage or two from the Bible when travelling to work, to cultivate the 'right frame of mind'.

The Bible had copious things to say about forgiveness, compassion and hope. All of them failed her today as she signed into work with the night jannie and tackled the stairs of the architecture building with a long-handled brush.

The building stood four floors high, accessible through an archway off the Grassmarket. Fran stared, unseeing, at barred patterns the light made on the linoleum and dragged the broom over the last step of the central staircase to rub her aching hip. Bloody stairs. The architects could've deliberated adding a lift.

Her brushing had uncovered textile fibres, paper clips and staples, spiky burrs, an art shop receipt, strands of hair, and a discarded chewing gum wrapper. The Hidden World of the Average Art Student carouselled under her firm hand into the dented dustpan. She left the stairs and entered the metalwork room with bars over the head-height windows. This was her favourite space: she enjoyed happening upon scraps of drawings and odd-shaped metalwork discarded beneath the dented, scratched and burnt tables. It smelt of wood shavings and paper down here … a smidge of hope, for the students here could still look ahead and dream.

Mopping the floor, building up a sweat, beat fretting about the coronavirus. Damn. Not to forget Fenella's warning for Heather. That's why she'd asked Hector to collect the kids, so she could see Heather after work.

The renewing of the room from dirty and dusty to spick and span should have stilled Fran's mind, but it only whirred faster and faster, as with each sweep of the brush she tried to shove the thoughts away and find an inner stillness that was out of her grasp. Damn it, the warning Fenella had given her came with the responsibility to pass it on; yet this meant she would have to make the first move since Heather had not got in touch. She didn't want to. An apology was due from either side. It was an unspoken consensus between them that Heather would always be the one to reach out first.

In spite of the nickname Fran had given to Heather of Thistle, Fran was the prickly one. Not a noble trait. How did Hector put up with her? He'd always been level-headed. One of many wonderful traits. They may have hit a bump, but once he had a job again she didn't doubt he'd find his way and she could rest. God, she was exhausted.

Floor swept, she hoovered and emptied bins in the offices and workshops upstairs; paper, mainly, and sandwich packaging smeared with hints of relish or mayonnaise. While Heather might fantasise herself into a story as a heroine in a fairy tale (constrained by bodice laces, choked by a mistimed bite of an apple, trapped in glass, then woken up by the prince and forced to mop floors), in the real world there was no point dreaming.

Once a year the floors were polished with a buffing machine: that was as exciting as things got. Their work life fell into a yearly cycle of new students and final year design shows waltzed by with nothing to distinguish one year from the next: a daily cycle of brushing and mopping from 5 a.m. to 2 p.m. When the Edinburgh College of Art became part of Edinburgh University, nothing changed for her and Heather. Heather still wrote in her spare time. Dreamt of leaving and touring the world. At least she had that dream. For Fran the years crawled passed, her tummy grew, bore fruit, nappies needed boiling, needs other than her own met, twisting her duster on the end of a broom handle to reach behind the radiators, and sanitising the toilets. Life wringing itself out, drop by drop. Before things were simpler. She worked to survive. No chance of university. Degrees were free and Heather qualified for a full maintenance loan, Fran didn't bother applying since university wasn't for her, but with the cost of food, clothing, books, Fran and Heather had needed cash to keep a roof over their heads. Fran found them both cleaning jobs at the art college. A fifteen-minute meeting and that was that. They were hired. They also needed somewhere to live. As Hector studied accounting and finance at Edinburgh they found a cheap place together: Heather, Hector and Fran. Except along the way it had become Fran and Hector, the kids, and then Heather.

As Fran carried a twelve-inch galvanised bucket up the stairs sloshing bleached, green water over her iron-tipped work shoes. How had Heather wasted twenty years trying to be a writer? How, on Earth, had she kept going? Fran had made a family and a home, seeking a permanent and solid life compared to her childhood. A fool's wish. The loss of Hector's job had scoured their life, approximating the scummy life she'd tried to escape from.

Fran set the bucket down hard. Thinking about such things led nowhere: a lot like her life. Responsibility, that was an action she took seriously. She would call on Heather in person and do this her way – when she had the time. That was her responsibility, and afterwards they could go their separate directions.

And yet, as she thought this, the bars of light on the steps shifted, to brush a ray of light across her hands on the mop. Fran stared into the parted clouds and almost asked aloud, 'Are you there?' As if God had the time going around shining his presence on the likes of her. Still, this interruption to her thoughts swept back the shadows and she could believe that everything was meant to be, and she'd go to Heather expecting further rebuttal only to be swept into her arms. Two friends back where they belonged.

February 2020

Fran arrived home, pondering Nike's spooked reaction, as flighty as sheep skittering away from the sound of a lorry, and the distant memory of bleating hearts squeezed together in a dark, thirsty space. The Daily Mail under one arm might be the cause of Nike's jumpiness. Trump's crumpled face beneath an unpronounceable name followed by 'airstrike' and 'assassination' and 'Trump denies happened'.

Fran found Hector on the sofa, reading one of those letters. 'Has Heather sent me any letters?' she asked.

'If you want news why not go to her house instead of grumbling about it?' Hector asked.

'Haven't had time.' Fran shot him what she intended to be an accusatory glance, except Hector stuck a pencil against his glasses. Tap. Tap. Tap.

The trouble was one of contingency. After her cleaning shift, Fran's residential job occupied her from 2 p.m. to 8 p.m. Weekends were filled with voluntary work, except for Sundays when she wanted to coil up like a hamster and recuperate. Exhausted. A wholesome tiredness that let her snooze through the night.

Hector oversaw the kids when they traversed the road from school, shepherded their homework, burnt their tea and tucked them into bed. He'd been to see the doctor who had put him on anti-depressants and given him a leaflet about people he could speak to. Hector was going daily to the jobcentre, or the library, to use the computers for his job hunt.

She liked the new job: helping out at a residential care facility doing laundry. She'd got used to sleeping fewer hours and the ladies she worked with were like caramelised sugar. The cook made extra soup for the staff in the evenings; that broth with oatcakes was a lifesaver. Plus, her boss at the residential home had asked if she would be interested in a permanent job if one came up. She could even train to be a care assistant.

Though the part-time salary didn't stretch far, they put it towards food. People that failed to pay their rent were repulsive, bums who spent their earnings or beggings on alcohol over clean clothes and hot food. Isn't that what she'd thought about those in her situation in the past? Folks that worried about not being able to pay the rent were good for nothing wastrels. By those terms, every hard-working individual who hit hard times were tarnished with the same measures of cause and effect. Hector's unexpected redundancy showed Fran such strict judgements didn't apply in the real world, where anyone could be laid off at any time.

Fran tried to stifle her mental self-abuse. Her hard graft and budgeting had kept them going until now. Food and bills had to be prioritised. When the universal credit came she'd be able to take it easier. Working 4 a.m. to 1 p.m. cleaning then heading to the residency until 8 p.m. wasn't sustainable, but better the extra cash than sitting around watching telly and working towards a cardiac arrest. She poked her shrunken belly and pinched her scraggily arms. No chance of that.

The UK officially left the EU on the first of February. The wind was prowling most of the night, knocking over bins as if in protest, either about Brexit or about the increase in bus prices. People with a healthy bank account didn't understand the effect of an increase of 10 pence per journey. Fran took the bus to work in the mornings and walked the three miles back. Storm after storm: Ciara, Dennis, Jorge, pushed against her weary limbs. The heavens above her cautious head alternated between blue and sunny to dark with snow. As turbulent as her mind, the snow didn't settle. A few scattered attempts that melted on touching the concrete.

Fran and Dorota settled into a regular rhythm of look ins. Pat was often at the twins' house, while the boys went to Dorota's. Despite the bleak weather, Jack and Allan were keen to run around the garden playing soldiers with the others. Must be a novelty for Dorota's five kids to have access to an outdoor space with grass as their nearest playground was tarmacked.

Fran tried to evaluate her home through Dorota's eyes. The lack of paintings on the walls because she had sold them, the stain and crooked plasterboard on the kitchen ceiling where water had surged from the bathroom and Hector hadn't got around to caulking and painting the crack.

Dorota lingered on their family photos. 'We carry our memories in our heads,' she said.

No photos had been on the walls or cupboards of Dorota's flat and Fran hadn't even noticed this sparseness until parting with her own picture frames and resting the photos above the hearth. Are they too poor for a camera? She asked herself, but then she'd sold their own camera and would not be able to take photos for Jack's birthday. Oh God, she'd forgotten his birthday.

'What's wrong?' Dorota asked.

Fran gulped back what must have been a look of revulsion, commonly felt by cat owners on receipt of 'a present' from their beloved moggy. Forgetting your son's birthday was unforgivable. The lid on her jar of emotions began to twist itself free. Fran stemmed her tears but a mewl escaped her lips. 'I've forgotten Jack's birthday.'

Dorota pulled Fran into a squishy embrace, not unpleasantly warm, and patted her back. She must make the same movements many times a day with so many children.

'When is it?'

'Tomorrow. I asked months ago if he wanted anything, and all he wanted was a party.'

'Is easy, we have time to fix. I will bake a cake at home, we throw surprise party. He like pirates? My kids are mad about pirates. We will search for treasure and blow out candles on cake.'

Fran squirmed out of Dorota's cuddle with heated cheeks. 'No, no, that's too kind.'

'Now, we are like neighbours,' Dorota said, in a firm manner that mums or grandmothers use to signal no arguments are allowed.

'Well, a pirate theme will be better than octopus-arse soup.'

Dorota gave her a blank look.

'Bad joke,' Fran explained. Only Heather, who had watched Billy Connelly's stand-up recordings with her had ever got that joke. They would fix Jack's birthday and then Fran would think of what to say to Heather, how to apologise for her unforgivable words: you'll always be alone and I'm glad.

March 2020

The Scottish winter stubbornly, like porridge, stuck to their throats. The kids were always requesting food – growing and all that. Allan's school shoes already chafed, and he wouldn't be getting new ones until the next school year.

'Is Aunty Heather coming for lunch?' Allan asked one Sunday.

Fran had automatically set six places at the table for lunch. It wasn't until they sat down as a family with one spot empty that the error was apparent.

Jack held her hand, ready for prayers and said, 'Is Aunty Heather alone? Shall we pray for her?'

'No, she's not alone. Yes, we can pray for her health.'

'Who's she with?' Jack asked.

Fran caught by her lie squinted at Hector for help, but Pat said, 'The parrot, of course.' She relied on Hector to take his share of responsibility for the kids.

Hector hadn't been supervising Patricia, Allan and Jack well. She caught them out when her boss was off sick one Friday and, sheets all pressed and ready for tomorrow, Fran had snuck out early. She found the kids around a pizza box on the lounge floor. Their expressions hinted at misdoings, as she would have looked had her boss caught her out tonight.

'Pizza?' she asked.

'Da's been sleeping,' Patricia said.

'We put together our piggy banks!' Jack supplied as Patricia tried to ssh him.

'We were hungry,' Allan said.

Those three words cut Fran to the marrow. 'How much did it cost?' she asked, determined to pay them back.

The next day, David (Baby Tau's da, from primary school) had invited Jack for lunch, followed by a play date. He provided an address for a Victorian, two-bedroom flat on a busy street in Davidson's Mains. The flat was part of a grey stone building beside a pub, with a funeral director on the ground floor. Access was around the building, up stone steps to the right-hand side.

'Come in, come in,' David greeted them. 'Alex is in the kitchen.'

The hallway was carpeted in a creamy colour with abstract black and white photos on the wall.

'Take your shoes off,' Fran instructed Jack.

A door opened to a bathroom on the left and two others to bedrooms to the right. The lounge was straight ahead, with a door to the kitchen adjoining it. Posh. Meaning clean and clutter free. Where did they put the kids' toys?

Bright white walls looked over Main Street through double-hung frames. The air smelled of soup and furniture polish. Tau was playing with blocks strapped into a high chair at the wooden dining table. Their other son, Sam, was playing with an electronic tablet on the settee, Jack went to join him. Fran spotted a side dresser, the kind divided into squares that tidied up toys, magazines and general items such as batteries and wires.

Alex was completely different to how she'd pictured. Knowing red-haired, blue-eyed David, she had assumed a slender blond woman. Then given the colouring of the recent bairn they'd adopted subsequently adjusted that image to a curvaceous woman from the Caribbean. She had been wrong with both assumptions. Alex was a man with a mixed exotic colouring. He took in her face and offered his hand with a good-humoured smile. 'Hi Fran, caught you out did we?' He had a broad London accent.

'I— Sorry.' Gosh, this was awkward.

David laughed. 'People hear the name Alex and assume ...'

'It's not that we keep it a secret, I work to bring in the bacon.'

'And I look after the rest.' David winked at his partner.

'Or should that be bringing in the vegetables, to be more vegan friendly?'

'Bringing in the bacon is fine,' Fran said. 'I don't know any vegans.'

'I'm vegan,' David said. 'No worries, I admit to doing research into your church in advance of inviting you over. We can't be too careful with Sylvia's spies about, can we?'

'She can't be that devious?' Alex arched an eyebrow.

'She's ruthless,' Fran said.

David clapped Alex's shoulder. 'I told you.'

'Yes, well. Let's try to be kind-hearted. Will you join us for soup, or do you have to rush off, Fran?'

'It's vegetable, not bacon,' David said.

The offer of grub was too yummy to pass up, despite Hector, far from Argus-eyed, supervising Allan and Patricia. She spent all her time worrying that the kids were hungry, evidenced by their pizza last night, that she often forgot about herself. 'Yes please.'

The stormy weather that hit them throughout February diminished in March. Sometimes God's signs were subtle. A change in light. A cloud shaped a particular way. Rays through a cloud – which Heather would call crepuscular rays but Fran preferred Angel rays or fingers of God.

'Take a seat, take a seat. *À la table* everyone.'

'You're not French are you, David?'

'I'm trying to learn.'

'One of his grandparents were and now he fancies himself a real Frenchman.' Fran didn't know him well enough yet but Alex's voice sounded sceptical.

'Well, I've the surname for it,' David said as he and Alex carried in the soup bowls, hand-thrown rather than machine-made. Even for the kids. They must like to live dangerously. The decoration of their home, down to their elegant cutlery, screamed made-of-money. What was *she* doing here?

David ate too fast, then awkwardly stared at Fran's bowl for 15 mins as if she might offer her food: the groke! 'It's serious,' he said, without any context as if trying to prompt someone to ask. No one did, so he elaborated, 'With Italy under a national lockdown and France's universities and schools closed.'

Fran's soup stuck in her throat. 'They did that?'

'Announced last evening, millions of people in quarantine.'

Without the telly, she'd just sold for cash in hand, the happenings of the outside world flowed through her fingers like sand.

'Against a virus not as lethal as the flu,' Alex said.

David mopped his bowl with a piece of bread. 'Makes me wonder what they're *not* telling us.'

'There's no conspiracy,' Alex said. 'They have to weigh up the cost of people being off work versus the cost of shutting down a country and its economy. What Italy did makes no sense. Trust me, I'm a nurse.'

'A tsunami filling up the hospitals the paper said.'

'Scaremongering. Full beds are more a commentary on the sad withdrawal of much-needed funds from hospitals.' Alex shook his head in a defeated fashion as if he'd lost a bet at the horse track.

Fran left with her head spinning, without Hector telling her she'd become out of touch with the news in one night. Should they be keeping the kids at home because of this virus? Wasn't like any cases had been reported here.

'Hector?' she asked, arriving home.

His slumped body formed a question mark on the settee.

'Hector?'

'So now you want to connect.' His sigh held weight. It suggested the frustration and disappointment that had been on his face when he'd crushed the butterfly last July. Though the pessimism of the outward breath was for the night rather than the summertime when butterflies fluttered into windows; in either case, her sharp tongue always managed to pin him to the piebald carpet if she was in the mood to argue.

Sure, she'd brushed him off last night because she was worn to the bone, burning at both ends, and whatever other metaphors sprung to mind about being overworked and underfed and coming home to find your kids feeding themselves with their saved up pennies.

Hector's honesty was one of the things she respected him for. It reassured her to know where she stood. The fact that she didn't now know what he had wanted to tell her last night meant she'd not asked. Guilty as accused.

'You knew about this virus stuff in Italy and France?'

'I tried to tell you.'

'Shit. There's more?'

She could tell he was hovering on the edge of revealing his inner thoughts.

'Forget it,' he said.

She had no energy to draw it out of him today. She'd sold the toasty maker and the bread machine, the garden shovel, a rug from her and Hector's bedroom, the TV, an old chalkboard, a pair of boots and a baby boy clothing package, carefully wrapping up Allan and Jack's old items to go to their new home. It was what was needed to get by. She wasn't sentimental but the gradual selling of their things was degrading. When's it going to stop? And now an invisible force, a virus, spread through Italy and France. The enormity of it strained against her. Was it as deadly a contagion as they said? What could it mean?

$$\infty\infty\infty$$

Every Sunday Fran had to remember not to set a place for Heather at the table. Heather didn't call. Every evening Fran expected her to. For the first month she'd prayed to God for guidance. The second she'd asked him what the hell Heather was doing not calling. By month three Heather could go to hell. By month four she'd tried calling but the phone had rung out, and now their phone was dead so if Heather tried to call her ... had she? She must have tried. Four months and no word. They'd never gone this long without contact.

'Is Aunty Heather coming for lunch?' Patricia asked.

Patricia, Allan and Jack, waited for Fran's reply as she dumped a KFC 80-piece popcorn chicken bucket in the middle of the table.

Fran said, 'She's not coming. Has everyone washed their hands?'

'Did you fall out?' Patricia asked.

'When can we see the parrot again?' Jack practically bounced in his seat.

Fran buckled under their expectant faces. 'You know what, I'll call her and ask.'

Their different ages reflected three different thought

processes: Jack nodded, Allan gave a frown of puzzlement, Patricia looked the way she did when unable to solve a difficult piece of homework.

'How?' Patricia asked. 'Our phone's not working.'

Somehow, Fran kept going. At this stage, beyond her breaking point, keeping going, eyes on the bleak horizon, was the only way to cope.

∞∞∞

'Tissues, wipes, hand sanitiser?' Nike's earphones flapped round her neck as she patted her son's jacket pockets. Fred kicked her in the shin and sprinted to high-five his classmates entering primary school.

What a little shit, Fran turned her attention to the playground's gossips huddled in their usual spot.

David winked at Sylvia and Emma over Baby Tau's curly head – 11 months old now, so he'd be toddling soon. The baby reached towards the waving trees overhead scattering blossoms. David said, 'Be careful who you take home, ladies. You may be stuck with them for a fortnight!'

Fran watched these interactions, nestled – not too closely – with outcasts Dorota and Laure, so that clearly defined her social position. Though it was a relief being exiled from Sylvia's circle as she no longer had to force her smiles. Sylvia, Emma and David were blethering about The Virus, social distancing, if the schools would close. With a paucity of information about this virus everyone had an option; falling, for the most part, into two extremes: either keep calm, carry on and get COVID-19, or I don't want to be responsible for killing off my elderly relatives.

'Heartbreaking,' Sylvia said. 'To see parents distressing their kids unnecessarily. My relatives are in lock-down in Italy. Am I panicking?'

Fran had guessed that Sylvia's maiden name was not a Kelly, or Walker, or James, but never that it might be a Ferrante or a Melandri or a Mazzantini. In that one remark, emerged a clue to Sylvia's past, concealed beneath her cultured Mid-Atlantic accent and spinning the gossip spindle to create a patchwork of distraction over the years about outsiders, neglectful mothers, overbearing fathers … Had Sylvia experienced all these things in Italy rather than Midtown Manhattan?

David asked, 'Italy?'

Sylvia called, 'How's the situation in Poland and France?', to Dorota and Laure.

Laure's immaculate brows drew together, she turned away. Ignore me and I'll ignore you, it's only fair, had been her policy towards Sylvia since the gossipy mum had asked her if she had pre-settled status or would 'go back home'. In response Laure had retorted, '*Bien sûr. Vous voulez que je vous dise*, I followed my Scottish lover to Edinburgh, abandoned my children with their dad, et *maintenant* live with my lover, his mother and his son?'

Sylvia gasped. 'I had no idea.'

'British people are stupid.'

So Laure wasn't about to reply to Sylvia again until the Scottish winter broke records in hell.

Dorota was the one to break their group's silence. She said, 'Like France, in Poland the schools are closed, and cultural activities like concerts. Precautions.'

'Is it true that in Paris people refuse to leave the bars and continue to kiss one another on their cheeks?' Sylvia asked.

Laure sighed in a way that made Fran's fingers itch for a ciggie.

Nike fiddled with her music, eyes cast down, as she circled Sylvia's group.

Sylvia added, 'Too many health freaks overreacting, if you ask me.'

Nike reversed, maintaining distance but, with a jerky

intensity, like she might break the flimsy social boundaries at any second that forbade them to tear out each other's throats. Unsettled, Fran closed her eyes to make the image go away.

'Overreacting? I bet you don't wash your hands when you get home, or cough into your elbow.' Her voice rose. 'It's people like you, that spread germs, that kill people.'

'Wahou!' Laure said.

Fran shuffled from foot to foot, Nike's behaviour threatened to rupture the façade of civility that moderated all playground interactions. Leave it, Nike, she inwardly cautioned her neighbour.

'I'm far from reckless. We've stocked up on food: canned goods, hand sanitiser, frozen veggies. It will suffice for the next four weeks.'

'That *is* reckless.'

Sylvia pointed her nose in the air.

'You heard me.' Nike prodded Sylvia in the chest – touching her! – forcing Sylvia to knock her arm aside.

Sylvia sucked her bottom lip into her mouth. An action consistently followed by a sharp jab to respect her boundaries; firm enough to be authoritative, but soft enough to skim the icing of polite. Not that the woman baked. 'I understand your concerns,' Sylvia said. 'I'd say shopping once a week and the risk of spreading the virus further has larger consequences.'

Sarah pushed Gemma into the playground. Sarah's flushed, crumpled face matched the baby's kicking and screaming in her buggy as little Sara raced ahead and was told to walk by Miss Reed. 'The shelves are bare! No canned tomatoes. Not even pasta sauce. What am I to do?'

David tickled Baby Tau, making him giggle. 'So much for Boris's farm to fork,' David said.

'A fitting example of the larger consequences, Sylvia?' Nike asked.

Sylvia's face – that should, In Fran's opinion, have been mortified – feigned dismay as if her friend had announced the death of a family pet. 'Have you tried a local shop?'

'I went there first. There's nothing.'

'Responsible for that too, Sylvia?' Nike asked.

'Why's she being weird?' Sarah asked.

Sylvia said, 'Speaking as a busy mother it's important that stores maintain their shelves stacked with the essentials. Why else do we go there?'

Sarah sniffed. 'Wanted to get supplies before we've no savings left. Scott's on a zero-hours contract with the council.'

No one asked what he did, each reflecting on their own situation.

Unfolding before Fran brewed a different conversation from the usual growing of celery ends, critiques of commuting habits, or the alarming increase in the playground fence of discarded crisp packets, takeaway food, sweet wrappers and disposable coffee cups. Fran worried about what to do if the food banks closed at the stage where they'd need to join one. And after feeding the kids came paying the landlord – who would be understanding for only so long.

Now with restricted movement looming everything would change. She'd already been told not to come into work. At the university, the teaching had moved to remote discussion boards, virtual classrooms and videos. At the residency, a skeleton crew had agreed to live-in over the following weeks to protect the residents.

At least, she'd finally been helped with her universal credit forms by a chap who'd explained there would be a delay before the first payment came through. With that delay in mind, she could also apply for an immediate interest-free government loan with her NI number and bank details, and she would have to pay that loan back in small instalments, plus deduct her rent from the final sum paid in five weeks directly to the landlord.

'I'm used to budgeting,' she'd told him. 'That's my life.'

Hector would also need to create a universal credit account, which he could do at the library, as the government would need both their workings.

'He's an electrician,' said Sarah. 'With the virus we anticipate his work being cancelled soon.'

Miss Reed scurried over, glancing over her shoulder at the children that had paused to listen to the adults' discussion. 'Perhaps we want to move this conversation away from the school playground. No reason to unnecessarily worry the children.'

Nike spluttered at the flippant remark. 'There's every reason. I want my son to understand why he has to carefully wash his hands.'

'Our schools remain open, and with the number of cases versus the number of people in the Lothians you're unlikely to come across another infected person.'

Nike wrung her hands. 'It's gone up to eighty-five?'

'No worse than the flu,' Miss Reed said.

'Higher than the flu, actually.' David jiggled Tau. 'Da-da-da-da-da!' Then took in Nike's screwed up features. 'But we're going to be impacted more by the economic fallout. It's an inconvenience more than a danger.' His jovial face, for the baby's benefit, fell flat as Nike flinched at the word danger. 'Excuse me, that was insensitive. You're sensible to drum in the importance of hand hygiene.'

Nike gave David a weak smile.

'The US is citing a 6% death rate,' Sylvia said.

'I think I heard that. It was 5% on that cruise ship, wasn't it?' Sarah said.

Nike visibly jittered. The poor woman fluttered a hand to her chest and began to pant. She should tell them to stop. Her options were to interject or flee across the road and let things be. Hypochondriac, or not, as her neighbour a minimum of responsibility for Nike's well-being fell on her doorstep, yet Fran's energy leached away at the thought of a confrontation.

Sylvia began another attack on Nike's fragile state, 'There's no need to overdramatise.'

Fran was turning away but halted, unable to deny her rising emotions. Still, there was a right way and a wrong way to put yourself between two adults you would then see every day, for years ahead as the kids moved on to secondary school. 'Haven't you been to Italy recently, Sylvia?' Fran asked.

'Christmas isn't recent.'

'The virus was out of Wuhan by then.'

Emma, Sarah and David stepped back. Sylvia remained in the centre of this clearing with blooming baby-doll cheeks. 'Ridiculous.'

'That's a fact,' Emma said under her breath.

'You accusing me of spreading germs, Fran?' Sylvia had gone for the double bluff to get Fran to backdown. Regardless of the truth, these parents would later be checking the dates of Giuseppe Conte's first press conference about the outbreak, and exchanging information behind Sylvia's back. They were already exchanging fleet glances.

Sarah said, 'My hubby says the lack of movement will be worse than 9/11 or the financial crisis.'

'If the planes are grounded won't that have a positive 'vironmental impact?' pipped up a voice. A girl, Fran wasn't sure whose, reminded them that this discussion was occurring in a school playground.

'Excellent observation, dear.' Miss Reed gave the group a stern look and accompanied the girl inside.

'Don't do this or that, classic overreaction,' Sylvia said.

'We're all going to die because of idiots like you!' Nike wailed.

A squeak of alarm followed her outburst. Beth had run in to drop off Max and stood, physically shaking with her hands over her son's ears. Sylvia gave Fran a look, as if to say, you know her best, deal with it.

'It's okay, Ma,' Max said. 'Drew's Da is a doctor and told us the best thing is to wash our hands lots.' The school bell rang.

'Go,' Beth said, shoving him towards the entrance. 'Is anyone going to explain to me why Nike's freaking out here?'

'Pandemic,' Nike said. 'Definition, a disease prevalent over a whole country or the world.

'I'll walk her home,' Fran said, as Nike shoved her earphones in her ears and fled. Fran heard her door slam from across the road.

'Did you hear the news?' Beth asked. 'The schools may close at the end of this week.'

'Better and better,' David said. 'Tell me when Boris gets it. That's news I want to hear.'

April 2020

Undisturbed by people, felines padded along the night streets creating new territories. Two toms scattered the ground with brown fur. The next morning a bluebird collected the tufts for his polygamy of nests, then announced with a puff of his lemon-yellow chest that he has the best nests, the best territory, the most attractive proposition.

Fran's world withdrew to the colours from the window: the yellow and blue of an insistent bluebird, the concrete and metal fence of the primary school, unfurling leaves, a bush covered with butter-coloured flowers, the flap of a red scarf around an elderly lady's face.

'Off to the shops!' Fran called upstairs to Hector and the kids.

'Later!' Patricia called back. Thank God for the help of her teenage daughter.

That morning Fran had taken the opportunity of the milder weather to get out the ladder and scrub the windows. In the upstairs windows she spied Allan doing dinosaur impressions to entertain Jack and Patricia who tried to guess the names, or whether the four-legged creature snapping its jaws could be a carnivore, herbivore or omnivore. Peering into her life from outside Fran hurriedly cleaned her and Hector's bedroom window. Curtains drawn. Hector was cocooned in bed again today; his moods swung up, then down when he forgot to take his medication. More often the medication didn't work. In most cases, they only partially worked: the old placebo effect. Otherwise, thank the Lord, he was transformed, putting out the rubbish, sweeping and mopping the kitchen floor and showing the kids how to make paper fortune tellers: pick a number, one two three?; pick a day of the week, Wednesday?; on Wednesday you'll dance with Michael Jackson while drinking mushy peas up a straw.

The government had placed the UK on lockdown from the 23rd of March with the advice to stay at home and work from there if you could. Trips were reserved for essential food or medicine only, and for one hour of exercise a day – though apparently DIY stores were essential for people to stock up on home improvements as 'basic necessities'. Though, Fran supposed, some things required fixing around the house. Leaking swimming pool, that sort of thing. 'Protect yourself, others and the NHS … we're in this together' government messages kept bleating.

Lockdown gave Fran zilch to do but scour the house: breakfast, clean, lunch, clean, cook tea, collapse, repeat. Heather once said when they were nine to do a silly thing, a different motion each night (stick out your tongue or dance around the bedroom) so it all wouldn't appear the same as their lives flashed before their eyes. So sometimes, if no one was around, Fran gave a wink or stuck out her tongue. Just in case. Because that way she coaxed Heather closer, especially while doing things like polishing windows. When lockdown was over the first thing Fran would do is go and see Heather and work things out. This further separation due to COVID-19 meant she couldn't warn Heather about Brother Baneshanks, though if God would be solicitous to claim him … no, she shouldn't think such things. That mode of thinking led to a downward spiral of thoughts, and she was determined to be in a more positive place.

Wiping the squeegee blade dry with a rag and surveying the clear reflection of each pane of glass she had taken a moment, that morning, to be grateful for what she had. Satisfying, as always, to see the results of one's labours glinting in the intermittent sun. Her emotions were more varied than her daily routine: thankful to spend more time with the kids, yawning constantly for the same reason, skin crawling due to the world being out of control, unable to sleep for the same reason, watchful … for what she wasn't quite sure yet … not just for which days were easy and which were a challenge for Hector. She waited for a sign from God.

Pulling her granny trolley down their street, Fran evaded a skinny guy with multiple nose rings packing food into a car: packets of cereal and biscuits, soup tins, rice, tinned meat, instant mash.

He waved a hand. 'Hey. I ain't stole it. For the food bank, innit. I live there.' He hooked a thumb at the druggie house. 'We're neighbours.'

Unsure what to reply – other than 'you seem relaxed for a potential thief' – Fran fell back on her churchgoing and said, 'God bless.'

'Stay safe,' he replied, clambering into the window of the car. The door beneath it dented at a sharp elbow and rusted into its frame.

At the supermarket near Telford Road, Fran halted her trolley two metres behind the last person in the queue outside the building. She squinted at her watch. Leaving the kids with Hector on a down day was practically leaving them unsupervised. Patricia, though responsible for her age, technically should have been sixteen to babysit.

An old man craned over the shoulder of his grey jacket to glower at her feet, making Fran aware she'd been impatiently tapping her foot.

'Sorry.'

The line shuffled forward, two-metre rule, two-metre rule. A teenager in a black fleece motioned a couple forward.

As well as supporting 80% of the full-time employed's wages, a government grant scheme had been announced for freelance workers at the end of March; shortly after which Boris got the virus: #StayHomeSaveLives. Hector sourced this news from his da's rusting analogue radio. The downside being that it could only tune into Radio 2. Their electricity had resumed in April due to an energy grant scheme. Thank God, Fran sent a silent thank you firework into the heavens, for the Citizen's Advice Bureaux for that one.

It took forever to reach the front of the queue. 'Two can enter,' the teenager said to Fran. 'Gary' according to his name badge. 'Mind if I let the couple after you go?'

Fran nodded in defeat at Name Badge Gary. She wanted to say, 'No, I don't have the time, Gary. Aren't we supposed to be one person to a trolley?' But social convention dictated that she display a façade of co-operation. Through this period of self-isolation, God was testing her patience.

Not the only one ticked off by these extra procedures a man ignored the line and sprinted his trolley at Gary. 'Effing ding-dong,' the man swore in an Australian accent, forcing Gary to move. His nine-year-old daughter gave an apologetic smile as they passed. Gary motioned a security guard over. 'That guy skipped the queue.'

'I'd leave it for now. Will have a word as he's heading off.'

'Two metres distance, please,' Gary reminded Fran when it was her turn.

It had never been so easy to walk down a supermarket aisle without dodging people, or those people's kids, or staff stacking the shelves with the requirement to block your every step with discarded boxes and packaging. Today, the staff were politely giving customers right of way. This must be what the royal family experienced daily. Why, it was like shopping at somewhere posher like Waitrose. What had Nike been worried about?

Pulling her trolley outside half an hour ago Fran had found Nike frozen to the entrance next door. 'Can't do it.' Nike gripped the door frame as if trying to force herself out. 'I need to – We're out of milk.'

'I can get you some milk, if you like?'

'Cheese, pizza, butter. This should cover it.' Nike handed Fran a ten-pound note with her shopping list.

So now Fran negotiated the aisles pulling a granny trolley

for her shopping and pushing a supermarket trolley for Nike's. She had no hypothesis about how she was going to cart this all home by herself. At times like this, she missed the convenience of a car.

Shoppers foraged the aisles alone, politely maintaining distance, allowing people to go first on the corners of aisles. No one was fighting each other for toilet roll, or elbowing the elderly aside for egg boxes. Though some folk were a bit slack with the two-metre rule, forcing Fran to sidestep once or twice.

She headed for the cold milk display. The woman in front of her wore blue latex gloves and a white mask. Fran waited until she'd chosen a two-litre carton. Another woman struggled to pick up a tub of margarine with woollen mittens. A scarf was pulled up over her nose. Were these people sick or paranoid?

Mandy, a member of staff with cropped hair who Fran said hello to at the cheese counter and occasionally got a free sample from, socialised with a younger staff member. '—it's worse than any Christmas,' Mandy spotted Fran, 'Hi there. Still coming on Wednesday as usual?'

'Aye.'

The Australian, his daughter dutifully at his heels, wedged his trolley between them muttering to himself more than to them or her. 'I'll buy this, just in case; I'll buy that, just in case.' He placed tin after tin in his trolley. 'Hey you!' He gestured at Mandy. 'Flour?'

Mandy eyed up his purchases so far.

'You've kept stock back, haven't you?'

'Sir, I assure you we have only packets of crisps and Easter eggs in the back.'

He stomped away.

'He's stressed,' said his daughter, and followed him on lighter feet.

Poor kid, and she had forgotten Easter entirely. The kids would have to go without this year unless the eggs were on discount the week after.

Fran drove her shoulders down and tried to relax. Odd to be here in a sterilised bubble. The whole sensation of food shopping had changed. People's trainers squeaked on the hard flooring, the steady whoosh of the air conditioning filling the space not padded by music and advertisements for 20% off sweetcorn today. Oddly, the music is what Fran missed the most. This is what the world would be like if half the population died. A sobering thought. And she thought of herself as a pragmatic person, no wonder Nike, unnerved, crumbled under the tension of a change to the routine of day-to-day life.

Fran retreated from a row of tinned vegetables as a man tried to reach across her. Sure, so she wasn't that relaxed either about this change of circumstances.

On the way home, she remembered that tonight was the 'big clap', or whatever they called it, for NHS workers. She'd told the kids it was a silly Americanised ritual to clap at everything. She had them draw rainbows for the windows instead.

Fran pictured David's husband Alex in a mask, reassuring patients who struggled to breathe, comforting patients that flinched from his colouring. Yet, to make up for it, she imagined, he was staying at a luxury hotel that had opened its doors to healthcare workers. The kind with incredibly huge beds, soft sheets and a minibar, because it must be too risky with Baby Tau and Sam at home to sleep in his own bed. A pity for families up and down the country.

Fran counted rainbows people had stuck in windows as she walked, to distract her arms from the weight of her and Nike's shopping. At least it was sunny and not pouring it down like ten minutes ago between mixed-pepper skies, and she could rest the bulk of the weight on the granny trolley.

'Look Ma!' Allan said, as she left Nike's shopping outside and entered the house. 'A letter from Boris.'

'I hope he didn't mail it personally.'

'Ew, germs!'

He looked so serious Fran took the opportunity to lighten

the mood. 'I'm a germ and I'm going to get you!'

Fran chased a squealing, giggling, Allan through the house. Pat and Jack joined in the chase, until they captured and tickled him to the point of almost peeing himself; happiness is fleeting but it was also always around them if they chose to see it. This was God's message for her today.

∞∞∞

Fran became aware of a rattle at the door at the end of the month. Not the postman but Nancy with a box of jam jars in her gloved hands.

'Och!' Nancy said. 'You made me jump. I'm trying to sneak these onto people's doorsteps before they wake up.'

Fran picked up the jar with its dark purple contents. 'Blackcurrant?'

'Plum. From the tree in my garden.' A black and white circle rolled by Nancy's feet. 'I think this is your youngest's. It wouldn't sit on the step. I get confused whose is whose when they sail into my garden. For some reason, the kids don't knock to claim them.'

'They think you're a witch.' Fran covered her mouth. 'I'm sorry that slipped out.'

Nancy threw back her head and laughed. 'Happy to be the resident witch. Guess that makes sense with my brewing of jam and the job.' She caught Fran's puzzled look. 'I'm a doula. I have a card somewhere.' Nancy patted her pockets and extracted a card with a blue background and a full moon. It read tenmoonsbirthkeeper.com in the curve of the moon. 'I guess the moon imagery also feeds into my reputation as a witch.'

Nancy kicked the football between her feet. 'Now the hospitals won't let me in – and we're not even living in form-filling lockdown like in France or Chile – I feel quite bored.'

This neighbourhood wasn't so atrocious as Nancy invited her around, if she dared to shun lockdown, for a game of cards one night.

Half an hour later Nike knocked at the door wearing grey woollen mittens, with a blue, white and grey tartan scarf around her mouth matching the sky above them. Nike held out a knitted cable jumper in a mustard colour.

Her words were muffled. 'I decided to go for bright and cheerful because I think this will contrast with your pale skin. I hope it fits.' Nike waited, expectantly. Fran slipped off her acrylic jumper and pulled the mustard yellow over her head. Immersed in its cheerful glow. Cosy, warm. Its ribbed sleeves gently hugged her wrists preventing the draft getting in. If they weren't in self-isolation she could have hugged Nike. 'This is the first time I've felt so warm in ages. Thank you.'

As she weeded mid-morning during a rare burst of sun, Rob with the impeccable garden gave them a wave and beckoned them closer towards the hedge that separated the gardens. 'I'll be out with the hedge cutter today, want me to trim your hedges?'

'If you don't mind.'

'Nah, gives me a task to busy my hands. My wife will thank you. I am a nightmare retiree, apparently.' He headed off to ready his equipment with a whistle.

After lunch, the man whose junk and a rusting van hadn't moved for over a year was throwing the junk into the van which was later towed away.

The noisy chap fixing up number 40 put a note through the door that he would clean everyone's gutters unless they objected. Young sycamore saplings waved overhead. No objection here. Her ladder wasn't long enough to reach, besides that was a messy task. How consoling to have others doing the heavy lifting for once.

Adrianne, with her own cleaning business, called around late-afternoon, 'Fancy a cuppa?'

'You have tea?' Fran must have looked desperate, for after their tea and chat over Adrianne's wall she left a whole box of tea on Fran's doorstep.

Fran hugged herself: jam, footballs and tennis balls, knitting, gutter cleaning, gardening, socialising and free tea! The young married couple who fostered children sent the kids around to offer, from a safe distance, to weed neighbour's gardens. Genius idea to keep kids out of trouble. And a flier appeared through their letterbox announcing a 'socially distanced street party' tomorrow evening. Jan, from number 47, started delivering fliers of science experiments with household objects: from water xylophones, baking soda volcanos, light refraction utilising a water-filled plastic bottle to more elaborate ideas: rock weathering using a household freezer and clingfilm, a static electricity butterfly constructed from cardboard and tissue, and how penguins stay dry with crayons and water. Everyone's offerings made the street a nicer place to live in, but she was stuck what she could contribute.

The next evening, despite the unstoppered rain people huddled under their umbrellas, starring dismally at DJ Mabel – shocking that all this time the whole street had assumed her son was the one making all the noise – as she tried to rally enthusiasm with her rainbow-coloured hair. 'Yeah, come on! Dance guys!' She'd set up her deck outside under a tarpaulin, a laptop synced with a speaker to baffle them with electronic Hip-hop. A kind of street party but with everyone wearing coats in the downpour, isolated in their own gardens. With gloved hands around hot drinks.

Fran watched Jack tried to catch raindrops in his mouth, opened wide to the sky. Ah, the playfulness of youth.

'Got anything classical?' yelled the guy with a face of piercings who'd had a car full of food the day before.

DJ Mabel grinned. 'Ah, taking the piss man, ALA!'

'Is she religious?' Hector asked. 'She keeps shouting Allah.'

Patricia doubled over with her characteristic chortle. 'A.L.A.,' she said, when she'd caught her breath. 'Not Allah. It means great.'

'Who's thirsty for tunes?' asked DJ Mabel.

'Thirsty, I know this one,' Hector said. 'It means desperate. We're certainly desperate for enjoyable music.'

The kids didn't care, Jack and Allan now danced in a game of mirror with Adrianna and Leon's two girls further down the street; where one pair danced several moves and the other pair copied.

'Got any ABBA?' Fran called.

'I said enjoyable music.' Hector shuddered.

'Yeah, well, you and your rock.'

'ABBA is pop rock.'

'No, no, pop is totally different from rock, it's disco.'

'It isn't though, they are both a subgenre of rock,' Hector said.

'Geek.'

Hector cupped his hands around his mouth and called, 'Got any Proclaimers?' He let his hands drop. 'There's some rock for you.'

'Thanks, sweetie.'

In the meantime, Mabel had got an order from her son, who had heard Fran's request, and began to play ABBA.

Fran and Patricia danced disco-style, turn and clap, turn and clap, pointing their arms up and diagonally across, towards the floor.

DJ Mabel's entertainment made one day different from the rest. Their gutters, along with the rest of the streets', had been cleaned, the eager volunteer splattering mud across the windows that the fine mist wasn't shifting. Just after scrubbing them. Typical. She squinted along the street. Perhaps everyone's windows would need a sluicing? She'd get up early tomorrow and get to work before people were up and about.

The next day the Priest from Fran's church showed up at door. 'I've been calling members of the congregation, to check how everyone is and to ask for volunteers. I couldn't get through to your number, so I hope everything is all right?'

'Thank you for checking on us, Father.' Fran ran a hand through her muddy hair, her dirt splattered clothes would have to do. 'I was about to get in touch to ask if I could volunteer at the food bank. I could pack boxes?'

'That would be appreciated. Your presence has been missed.'

She closed the door, feeling … feeling what exactly? As if God had sent a hug to remind her there was a place here for her if she would only reach out to others and take it.

Chapter 19

May 2020

Heather strolled beneath the expansive trees, examining their buds. The leaf shape of each tree was derived, in part, from its folding patterns within these buds. Soon, when they unfurled their leaves into the humid air there would be some of her favourites: black-leaved plums, beech trees, and willow (amongst others).

Dean cemetery was her spot to rearrange her thoughts. Her correspondence modules would end in June, and she struggled with the writing assignments without Irvin's help. She tried to think what advice he would give: that's not an introduction, use subheadings, how does this connect to that?

And, of course, Fran came to mind. Particularly during lockdown. Heather wondered how Fran, Hector, Trisha, Allan and Jack were doing in general. It had been her habit for months to redirect her mind whenever it headed in Fran's direction. By consciously redirecting the thoughts each time and focusing on her studies Heather had reached a place of calm.

She steeled herself as she neared the rubbish bin in the cemetery that five-year-old Trish, had called a 'wee house'. It stood like a miniature wooden cabin with a large rectangle to deposit the rubbish in. She missed their Sunday roasts, the chatter, the games, the outings to Inverleith Park with the bikes. Stillness and solitude embraced her life during confinement. More time to study and mute her fears that without Irvin this educational enterprise would be a failure.

As she approached the rubbish bin she spotted a lad of

about six. He withdrew his arm from the bin and stared at her with impassive brown eyes. He slunked around the cemetery most days, keeping his distance from others. Odd, in the deserted cemetery, that he hanged out between the graves of the forgotten while tourists came to visit photographer David Octavius Hill, or Robert Anstruther Goodsir who died exploring the Arctic.

Unkept hair, she noted closer up, more than one jumper, and the laces of his trainers were rotten. He held a discarded sandwich wrapper in his hand, his other hand picked at the skin on his wrist, that was bruised and scabbed over in places.

Heather went to the nearest local grocery store and returned to the park. This time she caught him with his entire front half in the bin, bottom sticking out like a mallard up-ending in the water for plants or insects. He wiggled back out of the bin and moved away, feet crunching on the gravel. Heather took the sandwich packaging, unopened, and threw the whole thing into the bin. The lad's eyes widened, he dove forward and tore it open. Swallowing without chewing. Dropped a frond of lettuce and scooped that up too and stuffed it in his mouth with the rest.

'I'm Heather,' she said. Moving away to read the names of a few graves. Any direct questions might spook him. 'I like coming here to read the names. Can you read?'

The lad's thin upper lip wobbled from its downward tilt into a line, his almond-shaped eyes squinted at the grave nearest him. 'I forget.' His accent was Scottish, yet there were strange symbols on his jumper in a language she couldn't identify – Polish?

'What language is that?'

'Russian. It says: If your face looks skewed don't blame the mirror.' He gave a crooked smile.

'I did not expect such a translation. You Russian?'

'My da was, I'm … Scottish, or half-and-half, like my ma.'

She nodded. He hadn't volunteered a name but didn't seem put off by her questions.

'That's why I'm called Harry,' he said.

'I don't know the link between being half-Scottish and half-Russian and a Harry.'

'They go crazy for Harry Potter in Russia.'

'Do they? I've never been to Russia.'

Now what? You couldn't invite a boy to follow a stranger. Stranger Danger and all that. He might also be a thief working for a gang or … the lad coughed … a carrier of the virus. A terrorist even – a low possibility, sure. She needed to know more about him.

'Where does your ma come from in Russia?'

'Kaliningrad.'

Heather pictured the map, blankly.

'Next question,' he said, with an abrupt laugh, as if aware she'd no idea where Kaliningrad was, and willing to play the game.

'What's that?' he asked, spotting the smooth green stone between her finger and thumb.

'Sea glass.' She hadn't been aware of fiddling with it whilst walking through the cemetery. 'It reminds me of my maither.'

Maither is a source of shelter, food, comfort, a sharp hand, your reason for being. Is she the sort of mother who waltzes with you through the house and onto the street? The imaginative kind with her nose squished between the pages of a story? A sipper of floral Bali, burnt oolong, or iced tea?

'She loved the sea,' Heather said, 'and people. Our door was always open to neighbours and "friends". Temporary lodgers.'

Maither would break-off mid-sentence to point out the way the light caught the iridescent wings of an insect. She sang The Beatles every morning while preparing porridge.

'Bright scarves,' Harry said, wistfully. 'Large earrings. Home-made *piroshki*.'

Harry followed her through the cemetery, grazing with his eyes on the hunt for scraps.

'Macaroni cheese,' she threw out, guessing that the word he'd spoken was connected to food. 'With a scoop of mustard in the sauce.'

'Honey cake.'

The promise of food had an impact where the offer of plasters and antiseptic had not. 'I have a Dundee cake at home.'

'Cake?'

'It's a fruitcake with sliced almonds on the top.'

He left him to decide whether to trail after her or not.

When she glanced back at every crossing and corner he followed with his bouncing gait. In Irvin's, no, in her garden Harry wolfed down two slices of cake and reached for a third and fourth.

'Can I?' She waved a bandage, pointing at his scabby arm. 'I'll put my mask on.'

Before he loped off she said, 'You can come here whenever you need food.'

The thought crossed her mind that he might return with a gang of street rats. Yet Edinburgh wasn't Victorian London in Dickens' day.

He returned three days later, pulling the bell rope then running to the edge of the driveway. She brought out a Shepherd's pie and a spoon.

A couple of days later he ate an entire lasagne, with tatties, and carrots. A smidge closer to the house. Then, one day later, a bowl of spaghetti bolognaise.

'The last of my pasta,' she explained. 'The shops are low.'

His eyes widened at the word low. Food clearly was always on this growing lad's mind.

'Don't worry, the supermarket shelves aren't empty. My cupboards are full.'

His eyes peered into the house. 'You like books.'

She followed his gaze to the stack beside the shoe rack. 'The person who owned this house before me, Irvin, worshipped books. So, so I keep them around.'

She awkwardly clasped her hands. The story of the Crescent Moon Bear came to mind, where a Japanese lady fed a wild bear, moving closer each day until she was close enough to pull a hair from the crescent slash of fur on his chest. The truth was: it was calming to have the company.

'Like books?' she asked.

'I prefer ice cream.'

Heather laughed. 'Nice hint.' The sky began to splutter. 'Why don't we see what's in the freezer?' She walked inside leaving the door ajar. She heard him step inside, shuffle out of his shoes and close the door. Polite kid, though she'd known that from the first moment she'd seen him.

∞∞∞

At the end of April, Fran discovered that residential and nursing homes had the majority – or at least 50% – of virus-related deaths across the UK. Into May, the authorities and experts argued about the best way to approach the virus. Boris confused the hell out of people up and down the country while Nicola Sturgeon, in Scotland, calmly suggested continuing to self-isolate. Herd immunity had been ruled out because you don't rely on a deadly infectious agent to create an immune population. Yet Finland was doing fine, throwing COVID-19's infection rates into doubt. No doubt, Fran assumed, social media threads in every media there was currently displayed activities parents were doing to keep their children entertained. Fran was cut off from it all, without internet or television, and she was glad.

Her neighbours appeared uber-chatty in the street: people that had never more than given her a nod before, a sure sign that folk were going doolally. Even the sun called in sick.

Fran borrowed Nike's mobile from next door. Listening to the phone ringing on the other end: two rings, four rings, her heart fluttered like a fish on a line. She'd been putting off this call for too long. There had been a food bank sign when she'd gone for a smear test at the new Pennywell All Care Centre. It might be worth popping in later if they had anything after the coronavirus panic. The Food For All scheme at the church was off limits because it would be awkward if parents whose kids went to the same school, or the people from church she volunteered with, delivered food to her front door.

'Yes?' a male voice answered, abrupt.

'This is Fran Walker, calling about the rent that's due this month.'

'There a problem?'

'I've heard there's been a delay with my universal credit.' Fran wetted her lips. 'I wouldn't bother you if I didn't need to. They told me I would have it by now. System flooded due to the freelance workers affected by the virus. Thought it would be best to let you know right away and see if we could arrange a payment plan until the grant comes through?'

'When do they expect it to come through?'

'Next month.' Though they said the same last time.

'Don't worry about the rent this month. Pay me when the payment arrives.'

'Aye? Thanks, that's a relief.'

His gruff voice softened. 'You've been reliable tenants for years.'

'Terrific. Thanks. I'll keep you updated.'

The face of her ma's clock on the mantelpiece gave off a reproachful vibe, like Donna near the end when the bowel cancer stole her will to live. Since she had the phone, might as well give Heather a call too. She dialled the number, as they'd both had the same numbers since the explosion of 2G cellular networks in the nineties.

Two rings. Four rings. The tangled shoelaces of her mind constricted. Like a house thief, she wrapped up her grandma's rings and snuck out of the house on her Saturday off. 'Give you …', the young man had appraised. He had acne around his jawline and might as well be appraising her life. Fran shrugged, although there had been the hope she would give the rings to Patricia one day, they were only rings. And here they only cared about the weight of the gold. Her ma's clock she took to a specialist, but it turned out to be a cheap knock-off. Fran had hugged it on the bus, dusted its dust-free face and placed it back on the mantelpiece. This didn't feel like getting by, almost selling Ma's clock was like giving up.

'Thanks for the loan of the mobile, Nike.' Fran handed the phone back not trying to conceal her disappointment that Heather hadn't picked up. Nike nodded and shut the door with no attempt at conversation. Fran nodded her gratitude, grateful to have avoided the awkwardness. She could at least have checked in with Nike, that she was okay. The abruptly changing sky, from slate grey to turquoise, almost mocked them: 'you can't control me'.

Her daily horoscope didn't help. It suggested: there's something you think you need. It may be that you're craving colour and something dynamic. You might not need to shop at all.

She prayed, 'Lord Jesus, give us peace in our mind, body, soul and spirit. Help us find forgiveness.'

The word forgiveness stuck in Fran's soul. Her palms perspired. Her gut rattled like paper clips caught in the washing machine. Bonds weren't unbreakable or effortless, she'd been too complacent by assuming her and Heather would always be in each other's lives. There was no one to fill the gap, not the other mothers or fathers at school, not her own children, not her husband. Forgiveness. Such a part of her church teachings, yet her ability to put it into action had never been tested. Sure, she'd forgiven her mother. Forgiven Dougie, forgiven Scott, forgiven herself – who was most at blame.

Sod that, it had been Dougie who was most at fault.

Then again, if she still sought a person to blame she had not truly forgiven the events of the past, so she still had to work on absolution after all.

∞∞∞

After a certain number of married years, there were instances where you'd had to pause while making love to bring in the washing, or evade curious children, but the important thing was her and Hector's commitment to one another. And Hector had always been there for Fran during the grimmest times of her life – so had Heather for that matter.

'Remember when we built that shelter?' Fran asked one evening with the kids tucked into bed, curling into Hector's warmth. He'd taken a shower and smelled of patchouli and orange according to the shower gel.

'When *I did* you mean.'

'With help.'

The day after running away from home, during first break, Hector had Fran, Heather and Scott scour the woods behind the school for five long poles and sent them to find more. They messed about, hiding behind trees and playing Indians, during which time Hector had constructed a central pole with four radiating off it, like a tepee, lashed together with tree bark.

'This is so cool,' Scott said. He hopped from foot to foot, face glowing with excitement and the cold. Fran checked he had his gloves on and his scarf wound snug around his neck.

'We could just lean a few sticks against a tree,' Fran said.

Hector wiped his hands on his jeans and pushed his glasses up his nose as he said, 'I'm not going to let you sleep outside tonight without adequate protection.'

At lunchtime, Hector had them gather piles and piles of ferns as he tied sticks over the central tepee until the structure took on a tent shape Fran was more familiar with. Fortunately, they were hidden from sight where their activity did not raise curious looks from pupils or teachers. As they tied bundles of five ferns together and knotted them at one end from a ball of string, Hector rested thinner sticks horizontally across these vertical logs. It was beginning to look like a spider's web. Hector picked up one fern bundle at a time and wove them into the structure.

'Now it makes sense,' Heather said.

Fran would have laughed, only Hector's eyes were swollen and streaming.

'Hay fever. Don't worry about it,' he said.

'In February?' Scott asked.

'Fern spores,' Hector explained and showed the rest of them how to weave the ferns.

It took hours, taking up afternoon break and labouring in the dark long after the final rays of the sun vanished from between the trees. Until from the outside they had constructed a typical tent silhouette, decorated in green. Inside Hector placed two foldable beds his da wouldn't miss until the summer, and camping bags for Fran and Scott to sleep in. Heather topped those with blankets.

Fran flung her arms around Hector. 'You're a genius!'

Hector pushed back his glasses and sneezed. As he wiped his cheeks with a handkerchief, he said, 'Puts that Scout training to use.'

'You're not in the Scouts,' Heather said.

'Am too. My da's a Scouter.'

The wind shook sounds out of the night: tree trunks creaked, branches cracked, a car skidded. Unseen objects clattered near the school. Though a tree might fall on their head, Fran didn't worry about that because Hector had built this shelter with kind, solid hands; They all had. Scott and Fran were protected by their pals in a way Ma never managed; otherwise they'd be in their beds right now beneath cartoon duvets, listening to the wind buffeting the house. If she'd chosen them over Dougie.

Now, twenty-one years later she breathed in the smell of patchouli and orange wafting from the bedsheets and whispered, 'Listening to the wind that night, cosy inside, that was the moment I fell in love with you.'

'That was two years before we dated,' Hector said.

Aye, he was still hung up on Heather then. 'When I had my chance, I took it. This month is our wedding anniversary.'

His fingers explored her skin beneath the bedsheets, moving her pyjamas aside. It had been too long. As Hector let out a gasp of release the bedroom door swung open.

Allan sleepily rubbed his eyes. 'Ma, Da, I—' He gave them a quizzical look and scampered.

'Yikes, time for the conversation,' Hector joked.

'Last time I had to do it.'

'Well, I could hardly heart-to-heart about periods with my daughter.' Hector's ears were flushed from their lovemaking as she tucked his springy hair behind his ears.

Allan reappeared in the doorway holding Jack by the hand. 'Look what Ma and Da are doing!'

Jack grinned, 'Yahoo! Is it a boy or a girl?'

Fran burst out laughing as Hector's ears reddened further. 'I'll leave this one for you to explain, shall I?'

As well as the moment she fell in love building the shelter had also been an occasion Heather had been there for her, as she'd been there after Heather's ma died. She let Hector in, Heather too, and back then, like now, that was a rare risk for her to take. Now she considered how far she had come, building relationships with parents such as Dorota, David, and Nike, reconnecting to her church community and playing cards with one of the neighbours. The one thing missing in her life right now was Heather. While Hector stammered over an explanation as to why another brother or sister wasn't imminent, Fran pondered what Heather was doing at this moment …

∞ ∞ ∞

What is Fran doing at this moment? Heather asked herself, checking on Harry curled on the settee where he'd fallen asleep and she's placed a blanket over him. Her heart constricted like a hole puncher. Not knowing all of Harry's situation, her mind turned to her own. Mother is a word that conjures emotions through fragments of memory and smell and touch. Talc powder mixed with rose perfume as she cuddles close to tell a story after bath time. Heather had told Harry the folk tale of the Handless Maiden, channelling her maither's expressions into its telling.

'Due to a bargain made by her da, a lass loses her hands. They are chopped off in a spraying of blood! So said my maither. And the lass wanders the world in grief, living from the generosity of others before encountering a king who fashions her a pair of silver hands, like gleaming moonlight. Can you imagine having a pair of hands like that? While the king is called away to fight the lass – now the queen – has their child, and a message is sent to the king of the happy news. Unfortunately, the scroll is intercepted by the devil and is rewritten to say the child is half-human half-dog! The king responds with a compassionate message to his mother: please care for the child and my wife. This scroll is, again, intercepted and is changed to direct her to kill the queen and the child. The mother horrified by the message tells the woman to flee with her child. She flees to the forest and the wild lands beyond. Living in the forest, bringing up her child, nourishing her. And her hands grow back over time.'

Maither admired that the lass had saved her father, voluntary given her hands and wandered the world surviving adventures until reclaiming her fingers. Maither used to ask Heather, and sometimes Fran when she stayed over, 'Does the tale reflect powerlessness or finding one's strength?' Fran used to think the former, but in the act of earning back her hands Heather had believed in the maiden's redemption. Ironic considering who was the believer in God and horoscopes.

Heather had clung to the story after Maither's death. The mental abuse at the hands of her uncle – maltreatment that, paradoxically, Maither would have died to protect Heather from if she hadn't been already dead – could be compared to the lass's wandering across the earth to find a better place.

How envious Heather had first been that Fran still had a maither. Only later had they learnt that Donna wasn't the class of maither to cease a step-da's fists. Then Scott died. Neither of them should have had to live through those circumstances. Nor should Harry be here with her. He needed an adult to take care of him, like Aunt and Uncle with all their faults had taken her in, like Donna with all her faults after Scott's death had kicked Dougie out and taken Fran back home.

The deficient father is a fairy-tale staple; in contrast, Heather imagined her da through stories. She'd never met him and never would. 'Father unknown' on the birth certificate. Instead, Maither told her stories where mothers left widowers, such as *Snow White, Rose Red, or* were abusive to their children, as in *Hansel and Gretel* and *Donkey Skin.* Heather used to dream that her father secretly lived in a castle in the highlands because Maither had asked for a rose and her grandfather stopped to pluck one from a beast's garden who then demanded he stayed.

Roses were Maither's favourite flower. The signs of the sickness were there if she'd known what to look for: sudden breathlessness and fatigue, confusing her words, unsteady footing, she picked at her food.

Later Heather had learnt what cancer meant, and asked the school librarian more specific questions about lung cancer who mistakenly thinking it was a biology project gave her books with pictures.

Heather recalled visiting her maither's brother and his wife on one birthday. She only gleaned a fragment of their conversation as she returned from the bathroom to ask for another slice of birthday cake.

'You're wasting your life.'

'She *is* my life. We're going.' Maither pulled her outside, away from their neat flower beds, wearing a look like thorns had left several red lines on her palm.

'Why?' Heather asked, baffled about what had happened between eating a slice of cake and returning from the bathroom.

'They're suffocating.'

As they caught the bus, she explained further by saying, 'They're jealous that I have you.'

That night she told Heather a tale of a sister and mother who set a fire and locked the 'good' sister in a bathroom, and ran away so that the 'good' sister was suffocated to death. Looking back were those twisted tales a way of preparing her daughter for life? For the disappointments and betrayals she'd yet to face?

Heather's phone lit up with an unrecognised number. She left the person to leave a voicemail and considered trying Fran's number again. Lockdown had begun to ease and people were able to visit others' gardens. Concerned by the disconnected message on the phone line Heather had walked all the way to Pilton. Fran had been chatting to a person over a low hedge. Clearly, she was okay without her. Turning away. A heart of briars like those that climbed the side of her conservatory.

No, there was little point in calling Fran. She'd clearly disconnected her number to cut off all contact and moved on. So would she, even with a heart wreathed in brambles.

Part 4

Tearin' the tartan (a good blether)

Chapter 20

May 2020

A phased deconfinement began with Phase One on the 28th of May, all Scots were allowed to meet up with two people outside their own household, outdoors, with social distancing measures, within a five-mile radius.

Throughout a blustery May and June Fran volunteered where she could. She made up food parcels at the church hall, and walked number 43's three Labradors, one Border Collie and a Jack Russell, as Mirren had hurt her ankle.

A heatwave hit Edinburgh in June, people in Europe whose idea of a heatwave was forty degrees Celsius must be laughing at those in Scotland for flocking to the beach for twenty-five. By Phase Two on the 19th of June some businesses began to reopen, and folk were allowed to meet with people from up to two other households, outdoors and, as a bonus, with indoor toilet access.

Though this didn't stop large groups of teenagers, possibly students, congregating on The Meadows parkland, at the end of June. According to the paper this social gathering resulted in a 'mass brawl' and 'anti-social behaviour', but it wasn't just teenagers who left the grassy fields framed by trees covered in glass bottles, aluminium cans, plastic bags, and burnt holes in the grass from instant barbecues.

Nike waved at her across the waist-high hedge, 'You'd expect this sort of thing in France, but Scotland?'

'Aye,' Fran agreed. She had popped out to leave the bins on the curb: the laundry had to be taken in before those black clouds undid her afternoon chores, and the kid's tea had to be cooked. She tried to think of an excuse to avoid Nike's querulous mood if rescuing the drying laundry wasn't sufficient.

Nike thumped a fist against her jean-clad thigh. 'They'll create a second wave!'

Second-wave panic, more like, Fran grimaced; though at times she remained unsure of what to believe: was it rising cases or number of deaths that mattered?

'Huh, improbable,' a gruff voice contradicted Nike from the pavement. Jan, the retired teacher at number 47, had paused at the other side of the metal gate. 'Case counts are rising, but some of that is due to testing. And I wouldn't trust the mortality figures.'

'How come?' Fran asked.

'Inaccurate recording. Happened to a friend of mine. Died of a heart attack, and it was recorded as COVID-19.'

Nike's breathing undulated in waves, as Fran murmured some appropriate condolences Nike crossed her arms and dug her nails into her lean biceps. 'Rubbish, the US has peaks.'

'Appears that way.' Jan scratched her head. 'However, America is an expansive country. There were outbreaks in New York, for example in March, and first outbreaks have occurred subsequently in other areas. No point lumping the data together. Should be split.'

Jan's open debate revealed the type of educator she was. Fran would rather agree and avoid Nike right now, preferring a peaceful life. Yet even disputing Nike's ideas Jan's face was calm and as clear as a freshly buffed floor.

Nike puffed. 'Pah! Remember Italy?' she asked. 'Low hospital admissions lag behind, and by the time they rise here it will be too late to stop it.'

Jan gave a hint of a smile. 'Conversely, since hospital admissions are low, I'm not worried.'

'And ... and ... the British Medical Association, warned that measures were scant.'

'Since I used to be a science teacher, I know that scientists are overly cautious. The key is controlling the spread.'

'You don't have a son who's at risk!'

'True, our only son died in Afghan.' A look crossed Jan's face, Fran instantly put herself in this woman's shoes, her expression a reflection of what life could have been had he been alive today: family meals, and trips to the beach with grandchildren and plastic buckets and spaces. 'How's your wee one?' Jan asked Nike.

Nike wilted. Fred had been diagnosed with a rare genetic condition as a baby. Fran could never recall the name of it but he often skipped school. During lockdown, she had begun to appreciate how isolated Nike must feel as her son's home carer. Did they even have any support groups in Edinburgh for what her son had?

Jan cast a keek at her sturdy hiking boots. 'The trick is to protect at-risk groups, so that they basically don't catch the disease, and by the time they come out of their cocooning herd immunity's been achieved in the rest of the population.'

'Herd immunity,' Nike repeated. Fran vaguely recalled the term being used in March but not since the government made it clear that this would not be their approach. Were they scared of the backlash if it came across as if any member of the population was dispensable? That customarily didn't bother politicians if you took their policies at face value.

'The difficulty is,' Jan continued, 'we don't know if herd immunity is plausible, as this virus is related to the flu. Less deadly, actually.'

'It could mutate, like the Spanish Flu which wiped out more people than WW1,' said Nike.

'Wow, it did?' Fran asked.

Jan tilted her head. 'Nike's right, scientists are learning about new viruses all the time.'

Nike reacted with a half-smile half-grimace, which struck Fran as odd … unless Nike didn't know how to repudiate Jan's validation.

'Pandemics are a part of our history,' Jan said and hitched

and lowered her shoulders like being pulled by strings from above. 'Leprosy in the Middle Ages; the plague that killed off one third of the population; the Columbian exchange which introduced smallpox, measles and bubonic plague to the Caribbean. AIDS, SARS, I could keep going. They're numerous.'

If Hector had asked her how hearing a list of pandemics would make her feel, the word 'terrified' would have been at the top. And yet Jan's matter of fact explanation was soothing in its assurance, like receiving a hug after an abysmal day.

Jan said, 'I'm in the vulnerable population and I understand I can't expect the economy to screak to a halt. I'm too auld to be living under restrictions, that's my choice, dear, but you look after your wee one.'

As Nike waved a parting goodbye to Jan a splatter of rain hit her hand. 'Looks like the rain is starting.'

'My washing!' Fran dashed to the back of the house.

Chapter 21

July 2020

Heather wriggled her slippered feet, this was her home now. Not Irvin's or his family's. Heather's and Harry's place. The kitchen, the front room. Hers. The tea cupboard. The study with its beautiful desk overlooking the rainy garden surrounded by books, her books.

Despite missing Fran, Heather decided to move on. She considered learning the art of Bonsai cultivation. To take a wicker weaving class when restrictions eased. Learn how to construct stained glass, or speak another language. Watercolour. Conservation work. Anything to fill her days. Plus, she needed to write. Passing the second year of her Open University degree had required critical essays for each module. Shaping thoughts on paper, she'd found, had been like slipping into a well-loved pair of slippers.

Heather took up her notebook and pen. She'd been getting in her own way too long.

A floorboard creaked behind her, and reminded her of Harry's presence in her life. 'Is it snack time?' he asked.

'Not yet.'

He retreated. After he'd slept on the couch the first night, she'd offered him one of the spare bedrooms. She found it satisfying doing wee things, buying some clothes for him (all too long for his limbs, but never mind), placing a toothbrush and extra towel in the bathroom, planning meals for two people instead of one. Boy, did the lad adore to eat!

His simple happiness – gobbling his cereal and going for walks, returning to bite into a sandwich and running out again

– was infectious. Heather found a routine in the spaces in-between his apparitions and began to write.

'Write,' Irvin had ordered, as if the faint grey lines on the pages would open the gate to her imagination. If only they would shift and reveal a novel underneath. But the lines were printed tightropes wobbling with every press of the pen; one slip and their unfolding would dump her in a batch of white pulp. Death by pulping machine. The factory owner would wonder why every page of his new journals were decorated with tiny figures.

She and Fran's science teacher had shown them Horner's zoetrope; where a spun drum revealed the image of a horse appearing to gallop. Heather had imagined a trapped impression of a horse racing to be free.

Death by pulping machine. Flick the edges and the figure would scream.

Heather rubbed her eyes. The overcast day brought a gloom to everything, her body had moved slowly this morning since she'd woken.

She wanted to craft a story about two imperfect women and their lives. About their friendship but also a sociological narrative aware of its positioning in the world: what it captures and provides commentary on. Yet it didn't have to be overtly academic or based in the lives of the privileged because to write with a purpose, about what she found important, was to tell the story of her and Fran and how she wanted it to end.

So while, on the microscale, it's a story about two women and jealousy, followed by compassion; on a wider scale, it would be about how social structure and class determine people's lives. Not due to a lack of 'intelligence' or hard work. Due to the organisation of society: governmental policies, organisations and institutions, and any social group working to promote their self-interests against mutual ones.

Heather outlined a story around two women's breaking friendship caused by their petty jealousies, revealed via the events they lived through whilst estranged. The reconciliation was tricky … what could compel two people to reunite?

What, why and how? She wrote on a sheet of paper. What? Two close childhood friends are broken apart by circumstances and accumulated jealousy in their lives, can they find a way to reconcile their differences? Why? To show how it is thinkable to overcome jealousy. How? Through their relationship and memories of childhood. Key event: inheritance of a parrot and house leading to a social class disunity between them.

How to overcome jealousy? Heather squirmed in her seat. Before meeting Irvin, the most important thing to her was the friendship between her and Fran. This book, she hoped, was a technique to decipher how to put past jealousies aside.

Heather kneaded her chest, tight beneath her Merino knitwear. A break would be worthwhile. And Harry was loitering behind her again. They shared a hazelnut and chocolate wafer in the kitchen with a hot chocolate and then Heather returned to the desk, stifling a cough.

What do I want to say? What characters do I want to tell it? She paced adjacent to the desk, the notebook, the pen. She hadn't a clue. Then her eye fell on *My Brilliant Friend* by Elena Ferrante. Write what you know. She picked up the pen: Fran is the kind of friend who becomes your whole life and takes it from you.

By the end of the day, Heather had made some progress, though her cough had worsened until the point where breathing was arduous. The world came and went for a while. The desk. Harry's concerned face. Being strapped into a wheeled stretcher. Harry being told he couldn't go with her in the ambulance, an overly white room, an oxygen mask, Fran smoking a ciggie. Heather reached for her. 'Fran,' she called, 'Fran?'

∞∞∞

Jan had been right: there were initial outbreaks in parts of the US in July that had avoided the virus, like in Florida, and therefore these were not a second wave. The weeks blurred together. Between jobs and church work, Fran couldn't find the time to go to Heather's. It wasn't as if she hadn't tried calling. Then the lockdown happened mid-March. So, it wasn't until July under lifting restrictions that she forced her feet in the direction of Heather's place.

Last night, Fran had prodded Hector who had growled like a Grizzly woken from hibernation.

'Can I trust you to pick the kid's up from school?'

'Mm-hmm?'

'School. Kids.'

'Pick kids up, got it.' He collapsed back into slumber. What was he doing that tired him out more than her day spent cleaning up after people at the art college, and packing carrier bags at the food bank to come home and tidy up after her family?

At Heather's house the next afternoon all the curtains were open, lights off – in spite of the overcast sky. Fran keeked through the letterbox. Junk mail filled the letter cage.

'I know your secret!' she yelled through its brass mouth.

Fran cocked her head; no sounds, that she could detect, from the parrot either. Heather wasn't here. *Where has she gone?* Travelling around the world with all that cash, letting me worry on purpose. Serve her right if she was trapped in quarantine in Santiago.

Shivering, Fran lit a ciggie and tapped a fingernail against the brass bell so it swung on its cord.

Mucky footprints soiled the doorstep: a smaller shoe-size than Heather's.

At least here Fran didn't need to hide from the kids by cranking open the bathroom window and spraying Febreze. Chemical products might be carcinogenic but so were ciggies. Ma had smoked all her life before bowel cancer claimed her, similar to Uncle Fraser and his ruptured intestines. It didn't seem feasible that nicotine and the bowel cancer could be related. Giving up is a preventable measure, they said, Ma's doctors, Fran's doctor too. Unfortunate that smoking felt slipping-into-a-warm-bath … gratifying …

Fran hovered the ciggie over her inner forearm, then brushed away the end of the ash where it fell. She could never bear to do it. One late afternoon when Scott was ten and she was sixteen (not long before they ran away) Dougie had dragged Scot into the bathroom by his hair, and bowled him back into the living room with a burn on his inner arm.

'Don't have me called in again.' Dougie growled, in a half-decent imitation of a wildcat, and stalked out.

Scott curled in a ball beside the settee. Fran curled up next to him.

'A teacher asked who had trod on my lunch,' Scott said. Fran understood, she'd pretended not to see Dougie tread on Scott's tuna sandwich that morning. It was Friday and he'd been drinking all week. 'I panicked and pointed to Ted, who said I was lying. They tried to call Ma, but got Dougie.' A tear ran down his face. Jack reminded her of Scott because he was such a sensitive lad. The same fear clenched in her ribs for him, growing up in this world.

Fran recoiled as a pigeon flapped overhead, releasing one white feather-like a sign from God. Mayhap it was Scott watching over her.

The bird reminded Fran that Heather liked to think of pigeons as escapees from amateur pigeon keepers; revolutionaries (in a sense) who got tired of being driven away from home only to return, and thus rebelled and decided to flock it on their own.

Fran stroked the soft, waxy feather and practised her signature smoke circles. She should give it up. Hector didn't smoke. He didn't mind the smoke either: largely worried about her health. And it wasn't something she wanted for their kids.

Fran bent down and hollered into the letterbox, 'Liar!'

She stubbed out the ciggie in the middle of Heather's door, attempted to scrawl the word liar though it only left a broad smudge. She tutted, leaving the stub where it fell as a calling card for Heather to find, and caught the bus back home.

Her daily horoscope had referred to her faith this morning: Remember that others have faith in you, and remember where you place your faith in turn. She'd chuckled, *nice try, God. I'm not ready yet to forgive either you or Heather.*

She couldn't wait to get her work shoes off; however, Nike waved across the low hedge as she slotted the key into the door. Fran sped up, not in the mood for another hypochondriac rant, but tripped over a pair of shoes on the threshold. Drat.

'Fran!' Nike called. 'I have the boys, don't worry!'

Why would Nike have the boys? Fran had told Hector to pick them up today, so that she could go see Heather.

'Come have a coffee,' Nike said, and left the door open behind her. Fran followed, at her own pace, still confused about why their neighbour would be watching Allan and Jack.

Jack and Allan and Nike's son, Fred, were working on a jigsaw puzzle in the middle of the lounge. Nike had a turquoise corner settee and the boys sat on its fabric cushions and leaned over a glass-topped table.

'Did Hector ask you …?'

Nike emerged from the kitchen with two mugs of coffee in hand. 'The boys will be finished with their puzzle soon.'

Fran sat, careful not to spill her drink, which wasn't an issue at home with their wipeable settee. 'Thanks for collecting them.'

Nike flapped a hand. 'I understand things haven't been easy lately. Well, that's being a parent, isn't it?'

The boys had constructed the outer edges of the jigsaw and were working their way in towards the centre of a cityscape.

'Hector would normally tell me, but our phone isn't working.' Fran tentatively sipped the black liquid, one too many sugars, the additional sweetness was comforting. She wasn't a fan of coffee which, despite what other cultures might think, was a common British staple since tea plantations devastated by a fungal disease in the 1800s and an alternative drink was needed to fill the gap.

Fran still didn't understand what happened. Her stomach curmurred, noisily. Shame there weren't some biscuits.

Nike pulled out a draw and a box of shortbread rounds. 'I thought it best that I bring them here. Everyone knows we're neighbours; otherwise, Miss Reed would have had to stay with them until someone came. Your phone number didn't work. She has much to organise before February half-term, so I offered to help.'

'Hector didn't show?'

'Perhaps he got confused with the days. It's hard to keep track, isn't it?'

Fran shoved a biscuit in her mouth before she used jibes against her hubby that she didn't want the whole playground to know about.

'And since we also go to the same church ...'

Fran nodded and dunked a biscuit. What she wanted right now was to scream and hurl things at Hector, but that wouldn't help either of them. The corner of Fran's eyes prickled. Things *would* be fine. They qualified for universal credit now which would cover their rent in four weeks. Hector, generally speaking, filled that place in her life and asked those sorts of questions – how are you feeling?, has anything had happened at work? – yet, having thought that, he hadn't been himself for a long time, which left her to carry their recent burdens alone. Not that she'd ever think of the kids that way – as a burden. They were the joy in her life. It was the financial side of things that was drowning her.

'It's taxing,' Nike said. She sighed. 'I miss Robert when he's overseas.'

No wonder she was always afeart, quick to rattle; strained relations between countries and Robert in the middle of it. Fran vaguely remembered Hector ranting about dissent between Iraq and the US.

Nike checked the boys; engrossed in pieces of sky. 'All it takes is mentioning "foreign terrorist organisation" and they think they can do what they want.'

'Hector follows this stuff, me less.' Fran wondered about discussing this in front of the children, but they heard worse at school. Fran asked, 'How did the US get from the attack to Trump threatening Iranian cultural sites and then backtracking?'

'It was a defensive strategy' – Nike dipped a biscuit in her tea – 'against a lash back from Iraq about US actions.'

Fran laced her eyebrows together. The story, if she'd paid attention to Hector correctly, was … Ah, she couldn't remember. Clearly, she hadn't been paying attention.

Nike added, 'The important thing to know is that attacking cultural sites would be regarded as a war crime. Trump had to backdown. Makes you wonder who the real terrorists are – though don't repeat that to my husband. Even if the aggression in Baghdad is aimed at America, I can't help but feel we're in the middle.'

Fred asked his ma for some shortbread. Nike looked to Fran for permission before offering some to her boys as well.

Nike's words rang a bell with Fran. Hector had told her that the UK had an international relationship with Iraq, as it did with the US. The US were working with Iraq until the country asked them to withdraw their troops. Trump came back hard with his refusal, threatening sanctions against Iraq if his troops were forced out.

'What's the situation now?' Fran asked.

'Escalating tensions. That's why I'm worried for Robert.' Nike put down her mug, leaned on one hand and supported the elbow of that arm by the other hand, playing a lonely game of Twister.

'Robert's in Iraq?'

'He's training Iraqi soldiers. The UK isn't fighting there or providing military support in that sense. Only with training and equipment.'

Meaning guns … Fran wrinkled her nose.

'You disapprove?'

Fran eyeballed the boys. 'I disapprove of any actions by any armies that place families at risk.'

'Robert wants to keep our families safe.'

'I get that.' She didn't want to start an argument over the pointlessness of war. It was awkward enough wearing a white poppy every Remembrance Day knowing a military man lived next door.

Fran watched the boys cooperatively sorting the jigsaw pieces and slotting them into place. Any of them might later want to join the army and take up a more practical career path over studying for four years at university. For many working-class lads that was their only option. The red poppies supported only the British Armed Forces, while the white ones commemorated the millions made sick or homeless by war, the families and communities torn apart, and those killed or imprisoned for refusing to fight and for resisting war. Lads like these who might one day fight and die for their country, or take a stand against violence.

Back home, Fran set to cooking tea.

'Beans on toast again?' Allan asked.

'Tomorrow you'll be saying "cheese on toast again".' Jack joked.

'Or Spaghetti on toast again,' Patricia said.

'Can I have some squash?' Jack asked, holding out his glass of water.

'There's none left, sweetie.'

'That's okay, Ma. Water is healthy for you.'

Fran's stomach contorted, not from hunger this time; she constantly tried to ignore her demanding belly. The kids came first.

'Time to say grace,' she said, surprising Patricia whose fork was halfway to her mouth, and surprising herself given her current inconsistencies with ritual and faith. Old habits? Or was she ready to forgive and accept the lessons he was trying to teach her?

Chapter 22

August 2020

Fran tracked the scuffed smears from the front step to the pile of shoes beside the stairs, and crumpled the civil court letter in her balled fist. While she'd disinfected every surface, inside and out, during confinement, she'd abandoned her cleaning since returning to work and volunteering for the church. Without Hector's assistance the house was reverting to its pre-evolutionary state: dust lingered on every surface; balls of hair trundled at the bottom of the bed; mould spores expanded around the bathtub; ants invaded the kitchen; moss competed with Jack's cress head on the damp windowsill, and now soil made snail-like trails along the hallway.

Yet, Fran smiled. Consoled after crumpling the civil court notification letter. They'd set the hearing date for February 2022, 18 months in advance. Fran gave a half-amused yap. Hector, pray to God, would have a job by then – or they'd have their universal credit sorted. Life might even be back to normal on a global scale. Or, at least, what the Guardian-reading mums at school termed the 'new normal'.

Fran stifled a belch. She'd been gassy lately, acid churning in her stomach, a side effect of her limited diet. Stepping forward she found another letter stuck with chewing gum to her shoe; urgh!, thanks to whatever buggers had spat it on the street.

From the HMRC from the official stamp on the envelope. The contents notified her of her benefit claim – good news! – with information about how her emergency advance issued in April would be deducted on a monthly basis. What advance? Her smile fled. She'd applied but not received anything. There was a free number to call which would have been useful if she had a phone. She didn't fancy asking Nike again since the embarrassment of Hector forgetting the kids.

'Is that a final notice bill?' Hector asked, from the stairs.

Fran almost threw her house keys in the air. She stuffed the official-looking envelope into her cardigan pocket, torn down one seam so the paper poked through. No point burdening him with additional pressure.

He wavered on the top step, his face pale as a mosquito's wing above his sombre dressing gown.

'It's nothing. How did the visit to the surgery go? Great to see you on your feet.'

'Sure, that's why you jumped like a cat with zero lives left.' He shambled into the lounge towards the kitchen.

Fran almost screamed with frustration, tugging at the top of her trousers which pressed against her gassy, swollen belly. The letter outlined the pitiful offering due to go into her account this week. She bit down on her fist, glad she could hear the kids playing Cowboys and Indians upstairs, their feet beating a quirky rhythm against the floorboards.

There was a knock on the door. Fran listened in case it had been accidental or they would, hopefully, go away. Another round of taps. Fran pasted a smile to her face and flattened the second letter to join the first in her pocket with a determined slap.

Beth, her corn-coloured hair like a deflated balloon, an apology on her face, said, 'I wasn't able to reach you by phone.'

'Broken,' Fran said, to avoid having to explain their financial situation. What did the woman want *now*? Between voluntary work, two jobs, Hector and the kids, all free babysitting services were off limits.

'I wondered if the kids would like to come around mine for regular sleepovers in the summer hols?'

Fran struggled to reply. She wanted to say, 'Sure, that would be useful for the last two weeks of the holidays. Where were you earlier?' Instead, she said, 'My prayers have been answered.

Can you take them now?' Fran smiled as she asked.

Beth laughed. 'Things are steady. It's the least I can do for your support over this year. Sorry, it wasn't sooner. Really, sorry. It's been a hard year, hasn't it?'

Fran's breath shallowed, and her sinuses ached as she fought back tears and restrained herself from allowing Beth to see her moment of weakness. Nike's curtains were twitching.

Beth refrained from asking if Fran was okay, and arranged a date and time when she could take the kids. 'So you and Hector can have some alone time.'

Fran thanked her, shut the door, and pinched the bridge of her nose to force her tears to retreat. Memories of previous times Hector had danced or chased the kids through these rooms flickered in her head. A sharp contrast to his mummified form today, newly awaken and unsteady on its feet. The air in the house smelled stale. Fran began to open all the windows.

She walked into the kitchen fifteen minutes later, feeling calmer.

Hector idled by the kettle. 'The nurse took a blood sample. They'll call with the results.'

'Our phone's out of order,' she reminded him. It wasn't the only dead object round here: the cactus plant on the top of the fridge – that Jack had glued googly eyes onto – was discoloured, droopy and had a foul smell.

'Fuck it, Fran. I can go to the surgery in person.'

'Okay, no need to snap.' She watched him pour the kettle in shaky, hesitant movements. She'd found him in the bathroom three days ago, knelt beside the toilet. 'I'm pure done in,' Hector had said.

'You're out your face.' If there had been a bottle of vodka on the linoleum, she'd have kicked it.

'Nah,' he'd said. 'No more dosh for booze. No more bottles. I've worked myself through the Christmas and birthday gifts we didn't want. The Armagnac wasn't that dreadful after those strange botanical liqueurs.' He had clutched the toilet rim.

'Fucking, Armagnac.'

'Sure, after that bottle of Scotch my ma bought you.'

'I've kept that for years. Time it was drunk.'

His words returned her in an instant to their last Christmas with Donna, insisting they pull cheap crackers and wear the hats. This Christmas Fran hadn't bought crackers.

'All that Scotch in one night?' she had asked.

He had kneaded his forehead. 'Don't Fran, don't. My head's loupin'. I've already thrown up once today.'

'You vomited?' She had tested his forehead with the back of her hand: it hadn't felt feverish. 'Let's get you a doctor's appointment.'

'You want to claim extra benefits, aye?' Hector asked.

'No, to get you checked out. Okay?'

'Fine, but it will be a waste of the doc's time.' He folded over the toilet with a groan.

A Robin tweeted from the sunny garden, the house the warmest it had been in a long time. Yet Fran fretted that the results they waited on might confirm liver poisoning from all the gifted schnapps, whisky, beer, vodka, he'd worked his way through this winter. Now wasn't the time to show him the official legal letter or the one from the HMRC. Rent arrears letters had arrived each month over the winter. The landlord wasn't giving them any leeway now. Emergency legislation had been enacted mid-March preventing landlords evicting tenants who couldn't pay the rent. Now the crisis was over, in that people were gradually going back to work and schools were due to reopen mid-August, he wanted the rent or his property back. At least he couldn't evict them until after the court date. She'd filled out council forms, in secret at the local library, so they were on the list waiting for social housing. But the woman had informed her, 'To be brutally honest the wait list is three to five years. Got anyone you can stay with?'

Ma had lived in a studio council flat that had been reassigned after her hospitalisation. Hector's parents were dead. And Heather who had moved into an enormous house – Irvin

Flaubert's house – the span of the wooden floorboards, that fancy kitchen, and the leafy garden? If Heather had thought to ask, Fran would have thrown coffee grounds in her eyes for suggesting they needed charity to put a roof over their kid's heads. Or at least fantasied about it, to rein in the violent tendencies she'd 'inherited' from her temporary step-da. She had always been able to feed and clothe her own kid's … until now. It was bloody unfair.

A click of high heels approached; Fran had let the front door hang open after Beth's visit to let in the warm air.

'Morning, Mrs Reid? I'm Brenda Brown from Social Care Direct.'

'What you here for?'

'I sent a letter to arrange an assessment meeting?'

'I'm here, ain't I?' Shit, she'd forgotten.

'I can understand your concern, ours is a misunderstood job. Let me reassure you I've come round to check on the kids. We're here to assess what help you might need due to illness, frailty, disability or concerns about safety.'

Gunshots and Indian war cries floated down the stairs.

'I'm a capable ma. I'm not a druggy or an alcoholic taking advantage of child benefits. It's a sore fight for half a loaf, to provide for my kids while my husband's unemployed.'

'Let me be clearer, this isn't a judgement on your parenting skills, or your financial situation. This is an assessment meeting to see if we can provide support. From what I understand your children are fortunate you've been working hard for them.'

Fran slumped. 'I'm useless. There's no way to make any extra money on top of all the hours I'm working.'

'Let's gather our wool and see what can be done. There's an assessment form to complete, which I will give you a copy of.'

'Then what?'

'We consider how we can help and discuss your options with you. For example, you might qualify for housing benefit to help pay rent, and we can help you complete the application.'

'Do you know anything about this?' Fran held out the HMRC letter.

Brenda glanced over the contents. 'I'm not a financial adviser, the Citizen's Advice Bureaux might be better placed to help you.'

'It's just, they say I'm to pay money back, which would be fine if I'd received any.'

Brenda's eyebrows arched. 'Did you provide personal information to anyone over the phone?' she asked.

'Yes.'

'Bank details?'

'Yes.'

'I don't want to alarm you, but that may have been a fraud call. HMRC never ask for such information on the phone, just online.'

'I was getting help from a chap about the online application. We don't have internet.'

'Did you call him, or did he call you?'

'He called. Shit.' Fran rested her head in her hands. 'Identity theft. I didn't even consider it.'

Summer days flipped by like damp pancakes, and soon it was the start of the school year. Thankfully, the start of the term was unaffected by the citywide lockdown that hit Aberdeen at the start of August, and a localised confinement in Glasgow. The school parent council had decided to allow parents onto the playground because it held more space than the pavements for social distancing, and there had been concerns that not all parents would wear masks. Fran didn't own a mask; she used a scarf when she needed to enter a shop. She was counting the months. One. Two. Three. No, that couldn't be right ...

Sylvia approached. 'David is gay!' Sylvia spat into Fran's face. Not a queen bee then but a Dilophosaurus – though Allan would protest such a comparison because he could cite more about dinosaurs than Jurassic Park director Steven Spielberg. Sylvia must have run out of people to tell if she deemed to acknowledge Fran's presence.

'Gay?' Dorota asked.

Laure merely exhaled in response to Sylvia's interruption.

Fran took a step away from Sylvia to get her out of her face.

'Alex isn't *a she*, she's *a he*. How could we have any idea?' Sylvia asked. 'I guess it could be worse these days with teenagers defining themselves as transgender. Homosexual now seems rather commonplace.'

Had she seriously said that? Fran shamefully recognised her own, old opinions in Sylvia's prejudices.

Connecting to Laure and Dorota – and David and Alex, for that matter – had shifted the way Fran appreciated Scottishness and its capital. A photographic study of Edinburgh Castle under sun or snow failed to capture the city because it neglected the people. The international community might have been outnumbered by rowan, sweet chestnut, whitebeam, walnut and lime but developed numerous relationships a map of the city couldn't show. Some connections were obvious, such as a mum-to-be with her baby bump or a grandparent squeezing a pudgy hand. Other roots were subtle: fifth-, third-, first-generation, who could auspicate on appearances? And throughout the country's narrative of Celtic tribes, Romans, Anglo-Saxons, Vikings, slavery and immigration, Scotland couldn't dub herself, by a touching of a sword to a shoulder, separate from the world. Scottishness had never been an accent or a birthright. She understood now when Heather had said Scottishness was 'a multi-ethnic hybrid of a future to come'. Fran's face heated as she recalled her response, at the time, 'Why do we need more scrounging migrants?' She'd had no idea that she'd more in common with these so-called migrants, like Dorota and Laure, than Sylvia and her privileged life choices.

Fran regarded Sylvia as the stay-at-home mum awaited her response. What lifestyle are you lucky enough to be born into to get a honeyed, if poisonous, voice like that: a loving ma and da, financial security, a roof over your head, bountiful food on the table? The opportunities others did not get. Due to class.

'I—' Fran began, feeling her back teeth clunk as she thought better of replying. Sylvia expected Fran to agree as if they could both pay their energy bills and feed their kids.

Laure asked Dorota, 'I thought Scotland was a liberal country?'

'Usually.' Dorota gave Sylvia a glare, given her brother's situation and her beliefs on that score.

'We can all admit it between us, can't we ladies, that taking it up the arse is disgusting.'

'Sylvia, that's inappropriate prattle,' Miss Reed's voice cut through their conversation.

'Well, I – Can't take an interest in one's community these days!' Sylvia stormed off.

Fran gave Dorota and Laure an awkward smile – though it was hardly her place to apologise for the other Scottish mums in the playground.

Besides, she had a nagging intuition ... She left Allan and Jack with Hector to pop to the Pharmacy. One reason she'd been so fatigued over the past months could be due to lack of iron, may be caused by her diet. More likely ... because she couldn't remember the date of her last period ... shit, this would be bad timing.

She paced over the arrows on the floor, though the small corner shop wasn't busy, so no one shouted as she walked the wrong way along the aisles marked by black arrows underfoot. It was only at the counter when she thought to ask for a pregnancy kit that the plastic shielding between her and the young blonde lady at the counter caught her attention. Self-consciously, Fran pulled up the scarf she'd forgotten to tug over her face. As she requested a pregnancy kit her eyes flickered to the yellow and black tape across the public toilet.

'Your loo's closed?'

'Yes, sorry. But the supermarket over the road has one open.'

Finding oneself peeing on a stick on the wrong side of forty – only because she'd been there three times already with Patricia, Allan and Jack – made her feel like a chicken with a knife; chickens had no use for cutlery. Sure, things happen when they aren't supposed to … yet what could she do? Fran recalled the first split condom in eight years. The first sex between them for months.

She stared at the result: an unexpected gift from God.

When she'd asked for an answer … well, He'd a sense of humour this year. There go the business plans. Unlikely with three kids anyhow. Hector redundant. Their financial situation and the further economic fears with it.

Bullshit, Hector refuted the government's spin on yet another recession (that COVID-19 equalled an economic downturn) because the banks had been rigging the system for years, creating too much currency so that the price of gold no longer reflected its own worth. All those films, music and consumer slogans: you can be what you want to be bullshit, when life's nothing but a series of black sheep with the rich reaping the wool.

As she stood, the reaction in her cracking knees was as strong as though called and told 'Hector's dead'. Fran grabbed onto the hand drier. Letting its weight solidify her.

Familiar objects around her lost form. The spaces between things growing wider revealed the nothingness of the everythingness beneath. She sat on a toilet and waited until her vision cleared. It was at times like this she immediately thought of telling Heather. Fran rocked herself forwards and back. Life starting to resume itself in many ways. This was the last thing they needed, the last thing she needed.

Chapter 23

October 2020

She managed to keep her pregnancy secret as throughout September her baby bump, not gas after all, was just about concealable beneath baggy clothing. The cold turn in the weather aided the switch into large jumpers. Restrictions were reintroduced in Scotland near the end of the month, no more house calls, while in England Johnson emphasised *hands, face, space.*

Dorota suggested they go for walks instead of sitting indoors, her eyes skimmed Fran's face frequently for what she was trying to hide, but she didn't ask about the pregnancy.

However, Fran could not hide the court letter from Hector. She had to prepare him to either get his butt moving and find a job or to move out whenever the court proceedings were complete, which might not be until well into next year.

'You're lying,' Hector said. Fran couldn't understand his denial. This was hardly a practical joke.

The hum of the fridge filled his silence.

Steam fogged his glasses. He'd poured her a three o'clock mug, even though the teabags had been dunked to death and came out like pond water. She had hidden the box the neighbour had given her because Hector had a habit of eating or using everything up without giving her a second thought. She tried to blame his depression instead of him. A year ago such behaviour would have been uncharacteristic.

'They will kick us out, won't they?' His voice slowed, the way a watering can drips when emptied out. 'Because ... I ... failed.'

'Don't start. The responsibility ain't solely yours. Man of the house and all that crap. We're in this together.' As worn as the bar of soap beside the sink; it took effort, as if her limbs were weighted, to reach out and squeeze his shoulder, only for him to shrug off the gesture. Why did she bother?

'I was the one that lost my job, and couldn't get another one. It's my fault if our kids become homeless.'

'Shut it!' She wanted to fling scalding water from the kettle in his face to prompt a reaction from him other than defeat. She clutched the mug to her chest to feel its warmth. 'Stop feeling sorry for yourself all the time.'

'You're being selfish, Fran. It's hard. Can't you understand?'

Hard. For him? It was he who understood nothing. Saw nothing. Everything she'd done since his lay-off had been for her family. How dare he. She fought her anger, though it wasn't like she could flick the switch off like she could on a kettle.

'It would be best if I go.' The cutlery draw rattled as he seized a spoon. They were all out. She had even scraped the hardened bits of old sugar encrusted at the bottom of the sugar container. Grains that would dissolve into the stained mugs like their unravelling marriage – how could he calmly make tea when their marriage was falling apart?

Fran spluttered. 'Leave me to deal with this alone and I won't take you back.'

'You're not alone, you have Heather.'

'Heather isn't here,' Fran heard her voice hitch.

'For Christ's sake,' he said, 'make it up with her.'

Fran opened and then slammed closed the fridge door, forgetting what she wanted. 'She hasn't called, hasn't been around, doesn't give a damn about us!'

'You know that ain't true, Fran. She's hurting, you're both hurt.'

He held out her watery mug of tea to her.

Fran squeezed back her tears. 'I know what this is. You think you made the wrong choice between us: me and Heather.'

His eyes widened. 'Fran. I never.'

Of course. She'd uncovered the truth. Because here he was

defending Heather over his own wife.

'Go to your Heather,' she said. 'Get out.'

'I won't do that. This is ridiculous.'

'Get, out. I don't want you here. I'm sick of it. I'm having to do everything alone while you're – get out! I can't deal with you anymore. I can't bear to see your face.' She turned towards the clock on the kitchen wall to hide her wobbling features from his worried gaze. 'Away and boil your head,' she added.

The weight of all those years trying to be the best wife she could be so that he wouldn't be tempted to regret his decision between his two best pals, hit her with a force that turned her bones to steel. Because if it wasn't that strong she would crumble. The burden would be too much: life without Hector. A life she was practically living now. What difference did it make if he physically left?

'Fran …' His fingers grazed her hunched back.

'Go away!'

'Right, I'm going for a walk.' He gulped down his hot water and removed the dressing gown. He wore a worn, grey trackie underneath. He'd get wet wearing that as the lazy melody of rain against glass accompanying hadn't eased all day – that always happened when she had a day off. The part of her that still saw her husband wanted to remind him to take a coat; the other part of her didn't care if he caught the flu from being out in the damp air.

'Don't be back,' she said. 'I'll have the locks changed before you do.'

'How could you afford it?' he asked. If it was a joke it was a lousy one.

He placed his mug in the kitchen sink for once, and grabbed his raincoat.

She fell to her knees on the baltic linoleum, palms caressing the baby. 'Heavenly Father, I give you all praise and adoration, because your word is ever true. I give you thanks because no weapon formed against this marriage will stand. No weapon, no weapon … please, no weapon … Lord heal each one of our emotional wounds and cause our hearts to be drawn towards each other in Jesus' name. Amen, amen.'

She pushed herself to her feet to tackle the overflowing laundry basket; a good scrub of the kitchen and laying out some flour would get rid of those ants. She had to start somewhere because the alternative wasn't worth thinking about.

∞ ∞ ∞

Heather sipped her green tea. Reflecting on the Japanese feeling of *mottainai*, from one of Irvin's books, which expresses regret when something is wasted, as well as *mushin*, the acceptance of change. The late-blooming hydrangea was exploding into colour stalk by stalk outside the kitchen window. As she waited for Hector to speak, Heather tried to match the exact shade of blue but kept circling back to other flowers. The parting misty light cast a rich glow on the leaves of the garden, so delicious looking that she wanted to pluck and bite into one like a ripe apple. She imagined Fran and Hector's place filled with the bustle of packed lunches, fights over the single bathroom, burnt toast, a quick peck on the cheek – no, more likely on the lips. Heather ran the rim of her mug over her lips.

'Remember how it used to be?' Hector asked. He scratched the end of his nose. 'Me and you, and afterwards Fran.'

Heather nodded to show Hector that she remembered, and gave him a smile of encouragement. Though her knee-jerk reaction towards Fran these days wasn't warm. She'd returned from hospital to find not one card, letter, or message from Fran. Clearly, their friendship was over. Evidenced by the ciggie stub purposefully thrown on the front step that the rain hadn't washed away.

Hector sipped his tea until Heather couldn't stomach not knowing.

'And? Why aren't you with your wife?' she asked.

'We don't work without each other, Heather. You're family.'

My family's dead. I'm alone. The derision ping-ponged around her head until she let them out, 'I'm alone.'

Out of her head the words 'I'm alone' were counterfeit emotions – he's right; they're my family, and I've missed them. Besides, these days there was also Harry, currently re-enrolled in school and living with his grandmother while his mother got the help she needed to cope with his father's death.

'Egotistical, self-centred,' he said, trailing off.

'Aye, all of those. I shouldn't have let you both go through whatever you have been going through alone. No matter what.' She reached out a hand for his. 'You're all bones. Tell me what's up.'

'You … You …' he stopped, raised a fist to his forehead then let it fall. 'Heather, you've distanced yourself from us, it's not the other way around.'

'Aye, I'm agreeing with you. You're right. No one's been right on both sides.'

It had been a long time since she'd seen him lose his temper, yet his fury fizzled out as soon as it left his lips, his eyes dulled as if he didn't have the energy to go on. 'Did Fran tell you?' he asked. 'I lost my job. Made redundant. Everything. My fault.'

She sucked in a breath. 'Redundancy is hardly your fault.' No wonder Fran had been sensitive about charity. 'Wait, when did this happen exactly?'

He didn't answer her questions but continued to let his speech flow. 'I couldn't find a new job. The endless job applications, and they hire younger people. People that don't appreciate what financial services organisations are, or what a secure job is. It's been frustrating for me, and I see the consequences for Fran. She's been carrying us on her cleaning salary while I wallowed at home.'

'Why didn't she say?'

'She didn't want it to seem like she was asking for freebies. Friends don't. I'm not now.' He paused to fix her with a look. 'We don't want a thing.'

She nodded. Not once had she thought about giving any of Irvin's earnings away; if she'd been in touch with Fran would she have thought of offering then, or kept it all to herself?

'How could you not notice?' he asked.

'Benefits?' she asked, unsure of how to answer his question. She hadn't noticed because she had cut Fran out of her life, rather than be there for them. It had been easier at the time. What did that say about the grade of friend she truly was?

'Benefits aren't enough to cover the food for three growing kids and a Hector.' His lips twitched.

Her head swelled as if lodged in a fishbowl, still with a fish inside. She'd share that image with him but his now serious face regarded the smashed mug. Whether he dropped it or knocked the mug off the countertop, they were both startled by the noise of the splintered fragments.

He said, 'Fran needs her oldest friend. I need you.'

'What's wrong?' she asked.

He bent down towards the pieces on the floor.

'Leave it. That's not important,' she said.

He knelt in front of the fragments, and she recalled Irvin telling her how the Japanese repaired broken pottery with special tree sap lacquer dusted with gold or silver, and the repaired piece was beautiful. An imperfect beauty like a person patched and repaired so many times they were a new person.

Hector acted fractured now, unable to say what he wanted to say for he began to pick up the shattered pieces.

She knelt beside him and helped. When all the pieces were collected he said, 'I'm sick, Heather. And I haven't told Fran.'

'Sick as in it will take time to get better, or sick as in …?'

The truth of it was clear from the uneven fluttering of his lashes, and the lines furrowing his forehead. She reached out to erase them; he drew away.

'The second one,' he said. 'Maybe the first.'

'Hector, go home to your wife.'

'I can't.'

'You must, you told her you were sick and walked away.'

'I can't.'

'And I can guess that she thinks you've walked out on her instead. You, numpty. Avoiding this is making it worse.'

'Can I stay the night?'

Heather bit the inside of her cheek. Would Fran understand a night's absence?

'And borrow a pen and paper?' he continued. 'There are some things I should write down before it's too late.'

She fetched him the paper. *Before it's too late*. This thing in his brain was serious then. She laced her hands behind her back to stop her flinging them around him. The thought of his parting … she couldn't go there.

'I'll come with you, tomorrow,' she said. Knowing Fran she'd have Hector's bags beside the door, but they couldn't risk waiting longer – the next stage would be heaving his things into the River Forth.

Chapter 24

Jack, my wee man,

I like to imagine you fully grown as I write this letter. I'm writing this because those raspberry-coloured cells the doctor tried to remove were more stubborn that he thought. It's not the doctors' or anyone's fault – life moves in circuitous loops the dreadful with the wonderful. These unexpected detours are not something to fear. Life is the way it is. I wish I could explain it better. Enjoy, is what I am trying to say, in clumsy terms. I certainly have. I am the luckiest man in the world to have been your da. If there's a life lesson to leave you with, it's that a sense of humour can get you through everything.

Allan has some more 'rules to live by' in his letter that my dad taught me. I wrote them down for you, both of my boys. I left my grandfather's watch with your ma for you when you're old enough for it to fit. It's expensive, so don't be annoyed with her if she keeps it safe until you're eighteen.

I want you to know how much you are loved. Always by me and your ma. As we've told you, when you were born we weren't able to hold you in our arms. The hospital placed you in a plastic bubble to monitor and help you breathe. Either me, or your ma, stayed with you at all times – your grandparents too. Because the nurses said that those babies who had someone to stroke their hand and spoke and sang them songs were most likely to survive, your ma got it in her head that singing would be even better. Of course, having buried my head in science books for most of my life I didn't know many lullabies, so I sang Mull of Kintyre, and Like a Red, Red Rose (the one your ma likes). Ma sang you a rhyme from Thumbelina. I've forgotten the name. The one that ends with 'when you are sad, afraid or alone, think of these things, you'll be happy, I know.'

I thought I'd record some of my favourite memories of you and I here. When you were born is the most obvious. The intoxicating smell of your milky hair when we finally held you. Your ma's obsession with stamping your wee foot in paint every Christmas and birthday as we couldn't get over how wee you were. There's a box of copies in the attic of your feet up to the age of five and a half, when you rebelled. We named you Jack after your great-great-great grandfather on my side who was a Jack of all trades, plumber, carpenter, you name it. Though Fran also liked the fact that Jack was a name "from the Bible", traditionally a diminutive form of John, as in John the Baptist. And if you are at all interested … you were conceived in a B&B on North Berwick's seafront. You've always loved to swim, even as a baby. Part merman, I used to joke with your ma.

Since your ma has a tendency to forget, I should record that your first word was Nanna – I suspect Nanna Donna and Nanna Florence said nothing else when they held you, a double conspiracy, and your first sentence was 'I want banana.'

When you were about two, we went to Blair Drummond Safari Park where you rode a real donkey, which you complained didn't smell like your stuffed Eeyore. Remember that? Then I bought you a strawberry ice cream to rid the smell from your nose. Your favourite animal at that time was the giraffe because it was the tallest. I told you, Allan and Patricia, that the giraffe's tongue was one meter long and blue and only you believed me. Your early obsessions were giraffe's or shells, always begging me to take you to Cramond to collect and play with the seashells. Disappointed that I wouldn't let you bring them back to the house for environmental reasons.

I hope a full life stretches ahead of you with a satisfying occupation, work can provide a sense of purpose until you retire and learn how to get the best yield from strawberries. And I wish you a family of your own as wonderful as mine has been. Perhaps. One day. Or not, if you prefer to take a different path.

Remember that every time you smile or laugh. I'll be there with you if I can be.

Your invisible angel,

always,

Da

∞∞∞

Allan, my son,

I see the glimmer of the man in you that you are going to be. It must have been hard for you as the middle child when so much of our attention went to Jack. Yet you took it all in your stride, and I am proud of you for the way you care deeply for your little brother and don't seem to mind putting all the attention on him. We hope as parents that we will love our children unconditionally and you make it so easy to do so. I will state it again: I am proud of the caring brother and son I see in you. Nurture those good qualities in the eyes of God, always, and you won't go far wrong.

My father taught me four lessons to live by that I hoped to pass along to you, and Jack, in turn:

1/ be well intentioned
2/ have faith in God's plan
3/ be your own kind of man
4/ pick a wife wisely and treat her with kindness and patience

I'm sure your ma will argue point two should be at the top, followed by four! I had hoped to be around to illustrate what each of these values means to me. I should add another: forge your own path, be an entrepreneur. Certainly don't work in the financial services unless you enjoy giving blood. You give the corporate bosses everything but bone marrow, then you're cast aside. So don't bother. Thank goodness for Fran and you kids. Footie in the park. Swimming lessons. Scouts. These are the activities that kept me sane for twenty-odd years.

Although your favourite stories these days are often about the herbivorous Oryctodromeus who digs its burrows in the forest floor, I think that some day you might want to know more about our family history. This is my gift to you. Your grandfather, Richard, was a mechanic able to take anything electrical apart and fix it. He got this love of moving parts from your great-grandfather, Albert. Albert was born in Newcastle in 1914, but grew up in Brussels. The way he told me the story of his coming to the UK was that his father, a butcher, – coming from a longline of horse breeders before the war – worked for the resistance. I'm not sure whether he bombed railways, broke lines of communication by other means or printed propaganda; either way, when the Nazi's occupied Belgium he knew that things would turn bad for him and his boys, so he handed them a banknote and told them to flee. They never saw their father again, and never spoke of their mother; there being a hint of abandoning her family in our oral family history to take up with a German lover.

This would have been in the early 1940s, when Albert and his brother were in their twenties. Albert and Johnny hiked their way to the coast and bribed a fisherman to take them across the channel at Dunkirk. They spoke no English, and trying to communicate in Dutch, French, and German, were arrested on arrival to Britain as German spies until it was figured out that they had been born in the UK. From there they both joined the British army because all they wanted to do was fight the Germans. Albert told me that he was tremendously excited that he would go for training in Hollywood; until he discovered it was Hollywood, Ireland, and there wouldn't be a chance of seeing any glamourous film stars on the Irish beaches.

Albert went to Africa and Italy with the 16/5th Lancers, Royal Armoured Corps, which, basically, means the tank division. He drove Valentine and Matilda tanks. He often joked that the American army had good equipment but kept leaving it behind. He gave up his old Valentine and clambered into one of the more solid looking American Shermans. A good thing too because he was bombed multiple times and survived! I'm not able to verify that, or any of his stories, as a fellow lieutenant told me at his funeral that American tanks were shipped across for British use, apparently a language mix up on Albert's part. After Africa, his division went to Naples, Italy. Unlike the open African desert, Italy's countryside wound around mountainous vineyards and olive groves. Terrain unsuitable for the tanks. They drove along the roads in tanks, then fought in close combat. Sounds terrifying! He got shrapnel in his leg and ended up in an Italian hospital where he learnt Italian. By this time he knew Dutch, French, German, English and Italian, as well as Latin from his schooling. His school-boy Latin came in handy for learning languages.

During the reconstruction of Europe Albert was based in Austria. There he met your great-grandmother, Ernestina, a riveting dancer and singer. They won tango awards. And they settled in Scotland, eventually, after moving about for his work all over the world. One time an historian turned up at the house and wanted to record him. He declined. But I'll tell you what he told me about what that chap was keen to hear first-hand.

Your great-grandfather received a commendation from King George VI, the Military Medal, in 1944. Albert was sitting with his pal in a trench in North Africa. Funnily enough he and a pal had the same surname of Rodd (one that Albert had chosen to avoid using his foreign sounding name in Britain). 'We weren't going to sit there and get bombed again!' he said, moustache bristling. 'Had enough of that in the tanks!' So, against orders to stay put, they took off and entered enemy territory, going in separate directions. They had weapons but were out of bullets. Albert came across a group of Germans. From above he could see he was outnumbered and outweaponed. So he came up with a plan. From his hiding spot he called down for them to put down their weapons and surrender because they were surrounded by the British Army. And they believed him! He marched back a group of German soldiers single-handedly that day with an empty weapon. His pal had done the same. Between them they rounded up 35 prisoners of war that day without loss of life.

Your great-grandfather was a character, a quick and lively mind, a boxer, a gymnast too; he often looped his legs over his arms and swung on them whenever he fancied. There wasn't a serious photo we could find for his funeral as in every shot he pulled a comical face beneath that moustache.

I had hoped to show you how to shoot a rifle when you were

older, like my Dad taught me, and his Dad taught him. Patricia can take you, she's a good shot with that keen left eye of hers.

One last piece of advice – since you love to cook as much as you love the Triassic-Jurassic period – but please forgive the following metaphor: what makes a man is not a fixed list of ingredients, like weigh 90 kg of flesh into a bowl and add a dash of machismo. It's not necessary for you to try to be the man of the house in my absence. You can all take care of one another together, including Auntie Heather.

If I could have beaten this thing to stay one more day with you, then I would have. I don't want to leave you, and unfortunately the doctors have done all they could and failed, if you are reading this. However, I have lived a life that I consider worthwhile, knowing that the result is that you will be in the world after I go.

Watching over you,

love,

Da

∞ ∞ ∞

Patricia, my darling daughter,

I am graced to have a strong, intelligent and kind daughter like you. You have surprised me in so many ways, from that first time I held you in my arms, rested my hand on your stomach and felt your legs kicking out, I wanted to lay the world at your feet, to shelter you from the worst of it. But that's not the role of a parent. I have no wish to stop you exploring and making your own mistakes. I had hoped to be around a little longer to see you taking further steps out into the world. I am proud of you whether you get the grades for university or not, when you start university or not, when you graduate and get your dream job or not, meet a life partner or not, have children or not … I am proud, regardless. I would have liked to see the woman you will become. Though, I think, I can see her in the teenager you are now. She is thoughtful towards others as she is towards her brothers. Demonstrating to them how to tie their shoelaces, to take their first glides at Murrayfield ice rink, and cleaning out the scrapes on their knees.

There are hundreds of memories I could relive with you on these pages, like when we went to the caravan park around your twelfth birthday and I watched you running after the entertainers dressed as pirates – them, not you! I think those entertainers were scared for their lives! There are hundreds of memories I could write about; instead, there's one story you have always requested. When you were small you loved to hear the story about how your ma and I met. Reflecting on the version of the story you were given, it was always your ma's or Auntie Heather's version of events. I never got to tell mine. So, especially for you, I want to unravel the thread of our trio to explain from my perspective what your ma and you mean to me.

It was during an afternoon break at university that I arranged to meet Fran and Heather for a coffee. Or rather Fran arranged it. She suggested one of a number of chain restaurants in the city centre not far from George Square Gardens as it was an easy walk from where her and Heather worked and where I studied. I arrived first and reserved us a table. The other seats were filled with grey-haired ladies enjoying a cake and a natter. I ordered a lemonade, freshly squeezed, covered the stains on the wooden table with my book on rocket engines, and raised my head whenever the door jangled. Fran arrived next, shaking her umbrella over her shoes. There was something different about her. When she slid into the opposite creaking seat I realised it was make-up that made the difference. The unattractive trend the university girls also preferred of darkening their eyelashes and lids as if wanting to conceal themselves in the shadows of their eye sockets. This was in the nineteen nineties.

'You've changed out of your work clothes,' I commented.

'Hot choc,' she replied, a strange retort until I realised the waiter stood behind me. Then she turned her darkened eyes towards me. 'I do own normal clothes, rocket man. How's the studying going?' She peered around the café, looking uninterested in my reply which I assumed was because she called all university goers 'morons with money to waste'.

'I'm learning about economics, draw your own conclusions about how interesting that is.'

She scoffed, as her watery chocolate arrived, undissolved powder melting on the surface. It came in a glass. I dislike that. It makes the drinks go colder faster and doesn't improve the quality. Plus I don't need to see what I'm drinking: it's the same principle as the contents of Haggis being described in detail.

The bell rang. I expected Heather and Fran but it was Fran on her own.

Fran fidgeted in her seat. 'It's just us today,' she said.

I'd like to be able to say something like, Fran then told me how much she admired me and would like to go out on a date, and I graciously, and modestly, despite being aware of my physical prowess, replied coolly, like guys I'd seen around campus, slouching in their leather jackets.

'Heather text me "see you later",' I said.

'Miscommunication.' Fran pulled her seat closer. 'We can talk, just the two of us.'

Instead of being cool, I stuttered, unable to get my words out. Feeling under pressure with her sole attention focused on me. 'Y-You're being weird.'

Fran frowned, giggled, straightened her features.

My mobile buzzed as some messages came through. I usually ignore it in company but checked in case it was from Heather. And they were. 'Heather's at the café and wondered where we are. What have you done, Fran?'

Fran touched the back of my hand lightly, just brief enough to raise the hairs on my arms. 'Don't reply.' She flicked her hair, around shoulder length then, leant over her drink a bit too much so I could see down her cleavage. Was she flirting? I admit, I'm a bit dense when it comes to things like that. My ears felt unpleasantly hot. I realised I still had my beanie on my head, ripped it off and puffed up my curls a bit. It was impossible not to be aware of the curious gazes of the older women sipping their tea at the nearby tables, their conversations lulling.

'I'd like it to just be us today,' Fran said.

She was flirting then. 'You don't have to manipulate me to get me to like you, or be cruel to Heather.'

'You like me?' Fran asked.

'Course.'

Hardly the romantic dialogue, or the dramatic tale Fran re-enacted. Heather, if I recall correctly, said she'd misunderstood where to meet us, and I didn't see her messages. While Fran overplayed how she contrived to get me alone. The truth of it is, it was an awkward and embarrassing first date, what with my geekiness and the betrayal I felt towards Heather, and on Heather's behalf. And I hadn't considered Fran or Heather in a romantic way before. I needed time to think it over, and your ma took offense that I didn't respond well. Though, thankfully I made up for it when I asked her out officially a couple of weeks later. I even bought her flowers. Granted the wrong type, but from then on I knew to buy daffodils, or tulips, not carnations. I'm still not certain why these are not a valid flower choice but I pay attention to the little things. And I hope that if you find someone in the future that they will be considerate above all else, and pay attention to the little things that matter to you.

I don't want to stop writing this letter. I think it's been the hardest to write, because what can you possibly write to your daughter in these circumstances. Well, the most important thing is, though you might be a bit old for this expression, I love you to the moon and back. There I've written it anyway,

Love you, <u>more</u> than to the moon and back,

Da

∞ ∞ ∞

Dearest Heather,

Thank you for your letters. Sorry for not responding. I've been in a bad mental state, and it took me a long while to break the gummy seals on your handwritten letters. I appreciate each one, reminding me of our friendship and the memories I keep close of you, me and Fran. At the same time, I admit I felt fashed and discouraged. As well you know, a letter is no substitute for coming round in person. Sorry, I didn't intend to write this letter to tell you off. On the contrary, because I've been in a bad way, I feel responsible for not being able to bring you and Fran back together. Usually I'd trick the two of you into the same place, and the two of you would shoogle your heads at each other, and one laugh at me would smooth over the awkwardness, but with all this Covid-19 business ... I should have acted more quickly before the March lockdown.

Didn't expect things to drag out so long. My hopes however are that in the event of my death at least this letter will bring you together on that first step towards forgiveness. Can I continue to fill my peace-pipe role from beyond the grave? You and Fran are both contermacious in your own ways but enough is enough. Agreed? Well then, go and give her a hug.

Returning to the subject of me and you, what a boon that we met at all. Things seem so random and unlikely when you look back, don't they? I'm glad that I only felt like an only child until you came into my life. Fran may carry some ill-founded notion I once adored you as something more, but we know the pull that two lonely children have for one another. Thank you for being a sister to me. Thank you for the acting and writing of plays together, for reading science books and conducting home experiments with baking soda. Especially, anything that exploded and made mum shout at us for the mess, even if we intended to tidy up. Thank you for sticking up for Fran when she joined our school and making her a part of our trio. Some of my fondest memories are when we listened to music, drank coffee in cafes, played Robin Hood and King Arthur. I think I have the order messed up, somewhat.

From day one you reminded me, in part, of my mum. Dad and mum grew up in post-war Britain. If they had lived to see it they would have been anti-Brexit, believing implicitly in the EU, blind to its ideological corruption. Mum remains in my mind a counterbalance to Dad's practical mannered faith. She carried an air of whimsy. Her fiddle-faddle, as Dad fondly said, never in forty years known to take his wife seriously. Her quirkiness extended to eclectic reading material from the library: books of philosophy, mathematics, knitting – or fiddle-faddle, does this remind you of anyone? – while the other housewives did the laundry and ours piled up. I dipped into these books. Dad was a scout leader in his spare time in the evenings and at weekends, by day working for Mike's Motors, grounding me in morals and a love of mechanics.

So when an inquisitive Hector met a creative Heather we understood that we weren't like the others in our school year – too babyish to hold a real conversation. As I devoured science books years ahead, you entertained me with stories of castles in the clouds, and a prism that went on adventures to outer space. What cemented our friendship, for me, was the day Phil Mathers said that girls and boys couldn't be friends. As if us sitting together in the school library was an affront to human evolution! I can't remember what either of us responded. But I do remember Phil Mathers insulting your mum with the word 'hippie', winding you up, and up, like that clockwork shark I used to play with. And then I got in trouble for hurling a book at his forehead, which, unfortunately angled, broke the skin, which, if I remember correctly, and I think I do, was because he begged me to take the blame, because he didn't want it getting round the school that a girl injured him. I've never hit someone in my life, not then and not now. You surprised me that day by your defensive nature. Concealed till you gave Fran a talking to during your falling out. We all have our dark side. No, that's not what I want to say, it's too judgemental, as if our animalistic nature is a vile thing when it's pure survival. You should bear your teeth more often to the world. Yes, that's closer to what I mean.

Would it surprise you to know that I didn't trust Fran at that first meeting? Just like Heather, I thought, to invite the awkward new girl to eat with us. Confrontation in her gaze, spiked hair, oozing trouble. All that was missing was a nose ring. I know, I know, we were too young to know any better. As you can tell, by the outcome, she grew on me. Fran is what she is on the surface and I love that directness about her. If she's angry or happy you know about it in that practical offhand way of hers. She uses it to protect herself. In this way Fran comes across as abrasive to those who don't know her, and 'brutally honest' to those who are being polite. If you are the whimsy in my life Fran is the spreadsheet.

Yet you're both contermacious in your own ways. Fran appears abrasive and you appear sweet. When, really, it's the vanishing into your head that enables you to cope. With your made-up characters, you can withdraw into creating a safe space in a world that took your mum away. By avoiding conflict at all costs I don't think you and Fran properly talked. Not like we can. Cause I knew you on a deeper level before the greatest loss of your life. I always got the sense that you were hiding from others. I guess this is your tendency to bottle things up, in contrast to Fran. You hid when you lost your mum. Your open nature ricocheted from a hurt I'm uncertain you completely shared with us, a private wound. Yet at least you have your writing through which to work out your emotions, and your compassionate nature stuck you to us through Jack's illness. And I hope this will bring you back to Fran and the kids. Fran, in contrast, was distrusting before the loss of her brother Scott, easily distempered. Afterwards, I suppose I could say, I see her like an inversed apricot displaying its pitted woody layer on the outside, while the sweet flesh within is protected by the seed's carapace. Fran has more layers of self-defence to breach than you do.

There are complex and there are simple-minded people in the world. I think of myself as the latter and you as the former, with your castles in the air. And then Fran joined us. It's more fun blowing things up with friends. I hope that you and Fran can continue that tradition of mine with the kids. Don't let them forget how much a geek I was. It makes me feel better knowing you'll look out for one another.

I'm sorry to have to break our trio. Fran can fill you in on the details of my illness. I'm struggling to know how to end this letter as you fuss about me in the kitchen. There's a limit to words that I hope our final hug, our final glance, can fill.

Thank you for being a sister to me, a best friend to Fran and an auntie to our children,

always yours,

Hector

∞ ∞ ∞

To Fran, my little penguin,

~~My doctor told me to – In case I don't survive this operation – If you've found this letter –~~

I've written this letter for you, one for Heather, and one each for Patricia, Allan and Jack. It felt too awkward to write anything to my scouting pals since most of them are boys under seventeen.

You see the trap I've laid for you? You'll have to make things up with Heather, our closest and, nearly, only friend – if only to hand her this letter. In my mind it's never in doubt that you will find your way back to one another. Please go and say you are sorry if she hasn't already approached you or you her.

Sorry I've been so difficult to live with. I think my dad's way of facing difficult times was to do DIY, and my mum's was to take up a new hobby. Alas, I wasn't up to the challenge. Going to blame the malfunctioning brain on that one.

There are many things I want to, and have to, thank you for. First, that you stick with me whatever life catapults our way. That you tried to inject some sense into me, and when that didn't work went with me to the doctors to hold my hand through multiple appointments. It helped to know that you were nearby. Even when you couldn't come into the MRI room. You camouflaged it well but your husband knows you, my selfless Fran. I could see it in the set of your face how much it was costing you to accompany me inside the hospital you detest so much.

Second, thank you for supporting our family financially, and being equally supportive throughout the job search. It helped immensely that you didn't place additional pressure on this malfunctioning brain. Well, you know, that I put enough of that on myself. It feels bad enough having put you in a difficult financial situation, let alone the excessive pressure of my illness. Gosh, this letter sounds like a work memorandum. What I'm trying to say, badly, is thank you for being on this planet and loving me unconditionally.

I remember when we first met, thanks to Heather, and how we hung out as a group as we grew up. The science experiments and games replaced by coffee and music, before you tricked me on our first date. As you know I was a bit dense. Nose in a book and all that! You have brought an unexpected richness to my life, with your love and support. For instance, when my parents hit a deer while driving, not long after Donna's prolonged hospitalisation.

The recent epidemic has changed my perspective. They've said, for as long as I can remember, 'we're screwing up the planet'. That future generations, us, now even, will face what's coming to them. In my opinion, we all buy crap but politicians make it possible as the consumerist culture has been set in motion by the privileged for profit. In my case, I think, it was the inability to believe that anything catastrophic would happen to the planet. Now, I see that the stability we craft of our lives is a temporary state with the most valuable item we possess being the amount of time we have on this planet. So, in preparing to leave Earth my brain is stuck on repeat like Dad's old vinyl. So this is it? Have I spent my time wisely?

I, we, built a life out of our time. In retrospect, doesn't it pass quickly. After university I settled into a job, learnt all I could about retirement benefits, anti-money laundering, death and spouse benefits in five years. As the work progress slowed life skuttled faster: marriage, rented house, kid one, two and three. Suddenly I'm over forty putting out the rubbish for the umpteenth time with a sense of accomplishment and considering training to run a half marathon. Gradually I stepped into my father's shoes, fulfilling the role set before me: work, family, proud parents, happy wife. Thank goodness for helping out with the local scout's group. This was always the person I was meant to be, raising three kids with you, teaching other kids the values my dad raised me on.

From some aspects it's been a minuscule life: I worked in an open-plan office; forked out now and again for charity; separated rubbish into cardboard, glass and composting; followed politics and otherwise kept my head down. Is this enough? Compared to my wife I've hardly lived. You gave birth, worked multiple jobs, helped out the local community when you could. I am in awe of you managing all that. I'm hopeful, because our lives are intertwined that all these aspects of our lives and connections to others is a combined contribution. Raising our kids to be polite, respectful and thoughtful, for instance, is one of the most important of our contributions to society.

Sorry, my love, forgive me slipping into politics and thoughts about life choices. Everything I am the most proud of involves you, my penguin. Right now, I am waiting to see how long it takes you to forgive me. You have a big heart. I know how deeply you care. You care about me and the kids and what their future will be, you care about giving back to those around you and following Christian ways of living. And though I cannot say to believe in God fully, or claim to know where I will go when I part from you. I find that your faith has also added something to the lives of those around you, including me. Your willingness to forgive and be open to others. I don't think you realise that it's not a trait everyone shares. And while other's saw a misfit – a spiky, suspicious kid – I saw you open up, thanks to Heather, and even relax a wee bit and share the best parts of yourself with me. Thank you for taking that risk. We worked, work well together, don't we?

It's as hard for me to write this as for you to read it: if I don't make it and if you find yourself alone don't feel the need to be a martyr. Live, live for yourself, for us both. You're still young and sexy after all! Sexy to me. To many men I'm sure. Part of me wants to forbid all contact with other men. It should be me, I'm thinking. But the last thing I would ever wish is for you to be alone, or hesitate because you are worried about me coming back to haunt you – whoo! I won't Fran, speaking seriously now, because what I want most of all is for you to be happy. That's all I have ever wanted for you. I wish it could be with me. I don't want to go. To leave you, or the kids. Since we may not have a choice in the matter, the next best thing is that if another decent fellow crosses your path, let it happen. Continue, knowing that I love you, I want the best for you, I want you to feel loved, always.

With more love than I can say,

your Hector

Chapter 25

'Ma! Ma!' Allan's voice was panicked enough to get her attention.

A damp patch covered the ceiling beneath the bathroom – again. Fran moved stiffly up the steps. Patricia was showering. The bathroom floor was sodden.

'Rinse your hair, darling. There's a leak. I'll turn the water off.' Fran unscrewed the plastic side of the bath. Black mound grew on the floorboards beneath. 'Damn it.' Tears rolled off her nose as she lay down a towel.

'You okay, Ma?' Pat asked.

'Fine, darling.'

'Stop saying that everything will be fine,' Pat said as she twisted her hair into a dry towel. 'It won't be fine will it?' She added, her voice growing smaller and smaller. 'We don't have any money.'

Jack hugged her legs. 'It will be okay, Ma,' he said. 'I'll pray harder every night.'

'You can sell all my cars,' Allan offered.

'Thank you, darling, you keep those.'

Typical reactions from her three darlings: Patricia demanding the truth and accepting no lies, Allan offering help, and Jack comfort.

'Someone's at the door,' Allan said.

Fran listened; she hadn't heard anything. Hector hadn't come back from his walk.

'I heard a key in the door,' Allan insisted.

The doorbell rang.

'Is it Da?' Patricia asked.

'Go your rooms.'

'But we haven't done anything.'

'Da and I need some time to talk.'

'Come on, we can fish for our toys off the bed,' Patricia said, leading the way into the boys' room.

Hector swayed unsteadily on the doorstep like he was preparing to step onto dry land. The sun was setting behind him and concealing his face. 'Drinking again?' She was about to say. A second figure caught her eye behind Hector. 'Heather?'

Heather said, 'You're all bones.'

'Kind of you to bring my husband back,' rasped Fran.

'Hector has something to tell you.'

Fran drifted from the door … and sunk unto the darkness of the house. It was as if they were caught in her net, impelled to follow or give chase, to the bone woman, across the hallway and into the lounge, to sit around the coffee table. As shadows trailed into the house, painting the walls and furniture with a chiaroscuro effect. None of the lights were on.

Hector tried to sit at the furthest point from Fran. Heather prodded him to scooch over a bit.

Hector, his eyes hollowed out, churned in the currents of his emotions; from the shadows of his face in the dim house fish might have plucked at his cheeks and sucked his eye sockets clean. Fran turned away to stare at a distant point through timber and plasterboard, she was responsible for his withdrawn look: kicked him out.

Heather tripped on the suitcase Fran had packed with some of Hector's things, as she fumbled for the light switch and flicked it back and forth. 'You don't have electricity?'

'No more bulbs,' Fran said, in the diffusing darkness. She'd left the working bulbs in the kid's rooms and the kitchen.

When she checked what Hector was doing he hung his head, sitting beside her in the gloom. Fran's heart wrung itself out as Heather gave Hector a pointed look, trying to communicate – start speaking, you numpty – Fran knew that look well when it turned on her.

As Fran opened her mouth Hector said, 'I'm sorry for walking out. I needed space to think, and I needed Heather to be here because I think it's only in me to say it once.'

'I packed a bag.' Fran nodded at the suitcase. 'I don't want to know the details.'

Hector reached a hand towards her, then curled his fingers away as Fran flinched. His head turned towards Heather. In the gloom his features crumpled. Whatever look he gave their ex-best friend prompted Heather to speak.

'I'm here for both of you,' Heather said. 'Go on, Hector. Tell her.'

'I prayed on it,' Fran said, 'and, as I love you, I've to let you go. To be happy. I've failed as a wife and I-I—'

'I'm the failure,' Hector said. 'Failed to keep my job, failed to support you, failed to pull it together and tell you the truth.'

'Well, it's out now,' Fran said.

'I'm not sure it is,' Heather interceded.

'Want me to say it aloud that you've won, you HOME WRECKER!'

Hector groaned. 'What, on earth Fran? It's not her fault.'

'Don't you dare take the blame. It takes two, that's what they say.'

'We're not having an affair, Fran,' Heather said.

'You probably don't think so, 'cause he was yours, right?' Fran asked.

'No, because Hector chose you. He cherishes you.'

'Then why is he leaving?'

'Fran, I'm sick.'

'Sick. That's what this is.'

'I'm properly poorly.' Hector tore his crumpled test results from his trackie top, held out the dampened sheet of paper, and when she didn't move he rested it on her lap.

Her eyes fell, but it was too dark to read. 'I can't see it.'

'It's a letter from the doctor.'

Her mother's clock ticked on the mantlepiece. A rubbish

lorry upended bins, the odd carton of milk escaping the recycling bins as they were emptied. Tears fell on the sheet of paper. Her tears.

'I think I should leave you to ...' Heather bolted before either of them could call her back.

Hector told Fran his secrets.

Chapter 26

October 2020

Fran lay awake listening to Hector's whistling nose. Sometimes she had thought what it would be like when one of them died: and, for that matter, who would be the first to go? Either option caused grief for the other person, a vacuuming of one's insides, a cobweb free emptiness. But reasoning that women tended to live longer she'd intended to outlast Hector and spare him the anguish. Only she hadn't recognised the alternative: that he could be the first to go. She wasn't ready for that, she stared at the cobwebs on their textured ceiling, her insides drying out. She'd rather die too, found curled against his body like a spider's discarded exoskeleton.

Fran called in sick the next day to spend it with Hector. When the doorbell rang Fran found Heather huddled under a waterproof and umbrella sheltered from a sudden spill. Disparate from last night, when Heather had come to support Hector tell his wretched news, this morning Fran got the impression, as the confidence returned to Heather's cheeks, of watching the process of patina in reverse: from an age-spotted patina of lead and copper to fresh patches of copper.

'Come for a walk,' Heather said.

No, Heather demanded it which didn't match her usually amiable manner and a tendency to avoid confrontation.

'What for?' Fran crossed her arms, shivering against the fading raindrops.

'I can give you three reasons. One, to heal our friendship. Two, for Hector's sake as he's friends with both of us. Three, for the kids. Technically another three reasons right there.'

'What've the kids got to do with—? Oh. Well. Aunty Heather, tell that to Allan who can't go on his school trip, or Patricia who needs a new pair of shoes, or Jack who wants to play hide-and-seek with you when you're forever absent.'

Heather had the grace to flinch and semi-turn away. Then she set her features determinedly. 'Walk. Now,' she said, moving away as if Fran had agreed to join her.

Fran couldn't exactly say what compelled her to yell back into the house she needed a stroll.

A rope of connection ran the gauntlet between her and Heather, its tug as natural as breathing. They'd come a long way from primary and secondary school together: through the skirt-flicking boys in gym class, and the bra-flicking boys who hung out smoking behind the music room; through their working lives; through multiple births and deaths. To be walking together in this moment.

Rapidly moving grey-bellied clouds slide across the sky like damp sponges. The coat she had grabbed turned out to be Hector's and hung off her.

They headed off Granton way treading over the yellow leaves of the sycamores. Or rather, Heather set the pace and Fran tried to keep up. The concrete path they followed was part of Edinburgh's cycle network. Most of Edinburgh's cycle paths had been created from the disused railway network in the eighties by the landscape architect Mr Ian Temple, except for the section they followed via West Shore Road to Silverknowes Esplanade.

Heather soon slowed, a sheen of sweat on her forehead as though she hadn't exercised all summer.

They walked over cobbles where metal benches rusted between the sea and the towering metal frame of the former gas works. The frame was comprised of four circular tiers connected by poles and intersected by a scaffolding of criss-crosses to form an enormous game of noughts and crosses.

First-class talk this. Will she apologise, or not? Then again, does she need to? They'd both said things. Relief flooded Fran that their laborious apologies and conflicting emotions could be skipped, like the couple to their right skipping stones with matching bobble hats.

The patchwork clouds gave way to sun, shadow, sun, an ever-changing jumble like the ball of shoelaces tangled in Fran's brain. How to reconcile such strong emotions? Her suspicion and jealousy had led her to call Heather a homewrecker, one she wished would die old and alone. If she was honest, those spiteful words were a knee-jerk reaction to Heather's rejection of her during lockdown. Fran had been cut up by Heather moving on with her life without a backward glance. Could a friendship come back from that? Conflicting emotions dangled on the end of Fran's tongue.

As they drew near the fields where people walked their dogs who stopped to sniff one another – the dogs not the people – Heather said, 'I owe you an apology, Fran.'

'There's a lot of shit under that bridge.' It was grudging humour. It was there so Heather would know Fran was willing to hash out their disparities.

Heather's lips twitched. 'Before you crack me up with one of your expressions, I want to be serious. I fucked up.'

'Continue.' Fran stopped, to narrowly avoid a lad on a rusty bicycle.

'It's been a weird year. I'm not blaming my bereavement. Irvin is— was— anyway, the most important thing to me is that I don't want to lose you and Hector and the kids. If that's realistic.'

Fran sucked on the inside of her cheek. If Heather was going to be that grudging about repairing their friendship, then why bother? Fran replied, 'We can carry on without you, I'm sure.' A seagull cried out, echoing Fran's wretchedness.

'I can't.'

'Course you can't. We're the best mates you've got.'

'But I haven't been here for you – recently, I mean.'

Fran ruminated. This wasn't a situation that could be rushed. They'd passed the Gypsy Brae Recreation Ground where sand, rock, and decomposing seaweed, became visible as the tide drew away from them, and they reached the busier part by the overpriced café where people drove to walk to Cramond, and planes, usually, flew overhead on their way to Edinburgh Airport. A mizzle began to obscure their vision of the rocky islands dotted about the estuary.

Fran crunched a shell that had been kicked up from the sea to the promenade under her heel. 'Doesn't take a walk in the wet to ken that. And it goes both ways.'

'Forgive me?'

Fran took a moment to ask herself that question. That Heather – her Thistle – asked it made her heart implode. Here are two people walking together, she reflected, that both desperately want to remain pals. Compassion would be a step in the right direction.

'You know how my God feels about forgiveness,' Fran said. Not able to say it yet in a way other than indirectly.

'I'm not sure about how you feel about forgiveness. Are we broken?' Heather asked.

Each question Fran had to respond to jarred like pulling teeth. Part of her was ready to flee home, to spend time with Hector (however long he had), and tell Heather where to stick her company. On the surface, Heather had once accused Fran being rough cobblestones.

Heather coughed, levering herself onto a bench with a sigh as if their stroll had been a marathon. 'I feel like a hollow chocolate bunny without you, Hector and the kids.' Heather tugged down the zip of her waterproof, revealing a sea-green cashmere sweater.

Fran wandered onto the beach, even though sand would end up in her trainers. The Firth of the Forth was grey and flat. Fran, worn down by life, ironed flat between the concrete and the matching grey sky, so that it was hard to draw breath, picked up a white fragment of glass, eroded into a smooth pebble.

Heather said, from beside her. 'I used to think of broken

bits of glass as the fragments of people's hearts … crystallised suffering. Tiny bits of grief migrating to the ocean to have their sharp edges smoothed.

Fran bowed her head, releasing a silent internal prayer, and on an aching outward breath rasped, 'Friendship is more important than retaining grudges.'

With the kind of understanding that grows over the years their bodies broke onto each other like the waves by their feet.

'It'll be all right, Thistle,' Fran muttered, because eventually it would be true.

'You haven't called me that in a while.'

'Well, you've been a bampot.' Fran pushed her away and crossed her arms. 'Let's get the fuck home. Else it'll pour down and shrivel up that cashmere sweater of yours, like a sheep in a sausage sock.'

Heather laughed. 'That makes no sense.'

'Careful, you're about to cross enemy lines, don't spoil it.'

'I've missed your frankness.'

Fran stretched her hands wide in the oversized pockets of Hector's coat. 'Well, there's frankness and meanness. Hector scolded me for being too harsh with you. And with him …'

They had months to catch up on, sat in the brown-carpeted lounge on the green faux-leather sofa, mugs of tea in hand. Fran puffed out some air, 'Right, apologise away.'

'You're tough. Don't you think it's your turn?' Heather asked.

Fran's ears that began to tingle. Her gut reaction to the word 'sorry' was to punch something. Hard. 'I am,' she said. 'I'm sorry. I could say that till I'm blue in the face, wouldn't change anything.'

'Would a little.'

'I'm sorry, I'm sorry, I'm sorr—'

'Stop. Stop.' Heather giggled.

Fran eyeballed the worn-out patch of carpet where she'd scrubbed the tea stain. 'I shouldn't have said the hurtful, untrue things I did … Have you ever got over it? And don't pretend not to understand.'

'The wedding.'

'Exactly.'

Heather said, 'Wasn't your fault.'

'I saw Hector adored you long before we were a possibility. You hadn't examined your feelings properly. I could tell when I asked at my eighteenth. The problem was that neither of us wanted to get in the way of the other's happiness. Yet I also wanted to be happy. And he made me happy. Still, don't think life's easy with three kids and everything that goes along with that: rent, bus fare, clothing, food … You see that average wages chart in the paper? Seriously, are they trying to make us more seriously depressed?'

Heather gave the tiniest of smiles. One which said two things: you're right, and if you thought life was going to be easy the joke's on you.

Fran recalled when they'd first met: an easier subject to broach. 'You used to be brave. Why'd you help me with Alex that day? You didn't know me.'

Heather steepled her hands above the mug on her lap. 'I used to think that fairness was the most important thingy in the world.'

'Well, thirty-odd years later it certainly ain't friendship.'

'United over roast dinner?' Heather tried.

'Don't.' Fran's core drained of emotion, at the point of fossilisation which Allan had learnt about in his quest to become a dinosaur archaeologist. It was the long hours and family right now added to her workload. 'As I said, you used to be brave. Not anymore.'

'Family is important, Fran. I need you.'

'Nah, I don't buy it.' They'd taken a step. A ridiculously small one. But Fran wanted to know if Heather still had space in her life for an old acquaintance. Doubts resurfaced.

'I thought it was a pleasure never a chore?' Heather asked.

'With you, always a chore. You're different, in that you think you're better than everyone else.'

'Nae, I dinnae.'

'I didn't say it was true, though it comes across that way.'

Heather sat a while in introspection. 'Okay,' she said. 'I'm nae different. I'm the same as other folks … yet, I'm also a bitty different. That's personality. Each a bitty different from the other, that's natural.' Heather sighed the air out between her teeth as she did when she fought annoyance. 'I'm proud, like Mr Darcy.'

Fran got the Pride and Prejudice reference but not why it was relevant. 'Pfff! Everything is related to writing with you.'

Heather continued, 'Aye, I idolise books and you don't do books. So what? Just different preferences.'

'There's differences between us.' Fran could picture them as separate high-rises with a gulf between them: it's a long swift drop to the concrete, trees and grass below.

'You need to explain to me what you're thinking, Fran.'

'I know my faults. I didn't think jealousy was one. Self-reliance can cross a line sometimes into not asking for help when you need it, and I think that's what's built up my resentment.' She paused, struggling to share what she'd kept to herself all these months. 'Things have been hard during lockdown without Hector's wages, we're losing the house. I had to choose between food and paying the rent. My two salaries didn't make a dent in what we need to live.'

Fran kept blethering because this was the only way she would get this out. 'He lost his job and I took a second one. Our welfare payments were delayed, and then I discovered someone stole our details and money that was due to us. An emergency fund.' Fran glanced sidewards at Heather who was listening intently, a flicker of shared agony in the depths of her eyes. 'From my point-of-view,' Fran said, 'you had a house, money, a posh new life, and were zeroing in on my husband.'

Fran understood now, she'd been measuring their relationship in terms of wins and losses. A win-lose perspective (where Heather was the victor) while there was another path here: win-win. A direction that involved being more vulnerable than she'd allowed herself to be in all her life. The end of all things is at hand, she recited internally, therefore be self-controlled and sober-minded for the sake of your prayers.

Heather reached out and rubbed Fran's arm.

'Hector's brain cancer is an additional stress. What cuts me to bits is when my kids who've been living on beans and toast and spaghetti on toast, and not complaining when the electricity is cut, use their own piggy banks to buy a pizza, and ask me if I'm okay. I'm supposed to be the parent.'

'That sounds impossibly hard. Can you forgive me?'

'Forgiveness,' Fran echoed. What was it about that word that made her stomach churn like a washing machine and her palms sweat?

'Are you relating this to what happened with your step-da?'

Bullseye! How could she pardon others when she struggled to absolve herself? Her decisions had caused Scott's death. Her decisions had led them to where they were now.

'There's no comparison, Fran. You weren't culpable for Scott's death. I agree with calling you harsh. The only Fran I've ever known is harshly protective of the ones she loves.'

Yes, the priest in the hospital chapel that day had also informed her about intentions. Her intention had been to help Scott, to protect her family. He'd then told the story of Lazarus. If we have no power over death, only God, then why beat herself up about it? She'd carried the burden of guilt for so long to keep him close, because she kept concealed under roughened edges that she cared for others. The scars she bore – from Dougie, Donna, Scott's death – mostly came from the inability to forgive what she had perceived as a child as an unforgivable failure to protect her brother.

'I'm a – I don't have the word,' she said, 'for hauling this self-reproach around, and I pulled us into a brabble for nothing.'

'Abso-bloody-lutely.'

Heather's hearty agreement made Fran laugh.

Heather squeezed her arm and said, 'I'm sorry for being so self-absorbed. I needed space to figure things out. You were right I had secrets … just not the ones you imagined.'

Fran raised her eyebrows.

'Irvin helped me access a university degree.'

Fran listened as Heather explained everything she'd been holding back: how she'd felt jealous of Fran's family life, how Irvin had encouraged and supported her studies, how she'd struggled with her courses after his death, meeting Harry and being hospitalised.

'I should have supported you more. You have my support a hundred per cent from now on. We're family.'

Jealous of me, Fran reflected, who could have known that as Fran envied Heather's freedoms, Heather coveted Fran's family.

'Shit,' Fran said. 'I forgot about Baneshanks. Fenella gave me a warning for you.'

Baneshanks pounded on the door. 'I know you're in!'

Heather dug her toes into her sheepskin slippers. Madness to answer.

Fenella's voice joined his, 'She never claimed to be a nurse. You're taking this too far.'

The door moved away from her, or her from it, as she reversed down the hallway, resting a hand against the stripy wallpaper.

What would Fran do? Nut him in the head and kick him in the knob. Heather dried her wet palms on her flared skirt.

'Stop this!' Fenella said.

The rasp of a key, a usually soothing sound, one of homecoming, turned against her as Blair opened her door. She pressed her shoulder blades against the wall. Why wouldn't it open behind her?

'A sneak as well as a thief,' Blair said.

Fenella's cheeks, rouged with embarrassment, as she turned to Lochlann. 'Don't follow him into this foolery.'

Lochlann's heavy-set face remained impassive.

She wanted to say, you have no right to those keys. She wanted to add *or this house.*

'I'm sorry. I didn't realise he had my key,' Fenella said.

The after-effects of the virus, a lingering cough stole her voice. Blair's lips twisted –amusement? Disgust? Fenella slipped past her father and brother and lay the back of her hand against Heather's forehead. Fenella's skin felt icy.

'No longer contagious,' Heather managed.

'Let's sit you down at least with a cuppa.'

The words could have come from Fran's lips. The vein-sized fissure in Heather's soul swelled a little. It took energy to join the edges and by then Fenella, Heather and Lochlann sat in the lounge with warm china, while Blair continued to persuade her to give in.

'After all,' he said. 'I helped him make his way in the world.'

Heather tried to convey a look which said, if your threats didn't work why would persuasion?

'Lies,' Fenella gritted through clenched teeth. 'You have no right to contradict Irvin's wishes. This isn't about justice, it's about revenge for his mother marrying your father. Aren't you tired of being manipulated?' she asked, cutting to the bone as only a daughter knows how.

Blair and Lochlann blinked and contorted their faces, giving the impression of castle guards waking from a hundred-year-old slumber. Father and son spoke at once, 'That's what you think of me?' they said. One groggy and the other diminished in his power, an emptying hourglass.

'I do my own thing, Fenella. I happen to agree with father. This house is ours.'

Blair clapped a hand on his son's shoulder.

'The difference is, the difference is I always adored Uncle Irvin.' Fenella met Heather's eyes, mouthing the word sorry. 'It's only because I respected Irvin that I haven't filed a complaint against you on Heather's behalf. Don't test me when you taught me so well.'

'You're always welcome,' Heather said. 'You two aren't. Get out.'

'Of course she's welcome to our house,' Lochlann tittered. 'Look, F—'

Fenella said, 'Leave now, and we won't file charges and sue you for harassment. I've a lifetime's knowledge of your bullying and legal harassment to be able to utilise it against you.' She stood, unflinchingly facing Blair's gradually rising temper and bullying language. Lochlann's pale eyes remained glued on his father during his rant, they all were. It was only then he spun and left.

Lochlann followed, with a flap of his wrist. Heather breathed again.

'I think Irvin would have approved.' Fenella gave her a smile of conspiracy.

November 2020

Irvin's house, now their house, had five bedrooms: the two with the en suite bathrooms for the adults, and the remaining three designated to Patricia, Allan and Jack. After playing a game of run-about-and-claim-your-room the kids returned to the dining room to claim several small boxes with their names on them, temporarily distracting themselves by playing with Irvin's Tibetan bell, which Heather, on returning to the house from hospital, had taken down saying, 'No one needs to be cleansed here, imperfect works just fine.'

Allan stacked two boxes one on top of the other that held clothes. 'I'm as strong as a giant,' he told Jack.

The three kids giggled; laughter bounced off the walls like putting your feet in a cool stream on a warm day – granted, a rare one in Scotland.

'Plenty of books in this house,' Fran said, nodding at Irvin's masses of books Heather still hadn't cleared away.

'I'm going to read them all,' Heather said. 'Though we better move them all into the library. Knowing Hector's allergies ...'

'How does a person find time to read?' Fran asked. She only managed to flick over her magazines in the bathroom with the door locked; and that was before one of the kids got curious and knocked on the door to hurry her up.

'When will he be out?' Heather asked Fran as they began to reorganise the lounge into a cosy nook for a family of five.

Irvin had decorated the floors with stainable cream rugs which they rolled up, and glass-topped coffee tables which they replaced with sturdy wooden ones from the attic. The brown leather sofas and cream blinds would remain, and the paisley armchairs in cream and pastel green, orange and yellow like a spring field.

Fran fiddled with a scratch on her arm and said, 'Could be any time Wednesday to the following Saturday, depending on how well he's recovering.'

Jack, his plastic stethoscope swung to one side, a box in his arms as he headed towards the stairs said, 'Daddy had to drink Gio-lan.'

'Gliolan,' Allan corrected, a few steps behind him.

'That a new fizzy drink?' Heather asked. Although Allan smiled at her joke, Patricia's face was pale and withdrawn as she hugged her box of clothes to her chest.

'Noooo, Silly!' Jack cried. 'It's a special drink so that Daddy's brain glows pink and blue.'

'That's right,' Fran said. 'The healthy tissue is blue, and the cancer tissue is pink, so the surgeon can remove it.'

Jack placed his box by his feet and said, 'You already told us that. Daddy will be better, Aunty Heather, when all his hair has grown back.' Jack's expression changed to one of school-teacher seriousness as he mimicked Dr Laurent – his rolling of the r in recovery an attempt to mimic the doctor's French accent. 'It's a long road to recovery.'

Fran ruffled Jack's hair. 'He's been asking the nurses and

doctors lots of questions. Go and unpack your things in your rooms.'

Fran waited until their footsteps reached the top of the staircase. 'You'd think I'd be used to their separate reactions by now. Patricia quietly observes everything while clinging to Hector, Allan asks questions, and Jack, after bursting into tears, seems to have soaked up all the information.'

Heather smiled and said, 'A doctor in the making.'

Heather added, 'There's a rail in the shower in case Hector's unsteady on his feet. Did I show you already?'

'Aye. They give you a list of contingent after-effects, but I don't know what to expect. He might have to see physiotherapists, speech and language therapists, and later an occupational therapist to get him back to work. If that's possible.'

'Don't worry about all that. I got you.' Heather compacted Fran into a tight hug.

There was much in life to be thankful for. Heather had opened her home to them as she had opened her heart to Fran all those years ago in primary school. The stalwart friendship Fran couldn't have predicted falling on her barricaded doorstep, which had unsealed more than a crack due to Heather and Hector's influence on her life – and God, the church community, and her ex-neighbours. Nancy had already arranged their next game of Cribbage. Lockdown had revealed there was so much to be thankful for, even in a simple life where social connections were more important than material goods. A ceiling overhead, however, is a prerequisite to build a life.

'Owch! Crush cars much?' Fran rubbed one shoulder, pulling away from the embrace. 'Hard to take in what's happening, you know? Liable to experience muscle weakness, difficulty moving, fits, hearing and visual problems. That's hard enough … I worry … I worry that …' Fran squeezed her eyes shut.

'That he's not going to be the same man?'

Fran nodded. A tear escaped.

Heather used a napkin to dab Fran's face dry. The feel of the cloth against her face soothing, harking back to a forgotten time when her ma had comforted her as a child.

Heather said, 'It's an impossible situation to prepare for. Let's focus on being here for Hector, whatever happens. And don't forget, while everyone is focused on Hector that I'm here for you too, and you have to look after yourself not just your hands.'

Fran folded her hands to hide her chipped nails. She hadn't been looking after herself at all after hearing the news. Not taken the time to file or paint the nails of her work-beaten digits. She chuckled. Wrong to find humour in the situation, and yet it helped to break the tension munching through the tight muscles where her shoulders met her neck. At night without Hector's reassuring warmth beside her spine spasmed. With the room absent of his breathing it was too damn quiet to sleep. It made her want to crawl into one of the kids' beds and clasp them tightly. If she didn't have them she wouldn't get out of bed in the morning.

'You alright, Fran?' Heather asked.

'I remember when I was asking you that.'

Schelle, the parrot, ran through his favourite sounds: a goosey laugh, a barking puppy; the na-na of a squeaky bed; the chunk-chunk of a stapler.

'What about your writing?' Fran asked.

'I finished a novel.'

'That's fantastic, what now?'

'Waiting to hear back from an agent.'

'What's your book about?' Patricia asked.

Fran started, the boys were thumping about their rooms, Patricia's gentle footsteps hadn't been audible on the stairs.

'The breaking and mending of a friendship,' Heather said.

'How does it end?'

Heather shrugged. 'Endings aren't always obvious. How do you think a book should end, Trish?'

'A happy ending.'

'Nah.' Fran fingered her cross. 'With hope, goodness knows life's a sore fight for half a loaf.'

Hope, that's what they could call the bairn. A fitting name for this period of unexpected adaptation for not just their family and friends, for a whole country, for countries, for a small world spinning on its axis in an overwhelming universe.

Hope … the word slipped through a crack under the door, scattered windward over the city, and who knows how far its parachuting seeds might propagate …

Other books

Thank you, dear reader, for reading!

Shattered Roses

Sixteen-year-old Megan wants to be a doctor. When Megan volunteers at a residential home she meets Lady. Lady tells a fragmented and confusing story of a duke who never aged; his fate tied to the roses that grew in his garden. As Megan hears more of Lady's tale, she is intrigued to know whether the duke existed or if he is a figment of Lady's imagination. As Megan embarks on unravelling the mystery of the beast a hidden family secret emerges connected with her West Indian heritage ... will it shatter her life forever?

Recommendations:
"It's really interesting seeing the story told in a different way. The characters are the strong points in E.L. Parfitt's story. Megan is a likable, relatable girl who struggles to be the odd one out at school and in her extended family. She is mature and introspective and not as interested in "nail varnish colours, gossip and possible weddings" as her female cousins. It's also refreshing for Megan's family to be immigrants from the West Indies, an unusual heritage in YA stories. It helps that I'm also West Indian!" (silverpetticoat)

"If you like retellings you should read this book... There is much more going on than meets the eye and Megan is going to have the biggest shock in her life... The plot was very well thought through and involves some harsh subjects that you didn't see coming." (Desert Rose)

Seascape

I invite you into a world of fairy tales where the lines between fiction and reality blur, and melt and burst into flames. A selkie leaves the sea for the first time to go to university; three young boys find a genie in a can of Irn Bru; two friends think they see a firebird in an old housing estate; a boy discovers that people are not always who they seem to be; a man is spirited away by a snake charmer into a dark maze; goblins crawl through mirrors; an unwilling princess is "saved" from a tower; and Rapunzel is kidnapped by an automaton. A series of original short stories to amuse and entertain.

"I've absolutely laughed my butt off! You've taken all the classic fairy tale stereotypical characteristics and turned them into a ball of irony and laughter." (Rosa Fiore, Software Engineering student and writer)

Temptation & Mozzarella

In an unknown location in Scotland is a small village where the locals love to eat pizza. The story unfolds around Smith, just an average guy who is having a really bad week. Smith loses his job, his bicycle becomes sentient and runs away, one of his best friends reveals that he is an alien, and a guy who thinks he is the devil is stalking him. If you thought that things couldn't get more surreal than that think again. From invisible snooker to rogue FBI agents, join me for a bizarre and wonderful journey over one week in Smith's life.

Wee Stories

Now for the first time the entire collection of wee stories in one volume with some wee poems thrown in. Children's stories suitable for a wide range of ages. Including *How the Herring Became a Kipper, Dunn's Magnificent Idea* and *The Skeleton Cat.*

Recommendations:
"E.L. Parfitt had the most "fabulous, stupendous magnificent idea" when she decided to create a series of 'Wee Stories'. Whether she wrote them in her pyjamas, or not, I'll never know. But you will find out why 'Dunn's Magnificent Idea' is better than television. The book reads effortlessly and fast, and captures the imagination with ease and clarity. I found myself wanting a few illustrations in the style of Quinten Blake or Shel Silverstein to compliment the storyline. 'Dunn's Magnificent Idea' is truly an enjoyable book to read, and soon to be, classic of the children's literature." (Edward Szynalski, Goodreads)

"My 5-year-old son picked out Skeleton Cat as a bed time story. Without giving too much of the story away, this was a delightful light read and showed how Etheny was able to cope with her mom's passing. This is definitely for older elementary school kids going onto middle school, but my son had no complaints while I read it." (Diana Southammavong, Goodreads)

Young People, Learning & Storytelling

This book explores the lives of young people through the lens of storytelling. Using extensive qualitative and empirical data from young people's conversations following storytelling performances in secondary schools in the UK, the author considers the benefits of stories and storytelling for learning and the subsequent emotional, behavioural and social connections to story and other genres of narrative. Storytelling has both global and transnational relevance in education, as it allows individuals to compare their experiences to others: young people learn through discussion that their opinions matter, that they are both similar to and different from their peers. This in turn can facilitate the development of critical thinking skills as well as encouraging social learning, co-operation and cohesion. Drawing upon folklore and literary studies as well as sociology, philosophy, youth studies and theatre, this volume explores how storytelling can shape the lives of young people through storytelling projects.

Reviews:
"This book is an exceptional study of how storytelling cannot only help us understand children's experiences under difficult conditions, but also how children use storytelling to cope with problems facing them in their daily lives. Dr Parfitt has a firm grasp of the art of oral storytelling and interdisciplinary methods, and develops keen insights into the emotional behaviour of children as they tell and listen to stories. Her book is a significant contribution to the fields of childhood studies and folklore and will interest anyone concerned with improving relations with children in schools and at home."

(Jack Zipes, Professor Emeritus, University of Minnesota, USA)

"Beautifully written, with imaginative metaphors from the stories themselves, she offers really accessible theory and vivid compelling accounts infused with the real voices and personalities of the young people themselves. This is not a manual, but something more precious, a guide to reflective practice to inspire teachers and storytellers practically in the classroom."

(Nicola Grove, Founder of OpenStoryTellers, UK)

Acknowledgement

Merci, Jeanne and Phyllis for being fabulous beta readers. Thanks to Morgan for putting up with my do-not-disturb hours. And thank you to all the friends who I have been lucky enough to cross paths with, including the Book group girls.

Printed in Great Britain
by Amazon

80248284R00180